The Elder Edda

A Book of Viking Lore

Translated with Introduction and Notes by
ANDY ORCHARD

PENGUIN BOOKS

PENGUIN CLASSICS

Published by the Penguin Group
Penguin Books Ltd, 80 Strand, London WC2R ORL, England
Penguin Group (USA) Inc., 375 Hudson Street, New York, New York 10014, USA
Penguin Group (Canada), 90 Eglinton Avenue East, Suite 700, Toronto, Ontario,
Canada M4P 2Y3 (a division of Pearson Penguin Canada Inc.)
Penguin Ireland, 25 St Stephen's Green, Dublin 2, Ireland
(a division of Penguin Books Ltd)
Penguin Group (Australia), 250 Camberwell Road, Camberwell, Victoria 3124, Australia
(a division of Pearson Australia Group Pty Ltd)
Penguin Books India Pvt Ltd, 11 Community Centre, Panchsheel Park,
New Delhi – 110 017, India
Penguin Group (NZ), 67 Apollo Drive, Rosedale, Auckland 0632, New Zealand
(a division of Pearson New Zealand Ltd)
Penguin Books (South Africa) (Pty) Ltd, 24 Sturdee Avenue, Rosebank, Johannesburg 2196,
South Africa

Penguin Books Ltd, Registered Offices: 80 Strand, London WC2R ORL, England

www.penguin.com

This translation first published in Penguin Classics 2011
003

Translation and editorial material copyright © Andy Orchard, 2011
All rights reserved

The moral right of the translator has been asserted

Set in 10.25/12.25 pt PostScript Adobe Sabon
Typeset by Jouve (UK), Milton Keynes
Printed in England by Clays Ltd, St Ives plc

ISBN: 978-0-140-43585-6

www.greenpenguin.co.uk

MIX
Paper from
responsible sources
FSC
www.fsc.org   FSC™ C018179

Penguin Books is committed to a sustainable
future for our business, our readers and our planet.
This book is made from Forest Stewardship
Council™ certified paper.

ALWAYS LEARNING   **PEARSON**

Contents

Appendix
Some Eddic Poems Not Contained in the Codex Regius

Acknowledgements

My first debt, appropriately enough for a book that deals so much in myth and speculation, is to a man I never met, Roger Lancelyn Green, whose *Myths of the Norsemen* I read at the age of eleven and immediately resolved both to become a medievalist and to visit Iceland; the latter I have been doing for nearly thirty years now, and the former I still aspire to. As a shy but somehow surly and hitherto largely self-taught undergraduate, I was I now realize my own worst nightmare to teach, and yet it was my great luck (and certainly not theirs) to sit at the feet of the likes of Ursula Dronke, Michael Lapidge, Ray Page, Sverrir Tómasson and Maureen Thompson, where I learned much and very likely should have learnt very much more. But I did also (and do!) pay close attention to the superb work of contemporaries at Oxford and Cambridge much more gifted in many areas of Old Norse–Icelandic studies than I, including Paul Bibire, Vicky Cribb, Matthew Driscoll, Mike Fox, Carolyne Larrington, Guðrún Nordal, Richard North, Peter Robinson and Clive Tolley. I am grateful in various and different ways to them all. In addition, I have learnt much from those I sometime tried to teach, and it has been wondrous to share a classroom or a supervision or just the odd pint or three with the likes of Chris Abram, Shami Ghosh, Jonny Grove, Guðrún Edda Þórhannessdóttir, Alaric Hall, Roberta Hamilton, Paul Langeslag, Emily Lethbridge, Marteinn Helgi Sigurðsson, Ralph O'Connor, Helle Falcher Petersen, Emily Thornbury and Al Vining; Shami and Marteinn and Jonny I should single out for specific and invaluable help. I would also like to apologize to the successive generations of students in Cambridge and

Toronto that I subjected to earlier versions of these transla-
tions, as I tried to make the words sound less clumsy than they
sometimes seemed.

There are, again appropriately, giants in this field, even
beyond those named already, and I would urge anyone with a
serious interest in the material to consult anything and every-
thing written by several scholars it has been (largely through
the good offices of the above named, though serendipity played
its customary part) my privilege and pleasure to meet and even
to discuss these and other related texts: especially Paul Acker,
Fred Biggs, Bob Bjork, Anthony Faulkes, Chris Fell, Alison Fin-
lay, Peter Foote, Roberta Frank, Tom Hall, Joe Harris, Tom
Hill, Judy Jesch, David and Ian McDougall, John McKinnell,
Rory McTurk, Heather O'Donoghue, Russell Poole, Judy Quinn,
Margaret Clunies Ross, Tom Shippey, Andrew Wawn, David
Wilson and Charlie Wright; they won't need me to tell them
that the mistakes and infelicities are my own. I am deeply grate-
ful to everyone at Penguin for their patience and professionalism,
and especially to Lindeth Vasey for her eagle-eyed editing, superb
suggestions and extraordinary expertise. And then there are the
folks at Mullins, who mainly made me welcome and left me
alone, even if they occasionally wondered what I was up to. I
give my warmest thanks to all.

Translation, especially of poetry, is a fraught business, a
masking of another's words, and an overlaying of often intru-
sive and unnecessary interpretation. Only the outcome, if it
provokes those who know and piques the interest of those who
don't, can be judged successful, and if this effort to transmit
some of the wonder I feel every time I read these texts seems to
some simply a tissue of errors and an opportunity squandered,
then I trust others will step up and fill the gap. Even as I can
now see from the scholarly perspective how the simplifications,
mystifications and misunderstandings of a well-educated fan
like that man I never met can muddy the waters but still inspire,
I do hope that these pages will provoke others to go beyond
what I could. After all, these poems have been read and reread
and remembered for centuries, and for reason: they can speak
to us still.

For Steve, best of brothers and first of friends

Chronology

117 Death of Tacitus, who wrote *Germania* (*Germany and Her People*)

376 Death of Ermanaric the Goth (who appears here as Jörmunrekk)

453 Death of Attila the Hun (as Atli Budlason)

526 Death of Theoderic the Ostrogoth (as Thjódrek)

584 Death of Chilperic the Neustrian (as Hjálprek)

787–95/6 Paul the Deacon writes the *Historia Langobardorum* (*History of the Lombards*)

793 Viking raid on the monastery at Lindisfarne

***c.* 850** Beginnings of Norse settlement in Anglo-Saxon England; Bragi Boddason composes *Ragnarsdrápa* ('Poem for Ragnar')

***c.* 870** Beginnings of Norse settlement in Iceland (traditional date is 874)

871 Accession of Alfred the Great to the throne of Wessex

***c.* 885** Harold Fairhair becomes king of all Norway

***c.* 885–*c.* 920** Þjóðólfr of Hvinir composes *Haustlöng* ('Autumn-long')

899 Death of Alfred the Great

***c.* 900** Þorbjörn hornklofi composes *Hrafnsmál* ('The raven's lay') for Harald Fairhair

930 Foundation of the national parliament (Althing) in Iceland

954 Death of Eirík Bloodaxe; composition of *Eiríksmál* ('Poem for Eirík')

961 Death of Hákon the Good fighting the sons of Eirík Bloodaxe; composition of *Hákonarmál* ('Poem for Hákon') by Eyvíndr Finnsson skáldaspillir *c.* 980   Egill Skallagrímsson composes *Sonatorrek* ('Painful loss of sons')

982   Beginnings of Norse settlement in Greenland

c. 985   Úlfr Uggason composes *Húsdrápa* ('House-poem')

986   Beginnings of Norse settlement in North America

995   Ólafr Tryggvason becomes king of Norway

999–1000   Christianity accepted in Iceland at Althing

c. 1000   The *Beowulf* manuscript is written

1010   Burning of Njál

1014   Battle of Clontarf

1030   St Ólafr killed at the Battle of Stiklastadir

1056   First bishop at Skálholt, South Iceland
Sæmundr Sigfússon inn fróði ('the wise') is born

c. 1065   Arnórr jarlaskáld composes *Þorfinnsdrápa* ('Thorfinn's poem')

1066   Battle of Stamford Bridge; death of Harald Harðráði
Battle of Hastings; death of Harold Godwinsson

1067   Ari Þorgilsson inn fróði is born

c. 1085   Death of Adam of Bremen, author of *Gesta Hamaburgensis ecclesiae pontificum* (*History of the Bishops of the Church at Hamburg*)

1106   First bishop at Hólar, north Iceland

c. 1130   Ari compiles *Íslendingabók* (*Book of Icelanders*)

1130–36   Harald Gilli (Harald IV), king of Norway

1133   First monastery is founded in Iceland, at Thingeyrar
Sæmundr inn fróði dies

1136   Death of King Harald Gilli of Norway

c. 1175–1250/1   *Þiðreks saga* (*The saga of Thidrek*) written

1178/9   Snorri Sturluson is born

1185–1216   Saxo Grammaticus composes *Gesta Danorum* (*History of the Danes*)

c. 1210–59   Óláfr Þórðarson, the grammarian, active

1215–18   Snorri is Lawspeaker

1218/19   Death of Gunnlaugr Leifsson, author of *Merlínusspá* ('The prophecy of Merlin')

c. 1220   Snorri composes the Prose Edda

1222–31   Snorri is Lawspeaker for a second time

1241   Snorri is killed at his home Reykholt

c. 1250   *Laxdæla saga* (*The saga of the people of Laxdale*) is written

1259   Death of Óláfr Þórðarson, author of the *Third Grammatical Treatise*

c. 1260–70   *Völsung Saga* is written

1262   Icelandic Commonwealth ends; Iceland is ceded to the king of Norway

c. 1270   Codex Regius is written

c. 1275   *Gísla saga* (*The saga of Gísli*) is written

c. 1280   *Njáls saga* (*Saga of Njáll*) is written

1294   Haukr Erlendsson is Lawspeaker

c. 1300   AM 748 Ia 4to written

1302–10   Hauksbók (AM 544 4to) is written

1334   Death of Haukr Erlendsson, the main scribe of Hauksbók (*Haukr's Book*)

c. 1350   Codex Wormianus of Snorri's Prose Edda (AM 242 fol.) is written

1387–94   Flateyjarbók (*The Book of Flatey [Flat-island]*) is written

1643   Bishop Brynjólfur Sveinsson of Skálholt acquires the Codex Regius

1662   Codex Regius is given to the Danish king

1665   First edition of *Völuspá* and *Hávamál* by Peder Hansen Resen, with Latin translations

1787   Arnamagnaean Institute begins to publish editions of the Codex Regius poems with Latin translations

1797   Amos Cottle publishes the first English translation of the Codex Regius poems

1944   Iceland regains independence

1971   Codex Regius is returned by Denmark to Iceland

Introduction

Iceland owns one of the literary wonders of the medieval world. Little to look at, there survives in Reykjavík today a plain manuscript of only 45 brown and heavily written leaves, each measuring around 19 × 13 cm, more or less the same size as the pages you are holding now, bound as a book. It is called variously the Codex Regius ('Royal manuscript'), the Elder Edda, the Poetic Edda and Sæmundar Edda ('Sæmund's Edda'). The traditional and apocryphal association of the manuscript with the Icelander Sæmundr Sigfússon (1056–1133), also known as Sæmundr inn fróði ('the wise'), a priest who is said to have studied in Paris, again marks a clear desire to authenticate its contents as not only old, but worthy of sustained and serious study, sanctioned by the most celebrated and learned of early Christian Icelanders. Most of these titles likewise distinguish the Codex Regius from a composite treatise on similarly mythological and heroic themes by another learned and politically active Icelander, Snorri Sturluson (1178/9–1241), that also survives in several copies (predictably enough as the Younger Edda, the Prose Edda and Snorra Edda ('Snorri's Edda')). Although the term 'edda' appears first to have been coined with regard to Snorri's compilation, given the extent to which he seems to have employed many of the same poems and even prose texts found in the Codex Regius, albeit in sometimes different forms, it seems appropriate to designate the collection presented here by the more traditional name *Elder Edda*, even if the manuscript of the Codex Regius itself was clearly written roughly a generation after Snorri's death. The use of *Elder Edda* has the further advantage of reminding readers that the book contains authentic echoes of an age already aged when the words were written down.

The manuscript, which now carries the shelf mark of the Royal Library in Copenhagen where it once was held (as GkS 2635 4to), has over time suffered loss, misreading and botched repair, much like its texts, largely in verse, but also with connecting prose passages, and originally seems to have had 106 pages, rather than the 90 that now survive. Loss of probably eight leaves after folio 32 (the so-called 'great lacuna') has left a gap in the narrative of the life of the mighty hero Sigurd the Völsung that can partly be filled by the surviving mid-thirteenth-century *Völsunga saga*, which, as we shall see, itself bears witness to many of the same poems preserved in the Codex Regius. It seems feasible that the missing leaves offered, among other things, the further wisdom of a valkyrie (one of the supernatural warrior-women who picked the best of the dead warriors for the service of the god Odin) given to her chosen hero, as well as an account of a heroic wooing of a matchless man and a marvellous maid; it is possible that apart from the ending of one damaged poem and the beginning of another, the great lacuna contained the longest single account of Sigurd's exploits. As such, the self-contained booklet may not so much have been simply lost as removed for private perusal by an over-zealous reader. A naturally occurring hole in the stretched vellum of folio 41, which affects nine lines, is carefully written around by the scribe, and a stitched repair on folio 28 covers most of the width of the page; in such ways one can begin to guess at how much the texts were valued that the modest volume contains.

Each page is densely written, in an often abbreviated fashion that has sometimes compounded the problems of interpretation, but which again may suggest the poems were so well known that readers could reconstruct them without the full wording, and each page contains between thirty-one and thirty-eight lines of text, with the number of the lines increasing and the size of the writing decreasing as the single scribe comes to the end of his stint. As it is, he (and it was almost certainly a man writing) seems to have overcompensated somewhat for the need to finish before the vellum ran out: the last third of the final page is blank. Yet what that unknown scribe wrote in this plain manuscript comprises the bulk of what we now know of viking lore, and how that developed over several centuries. If some of its contents have been traced back to the ninth century, the manuscript seems only to have survived because in 1662 an Icelandic bishop with a keen interest in his country's past gave it as a gift to a Danish king, then overlord of Iceland. This together with the joyous reception and outpouring of national pride when the Codex Regius came home to Iceland under naval escort from Copenhagen in 1971 say much for the symbolic power of the extraordinary texts that this battered and basic book contains; we can only wish we had more.

The Codex Regius was written around 1270, and has been associated with similar productions from the Benedictine monastery of Thingeyrar, in North Iceland, founded in 1133, a wealthy estate rich in salmon and seals. Indeed, according to recent investigations, seals may have supplied the raw material for at least some medieval Icelandic manuscripts just as sheep, goats and calves did further south. On the first page of the Codex Regius there is the distinctive mark of Bishop Brynjólfur Sveinsson of Skálholt in South Iceland (1605–75): a pair of intertwined 'L's to signify *Lupus Loricatus* ('Armoured Wolf'), a Latinization of his Norse name. Brynjólfur, whose role as collector of manuscripts for the Danish King Frederick III (1609–70) is well documented, added the date 1643 (presumably the date he acquired it), and called the book 'Edda', a name that has since stuck, though its meaning is still debated. 'Edda' seems to signify 'Great-grandma' in the poem *Rígsthula*, which is composed in a similar style to many of the texts in the Codex Regius and is found in a single manuscript, the Codex Wormianus (AM 242 fol.), written about 1350, that largely contains the composite prose and poetry text on Norse mythological and legendary lore (also called 'Edda') composed by Snorri *c.* 1220 and now known as the Prose Edda. An attractive alternative suggestion is that 'edda' is formed after the model of *kredda*, which derives from the Latin *credo* ('I believe'; also used for the Christian Creed), and would then suggest that 'edda' derives from the Latin verb *edo* ('I produce', 'I publish'), which can have the specific sense 'I compose (poetry)'. If that argument is accepted, an Edda would be a kind of compilation of traditional poetry, which Snorri's work certainly is; the application of the term to the Codex Regius would then be an extension, in effect an acknowledgement of the distinct overlap between its poems and those in Snorri's collection.

The twenty-nine poems (and various prose pieces) to which the Codex Regius is the main or only witness are, then, whether complete, composite or otherwise compromised, compiled from various places and periods, the works of different poets of divergent powers and discrepant beliefs, but they all deal with a common stock of inherited stories that together speak of gods and heroes from an ancient era. They are projections back into the pagan past, yet evidently preserved over the years and in many manuscripts by the skill of Christian scribes long after Iceland's conversion to Christianity in 999–1000. Some of these pagan gods survive into English in the names of the days of the week (in so far as Tuesday, Wednesday, Thursday and Friday can still be claimed to commemorate Týr the war-god, Odin the psychopomp and god of frenzy, Thor the thunder-god and Freyja the goddess of love and sex), while some of the heroes likewise live on in legend in culture both high and low: opera-goers will readily recognize Siegfried, the direct descendant of the hero Sigurd, and others will easily identify the infamous cruelty of Attila (or Atli) the Hun, who here has his just deserts, unwittingly eating the flesh of his sons before being stabbed and burnt alive in his own hall. These and other poems like them, scattered in other medieval parchments and, after the medieval period, on paper that a combination of chance, careful antiquarianism and often careless copying has allowed to survive, comprise what is known as 'eddic' or 'eddaic' verse, a term used to distinguish these anonymous texts on mythological and heroic themes from the skaldic poetry, generally on contemporary topics composed in a different metre than those used in the eddic poems (see below) by mainly named and known poets (also known as skalds).

When the eddic texts in this volume were first collected we do not know, though some groups of poems seem to have circulated together in earlier compilations. But as the last of a long line, the

single scribe of the Codex Regius was evidently eager to save
every scrap of such lore – whether he understood it well or not –
to judge by the tidy wee writing and multiple abbreviations he
employed; indeed, there are so many of the latter that when the
same set of words and phrases recur, as they do often in orally
transmitted texts, the scribe simply gave the first letter of each
word. In other examples, such as in the brief prose text entitled
Frá dauda Sinfjötla ('About Sinfjötli's death'), the scribe has care-
fully left gaps for a character's name to be filled in when it became
available. He did well: we should realize that for every letter that
has lasted, and whose sense we can still guess, much more has
been lost in other texts, and much of what remains was changed
by chance or circumstance; so that in reconstructing whole stan-
zas and verses from these tiny traces, we run the risk of merely
repeating what we know from other sources, but it is simply all
we have. Despite these drawbacks, the Codex Regius is a crucial
witness to how viking lore developed, as well as to its preserva-
tion and alteration long after the viking era was over: it is an
eclectic, incomplete and composite collection of often augmented
and interpolated poems from various dates and provenances,
which individually and in groups have been butchered, badly
transmitted and recast elsewhere not only by Snorri in his Prose
Edda, but also, for example, by the anonymous author of the
Völsunga saga (*The saga of the Völsungs*). Certainly, these poems
were preserved in part for their agedness and authenticity, but
also surely for their intrinsic worth as verse, and for the pure
pleasure that they still bring. While it would be quite wrong to
regard the Codex Regius manuscript as a definitive collection, it
clearly represents the last link in a conscious chain of compil-
ation, with some of the poems having been copied in groups from
pre-existing gatherings, and with separately-titled prose passages
both within and between poems summarizing, introducing or
filling gaps. Often the prose, particularly in the heroic section of
the manuscript, explains the fate (and usually the death) of major
figures, and occasionally provides different perspectives, so help-
ing to connect a narrative from poetry that would otherwise offer
an even more disjointed story than it currently conveys.

*

The first eleven poems in the Codex Regius are all concerned broadly with mythological themes, and seem to have been arranged in clusters: the opening four texts, *Völuspá* ('The prophecy of the seeress'), *Hávamál* ('The lay of the High One'), *Vafthrúdnismál* ('The lay of Vafthrúdnir') and *Grímnismál* ('The lay of Grímnir'), all deal with various aspects of the god Odin as a searcher after and a source of wisdom. Much mythological lore is imparted, largely through a series of conversations and wisdom-contests between Odin and creatures of various kinds, specifically a dead seeress (*Völuspá*), a wise giant (*Vafthrúdnismál*) and a young prince (*Grímnismál*). The clearly composite nature of *Hávamál* precludes any obvious sense of audience, although the sections commonly known as *Loddfáfnismál* ('Loddfáfnir's lay'), stanzas 111–37, and *Rúnatals þattr* ('The episode of the tally of runes'), 138–63, are each based on wisdom-dialogues featuring Odin. The fifth poem, *För Skírnis* ('Skírnir's journey'), again concerns a dialogue between inhabitants of different worlds: Skírnir, the servant of the god Frey, and the giantess Gerd. Five of the next six poems feature the giant-slaying thunder-god Thor, who, along with Odin and Frey, seems to have been the most widely worshipped of the Norse gods. In the first poem of this group, *Hárbardsljód* ('Greybeard's poem'), Thor and Odin engage in an abusive versified dialogue or flyting, that invites comparison between them, while in the next three Thor is paired with the mischievous and disruptive Loki, both as a travelling companion on quests (in *Hymiskvida* ('The song of Hymir') for a giant cauldron (although earlier commentators and translators have assumed that Thor's companion was actually Týr: see its headnote); in *Thrymskvida* ('The song of Thrym') for his lost hammer, Mjöllnir); and as antagonist (in *Lokasenna* ('Loki's hometruths')). In *Lokasenna*, after Loki has abused many of the gods in an extended formal flyting, Thor returns from a giant-slaying adventure in the East (as he does in *Hárbardsljód* and *Hymiskvida*), and terminates the abuse with threats of violence. None of the gods emerges well from the poetic accounts, where Frey dithers, Thor quivers, and even Odin in multi-faceted majesty cuts such a figure that to call him two-faced is to limit the options. '[H]ow can his truth be trusted?' the text says (*Hávamál* 110), where we can suspect that the poet has already put his faith elsewhere.

The final two poems in the mythological section of the Codex Regius, *Völundarkvida* ('The song of Völund') and *Alvíssmál* ('The lay of All-wise'), are often considered to be out of sequence, since while *Alvíssmál* is a wisdom-dialogue between the rather unintellectual god Thor and All-wise (*Alvíss*), described as a 'pale-nosed' dwarf, *Völundarkvida* depicts the grim vengeance of a 'prince' or 'leader' of elves. In terms of the kind of distinction between beings, as well as of the morality represented by the gods, it is notable that male gods sleep freely with giant women (Odin often; Thor, Frey and Njörd on occasion), but goddesses are generally spared such attentions from the giants, with which indeed they are threatened. So, while various giants might covet the sex-goddess Freyja, who is one of the fertility gods, the Vanir, with a record of sexual adventuring, there is no record of her accommodating them. As ever, the giant-born Loki is an exception: he claims in *Lokasenna* to have cunningly conquered almost every goddess that we know, but he also has had sex with a giant stallion, and his all-embracing appetites are widely condemned in *Lokasenna* itself.

In the mythological world of the Codex Regius, women are largely scheming and suspect, when they are not simply victims or the objects of unwanted sexual attention. Indeed, even giant-women can be threatened with giant lust, as Gerd is as the unwilling object of Frey's passion in *För Skírnis*. In the course of threatening Gerd he condemns her to *ergi* (here translated as 'cock-craving'), an insatiable yearning to be sexually penetrated that is beyond the pale. When used, as in *För Skírnis* 36, of a female, it connotes a wanton lasciviousness that is greatly frowned upon (see further headnote to *Lokasenna*). By contrast, the heroic poems of the Codex Regius quite regularly present the female perspective, and often with great sympathy and a deep acknowledgement of feminine authority; one can hardly argue that heroines such as Gudrún, Grímhild or Brynhild lack authority, even as they endure deep suffering. Such a contrast underlines a chief concern of the heroic poems of the

Codex Regius: the tensions between the family ties of blood and marriage. In fact, the compiler foreshadows the subject: all three of the final mythological poems, *Thrymskvida*, *Völunda-rkvida* and *Alvíssmál* (not to mention *För Skírnis*), concern forced, failed or thwarted marriages, a theme that is to become a leitmotif throughout the tragic intertwined tale of the mighty families of the Völsungs, the Gjúkungs and the Niflungs (linked through the doomed marriages of Sigurd the Völsung to Gudrún, the daughter of King Gjúki, and of Gudrún in turn to Atli and Jónakr), which forms the background for the heroic poems of the Codex Regius. Other repeated motifs link the mythological and heroic poems: so, for example, just as many of the first eleven poems concern wisdom-dialogues and predictions between different kinds of creatures, with Odin playing a principal role, so too Sigurd, Odin's favoured hero among a great family of favourites, is involved with a number of dialogues of wisdom or prophecy with a wide range of beings, including his maternal uncle Grípir (*Grípisspá* ('Grípir's prophecy')), the disguised god Odin (*Reginsmál* ('Regin's lay') 16–25), the dying dragon Fáfnir (*Fáfnismál* ('Fáfnir's lay') 1–22), the wise giant Regin (*Fáfnismál* 23–27 and *Reginsmál* 13–14), several talking nuthatches (*Fáfnismál* 32–44), and the newly woken valkyrie Sigrdrífa (*Sigrdrífumál* ('Sigrdrífa's lay')).

Nonetheless, a particularly large capital marks the first line of *Helgakvida Hundingsbana in fyrri* ('The earlier song of Helgi, the slayer of Hunding') in the Codex Regius, and so highlights the sensitivity of the compiler to the differences between the mythological and heroic material. Indeed, many of the same themes of love, loyalty and longing for knowledge are shot through both sections. The poems document several phases in the family saga of the doomed Völsung family, beginning with Sigmund, and his three sons by three different liaisons: Sinfjötli, whom he conceived with his own sister, Signý; Helgi, born of Borghild; Sigurd, born of Hjördís. The first three heroic poems in the Codex Regius (*Helgakvida Hundingsbana I*, *Hel-gakvida Hjörvardssonar* ('The song of Helgi Hjörvardsson') and *Helgakvida Hundingsbana önnur* ('The second song of Helgi, the slayer of Hunding'), together known as the Helgi-lays), conclude with the death of Helgi. An intervening prose passage, *Frá dauda Sinfjötla* ('About Sinfjötli's death'), marks the death of Sinfjötli, as well as the birth of Sigurd, Sigmund's most famous son, and recounts the death of Sigmund himself.

Grípisspá, the poem that immediately follows, offers a complete prophecy of Sigurd's life made by his maternal uncle, Grípir: his revenge for his father, Sigmund, and the slaying of the dragon, Fáfnir, and his brother Regin, so acquiring the doomed treasure of the Völsungs; then Sigurd will journey to the court of King Gjúki, encounter an unnamed valkyrie, who will teach him runic wisdom, and travel to the court of King Heimir, where he will meet the lovely Brynhild, daughter of Budli, with whom he will fall madly in love. But the meeting marks a turning-point in Sigurd's fortunes, since on his return to King Gjúki's court he will be tricked by Grímhild, Gjúki's queen, and made to forget Brynhild, to woo her instead for Grímhild's son, Gunnar (by taking on his appearance), and to marry Grímhild's daughter, Gudrún, himself. In binding himself by ties of marriage and blood-brotherhood to Gjúki's family, Sigurd effectively seals his own fate: when Brynhild discovers how she has been tricked and betrayed, she asserts her seniority as Sigurd's first love, and drives Gudrún and Gunnar, with the help of their brothers Högni and Gutthorm, to contrive Sigurd's death. Sigurd and Grípir part with the much chastened young hero accepting his fate.

The events described in *Grípisspá* are duly played out in the succeeding poems, beginning with *Reginsmál*, which narrates Sigur further education at the hands of the mysterious Regin, described by the prose as '*handier than any man, and a dwarf in height: he was wise, stern and skilled in magic*'. *Reginsmál* begins by telling Regin's own family history, and how they acquired a cursed treasure-hoard, which his brother, Fáfnir, now transformed into the shape of a dragon, was guarding. Rather than comply immediately with Regin's request that he help him kill Fáfnir, Sigurd instead heads off to avenge his own father, and apparently meets up en route with the god Odin in disguise, who offers him still more useful advice. When Sigurd returns successful from the battlefield, he accedes to Regin's

request, and *Fáfnismál*, which immediately follows and indeed
is seamlessly connected with *Reginsmál* in the Codex Regius,
describes Sigurd in conversation with the dying dragon, in
what seems yet another form of wisdom-dialogue. Once Fáfnir
is dead, Sigurd and Regin engage in a discussion of bravery and
cowardice that appears to end with Sigurd spouting two pieces
of gnomic wisdom on the value of the former (stanzas 30–31),
even as he roasts the dragon's heart for Regin to eat, illustrated
alongside other scenes from the same part of the Sigurd legend
on the Ramsund rune-stone (usually dated around 1000) in
Södermanland in south-eastern Sweden. The hero tests the spit-
ted heart to see if it is done, burns his thumb on the dragon's
roasted heart-blood, and when he sucks it, finds that he can
miraculously understand the language of birds. Several nut-
hatches (the precise number is debated) perched nearby urge
him to kill Regin, which he duly does; they then direct him to a
hall surrounded by flames, where a valkyrie disobedient to the
wishes of the god Odin slumbers. The account of Sigurd's
encounter with Sigrdrífa, the name given to the valkyrie in both
Fáfnismál and *Sigrdrífumál*, the next poem in the Codex Regius,
is told in full in the latter text, where once she has been awak-
ened, the valkyrie offers the hero more runic lore and sound
advice very close in spirit to some sections of *Hávamál*. Unfor-
tunately, *Sigrdrífumál* breaks off after the valkyrie has given
Sigurd only eleven pieces of advice (compare the twenty-one
pieces in the *Loddfáfnismál* section of *Hávamál*), just before the
missing pages.

As far as the 'great lacuna' is concerned, a rough calculation
suggests that the Codex Regius scribe averages around 100–125
lines of verse per page (written as elsewhere in the manuscript
in 31–8 lines of text: the poetry was written continuously as
though it were prose to save space). Given differences of metre
and levels of abbreviation, this produces on average about 15
stanzas per page, so suggesting that the eight lost folios may have
contained roughly 200–250 stanzas, allowing for occasional
prose inserts. Given that, if the two poems affected, *Sigrdrífu-
mál* and *Brot af Sigurdarkvidu* ('A fragment of the song of
Sigurd'), are excluded, the average length in the Codex Regius

is about 50 stanzas, the loss could amount to as many as four complete poems. Later paper manuscripts of *Sigrdrífumál* help to supply the missing material, with the further clue of four stanzas in *Völsunga saga* 27–9. The very fact that the Codex Regius also contains a poem explicitly called *Sigurdarkvida in skamma* ('The short song of Sigurd'), which at 71 stanzas long is significantly above average length, may encourage us to speculate that a significant portion of the 'great lacuna' was made up with the missing ending and beginning (and no poems were lost). When J. R. R. Tolkien sought to repair the loss, he composed two new poems, which he called *Völsungakviða en nýja eða Sigurdarkviða en mesta* ('The new song of the Völ-sungs, or The longest song of Sigurd') and *Guðrúnarkviða en nýja eða Dráp Niflunga* ('The new song of Guðrún, or The kill-ing of the Niflungs'), using the existing poems, and bridging the gap from a combination of his own imagination and the some-times contradictory narratives of *Völsunga saga* and Snorri's Prose Edda. In so doing, Tolkien was effectively aligning him-self with the long line of poets who, across many centuries, added or elaborated further links to an existing chain of song. Albeit unwittingly offering him a fine opportunity to demon-strate both his command of the material and his own poetic imagination, whoever was responsible for the missing folios certainly ripped the heart out of the Codex Regius.

Again, there is a change of tone and style in the prose passage (*Frá dauda Sigurdar* ('About Sigurd's death')) that immediately follows *Brot af Sigurdarkvidu*. We are told that there are differ-ent versions of the killing of Sigurd, and even disagreements about whether he was killed inside or outside; that he was killed while in bed with Gudrún may represent a later tradition that recalls the similar death of Atli, Gudrún's second husband – a death-scene for Atli (as Attila) at the hands of a Gothic or Germanic bride is attested early (by for example Priscus in the fifth century, and Jordanes and Procopius in the sixth), and on to which the character of Gudrún herself seems to have been grafted. Like so many of the bridging passages in prose, here too we learn of the fate of key characters, so tying up the loose ends and allowing the broader poetic narrative to continue.

Certainly, the poems that follow all switch the focus from Sig-
urd, safely dead, to his young Gjúkung widow, Gudrún, whose
three marriages (Sigurd, Atli, Jónakr) echo the three liaisons of
Sigmund the Völsung (Signý, Borghild, Hjördís) with which the
heroic portion of the Codex Regius began.

Clearly, the focus of the next five poems is squarely on the
perspective of the hapless women in Sigurd's life. Starting with
the poignant account of his grieving widow in *Gudrúnarkvida in
fyrsta* ('The first song of Gudrún') and the flashback sequence of
Sigurdarkvida in skamma, the whole sorry sequence is blamed
on fate, the female norns and the feminine wiles of the wounded
Brynhild, who in stanzas 53–64 continues the tradition of proph-
ecy, outlining all the hideous events ahead, and then in 65–70
makes requests for her own funeral, concluding in the final stanza
with words that seem to echo those of the seeress in *Völuspá*.
Brynhild's rewritten role (now identified with Sigrdrífa) as a
valkyrie and prophetess is more sympathetically presented in
Helreid Byrnhildar ('Brynhild's Hel-ride'), where her tragic and
tainted love for Sigurd is laid bare, before the focus shifts back
to Gudrún in *Gudrúnarkvida in forna* ('The ancient song of
Gudrún'), and forward to her marriage to Atli, Brynhild's brother,
and his own foreboding dreams (stanzas 38–43), that pre-empt
(physically, if not necessarily chronologically) the dismal dreams
of *Atlamál in grænlenzku* ('The Greelandic lay of Atli'). The next
poems in the Codex Regius can best be regarded as bridging
passages or later additions to the final two vengeful phases
of Gudrún's life, recounting as they do her alleged adultery (in
Gudrúnarkvida in thridja ('The third song of Gudrún')) and the
role of Oddrún, (in *Oddrúnargrátr* ('Oddrún's lament')), sister
of Atli and lover of Gunnar (who therefore slept with both Bryn-
hild and her sister), in helping Borgný, daughter of King Heidrek,
to give birth. Oddrún's sorry tale, encompassing as it does Gun-
nar's death in a snake-pit (stanzas 25–33), looks forward to the
two poems that immediately follow, namely *Atlakvida* ('Atli's
song') and *Atlamál*. The former is brisk and brutal, the latter
languid and leisurely; though they may have been composed sev-
eral centuries apart, they both testify to the fascination of a lurid
and inherited tale that they treat in quite different ways.

So Gudrún's grief is renewed, as it were, for the third and final time in the closing pair of poems in the manuscript. Here Gudrún, whose actions hitherto have been those of wife or sister, becomes in *Gudrúnarhvöt* ('Gudrún's inciting') and *Hamdis-mál* ('Hamdir's lay') Gudrún the vengeful mother, sacrificing one set of children, those she had by Jónakr (Hamdir and Sörli), to avenge another child, by Sigurd (Svanhild). Given that the previous two poems (*Atlakvida* and *Atlamál*) document in detail the ways in which Gudrún is prepared to sacrifice her sons for her own concerns, such a redemption is limited, but does at least serve to emphasize the point that Sigurd remains her 'real' husband: she will happily sacrifice the sons of her next two husbands to reassert her loyalty both to her own birth-family and to the one she shared with Sigurd. Likewise, *Hamdismál* looks back to the texts dealing with the death of Sigurd, by echoing the pattern of two close brothers who act out of heroic pride (there Gunnar and Högni; Hamdir and Sörli here), and a third who is somehow seen as inferior or at least disposable (Gutthorm and Erp, respectively). Certainly, these final poems in the Codex Regius, focusing as they do on the plight of the later generations of the children of Gjúki and their heirs (the Gjúkungs), have a force and allure of their own, and appear to have had a particular following; two thirteenth-century sagas from the West of Iceland, *Gísla saga* (*The saga of Gísli*) and *Laxdæla saga* (*The saga of the people of Laxdale*) both contain traces of poems about the Gjúkungs, even if there seems little else to connect them. In such ways did these texts continue to exert their poetic power.

We may reasonably assume, as we likely should, that the Codex Regius was compiled by a thirteenth-century Icelandic cleric who – because he was aware of his countrymen's trad-itional role as collective keeper of Norse lore, because he could appreciate the intrinsic value of texts he could not always fathom or understand, and because he could see that the know-ledge of such ancient and traditional texts was dying out – chose to preserve texts that did not always agree with his own beliefs. Nonetheless, that cleric, his patron or whoever made it clear that such things should be saved, evidently had sufficient respect for the material that he assembled the texts in a specific pattern and order, demonstrating to Christian readers the extent to which the ancient world of gods and men was one, and that it ended in death and destruction. There are no great ethical lessons to be learnt from the poems of the Codex Regius, except a stubborn insistence, exemplified by the god Odin and the heroes Helgi, Sigurd, Gunnar and Hamdir, as well as the heroines Gudrún and Brynhild, to fight on in the face of unfriendly fate. Even when they know they are doomed, they enjoy whatever pleasures they may partake of on the way, happy in the sense of being individually gifted and specifically subject to individual doom.

Beyond the Codex Regius, its poems are variously witnessed mostly in fragments and often in strikingly different forms in those manuscripts. The next most important manuscript witnesses to eddic verse are two fragments of six leaves, AM 748 Ia 4to, written around 1300. The first two leaves begin partway through *Hárbardsljód* (towards the end of stanza 19), then give the full text of *Baldrs draumar* ('Baldr's dreams'; not in the Codex Regius), and the first twenty-seven stanzas of *För Skírnis*, here called *Skírnismál* ('The lay of Skírnir'); the other four leaves witness the final twenty-three stanzas of *Vafthrúdnismál*, all of *Grímnismál* and *Hymiskvida*, and the beginning of the prose introduction to *Völundarkvida*. We have no way of knowing how much has been lost from this manuscript, but even the two scraps show less conscious organization than the Codex Regius, mixing up primarily Odinic material with that pertaining to other gods, and with *Völundarkvida* again apparently appended to mythological lore.

A further important witness to eddic poetry is the Hauksbók manuscript (AM 544 4to), written between 1302 and 1310 by Haukr Erlendsson (who became Icelandic Lawspeaker in 1294 and died in 1334), and containing on folios 20r–22r a variant version of *Völuspá* that was added by another hand after Haukr's death, likely around the middle of the fourteenth century. Some twenty-eight stanzas of the same poem are found in various manuscripts of the part of Snorri Sturluson's Prose Edda known as *Gylfaginning* ('The beguiling of Gylfi'), as well as single stanzas of *Hávamál*, *Vafthrúdnismál*, *Grímnismál*,

Lokasenna, Alvíssmál and *Skírnismál*. Other verses from the Codex Regius are also attested in various manuscripts of Snorri's *Skáldskaparmál* ('Treatise on the art of poetry'), to which other eddic poems not found in the Codex Regius are also occasionally attached, notably *Rígsthula* ('Ríg's list') and *Grottasöngr* ('Grotti's chanting'). The late thirteenth-century *Völsunga saga* bears witness to eleven of the heroic poems of the Codex Regius, found in a single manuscript that was also at one point in the Royal Collection of Copenhagen (Ny Kgl. Sml. 1824 b 4to), written around 1400, and seems to be using *Helgakvida Hundingsbana in fyrsta, Gripisspá, Reginsmál, Sigrdrífumál* (called 'The song of Brynhild' in *Völsunga saga*), *Brot af Sigurdarkvidu, Sigurdarkvida in skamma, Gudrúnarkvida in forna, Atlakvida, Atlamál in grœnlenzku, Gudrúnarhvöt* and *Hamdismál*, as well as the prose passage known as *Frá dauda Sinfjötla*. From the citations in the saga, it seems clear that its author had access to a manuscript containing the poems in a form very close to but not identical with the Codex Regius. There are also a few citations from *Reginsmál* and *Helreid Brynhildar* in the *Nornagests páttr* ('Story of Nornagest') found uniquely in Flateyjarbók (GkS 1005 fol.), a huge manuscript of 225 leaves, written 1387–94, and which likewise uniquely contains *Hyndluljód*, including the section known as *Völuspá in skamma* ('The shorter Völuspá'). Many of the texts discussed here, sometimes in variant forms, were copied into paper manuscripts in the post-medieval period, again attesting to continuing interest in them. Likewise, certain other texts which can broadly be called eddic are either embedded within other texts, or, like *Svipdagsmál* consisting of *Grógaldr* and *Fjölsvinnsmál*, preserved in several paper manuscripts, of which the earliest is from around 1650. In this volume, I include as an appendix four further poems which share so many affinities with those in the Codex Regius that they have regularly been included in editions and translations of eddic verse.

The first published edition of the first two poems in the Codex Regius (*Völuspá* and *Hávamál*), together with Latin translations and a version of Snorri's Edda, was edited by Peder Hansen

Resen (1625–88), and published in Copenhagen in 1665 within just a few years of Brynjólfur's presentation of the Codex Regius to the king; more than a century later (in 1787), the Arnamagnaean Institute in Copenhagen began to publish a series of editions of the texts with Latin translations. It was those Latin versions that inspired the first English translation of substantial parts of the Codex Regius by Amos Cottle of Magdalene College, Cambridge, in 1797, with a preface by a young Robert Southey (1774–1843), who went on to become Poet Laureate for three decades from 1813 onwards. The Swiss writer Paul Henri Mallet (1730–1807), appointed a professor of belles-lettres in Copenhagen in 1752, proved himself sufficiently enamoured of his adoptive country to produce his *Introduction à l'histoire du Danemarch où l'on traite de la religion, des moeurs, des lois, et des usages des anciens Danois* ('Introduction to the history of Denmark, in which is discussed the religion, customs, laws, and manners of the ancient Danes') in 1755, and his *Monuments de la mythologie et de la poèsie des Celtes, et particulièrement des anciens Scandinaves* ('Monuments of the mythology and poetry of the Celts, and particularly of the ancient Scandinavians'), which followed a year later; both volumes contributed mightily to the vast upsurge of interest in non-classical cultures that underlay the 'Romantic Movement'. Thomas Percy (1729–1811), Lord Bishop of Dromore, is perhaps best known for his *Reliques of Ancient English Poetry* (1765), but his highly influential *Northern Antiquities* of 1770 is in effect a translation of Mallet's work into English, with supplementary material based on Percy's own work; he had already produced the remarkable *Five Pieces of Runic Poetry* in 1763, a rendering of several skaldic texts. And then the flood-gates opened.

Writers and artists as diverse in time and temperament as Thomas Gray (1716–77), Sir Walter Scott (1771–1832), Alfred Lord Tennyson (1809–92), Richard Wagner (1813–83), William Morris (1834–96), Gerard Manley Hopkins (1844–89), August Strindberg (1849–1912), J. R. R. Tolkien (1892–1973), Jorge Luis Borges (1899–1986) and W. H. Auden (1907–73) have felt so moved that they produced their own renderings and reshapings of the texts. The Norwegian Sigrid Undset (1882–1949) and the

Icelander Halldór Laxness (1902–98), who won the Nobel Prize
for Literature in 1928 and 1955 respectively, have held that these
poems have influenced their literary output, and the challenge for
a translator is to render again such established texts in a way that
makes sense for a new generation; there can never be a definitive
version at once so playful and so diverse, preserved so imperfectly,
and so purposefully plundered.

The poems of the Codex Regius are composed in a variety of
alliterative metres, of which the most widespread, fittingly de-
scribed as *fornyrðislag* ('old poetry metre'; the term is used by
Snorri), has close affiliations to an apparently common inher-
ited Germanic metre that is also witnessed in Old English in
Beowulf (preserved in a manuscript from *c.* 1000, but perhaps
composed up to two and a half centuries earlier), and in Old
Saxon in the *Heliand* (composed *c.* 825); the metre is apparent
in the very first stanza of *Völuspá*:

> Hljóðs bið ek allar   helgar kindir,
> meiri ok minni   mǫgu Heimdallar.
> Viltu at ek, Valfǫðr,   vel fyr telja
> forn spjǫll fira,   þau er fremst um man?

> [A hearing I ask of all holy offspring,
> the higher and lower of Heimdall's brood.
> Do you want me, Corpse-father, to tally up well
> ancient tales of folk, from the first I recall?]

Each line consists of four stressed syllables (indicated here by
underlining), divided into two half-lines separated by a caesura
(given here as a blank space) linked by structural alliteration (indi-
cated here in bold). The first stressed syllable of the second half-line
is called the 'head-stave' (e.g. l.1 'hel'), and alliterates with one or
both of the stressed syllables in the first half-line; the fourth stressed
syllable does not partake of the structural alliterative scheme. Note
that in addition to the structural alliteration, a good poet will also
often have ornamental alliteration and other artful effects of rhyme
and assonance both within and between lines (as in the sequences:

Valfǫðr vel fyr and *Vil-/Val-/vel* in line 3; *allar/-dallar* linking lines 1 and 2; *fyr/forn/fir-* linking lines 3 and 4). Each half-line and in *fornyrðislag* in general has between four and six syllables.

By contrast, an apparently variant form, *málaháttr* ('speech metre'), is also found, where the rules of *fornyrðislag* seem relaxed, and more syllables, both stressed and unstressed, are permitted. The only poem in the Codex Regius consistently composed in *málaháttr* is *Atlamál*; elsewhere, the metre can simply be seen as a slightly looser form of *fornyrðislag*. Stanza 1 of *Atlamál* illustrates:

Frétt hefir ǫld ófu,   þá er endr um gǫrðu
seggir samkundu,   sú var nýt fæstum.
Œxtu einmæli;   yggr var þeim síðan
ok it sama sonum Gjúka,   er vóru sannráðnir.

[Folk have heard of the strife when long ago
warriors held a meeting that helped very few;
they spoke together in private, then terror overwhelmed them,
as well as Gjúki's sons, who were wholly betrayed.]

Here each line has five rather than four stressed syllables, the first half-line routinely contains double alliteration, and each half-line contains between five and eight syllables; again, however, the first stressed syllable of the second half-line sets the structural alliterative pattern (note that all vowels alliterate, as they do in *fornyrðislag* too).

The other main metre is *ljóðaháttr* ('song metre'), where paired alliterating verses are capped by a third and self-alliterating verse, again with a variant form, *galdralag* ('spell metre'), where there is repetition of self-alliterating verses. Illustrative examples can be given from *Hávamál* 92 and *För Skírnis* 35 denoting different techniques for winning young ladies through compliments or curses, as required:

Fagurt skal mæla   ok fé bjóða
    sá er vill fljóðs ást fá,
líki leyfa   ins ljósa mans:
    sá fær er fríar.

[Fair speaking and fine gifts
will win the love of a lass;
praise the figure of a fine-looking girl:
the one who woos will win.]

Hrímgrímnir heitir þurs,   er þik hafa skal
    fyr nágrindr neðan;
þar þér vílmegir   á viðarrótum
    geitahland gefi;
æðri drykkju   fá þú aldregi,
    mær, af þínum munum,
    mær, at mínum munum.

['Hrímgrímnir is the ogre's name, who shall have you,
down below Corpse-gates;
rough thralls there under the roots of a tree
will give you the piss of goats;
you'll never get a better drink,
girl, whatever you want,
girl, after what I want.']

In general terms, *fornyrðislag* is used for narrative, and
ljóðaháttr for speech, particularly in wisdom-dialogues. It is not
unusual to find combinations of these metres within the same
poem (especially *Fáfnismál*) for specific effect, and such changes
need not indicate interpolation from another source. There is
then, as in all poetry, a peculiar music to the texts of the Codex
Regius, and while in attempting to recreate at least a distant
echo of that music I have not tried to adhere strictly to an 'Eng-
lished' version of the metres, I have taken full advantage of the
fact that English offers rich possibilities for artful alliteration of
exactly the kind employed much more regularly in Old Norse–
Icelandic verse.

   Like their metre, the language of the poems is generally
spare and unadorned. The assumption of an audience at least
partly aware of a wider mythological and legendary background
of shared story is evident from the 'kennings' (*kenningar*): in effect,
mini-riddles that rely for their solution either on a familiarity with

the genealogies and putative biographies of various gods and
heroes, or on a knowledge of the compressed and allusive dic-
tion of skaldic verse. Understanding the poems of the Codex
Regius requires knowledge of not only the many names that
the same gods or giants might go by, but also their family affil-
iations: the god Thor, for example, might be called Hlórridi,
son of Odin (or son of any other of Odin's many names), son
of Earth, father of Magni or slayer of Hrungnir (or almost
any other giant), as he is in several of the texts. Likewise, gold
might be designated as 'river-fire' or 'strife-metal' and ships as
'wave-steeds' or 'beasts of the deep' (cf. the range of related
gold-kennings in *HH I* 21; *Reg* 1; *Fáf* 42; *Gkv I* 26; *Sigsk* 16;
Odd 21; *Atk* 27; and for similar ship-kennings in *Hym* 20, 26;
HH I 29, 30, 49; *Reg* 16, 17; *Sigrd* 10 – for abbreviations, see
pp. 266–7); in such cases, rather than solve or mask the ken-
ning, I have opted for a marginal gloss; while in general eddic
verse is far less packed with kennings and specifically poetic
forms (*heiti*) than skaldic verse, this only makes these features
when they do appear all the more notable. Some poems, such
as *Atlamál*, are almost entirely free from kennings, while others
are dense with them, particularly *Hymiskvida*. It is precisely
those changes in style and tone that distinguish the texts from
each other. Longer explanations are given in the Notes, where
the interrelationships between poems are also explored. Indeed,
as a conscious compilation of viking lore, the Codex Regius
seems in many ways specifically designed to teach and reinforce
knowledge of the very traditions required to appreciate fully
the poems themselves.

Many of the poems in the *Elder Edda* appear in later manu-
scripts and editions with different titles from those found here,
which are more or less traditional. A further problem is that the
Codex Regius does not actually include titles for all the poems,
and several titles are supplied from other sources (in most cases
later manuscripts or Snorri); such additions include *Vsp* (there
is damage at the top of the first page: it may well have been
there once); *HH I*; *HHj*; *HH II*; *Gríp*; *Reg*; *Fáf*; *Sigrd*; *Brot*;
Odd. All three of the Gudrún-lays (*Gkv I, Gkv II* and *Gkv III*)
just appear in the Codex Regius as *Guðrúnarkviða*, while *Sigsk*

has the heading *kviða Sigurðar*, and *Hym* and *Hel* as the descriptive *Thór dró Miðgarðsorm* ('Thor hauled up the Midgard-serpent') and *Brynhildr reið helveg* ('Brynhild rode the path to Hel') respectively; *Atk* has the full (and, as I argue, misleading, title) *Atlakviða in grœnlenzka*. A different kind of problem surrounds the many prose passages found in the Codex Regius, several with titles of their own; in all cases I have tried to reflect both the patchy reality of the Codex Regius and the fact that many of these prose passages are self-evidently later additions meant to 'clarify' pre-existing verse. Likewise, extra-metrical attribution of individual verses is by no means consistent in the Codex Regius, and I have therefore taken a similarly minimalist approach. It is important to realize that the whole of the Codex Regius is written out as prose, with various space-saving measures (abbreviations, marginal annotations and even individual runes used to stand for the words they signify), and that all of these ingenious devices, doubtless familiar to the original compiler and his copyists, are less clear today. Sometimes it has been necessary to supply obvious defects in the manuscripts, whether by expanding abbreviations, such as the frequent use throughout *Háv* of runic ᛉ for 'man' or acronyms for the repeated phrases of (for example) *Vsp* 9, 23 and 25, or individual words or even whole stanzas that have clearly dropped out in copying (for example at *Hár* 28 or *Ríg* 18). Such necessarily speculative reconstruction of obviously damaged texts only serves to underline the fact that the edda given here is old, and all the more venerable for that.

But the gap at the heart of the Codex Regius should remind us that what we have is both limited and incomplete, just as the poems themselves point to the limitations of both gods and men. In considering the Codex Regius as a book of viking lore, we should always remember that the limitations of Odin's knowledge are explicit in *Grímnismál*, *Vafthrúdnismál* and *Hávamál*, where despite his many manifestations and connotations he is exposed as effectively out of date, a sage whose time has passed and whose end is both certain and predictable, except apparently by him. The fact that Christian scribes and commentators have preserved almost all that we have of Norse pagan faith should make us cautious about drawing conclusions that are too broad or too specific. What we do know is that none of the poems of the Codex Regius appears as if it would be truly useful in pagan worship; none offers prayers or propitiates the powers that they name; none asks for anything except to be remembered. Instead, we find spells, oaths, threats and curses, uttered even by the gods themselves. Antiquarians have expanded on the lore, as seen from a safe and suitable distance of time and space. The twin fatal flaws of Norse pagan belief were that it was fragmented and that it had an uncertain future: such a disparate set of locally dissimilar and varied versions of what was never a unified creed, and such a combination of geographically distinct cults, none of which seems to have sought to proselytize or crave converts, was surely no match for the well-defined, written doctrine of muscular Christianity that perhaps inevitably replaced it. As a best hope, paganism is depicted as offering an ill-defined afterlife of feasting and fighting for the few, to be terminated in an apocalyptic battle at Ragnarök ('The doom of the powers'), where many of the gods themselves will be slain; it will be left to others to see further ahead, and literally to pick up the playing-pieces again.

The parlous present state of this precious book of poems reminds us of the tenuous transmission of so much ancient lore, and how lucky we are still to be able to access and, at least in part, to understand verse that retains its power across the centuries to entertain, to educate and, perhaps above all, and in the spirit of the vikings, to enthral.

Further Reading

Useful websites

alvíssmál, journal of Old Norse–Icelandic studies <http://user page.fu-berlin.de/~alvismal/>

The Árni Magnússon Institute, Copenhagen (Den Arnamagnæanske Samling), the main repository of Old Norse–Icelandic manuscripts in Denmark

The Árni Magnússon Institute, Reykjavík (Stofnun Árna Magnússonar), the main repository of Old Norse–Icelandic manuscripts in Iceland

Eysteinn Björnsson's homepage, including texts of *Gylfaginning*, *Hymiskviða* and *Völuspá*, as well as a facsimile of AM 748 Ia 4to <notendur.hi.is/eybjorn/ugm/hymir/index.html>

Heimskringla, an online collection of Old Norse–Icelandic texts <www.heimskringla.no/wiki/Main_Page>

Poetic Edda, searchable electronic text of the 5th edn of Neckel/ Kuhn <titus.uni-frankfurt.de/texte/etcs/germ/anord/edda/edda. htm>

SagaNet, database of digitalized Icelandic manuscripts, early printed texts and editions

Septentrionalia, online collection of antiquarian texts and scholarly aids for Old Norse–Icelandic

Viking Society for Northern Research <www.le.ac.uk/ee/viking/>

Discography

Selected Readings from 'A New Introduction to Old Norse' (Chaucer Studio, 2003)

Sequentia, *Myths from Ancient Iceland* (Deutsche Harmonia Mundi, 1999)

Reference tools

Gillespie, George T., *A Catalogue of Persons Named in German Heroic Literature (700–1600), including Named Animals and Objects and Ethnic Names* (Oxford, 1973)

Kellogg, R. L., *A Concordance to Eddic Poetry* (East Lansing, MI, 1988)

La Farge, Beatrice, and P. Tucker, *Glossary to the Poetic Edda* (Heidelberg, 1992)

Pulsiano, Phillip, Kirsten Wolf, et al., eds, *Medieval Scandinavia: An Encyclopedia*, Garland Encyclopedia of the Middle Ages 1 (New York and London, 1993)

Editions, translations, facsimiles and commentaries

Auden, W. H., and Paul B. Taylor, trans., *Norse Poems*, rev. edn (London, 1981)

Bellows, Henry Adams, trans., *The Poetic Edda: Translated from the Icelandic with an Introduction and Notes* (New York, 1923)

Byock, Jesse, *The Saga of the Volsungs* (London, 1999)

Clarke, D. E. Martin, ed. and trans., *The Hávamál, with Selections from Other Poems of the Edda, Illustrating the Wisdom of the North in Heathen Times* (Cambridge, 1929)

Dronke, Ursula, ed., *The Poetic Edda I: Heroic Poems* (Oxford, 1969)

—, *The Poetic Edda II: Mythological Poems* (Oxford, 1997)

Evans, D. A. H., ed., *Hávamál* (London, 1987)

Faulkes, Anthony, *Hávamál: Glossary* (London, 1987)

—, trans., *Snorri Sturluson: Edda* (London, 1987)

—, ed., *Snorri Sturluson, Edda. Prologue and Gylfaginning* (Oxford, 1982)

—, ed., *Snorri Sturluson, Edda. Skáldskaparmál and Háttatal* (Oxford, 1998)

Gísli Sigurðsson, ed., *Eddukvæði* (Reykjavik, 1998)

Guðbrandur Vígfússon and F. York Powell, eds and trans., *Corpus Poeticum Boreale. The Poetry of the Old Northern Tongue*, 2 vols (Oxford, 1883; repr. New York, 1965)

Hollander, Lee M., trans., *The Poetic Edda, with Introduction and Explanatory Notes* (Austin, TX, 1962)

Kershaw, N., trans., *Stories and Ballads of the Far Past* (Cambridge, 1921)

Larrington, Carolyne, trans., *The Poetic Edda*, Oxford World's Classics (Oxford, 1996)

Machan, T. W., ed., *Vafþrúðnismál*, 2nd edn, Durham and St Andrews Medieval Texts 6 (Toronto, 2008)

Neckel, Gustav, ed., *Die Lieder des Codex Regius nebst verwandten Denkmälern I: Text*, rev. Hans Kuhn, 5th edn (Heidelberg, 1983)

See, Klaus von, Beatrice La Farge, Wolfgang Gerhold, Eve Picard, and Katja Schulz, eds, *Kommentar zu den Liedern der Edda*, 6 vols (Heidelberg, 1993–)

Sigurður Nordal, ed., *Völuspá*, trans. B. Benedikz and J. McKinnell, Durham and St Andrews Medieval Texts 1 (Durham, 1978)

Terry, Patricia, trans., *Poems of the Elder Edda*, rev. edn (Philadelphia, 1990)

Thorpe, Benjamin, trans., *Edda Sæmundar hins froða: The Edda of Sæmund the Learned*, 2 vols (London, 1866)

Tolley, Clive, ed., *Grottasöngr: The Song of Grotti* (London, 2008)

Vésteinn Ólason, ed., *Konungsbók Eddukvæða. Codex Regius, Stofnun Árna Magnússonar á Íslandi Gl. Kgl. Sml. 2365 4to*, Manuscripta Islandica Medii Aevi 3 (Reykjavik, 2001)

Wessén, Elias, ed., *Fragments of the Elder and the Younger Edda AM 748 I and II 4to*, Corpus Codicum Islandicorum Medii Aevi 17 (Copenhagen and Reykjavik, 1945)

General surveys and discussions

Acker, Paul, and Carolyne Larrington, eds, *The Poetic Edda: Essays on Old Norse Mythology* (New York, 2002)

Andersson, Theodore M., 'The Lays of the Lacuna of *Codex*

Regius', in *Speculum Norroenum: Norse Studies in Memory of Gabriel Turville-Petre*, ed. Ursula Dronke, Guðrún P. Helgadóttir, et al. (Odense, 1981), pp. 7–26

—, *The Legend of Brynhild*, Islandica 43 (Ithaca, NY, 1980)

Anlezark, Daniel, ed., *Now Shines the Sun: Essays on Old Norse and Old English Literature in Honour of John McKinnell* (Toronto, 2011)

Brink, Stefan, ed., *The Viking World* (London and New York, 2008)

Davidson, H. R. Ellis, *Gods and Myths of Northern Europe* (Harmondsworth, 1964)

—, *Pagan Scandinavia* (London, 1967)

Dronke, Ursula, 'The Contribution of Eddic Studies', in *Viking Revaluations: Viking Society Centenary Symposium 14–15 May 1992*, ed. Anthony Faulkes and Richard Perkins (London, 1993), pp. 121–7

—, *Myth and Fiction in Early Norse Lands* (Aldershot, 1996)

Ellis, H. R., *The Road to Hel: A Study of the Conception of the Dead in Old Norse Literature* (Cambridge, 1943)

Ewing, Thor, *Gods and Worshippers in the Viking and Germanic World* (Chalford, 2008)

Fidjestøl, Bjarne, *The Dating of Eddic Poetry* (Copenhagen, 1999)

Gísli Sigurðsson, 'On the Classification of Eddic Heroic Poetry in View of the Oral Theory', in *Poetry in the Scandinavian Middle Ages*, ed. Teresa Pàroli, Seventh International Saga Conference, Atti del XII Congresso internazionale di studi sull'alto medioevo (Spoleto, 1990), pp. 245–56

Glendinning, Robert J., and Haraldur Bessason, eds, *Edda: A Collection of Essays*, University of Manitoba Icelandic Studies 4 (Winnipeg, 1983)

Gould, Chester Nathan, 'Dwarf-Names: A Study in Old Icelandic Religion', *Publication of the Modern Language Association* 44 (1929), pp. 939–67

Gunnell, Terry, *The Origins of Drama in Scandinavia* (Cambridge, 1995)

Hall, Alaric, *Elves in Anglo-Saxon England: Matters of Belief, Health, Gender and Identity*, Anglo-Saxon Studies 8 (Woodbridge, 2007; repr. 2009)

Hallberg, Peter, 'Elements of Myth in the Heroic Lays of the Poetic Edda', in *German Dialects: Linguistic and Philological Investigations*, ed. Bela Brogyanyi and Thomas Krömmelbein (Amsterdam, 1986), pp. 213–47

—, *Old Icelandic Poetry: Eddic Lay and Skaldic Verse*, trans. Paul Schach and Sonja Lindgrenson (Lincoln, NE, 1975)

Harris, Joseph, 'Eddic Poetry', in *Old Norse-Icelandic Literature: A Critical Guide*, ed. Carol J. Clover and John Lindow, Islandica 45 (Ithaca, NY, 1985), pp. 157–96

—, 'Eddic Poetry as Oral Poetry: The Evidence of Parallel Passages in the Helgi Poems for Questions of Composition and Performance', in *Edda: A Collection of Essays*, ed. Glendinning and Haraldur Bessason, pp. 208–40

—, 'The Performance of Eddic Poetry: A Retrospective', in *The Oral Epic: Performance and Music*, ed. Karl Reichl, Intercultural Music Studies 12 (Berlin, 2000)

Haugen, Einar, 'The Edda as Ritual: Odin and his Masks', in *Edda: A Collection of Essays*, ed. Glendinning and Haraldur Bessason, pp. 3–24

Jackson, Elizabeth, 'Eddic Listing Techniques and the Coherence of *Rúnatal*', *Alvíssmál* 5 (1995), pp. 81–106

Jónas Kristjánsson, *Eddas and Sagas: Iceland's Medieval Literature* (Reykjavik, 1988)

—, 'Stages in the Composition of Eddic Poetry', in *Poetry in the Scandinavian Middle Ages*, ed. Teresa Pàroli, Seventh International Saga Conference, Atti del XII Congresso internazionale di studi sull'alto medioevo (Spoleto, 1990), pp. 201–18

Kellogg, Robert L., 'Literacy and Orality in the Poetic Edda', in *Vox intexta: Orality and Textuality in the Middle Ages*, ed. A. N. Doane and Carol Braun Pasternack (Madison, WI, 1991), pp. 89–101

Lindow, John, 'Mythology and Mythography', in *Old Norse-Icelandic Literature: A Critical Guide*, ed. Carol J. Clover and John Lindow, Islandica 45 (Ithaca, NY, 1985), pp. 21–67

—, *Scandinavian Mythology: An Annotated Bibliography*, Garland Folklore Bibliographies 13 (New York and London, 1988)

McKinnell, John, *Both One and Many: Essays on Change and Variety in Late Norse Heathenism* (Rome, 1994)

—, *Essays on Eddic Poetry*, ed. Donata Kick, Toronto Old Norse–Icelandic Studies (Toronto, 2011)

—, *Meeting the Other in Norse Myth and Legend* (Cambridge, 2005)

—, David Ashurst and Donata Kick, eds, *The Fantastic in Old Norse/Icelandic Literature: Sagas and the British Isles*, 2 vols (Durham, 2006)

Meletinskij, Eleazar M., 'Scandinavian Mythology as a System of Oppositions', in *Patterns in Oral Literature*, ed. Dimitri Segal and Heda Jason (The Hague, 1977), pp. 252–60

Motz, Lotte, *The Beauty and the Hag: Female Figures of Germanic Faith and Myth*, Philologica Germanica 15 (Vienna, 1993)

—, *The Wise One of the Mountain: Form, Function, and Significance of the Subterranean Smith: A Study in Folklore*, Göppinger Arbeiten zur Germanistik 379 (Göppingen, 1983)

Nerman, Birger, *The Poetic Edda in the Light of Archaeology* (Coventry, 1934)

Page, R. I., *Chronicles of the Vikings: Records, Memorials and Myths* (London, 1995)

Philpotts, Bertha S., *The Elder Edda and Ancient Scandinavian Drama* (Cambridge, 1920)

Quinn, Judy, 'Editing the Edda: The Case of *Völuspá*', *Scripta Islandica* 51 (2001), pp. 69–92

—, 'The Naming of Eddic Poems', *Parergon* 8:2 (1990), pp. 97–115

—, 'Verseform and Voice in Eddic Poems: The Discourses of *Fáfnismál*', *Arkiv för nordisk filologi* 107 (1992), pp. 100–30

—, Kate Heslop and Tarrin Wills, eds, *Learning and Understanding in the Old Norse World: Essays in Honour of Margaret Clunies Ross*, Medievala Texts and Cultures of Northern Europe 18 (Turnhout, 2007)

Ross, Margaret Clunies, *A History of Old Norse Poetry and Poetics* (Woodbridge, 2005)

—, ed., *Old Norse Myths, Literature, and Society* (Odense, 2003)

—, *Prolonged Echoes: Old Norse Myths in Medieval Northern Society. Volume I: The Myths; Volume II: The Reception of*

Norse Myths in Medieval Iceland, The Viking Collection 7, 10 (Odense, 1994, 1998)

Shippey, Tom, ed., *The Shadow-Walkers: Jacob Grimm's Mythology of the Monstrous* (Tempe, AZ, 2005)

Sims-Williams, Patrick, *The Iron House in Ireland*, H. M. Chadwick Memorial Lecture 16 (Cambridge, 2005)

Sørensen, Preben Meulengracht, *The Unmanly Man: Concepts of Sexual Defamation in Early Northern Society*, trans. Joan Turville-Petre, The Viking Collection 1 (Odense, 1983)

Steblin-Kamenskij, M. I., *Myth: The Icelandic Sagas and Eddas*, trans. Mary P. Coote (Ann Arbor, MI, 1982)

Turville-Petre, E. O. G., *Myth and Religion of the North: The Religion of Ancient Scandinavia* (London, 1964)

Ulvestad, Bjarne, 'How Old are the Mythological Eddic Poems?', *Scandinavian Studies* 26 (1954), pp. 49–69

Vries, Jan de, *Heroic Song and Heroic Legend*, trans. B. J. Timmer (London, 1963)

A Note on Spelling, Pronunciation and Translation

Spelling generally reflects 'normalized' Old Norse–Icelandic, but with the final consonant marking the nominative singular (generally -r, -n, or -l) generally removed, except where it follows a vowel. The digraphs 'æ/Æ' and 'œ/Œ', as well as accents, have been retained, but the less familiar 'ǫ' has been levelled to 'ö'. Likewise the ultimately Anglo-Saxon consonants 'ð/Ð' and 'þ/Þ' are generally simplified to 'd/D' and 'th/Th' respectively. In a few cases (notably 'Odin' and 'Thor'), I have retained the form most familiar to the general reader; it would be pedantic to insist upon the more accurate 'Óðin' and 'Thór'.

I have retained the original spelling where I quote original forms and for Modern Icelandic names; the resulting hybrid appearance of some notes is not, I hope, overly confusing, but emblematic of a deeper malaise: there are two quite separate systems for pronouncing Old Norse–Icelandic, depending on which side of the divide one wishes to jump. Some scholars encourage the use of Modern Icelandic pronunciation, since while the language has clearly developed greatly over the past millennium in ways which render such soundings inappropriate for the ancient tongue, there is great value in stressing the continuity of culture with a living language, and the fact that this poetry is ripe for performance (as witness the modest Discography in the Further Reading) makes modern approximations most attractive. Others urge the use of a reconstructed form of the language, in so far as that can be deduced from later developments and cognate forms, although alas such a procedure tends to render what were once vibrant patterns into artificiality. There is no simple solution, although consistency is the real key; detailed versions of both systems can be found in (for example) Michael Barnes, *A New Introduction to Old Norse, Part I: Grammar* (London, 1999), pp. 8–21. Given such disagreement, suffice it to say that the acute accent on vowels is a mark of length, not stress; and that most Norse words are stressed on the first syllable.

I have also taken various more-or-less arbitrary decisions with regard to the translation of more-or-less transparent names, acutely conscious of the fact that such random judgement-calls are often both unappealing and wide open to appeal. I have tried to mitigate this frankly indefensible position by making full use of an Index of Names that aims to be both comprehensive and comprehensible; I suspect that for many of the poems of the Codex Regius, collected, compiled and perhaps even composed by antiquarians, the confusing array of shared names of apparently different entities, of multiple names for the same individual and of seemingly transparent names that define specific attributes has contributed greatly to muddying the waters of understanding, and it seems only honest to reproduce, at least in part, that opacity here.

Of the attempts to render this often intractable material into more-or-less coherent and comprehensible English, I would signal in particular the sterling efforts of Benjamin Thorpe (1866), Guðbrandur Vígfússon (1883), Olive Bray (1908), Henry Adams Bellows (1923), J. R. R. Tolkien (composed in the earlier 1930s, and ed. Christopher Tolkien in 2009), Lee M. Hollander (1962), Patricia Terry (1969; reprinted 1990), W. H. Auden (with Paul B. Taylor, 1969, revised and expanded in 1981), Ursula Dronke (1969 and 1997), Ray Page (1995) and Carolyne Larrington (1996), all of which works I have consulted and made frequent use of both in tempering my own efforts and in compiling the Notes; likewise the recent magisterial and comprehensive multi-volume German edition, translation and commentary by Klaus von See and his team (1993–), to which I am also greatly indebted, provides a sure and splendid platform for future work.

The Elder Edda

THE MYTHOLOGICAL
POEMS OF THE
CODEX REGIUS

Völuspá: The prophecy of the seeress

1. A hearing I ask of all holy offspring,
    the higher and lower of Heimdall's brood.
    Do you want me, Corpse-father, to tally   *Corpse-father* Odin
        up well
    ancient tales of folk, from the first I recall?

2. I recall those giants, born early on,
    who long ago brought me up;
    nine worlds I recall, nine wood-dwelling witches,
    the famed tree of fate down under the earth.

3. It was early in ages when Ymir made   *Ymir* 'Groaner',
        his home,   primordial giant
    there was neither sand nor sea, nor cooling waves;
    no earth to be found, nor heaven above:
    a gulf beguiling, nor grass anywhere.

4. Before Bur's sons brought up the lands,   *Bur's sons* Odin and his
    they who moulded famed middle-earth;   brothers Vili and Vé
    Sun shone from the south on the stones of the hall:
    then the ground grew with the leek's green growth.

5. Sun, Moon's escort, flung from the south
    her right arm round heaven's rim.
    Sun did not know where she had a hall;
    the stars knew not where they had stations,
    Moon did not know what might he had.

6. Then all the powers went to their thrones of destiny,
    high-holy gods, and deliberated this:
    to Night and her children they gave their names:
    Morning they called one, another Mid-day,
    Afternoon and Evening, to tally up the years.

7. The Æsir assembled on Action-field,
    they who built high-timbered temples and altars;
    they set down forges, fashioned treasures,
    shaped tongs, and fabricated tools.

8. They played board-games in the meadow: they
            made merry;
    in no way for them was there want of gold
    until there came three ogres' daughters,
    vastly mighty, from Giants' Domain.

                        *

[*Dvergatal* ('The tally of dwarfs'):]

9. Then all the powers went to their thrones of destiny,
    high-holy gods, and deliberated this:
    who should shape the troop of dwarfs,
    from Brimir's blood, from Bláin's limbs.

10. There was Mótsognir made most esteemed
    of all the dwarfs, and Durin next;
    many man-shaped forms they made,
    dwarfs from earth, as Durin told:

11. New-moon, Moon-wane, North and South,
    East and West, All-stealer, Dawdler,
    Trembler, Grumbler, Tubby, Old Salt,
    Friend and Friendly, Great-grandpa, Mead-wolf.

12. Swig and Wand-elf, Wind-elf, Urge,
    Knowing and Daring, Spurt, Wise and Bright,
    Corpse and New-counsel – now the dwarfs –
    Regin and Cunning-counsel – have I reckoned aright.

13. Filer, Wedger, New-found, Needler,
    Handle, Slogger, Craftsman, Waster,
    Swift, Horn-bearer, Famed and Puddle,
    Mud-plain, Warrior, Oaken-shield.

14. Time it is to reckon back to Praiser,
    the dwarfs in Dawdler's band for the children of men:
    those who sought from halls of stone
    the dwellings of Mud-plains on Soily-flats.

15. There was Dripper and Eager-for-strife,
    Grey, Mound-treader, Shelter-plain, Glowing,
    Artisan, Stainer, Crooked-Finn, Great-grandpa.

16. Elf and Yngvi, Oaken-shield,
    Much-wise and Frosty, Finn and Beguiler;
    there will remain in memory while the world lasts,
    the lineage of Praiser, properly listed.

                                    *

[return to *Völuspá*:]

17. Until there came three from that company,
    powerful and pleasant Æsir to a house.
    They found on land, lacking vigour,
    Ash and Embla, free of fate.

18. Breath they had not, energy they held not,
    no warmth, nor motion, nor healthy looks;
    breath gave Odin, energy gave Hœnir,
    warmth gave Lódur, and healthy looks.

19. An ash I know stands, Yggdrasil by name,
    a high tree, drenched with bright white mud;
    from there come the dews that drop in the dales,
    it always stands green over Destiny's well.

20. From there come maidens, knowing much,
    three from the lake that stands under the tree:
    Destiny they called one, Becoming the second
    – they carved on wood-tablets – Shall-be the third;
    laws they laid down, lives they chose
    for the children of mankind, the fates of men.

21. She remembers the war, the first in the world,
    when they stabbed at Gold-draught with many spears,
    and in the hall of the High One they burned   *High One* Odin
        her body.
    Three times they burned the one thrice-born,
    often, over again; yet she lives still.

22. They called her Brightness, when she came to their
        homes,
    a witch who could foretell; she knew the skill of wands,
    she made magic where she could, made magic in a
        trance;
    she was always a delight to a wicked woman.

23. Then all the powers went to their thrones of destiny,
    high-holy gods, and deliberated this:
    whether the Æsir were obliged to render tribute,
    and all the gods were obliged to pay the price.

24. Odin flung his spear, cast it into the host,
    still that was the war, the first in the world;
    the shield-wall was shattered of the
        fortress of the Æsir,   *fortress of the Æsir* Ásgard
    the Vanir with war-spells trampled the battlefield.

25. Then all the powers went to their thrones of destiny,
    high-holy gods, and deliberated this:
    who had mixed the whole sky with mischief
    or given Óð's girl to giants' kin.   *Óð's girl* Freyja

26. Thor alone threw blows there, bursting with rage
    – he seldom sits still when he hears such things said –
    oaths were trampled, words and assurances,
    every binding pledge that had passed between.

27. She knows that Heimdall's hearing is hidden
    under that brilliant holy tree;
    she sees a river surge with a muddy stream
    from Corpse-father's pledge: do you know yet, or what?

28. Alone she sat out, when the aged one came,   *aged one* Odin
    the Dread One of the Æsir, and she looked   *Dread One of*
        in his eye: *the Æsir* Odin
    'What do you ask me? Why do you try me?
    I know it all, Odin: where you hid your eye,
    in the much-famed fountain of Mímir;
    Mímir sips mead every morning
    from Corpse-father's pledge: do you know yet, or what?'

29. War-father picked for her rings and circlets: *War-father* Odin
    he had back wise tidings and wands of prophecy;
    she saw widely and widely beyond, over every world.

30. She saw valkyries come from widely beyond,
    ready to ride to the people of the gods.
    Shall-be bore one shield, Brandisher another,
    Battle, War, Wand-maid and Spear-brandisher:
    now are reckoned War-lord's ladies,   *War-lord* Odin
    ready to ride over earth, valkyries.

31. I saw for Baldr, the blood-stained god,
    Odin's son, his fate fully settled;
    there stood blooming, above the ground,
    meagre, mighty beautiful: mistletoe.

32. From that plant, that seemed so slender,
    Höd learned to shoot a dangerous dart of harm;
    Baldr's brother was quickly born:
    that son of Odin learned to kill one night old.

33. He never washed hands nor combed his head,
    till he put to the pyre Baldr's foe;
    but Frigg lamented in Fen-halls,
    for Slain-hall's woe: do you know yet, or what?

[34. Then Váli's war-bands were woven   *Váli* Loki's son
    – rather hard were the bonds – out of his own guts.]

35. She saw a prisoner prostrate under Kettle-grove,
    in the likeness of Loki, ever eager for harm;
    there sits Sigyn, over her husband,
    but she feels little glee: do you know yet, or what?

36. A river flows from the East through venom-valleys
    with knives and swords: Stern is its name.

37. There stood to the north, on Moon-wane-plains,
    a hall of gold, of Sindri's line;   *Sindri* 'Sparky', a dwarf?
    a second stood, on Never-cooled,
    the beer-hall of a giant, the one called Brimir.

38. A hall she saw standing far from the sun,
    on Dead-body-strands: its doors face north;
    venom-drops flowed in through the roof-holes:
    that hall is plaited from serpents' spines.

39. She saw there wading through heavy currents,
    men false-sworn and murderous men,
    and those who gull another's faithfulest girl;
    there Spite-striker sucks the bodies of the dead
    – a wolf tore men – do you know yet, or what?

40. East sat an old crone in Iron-wood,
     and suckled there the seed of Fenrir: *seed of Fenrir*
     from them all shall emerge a certain one,   monstrous wolves
     a grabber of the moon in monstrous guise.

41. He is filled with the life-blood of doomed men,
     reddens the powers' dwellings with ruddy gore;
     the sun-beams turn black the following summer,
     all weather woeful: do you know yet, or what?

42. There sat on a grave-mound and plucked at a harp,
     the giantess's herdsman, happy Eggthér;
     over him there crowed in Gallows-wood,
     a bright-red cock, whose name is Much-wise.

43. Over the Æsir there crowed Golden-comb,
     who wakes the warriors at Host-father's home;
     another crows beneath the earth,
     a soot-red cock in the halls of Hel.

44. Garm howls loud before Looming-cave,
     the bond will break, and the ravenous one run;
     much lore she knows, I see further ahead,
     of the powers' fate, implacable, of the victory-gods.

45. Brothers will struggle and slaughter each other,
     and sisters' sons spoil kinship's bonds.
     It's hard on earth: great whoredom;
     axe-age, blade-age, shields are split;
     wind-age, wolf-age, before the world crumbles:
     no one shall spare another.

46. Mím's sons sport, the wood of destiny is   *wood of destiny*
          kindled   Yggdrasil
     at the ancient Sounding-horn.
     Heimdall blows loud, the horn is aloft,
     Odin speaks with Mím's head.

47. The standing ash of Yggdrasil shudders,
    the aged tree groans, and the giant breaks free.
    All are afraid on the paths of Hel,
    before Surt's kin swallows it up.   *Surt* fire-giant

48. What's with the Æsir? What's with the elves?
    All Giants' Domain groans, the Æsir hold council,
    the dwarfs murmur before their stone doors,
    lords of the cliff-wall: do you know yet, or what?

49. Garm now howls loud before Looming-cave,
    the bond will break, and the ravenous one run;
    much lore she knows, I see further ahead,
    of the powers' fate, implacable, of the victory-gods.

50. Hrym drives from the East, holds his shield   *Hrym* giant
        ahead,
    Great-wand writhes in giant-wrath;   *Great-wand* World-serpent
    the serpent strikes waves, the eagle screams,
    pale-beaked rips bodies, Nail-boat breaks free.

51. A vessel journeys from the East, Muspell's troops
        will come,
    over the waters, while Loki steers.
    All the monstrous offspring accompany the ravenous one,
    The brother of Býleist is with them on the   *brother of*
        trip.   *Býleist* Loki

52. Surt comes from the South with what damages   *damages*
        branches,   *branches* fire
    there shines from his sword the sun of corpse-gods;
    rock-cliffs clash, troll-wives crash,
    warriors tread Hel-roads, and heaven is rent.

53. Then there comes for Hlín a second sorrow,   *Hlín* Frigg
    when Odin goes to fight the wolf
    and Beli's bright bane against Surt: *Beli's bane* Frey
    then's when Frigg's beloved must fall.

[54. Then there comes the great son of Victory-   *Victory-father*
     father,   *Odin*
     Vídar, to fight against the slaughtering   *slaughtering beast* Fenrir
         beast;
     with his hand he sends his sword to the heart
     of Hvedrung's son: then his father is   *Hvedrung* Loki
         avenged.]

55. The earth's girdle gapes over heaven,   *earth's girdle*
    the dread serpent's jaws yawn on high,   *World-serpent*
    Odin's son must meet the serpent,   *Odin's son* Thor
    when the wolf is dead, and Vídar's kin.   *Vídar's kin* Odin

56. Then there comes the famous offspring   *offspring of*
        of Hlödyn,   *Hlödyn* Thor
    Odin's son goes to fight the serpent;
    the defender of middle-earth strikes in his   *defender of*
        wrath;   *middle-earth* Thor
    – all warriors must abandon their homesteads –
    he goes nine paces, the son of Fjörgyn,   *son of Fjörgyn* Thor
    spent, from the snake that fears no spite.

57. The sun turns black, land sinks into sea;
    the bright stars scatter from the sky.
    Flame flickers up against the world-tree;
    fire flies high against heaven itself.

58. Garm now howls loud before Looming-cave,
    the bond will break, and the ravenous one run;
    much lore she knows, I see further ahead,
    of the powers' fate, implacable, of the victory-gods.

59. She sees rising up a second time
    the earth from the ocean, ever-green;
    the cataracts tumble, an eagle flies above,
    hunting fish along the fell.

60. The Æsir come together on Action-field,
    and pass judgement on the powerful
            earth-coil,   *earth-coil* World-serpent
    and commemorate there the mighty events,
    and the ancient runes of Potent-god.   *Potent-god* Odin

61. Afterwards there will be found, wondrous,
    golden gaming-pieces in the grass,
    those which in ancient days they had owned.

62. All unsown the fields will grow,
    all harm will be healed, Baldr will come;
    Höd and Baldr will inhabit Hropt's victory-   *Hropt* Odin
            halls,
    sanctuaries of the slain-gods: do you know yet, or what?

63. Then Hœnir shall choose the wooden lots,
    and the sons of two brothers build   *two brothers* Vili and Vé?
            dwellings   or Höd and Baldr?
    in the wide wind-home: do you know yet, or what?

64. She sees a hall standing, more beautiful than the sun,
    better than gold, at Gimlé.
    Virtuous folk shall live there,
    and enjoy pleasure the live-long day.

[65. Then there comes the mighty one down from above,
    the strong one, who governs everything, to powerfulness.]

66. Then there comes there the dark dragon flying,
    the glittering snake up from Moon-wane-hills,
    it bears in its wings – and flies over the plain –
    dead bodies: Spite-striker; now she must sink.

Hávamál: The lay of the High One

1. Every gateway, before going ahead,
   one should peer at,
   one should glimpse at;
   no one knows for sure what enemies
   are sitting ahead in the hall.

2. Good luck to who gives; a guest has   *guest* or Gest: Odin
       entered;
   where should he find somewhere to sit?
   Very jumpy's the one who by the blaze
   must make a test of his luck.

3. Fire is required by one who's entered
   and is chilled to the knee;
   food and clothes are required by anyone
   who's journeyed over the fells.

4. Water is required by one come to dine:
   a towel and friendly welcome;
   a kind disposition, if it's to be had,
   speech and silence in return.

5. Sense is required by one who roams widely;
   at home all is easy to handle;
   he gets sidelong glances, who knows not a thing
   and sits among the wise.

6. No man ought to boast about his brains,
   but rather beware with his wits;
   when one sensible and silent comes to the house
   seldom wrong befalls the wary;
   no man ever had a friend more faithful
   than a good store of common sense.

7. The wary guest, who comes to dine,
    stays silent, but strains his ears:
    all smart men find things out for themselves.

8. Happy is he who gets for himself
    praise and warm regard;
    more difficult to deal with when a man must have
    what lies in another man's heart.

9. Happy is that man, who has for himself
    praise and wisdom while he lives;
    for ill advice has often been had
    that came from another man's heart.

10. No better burden is borne on the road
    than a good store of common sense;
    better than wealth will it seem in strange parts:
    such is a poor man's means.

11. No better burden is borne on the road
    than a good store of common sense;
    no worse provisions can be carried through country
    than to be too drunk on ale.

12. It's not as good as it's said to be good,
    the ale of the sons of men:
    for the more a man drinks, the less he knows
    about his own intentions.

13. It's the heron of forgetfulness that hovers over
        ale-gatherings,
    and steals the wits of men;
    with that fowl's feathers I was once fettered
    within the court of Gunnlöd.

14. Drunk I became, I became over-drunk
at smart Much-wise's home;
it's the best ale-gathering when afterwards
each man can claim back his wits.

15. Silent and prudent a princeling should be,
also bold in battle;
merry and mirthful each man should be,
until the time of his death.

16. A senseless man thinks to live for ever
if he bewares a war;
but old age won't grant him a truce,
whatever spears may grant.

17. A fool gawps when he comes to visit:
he mumbles to himself or acts dumb;
things come in a rush if he takes a swig:
the man's wits are wholly exposed.

18. He alone knows, who wanders widely
and has travelled much,
what wits every man controls:
he is a man with some sense.

19. A man shouldn't clutch at a cup, but moderately
    drink his mead;
he should be sparing of speech or shut up;
no man will blame you for bad behaviour
if you go early to bed.

20. A greedy bloke, unless he curbs his bent,
will eat himself into lifelong grief:
he's often derided when he comes among the wise,
a man who's a fool in the belly.

21. Herds and flocks know, when they have to head
       home,
    and then they go from the grass;
    but an unwise man never knows
    the measure of his own belly.

22. A wretched man, with cruel character,
    laughs at everything;
    he doesn't know what he ought to know:
    that he's not free from flaws.

23. An unwise man lies awake all night,
    brooding on everything;
    he's quite worn out, when morning comes,
    and it's all just as bad as before.

24. An unwise man thinks everyone
    who smiles at him is his friend;
    he doesn't notice when they bitch him up
    if he sits among the wise.

25. An unwise man thinks everyone
    who smiles at him is his friend;
    he soon notices when he comes to the Thing
    that his supporters are few.

26. An unwise man thinks he knows it all,
    if he finds an escape in a corner;
    but he doesn't know what he can reply
    when folk test him out.

27. An unwise man, when he comes in a crowd,
    does best, if he keeps quiet;
    no one will know that he isn't smart
    unless he's talking too much;
    but the man who knows nothing doesn't know
    just when he's talking too much.

28. That man seems clever who knows how to ask
    and answer just the same;
    the sons of men cannot conceal
    what's said about another person.

29. Enough is said by one never silent
    in nonsensical speech;
    a fast-talking tongue, unless held by its owner,
    often gabbles itself into grief.

30. A man must never look askance at another,
    though he comes on a visit;
    many seem clever if they go unquestioned
    and are able to linger unscathed.

31. He seems clever when he beats a retreat,
    a guest who mocks other guests;
    he can't know clearly, making fun at a feast,
    if he's making a row among foes.

32. Many folk are kindly disposed
    but end up fighting at feasts;
    arguments among men will always occur:
    guest brawling with guest.

33. An early meal a man should generally take
    unless he is off on a visit;
    he'll sit and stare greedily, act as if starved,
    and be quite unable to chat.

34. It's a big detour to a bad friend's house,
    even if he lives on the way;
    but the way to a good friend's a direct route,
    even if he lives far away.

35. One must go on, and not stay a guest
    for ever in just one place:
    a loved one is loathed if he lingers too long
    in someone else's hall.

36. A home of one's own is better, though small:
    each man's a hero at home;
    just two goats and rough-roofed hall:
    it's still better than begging.

37. A home of one's own is better, though small:
    each man's a hero at home;
    the heart becomes bloody, when one has to beg
    for food at every meal.

38. From his weapons in open country
    a man must move less than a pace;
    no man knows for sure, when he's out on a trip,
    when he might have need of his spear.

39. I've never met a man so generous or so food-free
    that he didn't count giving a gift;
    nor one so liberal with his goods
    that he'd not take an offered reward.

40. The goods that a man has acquired,
    he ought not stint to spend;
    he often spares for the loathed
    what he'd hoped for the loved:
    much turns out much worse than we want.

41. With weapons and cloth one should gladden one's
            friends
    that is quite clear of itself;
    those who give and receive stay longest friends,
    if things last and all is well.

42. To his friend a man must be a friend,
    and repay gift for gift;
    laughter for laughter folk should receive,
    and also falseness for lies.

43. To his friend a man must be a friend,
    and also to that man's friend,
    but no man must to his unfriend's friend
    ever be found a friend.

44. You know, if you've a friend that you trust well,
    and from him want nothing but good:
    share thoughts with him, and keep trading gifts,
    go and visit often.

45. If you've another that you trust ill,
    but from him want nothing but good:
    you must speak him fair and think him a fraud,
    and give him falseness for lies.

46. Another thing about him that you trust ill,
    and have no faith in his thoughts:
    you must smile at him and not speak your mind,
    gifts should be repaid in kind.

47. Young was I once, and I travelled alone:
    it turned out I'd wandered astray;
    I thought myself rich when another I found:
    mankind is man's delight.

48. Liberal and brave men live the best,
    they seldom foster sorrow;
    but a cowardly man fears everything
    and a mean man grieves at gifts.

49. I gave my clothes on the open plain
    to two men carved from wood;
    soldiers they seemed when they wore that garb:
    a naked man is ashamed.

50. The fir-tree fades that stands in the grove;
    its bark and needles give no shelter:
    so it is for a man whom nobody loves,
    how shall he live for long?

51. Hotter than fire among bad friends
    burns a friendship five days long;
    but it soon slackens when the sixth day comes,
    and all the affection turns ill.

52. Great gifts alone need no man give,
    praise often comes from a little:
    with half a loaf and a tilted cup
    I found myself a fellow.

53. On little shores, by little lakes,
    little are the minds of men;
    for all men are not equally smart:
    folk are half and half.

54. Middling-wise should each man be,
    never over-wise;
    for he lives the fairest life of folks
    who knows not over-much.

55. Middling-wise should each man be
    never over-wise;
    for a wise-man's heart is seldom glad,
    if he is truly wise.

56. Middling-wise should each man be,
    never over-wise;
    he never knows his fate before,
    whose spirit is freest from sorrow.

57. Fire-brand from fire-brand takes flame till it's burnt out,
    blaze is kindled from blaze;
    man from man becomes skilled of speech,
    but dumb from lack of words.

58. He must rise early, who will take
    another's life or goods;
    a wolf lying down seldom gets the ham
    nor a sleeping man victory.

59. He must rise early, who has few workers,
    and go to inspect his work;
    he delays much, who sleeps through the morning:
    the wealth's been half-won by the brisk.

60. Of dry sticks and roofing-bark
    a man can know the measure,
    and of the wood, which can last
    for three months or for six.

61. Washed and well-fed one should ride to a meeting,
    even if he isn't well-clothed;
    no man should feel shame for his shoes or breeches,
    nor yet of his horse, if it's no good.

62. It snatches and stretches when it comes to the sea,
    an eagle on the ancient ocean;
    so it is with a man, when he comes among many
    and his supporters are few.

63. Asking and answering, each clever man must master,
    who wants to be called wise;
    one can know, two should not:
    if three know, then so does the world.

64. Each prudent man must his might
    keep in moderation;
    he finds that out who comes among brave men,
    that no one is boldest of all.

65. For those words which one man says to another,
    he often gets recompense.

66. To many places I have come much too early,
    and too late to some;
    the ale was drunk or not yet brewed,
    the hated seldom hit the right spot.

67. Now and then I'd be invited home,
    when I had no need of a meal;
    or two hams hung at a trusty friend's
    when I had eaten one.

68. Fire is best for the sons of men,
    and a sight of the sun;
    his health, if a man can keep it,
    and living without taint.

69. No man is wholly wretched, though he is not well:
    one man is blessed in sons,
    another in friends, another with enough wealth,
    another well-blessed in his works.

70. Better to live, and blessed to live,
    the living always get the cow;
    I saw a blaze burn for the wealthy man,
    and he was dead out by the door.

71. The lame can ride horses, the handless drive herds;
    the deaf can fight and do well;
    better blind than to be burnt:
    no one has use for a corpse.

72. A son is better, however late-born,
    after his dad has died;
    memorial-stones seldom stand by the way,
    unless kin raise them for kin.

73. Two can kill one; and tongue can kill head;
    inside every fur cloak I search for the hand.

74. Night is welcome to the man with full provisions,
    short are the yards of a ship;
    an autumn night is variable:
    in five days the weather changes much,
    and more in the course of a month.

75. That man knows who knows nothing
    that many a man's fooled by cash;
    one man is rich, another poor,
    he shouldn't be blamed on that score.

76. Cattle die, kinsmen die,
    oneself dies just the same.
    But words of glory never die
    for the one who gets a good name.

77. Cattle die, kinsmen die,
    oneself dies just the same.
    I know one thing that never dies:
    the judgement on each one dead.

78. I saw full pens for Fitjung's sons,
    now they bear a beggar's staff;
    wealth is like the twinkle of an eye:
    it's the infirmest of friends.

79. An unwise man, if he manages to obtain
money or a lady's love:
his pride swells, but not his brains,
he strides on firmly into folly.

80. Now has been tested, what you asked of the runes,
come from potent powers,
which the great powers made,
and the mighty sage stained: *mighty sage* Odin?
he has it best who keeps quiet.

81. Praise the day at evening; a wife, when she's been burnt;
a sword, when it's been tested; a maid, when she's
been wed;
ice, when it's crossed over; ale, when it's drunk down.

82. Cut wood on a windy day, row to sea in fine weather,
murmur to friends in the darkness: many are the
eyes of day;
ask swiftness of a ship, protection from a shield,
sharpness from a sword, kisses from a girl.

83. Drink ale by the fireside, slide on ice,
buy a mount lean and a sword-blade bloody,
fatten a horse at home and a hound in the house.

84. One never must trust the words of a maid,
nor whatever a woman says:
on a whirling wheel their hearts are thrown,
fickleness fills their breasts.

85. A creaking bow, a crackling flame,
a gaping wolf, a croaking crow,
a squealing swine, a rootless tree,
a swelling wave, a bubbling pot,

86. a flying dart, a falling surge,
    overnight ice, a snake tight-sprung,
    a bride's bed-talk or a broken blade,
    a bear's play or a king's young boy,

87. a sick calf, a self-willed slave,
    a soothsayer's smooth talk, a fresh-killed corpse,

88. a field sown early: let no one trust them,
    nor a son too soon;
    weather creates crops, but wit makes a son,
    each of them lies in doubt.

89. Your brother's butcher, if you pass him in the street,
    a house half-burnt, a horse too frisky –
    a steed is useless if it breaks a leg –
    none is so assured as to trust all these.

90. The love of women whose hearts are false
    is like driving an unshod steed across slippery ice,
    a two-year-old, frolicsome, badly broken;
    or like being in a rudderless boat in a storm,
    or a cripple trying to catch reindeer on a thawing slope.

91. Now I speak plainly: since I know both sides:
    men's minds are fickle to women;
    the fairer we speak, the falser we think:
    that trips up any sensible soul.

92. Fair speaking and fine gifts
    will win the love of a lass;
    praise the figure of a fine looking girl:
    the one who woos will win.

93. No man should ever reproach
    another man for his love;
    they often snare the wise,
    what cannot catch the fool:
    the loveliest looks of all.

94. No one should reproach in any way
    what comes to many a man;
    almighty love takes the sons of men,
    and makes of wise men fools.

95. The mind alone knows what lives near the heart;
    alone it sees into the soul.
    Worse for the wise than any disease:
    finding nothing that makes one content.

96. I found that out when I sat in the reeds,
    and waited for my best-loved girl:
    body and soul was that wise lass to me,
    and yet I couldn't have her.

97. Billing's girl I found on the bed,
    sun-bright, all asleep;
    a nobleman's joys were as nothing to me
    unless I could be with that body.

98. 'Again at evening must you, Odin, return,
    if you will woo a woman;
    everything's lost, unless we alone know
    our wickedness together.'

99. Back I turned, intending love,
    back from certain delight;
    I really thought that I should have
    her whole lust, and her love.

100. When next I came there handy stood
     a war-band all awake;
     with burning torches and wood borne high:
     my wretched path was revealed.

101. Close to morning I came again,
     and saw the hall-band asleep;
     I found a bitch tied up on the bed
     of that wondrous woman.

102. Many a fine lass, once you know her well,
     proves fickle of heart towards men;
     I found that out, when I tried to seduce
     that learned lady to tricks.
     That wise woman showed me every disgrace,
     and I got not the girl for all that.

103. At home a man should be merry, mirthful with
          every guest
     and shrewd about himself;
     fine of memory and speech, if he wants to be wise,
     and always speaking good things.
     A dumb bum he's called, who has few things to say,
     that is the mark of a fool.

104. I sought the ancient giant; now I have   *ancient giant* Suttung
          returned,
     I got little there by being silent.
     With many words I wove my own fame
     inside Suttung's halls.

105. Gunnlöd gave me on the golden throne
     a drink of the dear-won mead.
     In return I gave her bad recompense,
     for her whole heart,
     for her sorrowful soul.

106. With the mouth of Rati, I made myself room,
     and nibbled my way through the rock;
     above and beneath were the giants'   *giants' paths* solid rock
          paths;
     in this way I hazarded my head.

107. I took advantage of my disguise:
     wise men want for little;
     and now Frenzy-stirrer has emerged
     inside the sacred boundaries of men.

108. I doubt I would have returned
     back from Giants' Domain,
     if I hadn't had Gunnlöd, that fine woman
     whom I laid in my arms.

109. The following day the frost-giants came
     and found Odin already in the High One's hall;
     they asked if Bale-worker had gone to the gods
     or if Suttung had slain him.

110. I reckon that Odin swore a ring-oath:
     how can his truth be trusted?
     He left Suttung deceived, without drink,
     and Gunnlöd, she was grieving.

111. It's time to declaim from the seat of the sage,
     by the well of Destiny;
     I saw and stayed silent, I saw and I pondered:
     I listened to the speech of men;
     I heard runes discussed, nor did they omit interpretation,
     at the High One's hall, in the High One's   *High One* Odin
         hall:
     I heard them say these things:

112. I advise you, Loddfáfnir, to take this advice:
     it'll help, if you take it,
     do you good, if you get it:
     don't get up at night, except to snoop,
     or to seek out a place for a pee.

113. I advise you, Loddfáfnir, to take this advice:
    it'll help, if you take it,
    do you good, if you get it:
    in a witch's embrace you should never sleep,
    when she enfolds you in her limbs.

114. She'll bring it about that you won't attend
    any meeting or prince's affairs;
    you won't want food or the delight of others:
    you'll go to sleep full of sorrow.

115. I advise you, Loddfáfnir, to take this advice:
    it'll help, if you take it,
    do you good, if you get it:
    never seduce another man's wife
    and make her your much-trusted girl.

116. I advise you, Loddfáfnir, to take this advice:
    it'll help, if you take it,
    do you good, if you get it:
    on the fell or the fjord, if you happen to go,
    stock yourself well up with food.

117. I advise you, Loddfáfnir, to take this advice:
    it'll help, if you take it,
    do you good, if you get it:
    never let a wicked man
    know of any distress of yours;
    from a wicked man you'll never get
    any good thought in return.

118. I saw a chap wounded high up
    by a wicked woman's words;
    an insidious tongue took him to his death,
    and there was no truth in the charge.

119. I advise you, Loddfáfnir, to take this advice:
    it'll help, if you take it,
    do you good, if you get it:
    you know, if you've a friend that you trust well,
    go and visit often;
    for brushwood grows, and tall grass,
    on a path that no one travels.

120. I advise you, Loddfáfnir, to take this advice:
    it'll help, if you take it,
    do you good, if you get it:
    lure a good man into intimacy,
    and learn healing charms as long as you live.

121. I advise you, Loddfáfnir, to take this advice:
    it'll help, if you take it,
    do you good, if you get it:
    with your friend never be
    the first to break things up,
    pain gnaws at the heart if there's no one
    to tell about all your thoughts.

122. I advise you, Loddfáfnir, to take this advice:
    it'll help, if you take it,
    do you good, if you get it:
    you never ought to bandy words
    with any dumb blockhead;

123. For never from a wicked man
    will you get a good return;
    but a good man will surely make you
    well-respected and praised.

124. Kinship's well mixed when one can really reveal
    all one's thoughts to another;
    anything is better than being deceitful:
    no friend only says the one thing.

125. I advise you, Loddfáfnir, to take this advice:
 it'll help, if you take it,
 do you good, if you get it:
 don't waste even three words quarrelling
 with someone worse than yourself;
 often the better man holds back,
 when the worse one fights on.

126. I advise you, Loddfáfnir, to take this advice:
 it'll help, if you take it,
 do you good, if you get it:
 never make shoes or shafts
 except for yourself alone;
 if the shoe is ill-shaped or the shaft is bent
 you'll just bring ill will on yourself.

127. I advise you, Loddfáfnir, to take this advice:
 it'll help, if you take it,
 do you good, if you get it:
 when you recognize ill will, speak out against ill will,
 and grant no peace to your foes.

128. I advise you, Loddfáfnir, to take this advice:
 it'll help, if you take it,
 do you good, if you get it:
 never be made happy by wicked things,
 but make yourself glad at the good.

129. I advise you, Loddfáfnir, to take this advice:
 it'll help, if you take it,
 do you good, if you get it:
 never look up in battle
 – the sons of men run wild –
 in case people bewitch you.

130. I advise you, Loddfáfnir, to take this advice:
    it'll help, if you take it,
    do you good, if you get it:
    if you wish to talk in intimacy with a fine woman,
    and take therefrom delight,
    you must make fair promises and keep them well:
    no one hates a good thing, if they can get it.

131. I advise you, Loddfáfnir, to take this advice:
    it'll help, if you take it,
    do you good, if you get it:
    I tell you, be wary, but not too wary;
    be most wary of ale and another man's wife,
    and third, that no thieves fool you.

132. I advise you, Loddfáfnir, to take this advice:
    it'll help, if you take it,
    do you good, if you get it:
    never hold up to scorn or to spite
    any guest or traveller.

133. They're often not sure, those who sit in the hall,
    whose kin they are who've come;
    no man is so good that he has no flaw,
    nor so bad that he's good for nothing.

134. I advise you, Loddfáfnir, to take this advice:
    it'll help, if you take it,
    do you good, if you get it:
    never laugh at a grey-haired sage;
    often old men say what is good;
    often from a shrivelled bag smart words emerge,
    from one that hangs with the hides,
    and dangles with the skins,
    and swings with the bags of tripe.

135. I advise you, Loddfáfnir, to take this advice:
     it'll help, if you take it,
     do you good, if you get it:
     don't insult a guest or chase him from the gate,
     be kind to those in need.

136. It's a stout beam that must be swung
     to grant an entrance to all;
     give a ring, or there shall be called upon you
     every ill on your limbs.

137. I advise you, Loddfáfnir, to take this advice:
     it'll help, if you take it,
     do you good, if you get it:
     when you drink ale, choose earth's might;
     for earth works against getting drunk, and fire
         against disease;
     oak against constipation, an ear of corn against
         witchcraft,
     elder against household strife – the moon must
         be invoked against malice –
     an earth-worm against a bite or sting, and runes
         against wickedness;
     soil must stand against flood.

138. I know that I hung on that windy tree,
     spear-wounded, nine full nights,
     given to Odin, myself to myself,
     on that tree that rose from roots
     that no man ever knows.

139. They gave me neither bread nor drink from horn,
     I peered down below.
     I clutched the runes, screaming I grabbed them,
     and then sank back.

140. I had nine mighty songs from that famed
     son of Bölthor, Bestla's father,   *Bölthor* Odin's grandfather; *Bestla*
     and one swig I snatched of that glorious   Odin's mother
         mead
     drained from Frenzy-stirrer.

141. Then I quickened and flourished,
     sprouted and throve.
     From a single word, another sprung:
     from a single deed, another sprung.

142. Runes must you find, and the meaningful symbols,
     very great symbols,
     very strong symbols,
     which the mighty sage stained,
     and the great powers made,
     and a runemaster cut from among the powers:

143. Odin among the Æsir, and for the elves Dead-one,
     Dawdler for the dwarfs, Ásvid for the giants;
     I have cut some myself.

144. Do you know how to cut? Do you know how
         to read?
     Do you know how to stain? Do you know how
         to test?
     Do you know how to invoke? Do you know how
         to sacrifice?
     Do you know how to dispatch? Do you know how
         to slaughter?

145. Better not invoked, than too much sacrificed:
     a gift always looks for a return;
     better not dispatched, than too much slaughtered:
     so Thund cut before the creation of nations: *Thund* Odin
     he rose up when he returned.

146. I know those spells no noble wife knows
     or the son of any man.
     One is called 'help', and it will help you
     against strife and sorrow and every grief.

147. I know another, that men's sons need
     who wish to live as doctors.

148. I know a third, if I feel pressing need,
     to hold those who hate me in check:
     I blunt the blades of my enemies,
     their weapons and bats just won't bite.

149. I know a fourth, if men bring forward
     shackles for my limbs:
     I utter the words, and I walk free;
     the fetter springs from my leg,
     the manacle from my arms.

150. I know a fifth if I see fly
     an arrow in the midst of fighting-men.
     It won't fly so straight that I can't stop it
     if I can fix it in my sight.

151. I know a sixth, if someone harms me,
     with the roots of a right-strong tree:
     then the man who means damage to me,
     himself rather gets the harm.

152. I know a seventh, if I see a high hall
     aflame above bench-companions;
     It won't burn so briskly that I can't save it;
     I know the charm to chant.

153. I know an eighth that's useful
     for everyone to learn.
     When hatred grows between a chieftain's sons,
     I can quickly cure it.

154. I know a ninth, if the need should arise
    to save my ship at sea.
    I quell the wind upon the wave
    and soothe the face of the sea.

155. I know a tenth, if I see hag-riders
    stream across the sky.
    I can cause them to wander
    away from their proper skins,
    away from their proper minds.

156. I know an eleventh, if I must take
    old friends to fight a battle:
    I chant under shields, and they pass with power,
    safely into battle,
    safely out of battle,
    safely wherever they walk.

157. I know a twelfth, if I see in a tree
    a hanged corpse dangle;
    I cut and colour certain runes,
    so that man walks
    and talks with me.

158. I know a thirteenth, if it falls to me,
    to sprinkle a young boy with water,
    he will never fall when he walks to war,
    that warrior will never sink under swords.

159. I know a fourteenth, if before a host
    I have to give a tally of the gods;
    I know something about all the Æsir and elves:
    few foolish men know the same.

160. I know a fifteenth, that Thjódrœrir the dwarf
    chanted before Delling's doors: *Delling* dwarf
    he chanted strength to the Æsir, success to the elves,
    knowledge to Tumult-god.   *Tumult-god* Odin

161. I know a sixteenth, if I want
     all a wise girl's lust and her love:
     I can change the mind of a white-armed lass,
     and totally turn her heart.

162. I know a seventeenth, to make a young maid
     slow to separate from me.
     These spells, Loddfáfnir,
     you will long be lacking,
     though they bring you good, if you get them,
     benefit, if you but learn them,
     profit, if you procure them.

163. I know an eighteenth, which I never tell
     a maid or any man's wife:
     much better if only one is aware
     (the last it is of my chants),
     except only her my arms enfold,
     or perhaps my sister.

164. Now are the words of the High One uttered
     within the High One's hall.
     Very useful to the sons of men,
     no use at all to the sons of giants.
     Good luck to whoever recited them,
     good luck to whoever knows them!
     Use them well, if you've learnt them:
     good luck to all who have listened!

Vafthrúdnismál: The lay of Vafthrúdnir

1. 'Advise me now, Frigg, since I feel keen to go
   to visit Vafthrúdnir;
   I'm very curious to contend in ancient lore
   with that all-wise giant.'

2. 'I'd rather keep home Host-father   *Host-father* Odin
   within the courts of the gods;
   for I count no giant the match in might
   of that Vafthrúdnir.'

3. 'Much have I travelled, much have I tried,
   much have I tested the powers;
   one thing I'd know: what company is kept
   within Vafthrúdnir's hall.'

4. 'Go in one piece; come back in one piece;
   stay in one piece on your trip.
   I hope your wit's up to it, Father of Men,   *Father of Men* Odin
   when you bandy words with that giant.'

5. Then Odin went to test the word-wisdom
   of that all-wise giant;
   he came to the hall that Ím's father   *Ím's father* Vafthrúdnir
       owned:
   Dread promptly entered in.   *Dread* Odin

6. 'Hail now, Vafthrúdnir; now I've come to your hall,
   to see your very self.
   The first thing I'll know is whether you're wise,
   or really all-wise, giant.'

7. 'What kind of person do I address
   inside my very hall?
   You'll never walk away from these walls
   unless you're the fuller of wisdom.'

8. 'Gagnrád is my name; now I've come   *Gagnrád* 'Gain-counsel'
       in my travels
   thirsty to your hall;
   I've been a long way in need of welcome,
   and of your reception, giant.'

9. 'Why then, Gagnrád, do you speak from the floor?
   Take a seat in the hall;
   we must find out which one knows more:
   the guest or the ancient sage.'

10. 'The poor man, when he visits the rich,
    should be sparing of speech or shut up;
    too much talk I reckon works none too well,
    when one comes up against a cold heart.'

11. 'Tell me, Gagnrád, since you wish from the floor
    to make a test of your talents,
    what's the name of the horse who always drags
    the day over troops of men?'

12. 'He's called Shining-mane who always drags
    the day over troops of men.
    The glorious Goths think him the best horse:
    his mane shines always aflame.'

13. 'Tell me, Gagnrád, since you wish from the floor
    to make a test of your talents,
    what that steed is called who draws from the East
    night over the gifted gods.'

14. 'He's called Frost-mane who draws in turn
    each night over the gifted gods.
    Foam from his bit falls each morning,
    from which comes the dew in the dales.'

15. 'Tell me, Gagnrád, since you wish from the floor
    to make a test of your talents,
    what that river's called that cuts off the land
    of the giants' sons from the gods.'

16. 'That river's called Ífing that cuts off the land   *Íting* 'Rushing'
    of the giants' sons from the gods;
    it runs unchecked throughout all time:
    on that river no ice will form.'

17. 'Tell me, Gagnrád, since you wish from the floor
    to make a test of your talents,
    what the place is called where battle will be joined
    between Surt and the splendid gods.'

Odin said:

18. 'The place is called Vígríd, where battle will   *Vígríd* 'Battle-field'
    be joined
    between Surt and the splendid gods;
    a hundred leagues in every direction
    it spreads, as all who know can tell.'

Vafthrúdnir said:

19. 'Now you're wise, guest: come join the giant's bench;
    and let's speak together on the seat.
    We shall wager our heads inside the hall,
    guest, on riddling wisdom.'

Odin said:

20. 'Tell me one thing, if your wit is up to it,
    and you, Vafthrúdnir, know:
    from where did the earth come, and heaven above,
    first of all, you wise giant?'

Vafthrúdnir said:

21. 'From Ymir's flesh the earth was formed,
    and the rocks from out of his bones;
    the sky from the skull of the ice-cold giant,
    and the sea from his blood.'

Odin said:

22. 'Tell me a second thing, if your wit is up to it,
    and you, Vafthrúdnir, know:
    from where did Moon come, that passes over men,
    and likewise Sun the same?'

Vafthrúdnir said:

23. 'Mundilfœri he is called, who is the father of Moon,
    and likewise of Sun the same.
    they must sweep through the sky every day,
    to mark off the years for men.'

Odin said:

24. 'Tell me a third thing, since they call you smart,
    and you, Vafthrúdnir, know:
    from where did Day come, that passes over people,
    or Night and the phases of Moon?'

Vafthrúdnir said:

25. 'Delling he is called, who is the father of Day,
    but Night was born of Nör,
    New-moon and Moon-wane the gifted powers created
    to mark off the years for men.'

Odin said:

26. 'Tell me a fourth thing, since they call you wise,
    and you, Vafthrúdnir, know:
    from where did Winter come, or warm Summer,
    first of all among the wise powers?'

Vafthrúdnir said:

27. 'Wind-cool he is called, who is father of Winter,
    but Sweetness that of Summer.'

Odin said:

28. 'Tell me a fifth thing, since they call you wise,
    and you, Vafthrúdnir, know:
    who was the eldest of the kin of Ymir or the Æsir
    to appear in ancient days?'

Vafthrúdnir said:

29. 'Countless years before the earth was created:
    then was Bergelmir born;
    Thrúdgelmir was that one's father,
    and Aurgelmir grandfather.'

Odin said:

30. 'Tell me a sixth thing, since they call you smart,
    and you, Vafthrúdnir, know:
    from where did Aurgelmir come among giants' sons,
    first of all, you wise giant?'

Vafthrúdnir said:

31. 'From Élivágar dripped venom-drops,
    which grew till a giant formed,
    [from there came all our lines together:
    so all is ever too awesome.']

Odin said:

32. 'Tell me a seventh thing, since they call you smart,
    and you, Vafthrúdnir, know:
    how did that grim giant get a child,
    when he had no joy of a giantess?'

Vafthrúdnir said:

33. 'They said that under that frost-giant's arm,
    at the same time a boy and girl grew;
    one leg with another of that wise giant
    got a six-headed son.'

Odin said:

34. 'Tell me an eighth thing, since they call you smart,
    and you, Vafthrúdnir, know:
    what first you recall, or earliest know?
    You are all-wise, giant!'

Vafthrúdnir said:

35. 'Countless years before the earth was created:
    then was Bergelmir born;
    the first I remember was when that wise giant
    was first placed in a cradle.

Odin said:

36. 'Tell me a ninth thing, since they call you smart,
    and you, Vafthrúdnir, know:
    from where comes the wind, that passes over the waves?
    Men never see the thing itself.'

Vafthrúdnir said:

37. 'Corpse-swallower he is called, who sits at heaven's edge,
    a giant in eagle's form;
    from his wings, they say, the wind does come
    over every man.'

Odin said:

38. 'Tell me a tenth thing, since the fate of the gods,
    Vafthrúdnir, you wholly know:
    from where did Njörd come among the sons of the Æsir?
    Temples and shrines he rules by the hundred,
    but he was not raised among the Æsir.'

Vafthrúdnir said:

39. 'In Vanaheim the clever powers created him,
    and gave him as hostage to the gods;
    at the end of time he will return
    home to the clever Vanir.'

Odin said:

40. 'Tell me an eleventh thing: in what enclosures
    do warriors fight together each day?'

Vafthrúdnir said:

41. ['All the Einherjar in Odin's enclosures
    fight together each day;]
    they choose the slain and ride from the fray:
    they sit settled together the more.'

Odin said:

42. 'Tell me a twelfth thing: how the fate of the gods,
     Vafthrúdnir, you wholly know?
     Of the secrets of giants and all of the gods
     you tell the whole truth,
     you all-wise giant.'

Vafthrúdnir said:

43. 'Of the secrets of giants and all of the gods,
     I can tell the truth,
     since I have travelled into every world,
     nine worlds I have travelled below Niflhel,
     where men die down from Hel.'

Odin said:

44. 'Much have I travelled, much have I tried,
     much have I tested the powers:
     which folk will live on when the famed Great Winter
     comes to pass among men?'

Vafthrúdnir said:

45. 'Life and Life-eager, and they will hide
     in Hoddmímir's wood;
     morning-dew they will have as their food
     – from them races will be raised.'

Odin said:

46. 'Much have I travelled, much have I tried,
     much have I tested the powers:
     how will a sun come into smooth heaven
     once Fenrir has overtaken this one?'

Vafthrúdnir said:

47. 'Elf-disk will bear a single daughter   *Elf-disk* Sun
    before Fenrir overtakes her:
    she shall ride, when the powers die,
    the daughter, her mother's paths.'

Odin said:

48. 'Much have I travelled, much have I tried,
    much have I tested the powers:
    who are those maidens who pass over the sea,
    travelling with wisdom of mind?'

Vafthrúdnir said:

49. 'Three of the race of the maidens of Kin-eager
    come to descend over dwellings;
    they alone are the guardian spirits in the world,
    though they were raised among giants.'

Odin said:

50. 'Much have I travelled, much have I tried,
    much have I tested the powers:
    which Æsir will govern the gods' effects
    when Surt's fire has died down?'

Vafthrúdnir said:

51. 'Vídar and Váli will inhabit the   *Vídar and Váli* Odin's sons
        gods' shrines
    when Surt's fire has died down;
    Módi and Magni shall have   *Módi and Magni* Thor's sons;
        Mjöllnir   *Mjöllnir* Thor's hammer
    to wield when war has waned.'

Odin said:

52. 'Much have I travelled, much have I tried,
    much have I tested the powers:
    what end of life will Odin have
    when the powers are rent?'

Vafthrúdnir said:

53. 'The wolf will swallow the Father of Men;
    this Vídar will avenge:
    he'll rip apart the wolf's cold jaws
    in battle with the beast.'

Odin said:

54. 'Much have I travelled, much have I tried,
    much have I tested the powers:
    what did Odin himself say into the ear of his son
    before he mounted the pyre?'

Vafthrúdnir said:

55. 'No one knows what you said in ancient days
    into the ear of your son;
    with a doomed mouth did I tell my ancient lore
    and speak of Ragnarök.
    It was with Odin I've now traded my wits:
    you are always the wisest of men.'

Grímnismál: The lay of Grímnir

Frá sonum Hraudungs: About King Hraudung's sons

King Hraudung had two sons: one was called Agnar, the other
Geirröd; Agnar was ten years old, and Geirröd eight. They
both rowed out in a boat with their fishing-lines after small

*fish. The wind drove them out into the ocean; in the darkness
of the night they were shipwrecked on land, and disembarked,
and found a cottager. They stayed there for the winter: the old
woman fostered Agnar, the old man Geirröd.*

*In the spring the old man got them a ship, and when he
and the old woman led them down to the shore, the old man
had a private talk with Geirröd. They had a fair wind, and
reached their father's landing-place. Geirröd was at the fore of
the ship: he jumped ashore, shoved the ship out and said: 'Get
off now, where the trolls can take you!' The ship drove out,
and Geirröd walked up to the house. He was well received;
his father was dead, and Geirröd was taken as king, and
became a magnificent man.*

*Odin and Frigg sat on Hlidskjálf and looked out over all
the worlds. Odin said: 'Do you see Agnar, your foster-son,
raising children with a troll-wife in a cave? But Geirröd, my
foster-son, is a king and now rules over his land.' Frigg said:
'He's mean with food, and abuses his guests, if he thinks too
many have come.' Odin called that the greatest lie, so they
placed a wager on it.*

*Frigg sent Fulla, her chambermaid, to Geirröd. She told
the king to beware lest he should be bewitched by a wizard,
who had arrived in the land, and said that he could be
recognized by the fact that no dog was so ferocious that it
would leap up at him. But it was the greatest calumny that
Geirröd was not generous with food. Still, he had that man
seized that the dogs would not attack. The man was in a blue
cloak, and called himself Grímnir; he said nothing else about
himself, though he was asked. The king had him tortured to
make him speak, and set him between two fires; he sat there
for eight nights. King Geirröd had a son, ten years old, called
Agnar after his brother. Agnar went to Grímnir and gave him
a full horn to drink; he said that the king was behaving
wickedly in having an innocent man tortured. Grímnir drank
it up; then the fire had come so close that the cloak was
burning off Grímnir. He said:*

1. 'Flames, you're too hot, and rather too big:
   get away from me, fire!
   My wool-cloak's singed, though I lift it aloft,
   my cape's burning in front of my eyes!

2. 'Eight nights I've sat here between these fires,
   and no one's offered me food,
   except Agnar alone, and alone he shall rule,
   Geirröd's son, in the land of the Goths.

3. 'You shall have luck, Agnar, since luck has been bidden
   for you by the Man-god of men;   *Man-god of men* Odin
   for a single sip you never shall
   receive a better reward.

4. 'The land is hallowed that I see lie
   near the Æsir and elves;
   but in Strength-home Thor must stay
   until the powers are rent.

5. 'It's called Yew-dales, the place where Ull
   has made himself a hall;
   Elf-home the gods gave to Frey
   in ancient days as a tooth-gift.

6. 'There is a third home where the kind powers
   thatched the hall with silver;
   Válaskjálf's the name of the place that in ancient days
   the god contrived for himself.

7. 'Sunken-bank a fourth is called, and there cool waves
   can thunder over the place;
   there Odin and Sága drink every day,
   gladly, from golden cups.

8. 'Happy-home the fifth is called, where, gold-bright,
   Slain-hall quietly lies;
   there Hropt makes his choice each day   *Hropt* Odin
   from men weapon-dead.

9. 'It's very familiar for those who've come
   to Odin to seek his company:
   spear-shafts serve as rafters, the hall is thatched
       with shields,
   mailcoats are massed along the benches.

10. 'It's very familiar for those who've come
    to Odin to seek his company:
    a wolf hangs in front of the western doors,
    and an eagle swings above.

11. 'Crash-home is the name of the sixth, where Thjazi dwelt,
    that gigantic giant.
    but now Skadi, bright bride of the gods,
    dwells in her father's old courts.

12. 'Broad-gleam is the seventh, where Baldr has
    made himself a hall;
    in that land, where I know lie
    the fewest evil plans.

13. 'Heavenly-hills the eighth, where Heimdall
    they say rules the shrines;
    there the watchman of the gods drinks good mead,
    happy in a homely hall.

14. 'Battle-field the ninth, where Freyja arrays
    the choice of seats in the hall;
    from half the slain she makes her choice each day:
    the other half Odin has.

15. 'Shining the tenth, supported by gold,
and thatched with silver the same;
there Forseti lives most every day
and settles every quarrel.

16. 'Naval-yard the eleventh, where Njörd has
made himself a hall;
the prince of men, free from malice,
rules the high-timbered temple.

17. 'Brushwood grows, and tall grass,
and wood, in Vídar's land;
there the son says from a horse's back,
brave, that he'll avenge his father.

18. 'Andhrímnir in Eldhrímnir
has Sæhrímnir boiled;
the best of bacons, though few know
how the Einherjar are fed.

19. 'Geri and Freki, the war-worn one feeds,   *war-worn one* Odin
that Host-father famed of old;   *Host-father* Odin
but on wine alone, weapon-fine,
Odin ever lives.

20. 'Hugin and Munin fly every day
across the Gaping Ground.
I worry that Hugin may not return,
but I am more worried about Munin.

21. 'Thund roars as Mighty Wolf's fish   *Thund* Odin? river?; *Mighty*
gambols in the flood,   *Wolf* Fenrir?
the river-stream seems too strong
for the slaughter-keen to wade.   *slaughter-keen* Einherjar

22. 'Corpse-gate, it's called, that stands on the plain,
    hallowed, before holy doors;
    ancient is that gate, but few know,
    how that bolt is barred.

23. 'Five hundred doors and forty
    I think that Slain-hall has;
    eight hundred Einherjar walk through each door,
    when they go off to battle the wolf.

24. 'Five hundred floors and forty
    I think Bilskírnir has in all;
    of all the dwellings that I know with roofs
    my son's I reckon the most.

25. 'Heidrún is the name of the goat
    standing on Host-father's hall,
    who bites off Lærad's limbs;   *Lærad* the World-tree?
    she fills a vat with shining mead,
    a draught that does not diminish.

26. 'Oak-antlered is the name of the hart,
    standing on Host-father's hall,
    who bites off Lærad's limbs;
    from his horns there drips into Hvergelmir
    the source from which all rivers run.

27. 'Wide and Broad, Hard and Harsh,
    Cool and Conflict-keen,
    Rage and Mighty-sage,
    Rhine and Running,
    Groaning and Gaping,
    Spent and Spear-tumbling,
    they flow round the gods' hoard,
    Roar and Dwindle, Swell and Slip,
    Greed and Battle-bold.

28. 'One is called the Dvina, a second Way-swift,
    a third Great-reservoir,
    Fish-rich and Fresh, Wild and Wave,
    Stern and Storm, Swallow and She-wolf,
    Wide and Wanting, Bad and Bank,
    Screaming and Lightning, they flow close to men,
    they flow down from here to Hel.

29. 'Körmt and Örmt, and the two Kettle-baths,
    Thor must wade through these
    each day, when he journeys to judgement
    close by the ash Yggdrasil,
    since the Æsir-bridge burns all aflame,
    the hallowed waters seethe.

30. 'Glad and Golden, Glær and Skeidbrimir,
    Silver-top and Sinir,
    Gísl and Falhófnir, Gold-top and Light-foot:
    these are the horses the Æsir ride,
    each day, when they journey to judgement
    close by the ash Yggdrasil.

31. 'Three roots spread in three directions
    under the ash Yggdrasil;
    under one Hel dwells, the second frost-ogres,
    the third the human race.

32. 'Ratatosk is the name of the squirrel who has to run,
    over the ash Yggdrasil;
    the eagle's words he must bring from above,
    and say to Spite-striker below.

33. 'There are also four harts, and the budding shoots
    they gnaw with necks thrown back:
    Dead-one and Dawdler,
    Duneyr and Durathrór.

34. 'More serpents lie under the ash Yggdrasil
    than any dumb blockhead can believe;
    Góin and Móin – Grafvitnir's sons –
    Grey-back and Grafvöllud;
    Ofnir and Sváfnir, I reckon must always
    bite on the branches of the tree.

35. 'The ash of Yggdrasil suffers grief,
    more than men can know;
    a hart bites above; on each side it rots,
    Spite-striker gnaws it below.

36. 'I want Wielder and Mist to bring me a horn;
    Axe-age and Brandisher,
    War and Strength, Clash and War-bonds,
    Smash and Spear-waver,
    Shield-truce and Counsel-truce and Power-trace:
    they bring the Einherjar ale.

37. 'Early-waker, All-swift: from here they have
    to drag wearily on Sun;
    but under their saddle-bows the Æsir have concealed,
    kind powers, cooling irons.

38. 'Chill is the name of what stands in front of Sun,
    a shield before the shining god;
    mountains and oceans I know should burn
    if it fell from in front.

39. 'Spite's the name of the wolf who chases
        the fair-faced god   *fair-faced god* Moon
    to the protection of the woods;
    a second is Hate, Famed Wolf's son,   *Famed Wolf* Fenrir
    who is after the bright bride of   *bright bride of heaven* Sun
        heaven.

40. 'From Ymir's flesh the earth was formed,
    and from his blood the sea;
    rocks from bones, trees from hair,
    and from his skull the sky.

41. 'And from his brows the kind powers made
    middle-earth for the sons of men;
    and from his brain, the cruel-hearted
    clouds were all created.

42. 'May he have Ull's help, and of all of the gods,
    who first takes hold of the flame;
    for worlds fall open to the sons of the Æsir,
    when they carry up cauldrons.

43. 'Ívaldi's sons went in ancient days
    to create Skídbladnir,
    the best of ships, for shining Frey,
    the capable son of Njörd.

44. 'The ash of Yggdrasil is the finest of trees,
    and Skídbladnir of ships;
    Odin of Æsir, Sleipnir of steeds,
    Bilröst of bridges, Bragi of skalds,
    High-breeches of hawks, Garm of hounds.

45. 'Now I've lifted my face before victory-gods' sons,
    so the wished-for sustenance will occur;
    it shall fetch in all the Æsir
    on Ægir's benches,
    at Ægir's feast.

46. 'I am called Battle-mask, I am called Wanderer,
    War-lord and Helm-bearer,
    Knowing and Third, Thund and Ud,
    Hel-blind and High,

47. 'Truth and Fleeting, and Truth-getter,
    Host-glad, Inciter,
    Feeble-eye, Blaze-eye, Bale-worker, Hider,
    Battle-mask and Masked One, Seducer and Much-wise,

48. 'Drooping-hat, Drooping-beard, Victory-father, Egger-on,
    All-father, Corpse-father, Attacking-rider, Cargo-god,
    by one name I have never been known,
    since I fared forth among folks.

49. 'Masked one they've called me at Geirröd's,
    but Gelding at Ásmund's hall;
    Nourisher, when I drove my sledge,
    Spurt at the assembly,
    Killer in battle,
    Wished-for and Boomer, Just-as-high and Shield-shaker,
    Wand-wielder and Grey-beard among gods.

50. 'Calmer and Cooler I was called at Sökkmímir's,
    and beguiled the aged giant,
    when I became of Midvitnir's famed boy
    the solitary slayer.

51. 'Drunk you are, Geirröd: you've drunk too much;
    you're robbed of much when robbed of my aid
    and that of the Einherjar, and Odin's help.

52. 'Much have I said, but little you've remembered:
    friends are proving deceitful:
    I see the sword of my friend lying
    all bespattered with blood.

53. 'A corpse edge-wearied will Dread have now;   *Dread* Odin
    I know your life is done;
    the *dísir* are hostile: now you can see Odin;
    come closer to me, if you can!

54. 'Now I'm called Odin; before I was called Dread;
     I was called Thund before that,
     Vigilant and Skilfing, Dangler and Tumult-god,
     Gaut and Gelding among gods.
     Ofnir and Sváfnir: I think they've become,
     all of these, one with me.'

King Geirröd was sitting with a sword on his knee, half-drawn. When he heard that it was Odin who had come there, he stood up and wanted to take Odin away from the fires. The sword slipped out of his hand, and turned hilt-down. The king stumbled and tripped and fell forward, and the sword went through him, and he died from that. Then Odin disappeared, and Agnar was king there for a long time afterwards.

För Skírnis: Skírnir's journey

One day Frey, the son of Njörd, had seated himself on Hlidskjálf, and looked out across all the worlds. He saw into Giants' Domain and saw there a beautiful girl, as she walked from her father's hall to the storehouse. From that he had great sickness of heart. Skírnir was the name of Frey's page. Njörd asked him to go and get Frey to talk. Then Skadi said:

1. 'Rise up now, Skírnir, and go and request
    the boy of us both to talk,
    and find out with whom is so greatly enflamed
    that kinsman's fertile brain.'

Skírnir said:

2. 'I expect wicked words from the son of you both,
    if I go to speak with the boy,
    and find out with whom is so greatly enflamed
    that kinsman's fertile brain.

3. 'Tell me, Frey, great general of the gods,
   what I would like to know:
   why you sit alone inside the long hall,
   my lord, throughout the days?'

Frey said:

4. 'Why tell it to you, young sir:
   the great grief of my heart?
   for Elf-disk shines throughout the days,   *Elf-disk* Sun
   but never the way I want.'

Skírnir said:

5. 'I don't think what you want can be so great,
   that you, sir, can't tell it to me;
   we were young together in ancient days:
   we two should trust each other well.'

Frey said:

6. 'In Gymir's yards I saw wander   *Gymir* Ægir?
   a maiden dear to me:
   her arms were bright, and from their light
   all sea and sky seemed to gleam.

7. 'A girl dearer to me than to any lad
   young in ancient days;
   but none of them wishes, neither Æsir nor elves,
   that we two should be as one.'

Skírnir said:

8. 'Give me a horse to bear me over the dark
   and famous flickering flame,
   and that sword, that of itself can fight
   against the giants' kin.'

Frey said:

9. 'I'll give you the horse to bear you over the dark
   and famous flickering flame,
   and that sword, that of itself can fight
   if the one who wields it is wise.'

Skírnir spoke to the horse:

10. 'It's dark outside; I think it's time that we two went,
    across the dewy mountains, across the ogres' land;
    we'll both return, or both be taken
    by that gigantic giant.'

*Skírnir rode into Giants' Domain to Gymir's courts. There
were ferocious dogs tied up in front of the wooden fence
surrounding Gerd's hall. He rode up to where a herdsman
was sitting on a burial-mound, and gave him a greeting:*

11. 'Tell me, herdsman, sitting on a burial-mound,
    watching over every way,
    how can I get that girl to talk
    in the face of Gymir's hounds?'

The herdsman said:

12. 'Are you doomed, or are you dead?
    [. . .]
    You'll never have the chance to talk
    with Gymir's splendid girl.'

Skírnir said:

13. 'There are better choices than bleating about it,
    for one who is keen to get on;
    a single day my fate was shaped,
    and all my life laid out.'

Gerd said:

14. 'What is that sound I hear resounding now
    in among our buildings?
    The earth shudders, and all the courts
    of Gymir shiver before it.'

The maid said:

15. 'There's a man out here, just stepped off a horse:
    he's letting his steed start to graze.'

Gerd said:

16. 'Ask him to enter inside our hall,
    and drink our much-famed mead,
    even though I fear there may be
    out there my brother's butcher.

17. 'Which are you of the elves or the Æsir's sons
    or of the wise Vanir?
    Why come alone over raging flames
    to seek our company?'

Skírnir said:

18. 'I'm not of the elves or the Æsir's sons,
    nor of the wise Vanir,
    though I came alone over raging flames
    to seek your company.

19. 'Apples against old age I have here, all gold,
    and those I'll give you, Gerd,
    to purchase peace, so you might call Frey
    not the loathsomest creature alive.'

Gerd said:

20. 'Apples against old age I shall never accept,
    whatever anyone may want,
    nor will Frey and I both live as one
    so long as our twin lives last.'

Skírnir said:

21. 'Then I'll give you that ring, the one that was burnt
    alongside Odin's young son:
    eight just as heavy drop from it
    upon every ninth night.'

Gerd said:

22. 'I'll not take a ring, although it was burnt
    alongside Odin's young son;
    I've no lack of gold in Gymir's courts
    sharing my father's fortune.'

Skírnir said:

23. 'Do you see this sword, girl, slender, inlaid,
    that I hold here in my hand?
    Your head I'll hew from off your neck
    unless you say we're set.'

Gerd said:

24. 'I won't ever put up with pressure like that,
    whatever anyone may want,
    though I guess that if you and Gymir meet,
    unsluggish to strike, there'll be strife.'

Skírnir said:

25. 'Do you see this sword, girl, slender, inlaid,
    that I hold here in my hand?
    Before this blade that old giant will buckle:
    your father will turn out fey.   *fey* doomed to die

26. 'I'll strike you with a taming wand, and I'll tame you,
    girl, for whatever I want:
    you'll have to go where the sons of men
    will never see you again.

27. 'On an eagle's perch early you'll have to sit,   *eagle's perch*
    gazing out of the world, anxious, at Hel;   mountain-top
    may food be to you more hateful than is to all folk
    the shining snake among men.

28. 'Monstrous to see you'll seem, when you emerge:
    on you Hrímnir will glare, and everything   *Hrímnir* frost-giant
        stare;
    you'll seem better-known than their guard   *their guard*
        to the gods   Heimdall
    as you gape out from the gates.

29. 'Howling and growling, teasing, impatience:
    may your tears increase with your trouble;
    sit down, and I'll say to you
    a sorry end to joy
    and a twin trouble too.

30. 'Fiends will plague you the whole day long
    inside the giants' courts;
    to the frost-ogres' hall you'll have to go every day,
    stagger with no choice,
    stagger lacking choice,
    pain for pleasure in return you'll get,
    hateful horror and troubling tears.

31. 'With a three-headed ogre you'll dally always
    or be without any man;
    let lust lasso you,
    hunger make you hungry!
    Be like the thistle, the one that was crushed
    at the harvest's end.

32. 'I went to the woods, to the right-strong wood,
    a wand of power to get;
    a wand of power I got.

33. 'Odin rages at you, the Æsir-prince rages   *Æsir prince* Thor?
        at you,
    Frey will think you foul;
    most evil girl, you've got yourself
    the powerful rage of the gods.

34. 'Listen, giants; listen, frost-ogres,
    Suttung's sons and the hosts of the Æsir   *Suttung's sons* giants
        themselves:
    how I forbid, how I proscribe,
    human gladness to the girl,
    human glee to the girl.

35. 'Hrímgrímnir is the ogre's name, who shall have you,
    down below Corpse-gates;
    rough thralls there under the roots of a tree
    will give you the piss of goats;
    you'll never get a better drink,
    girl, whatever you want,
    girl, after what I want.

36. ' "Ogre" I carve for you, and three other runes:
    "cock-craving", and "frenzy", and "impatience";
    I can cut away what I cut in,
    should any reason arise.'

Gerd said:

37. 'Your health, instead, young man:
     take this white-topped cup
     full of vintage mead;
     I never thought that I should love
     one of the Vanir so well.'

Skírnir said:

38. 'My message I will wholly know
     before I ride home from here,
     when you'll agree to a meeting
     with the sprightly son of Njörd.'

Gerd said:

39. 'Barri is the name, that we both know,
     of a calm and quiet grove;
     and after nine nights, to the son of Njörd
     Gerd will grant some sport.'

*Then Skírnir rode home. Frey stood outside, and greeted him,
and asked for the news:*

40. 'Tell me, Skírnir, before you cast saddle from steed,
     and take a single step further:
     what you accomplished in Giants' Domain
     that you or I might want.'

Skírnir said:

41. 'Barri is the name, that we both know,
     of a calm and quiet grove;
     and after nine nights, to the son of Njörd
     Gerd will grant some sport.'

Frey said:

42. 'A night is long; two are longer:
    how can I put up with three?
    Often a month has seemed to me less
    than half such a wait-wedding night.'

Hárbardsljód: Grey-beard's poem

Thor was journeying from his travels in the East, when he came to a sound. On the other side of the sound was the ferryman with his boat. Thor called out:

1. 'What lad of lads is that, standing on the other side
       of the straits?'

He answered:

2. 'What gramps of gramps is that, calling across the water?'

Thor said:

3. 'Take me over the sound and I'll feed you breakfast;
    I've a basket on my back and no food could be better;
    I ate at leisure, before I left home:
    herring and porridge, and I've had my fill.'

The ferryman said:

4. 'In early deeds you glory at mealtimes;
    you can't see so clearly ahead:
    your folks at home are unhappy; I think your
        mother's dead.'

Thor said:

5. 'What you say now would seem to many
   the most awful news: that my mother's dead.'

The ferryman said:

6. 'You don't look as if you own three fine farms;
   bare-legged you stand, and in beggar's gear:
   you don't even wear any breeches.'

Thor said:

7. 'Bring your ferry-boat here: I'll show you where to get off;
   but who owns the boat that you keep by the bank?'

The ferryman said:

8. 'Battle-wolf he's called, who told me to keep it,
   the counsel-wise warrior, from Counsel-island-sound;
   he told me not to carry brigands or horse-thieves,
   only good folk, and those I knew well;
   tell me your name if you'll traverse this sound!'

Thor said:

9. 'I'd tell you my name, even if I were an outlaw,
   and all of my lineage: I'm Odin's son,
   Meili's brother, Magni's father,
   the god's great champion; you're talking to Thor.
   Now I want to know what it is that you're called.'

The ferryman said:

10. 'I'm called Grey-beard: I don't often hide my name.'

Thor said:

11. 'Why should you hide your name, unless you have
        some quarrel?'

Grey-beard said:

12. 'Even though I were outlawed, from people like you
        I'd defend my life, unless I were doomed.'

Thor said:

13. 'It seems a dreadful pain to me,
        to wade over the water to you, and wet my balls:
        I'll get you back, you dribbling git,
        for your smarmy words, if I get over the straits.'

Grey-beard said:

14. 'I'll stand here and wait for you:
        you never found a harder foe, now that Hrungnir's dead.'

Thor said:

15. 'Now you bring up my battle with Hrungnir,
        the stout-hearted giant with a head of stone:
        nonetheless, I felled him and made him fall;
        what did you do meantime, Grey-beard?'

Grey-beard said:

16. 'I was with Fjölvar for five full years,
        on the island they call All-green;
        there we waged many battles, piled up the dead,
        passed many a test, tried many a maid.'

Thor said:

17. 'How did your women turn out for you?'

Grey-beard said:

18. 'We'd have had frisky women, if they'd been
          friendly to us;
     we'd have had smart women, if our course had
          run smooth;
     they wound their ropes from sand,
     and out of deep dales they dug the earth;
     alone I was able to outwit them all,
     I slept with seven sisters,
     and had all of their lust and their love.
     What did you do meantime, Thor?'

Thor said:

19. 'I slew Thjazi, the great-hearted giant,
     and cast up the eyes of Allvaldi's son
     into the shining sky;
     those are the greatest marks of my deeds,
     that all men can afterwards see.
     What did you do meantime, Grey-beard?'

Grey-beard said:

20. 'Great love-spells I used against witch-hags,
     those that I tricked from their men;
     I thought Hlébard was a harsh giant,
     but he gave me a wand of power:
     then I tricked him out of his wits.'

Thor said:

21. 'With a wicked heart you repaid good gifts.'

Grey-beard said:

22. 'One oak-tree thrives, when another's cut back:
    in such matters it's each for himself.
    What did you do meantime, Thor?'

Thor said:

23. 'I was in the East, battling giants,
    wicked-hearted women, who wandered the fells;
    great would be the giant-race, if they all lived:
    mankind would be nothing, under middle-earth.
    What did you do meantime, Grey-beard?'

Grey-beard said:

24. 'I was in Valland, waging war,
    I spurred on the princes, and never made peace:
    Odin gets the noblemen, who fall in the fight,
    but Thor gets the race of slaves.'

Thor said:

25. 'A bad share would you bring to the Æsir host
    if you'd as much might as you wish.'

Grey-beard said:

26. 'Thor has strength a-plenty, but not heart:
    in fear and cravenness you cowered in a glove,
    and scarcely did you seem then like Thor;
    you didn't then dare, because of your fear,
    to sneeze or fart, in case Much-wise might hear.'

Thor said:

27. 'Grey-beard, you cock-craver, I'd smash you into Hel,
    if I could just reach across this sound!'

Grey-beard said:

28. 'Why reach across this sound, when we've no quarrel?
      What did you do [meantime], Thor?'

Thor said:

29. 'I was in the East, protecting the river,   *river* Ífing?
      when Svárang's sons assailed me;
      they threw rocks at me, but gained no victory for that;
      they had to beg for peace at my hands.
      What did you do meantime, Grey-beard?'

Grey-beard said:

30. 'I was in the East, talking to a woman:
      I toyed with the linen-bright lady in tryst;
      I gladdened her gold-bright: the lass loved her love-play.'

Thor said:

31. 'Your sport with girls there was good!'

Grey-beard said:

32. 'I could have used your help then, Thor,
      to hold down that linen-bright lady!'

Thor said:

33. 'And I'd have offered it, if I could.'

Grey-beard said:

34. 'And I'd have trusted you, unless you'd tricked me.'

Thor said:

35. 'I'm no heel-biter, like an old leather shoe in the spring.'

Grey-beard said:

36. 'What did you do meantime, Thor?'

Thor said:

37. 'Berserk-women I battled on Hlésey;
    they'd acted most wickedly, bewitched the whole people.'

Grey-beard said:

38. 'You did a disgraceful deed, Thor, battling with women.'

Thor said:

39. 'They were wolf-bitches, and hardly women,
    they smashed my ship, when I'd put it on props,
    they threatened me with iron bars, and chased
        Thjálfi away.   *Thjálfi* Thor's servant
    What did you do meantime, Grey-beard?'

Grey-beard said:

40. 'I was with the host that travelled here
    to raise war-banners, and redden spears.'

Thor said:

41. 'Now you bring up the fact that you came to give us a
        fight.'

Grey-beard said:

42. 'I'll make it up to you with a ring for the arm:
      just as judges grant, who make a settlement between us.'

Thor said:

43. 'Where did you learn these biting words?
      I never heard more biting!'

Grey-beard said:

44. 'I learned them from those aged men, who live in
          the woods at home.'

Thor said:

45. 'You're giving a good name to burial cairns, to call
          them the woods at home.'

Grey-beard said:

46. 'That's what I reckon about such things.'

Thor said:

47. 'Your quick tongue will cause you grief
      if I can wade over the water;
      louder than a wolf, I reckon you'd howl
      if you had a blow from my hammer.'

Grey-beard said:

48. 'At home Sif's taken a lover: he's the one   *Sif* Thor's wife
          you want to meet,
      then you'll have a match more urgent for your energy.'

Thor said:

49. 'You say without thinking what should seem worst to me,
    you cowardly creep, I reckon you're lying!'

Grey-beard said:

50. 'I reckon I'm telling the truth; you're slow in your travels;
    you'd be long gone now, Thor, if you'd got in the skiff.'

Thor said:

51. 'Grey-beard, you cock-craver, now you've delayed me
        too long.'

Grey-beard said:

52. 'I never thought that Ása-Thor,   *Ása-Thor* Thor of the Æsir
    would be played for a fool by a ferryman.'

Thor said:

53. 'Now let me give you some advice: row the vessel here;
    let's leave off this banter: meet Magni's   *Magni's father* Thor
        father!'

Grey-beard said:

54. 'Get away from the sound: the crossing's denied!'

Thor said:

55. 'Show me the way, if you won't ferry me over.'

Grey-beard said:

56. 'It's easy to deny, but a long way to try;
    a skip to the stock, another to the stone;
    keep to the left, until you reach Verland: *Verland* 'Man-land'?
    then Fjörgyn will meet her son, Thor,
    and show him the family way to Odin's lands.'

Thor said:

57. 'Will I reach there today?'

Grey-beard said:

58. 'At sun-rise, if you take some toil and trouble,
    since I think there's a thaw.'

Thor said:

59. 'Our talk must be brief this time, since you only
              answer me with scorn;
    I'll repay your refusal, if we meet another time.'

Grey-beard said:

60. 'Get off now, where fiends can have you whole!'

Hymiskvida: The song of Hymir

Thór dró Midgardsorm: Thor hauled up the Midgard-serpent

1. Long ago the slaughter-gods were eating their
              hunting-prey
    in the mood for a drink, before they were full;
    they shook the sticks and looked at the lots:
    they learned that at Ægir's was a fine crop of cauldrons.

2.   The cliff-dweller sat there, child-cheerful,   *cliff-dweller* Ægir
     much like Miskorblindi's boy;
     the son of Dread, defiant, stared him in   *son of Dread* Thor
          the eye:
     'Often you'll have to prepare drinking-feasts for the Æsir.'

3.   The word-surly warrior gave trouble to the giant:
     he thought how next he might be revenged on the gods;
     he asked Sif's husband to bring him   *Sif's husband* Thor
          a cauldron
     'With which I can brew ale for you all.'

4.   The far-famed gods and the great powers
     couldn't get one anywhere,
     till, because of close ties, one was able to offer   *one* Loki?
     much welcome advice to Hlórridi alone.   *Hlórridi* Thor

5.   'East of Élivágar dwells
     hugely-wise Hymir at heaven's edge;
     my fierce father owns a pot,
     a capacious cauldron a league deep.'

6.   'Do you know if we can get that brew-kettle?'
     'If, friend, we two do it with cunning.'

7.   They travelled far away that day
     from Ásgard, until they reached Egil's.   *Egil* Thjalfi's father
     He took care of the goats with   *goats* that pull Thor's chariot
          their splendid horns,
     while they turned towards Hymir's hall.

8.   The lad met his granny, who seemed hateful   *lad* Loki?
          to him:
     she had nine hundred heads;
     another all-golden girl stepped ahead,
     bright-browed, to bring her son beer.

9. 'Offspring of giants, I'd like to hide
    you brave pair under the pots;
    my lovely husband, many a time,
    has been mean and bad-tempered to guests.'

10. The man malice-shapen came back late:
    hard-hearted Hymir, home from the hunt.
    When he walked in the hall, the icicles tinkled:
    the old guy's cheek-forest was frozen.   *cheek-forest* beard

11. 'Welcome, Hymir, in fine fettle:
    now your son has come home to your halls,
    one we've both missed on his long travels.
    Hród's adversary has come along   *Hród's adversary* Thor
          with him,
    a fighter's friend, Véur is his name.   *Véur* Thor

12. 'See, where they sit beneath the hall-gable,
    protecting themselves with the pillar in front?'
    The pillar split at the giant's gaze,
    and the pillar-beam broke in two.

13. Eight pots split, but one of them,
    fire-hardened, fell down whole from the post.
    They walked ahead, but the ancient giant
    followed his enemy with his eyes.

14. His heart sank, when he saw,
    the griever of giantesses walk across   *griever of giantesses* Thor
          the floor.
    Then three bulls were taken up,
    the giant had them quickly boiled.

15. Each one was made shorter by a head
    before being borne to be cooked.
    Sif's husband ate, before going to bed,
    two of Hymir's oxen all on his own.

16. To Hrungnir's hoary friend it seemed   *Hrungnir's ... friend* giant;
    that Hlórridi had had his fill.   here Hymir
    'Tomorrow evening we'll have to go hunt
    for food to feed us three.'

17. Véur said he wanted to row out to sea,
    if the brave giant would give him bait.
    'Turn to the herds, if you trust your guts,
    breaker of rock-Danes, to find some   *rock-Danes* giants, whose
            bait.   *breaker* is Thor

18. 'I expect it will prove easy for you
    to find some sea-bait from the oxen.'
    The lad swiftly slipped off to the woods,
    where a jet-black ox stood ahead.

19. There the ogre-exterminator broke from the bull,
    the lofty high pasture of both horns.   *lofty ... pasture of ...*
    [...]   *horns* head
    'Your act seems much worse to me,
    ship-steerer, than if you'd just sat still.'

20. The lord of goats told the offspring   *lord of goats* Thor; *offspring*
            of apes   *of apes* Hymir
    to put the roller-steed further out to sea;   *roller-steed* ship
    but the giant said that on his own reckoning
    he felt little urge to row further.

21. Famed Hymir then soon caught, full of wrath,
    alone two whales on a hook;
    but, back in the stern, Odin's kin,   *Odin's kin* Thor
    Véur, cunningly laid out his line.

22. He baited his hook, protector of men,   *protector of men* Thor
    the serpent's sole slayer, with the ox's   *serpent's sole slayer* Thor
        head;
    there gaped at the hook the one the gods   *one the gods hate*
        hate,   World-serpent
    from below, the girdle of all lands.   *girdle of all lands* World-serpent

23. Deed-brave Thor mightily dragged
    the venom-stained serpent up to the gunwale;
    he struck from above with his hammer
    the horrible hair-summit of the   *hair-summit* head; *wolf's*
        wolf's close-knit brother.   *close-knit brother* World-serpent

24. The rock-monsters groaned, the stone-fields thundered,
    the ancient earth all moved together;
    [. . .]
    then that fish sank back into the sea.   *fish* World-serpent

25. The giant was unhappy, when they rowed back:
    Hymir didn't say a word at his oar;
    he steered a quite different course:

26. 'Would you share out the work with me,
    by either bringing the whales home to the house,
    or tethering up our floating-goat?'   *floating-goat* ship

27. Hlórridi went and gripped the prow,
    he lifted up the sea-steed, bilge and all,   *sea-steed* boat
    along with the oars and bilge-bailer;
    he carried to the house the giant's surf-   *surf-swine* whales
        swine,
    and the basin, across the wood-ridge.   *basin* boat

28. Yet still the giant, when it came to strength of arm,
    obstinately quarrelled with Thor:
    he said no one was strong, although he could row
    robustly, unless he could smash his cup.

29. But Hlórridi, when it came to his hand,
    caused soon a stone column to shatter with the glass;
    from his seat he struck it at a pillar;
    but they bore it back to Hymir in one piece.

30. Until the lovely sweetheart told him
    some useful advice that she knew:
    'Hit it on Hymir's head when he's heavy with food:
    it's harder than any cup.'

31. The hardy lord of goats rose from his seat,
    summoned all his Æsir-strength;
    the old man's helmet-stump stayed whole   *helmet-stump* head
        above,
    but the round wine-vessel was ruptured.

32. 'Many a treasure has passed from me,
    when I see the cup smashed out of sight.'
    The old man spoke some more: 'I'll never say again:
    "Beer, now you're brewed!"'

33. 'It's up to you, if you can take
    the ale-kettle out of our home.'
    One god tried twice to stir it: *One god* Loki?
    the cauldron stayed both times quite still.

34. Módi's father grabbed it by the rim,   *Módi's father* Thor
    and his feet sank down into the floor of the hall;
    Sif's husband heaved the cauldron up on his head,
    and its rings jingled around his heels.

35. They'd journeyed long, when Odin's son   *Odin's son* Thor
    took a single look behind him;
    he saw from the rocks, from the East with Hymir,
    a mighty, many-headed troop approach.

36. He heaved the cauldron down from his shoulders,
    brandished murder-loving Mjöllnir,
    and killed all the vast lava-whales.   *lava-whales* giants

37. They'd not journeyed long, before there fell
    Hlórridi's goat, half-dead, ahead;
    the trace's team-mate was lame in the leg:
    vice-wise Loki had caused it.

38. But you have heard – someone more aware
    of the lore of the gods can tell better –
    how he took recompense from the lava-   *lava-dweller* giant;
        dweller: here Egil?
    he gave up both children he had.

39. The strength-mighty one came to the   *strength-mighty one* Thor
        gods' assembly,
    bringing the cauldron that Hymir had owned;
    and the sacred ones shall drink well
    ale-feasts at Ægir's at flax-cutting time.

Lokasenna: Loki's home-truths

Frá Ægi ok godum: About Ægir and the gods

*Ægir, who is called by another name Gymir, had prepared
ale for the Æsir, when he had obtained the great cauldron,
as has just been told. To the feast there came Odin and
Frigg, his wife. Thor did not come, because he was off in
the East. Sif, Thor's wife, was there, and Bragi, together
with Idunn, his wife. Týr was there; he had only one hand:
the wolf Fenrir ripped his hand off, when it was put in
fetters. Njörd was there, with his wife, Skadi, and Frey and
Freyja, and Vídar, Odin's son. Loki was there, and Frey's
servants, Byggvir and Beyla; many of the Æsir and elves
were there.*

*Ægir had two servants, Fimafeng ['Quick-service'] and
Eldir ['Kitchen-boy']; bright gold took the place of firelight,
and the ale served itself. There was a great place of sanctuary
there. Everyone had much praise for how good Ægir's
servants were; Loki couldn't stand that, and killed Fimafeng.
Then the Æsir shook their shields and screamed at Loki, and
drove him away to the woods, and then went back to
drinking.*

Loki turned back, and met Eldir outside. Loki spoke to him:

1. 'Tell me, Eldir, before you take
    a single step any further:
    what do they have inside here,
    those victory-gods' sons, for ale-speech?'

Eldir said:

2. 'They reckon up their weapons
    and their prowess in war,
    those sons of victory-gods.
    Of the Æsir and elves who are here inside,
    not a one has a good word for you.'

Loki said:

3. 'One ought to go into Ægir's halls,
    to see a feast like that;
    I bring strife and grief to the Æsir's sons,
    and so mix malice with their mead.'

Eldir said:

4. 'I tell you, if you go into Ægir's halls,
    to see a feast like that:
    spill insults and slander on the powers in the hall,
    and they'll wipe them off on to you.'

Loki said:

5. 'I tell you, Eldir, if it's just we two
    who wrangle with wounding words:
    I'll turn out rich in my replies,
    if you talk too much.'

*Then Loki walked into the hall. And when those inside saw
who had come in, everyone fell silent. Loki said:*

6. 'Thirsty I have come to these halls,
    Lopt travelling from long away,   *Lopt* Loki
    to ask the Æsir for just one draught
    of their much-famed mead.

7. 'Why so silent, you puffed-up gods:
    have you nothing to say to me at all?
    Find me a seat and a place at the feast,
    or tell me to go away from here!'

Bragi said:

8. 'To find you a seat and a place at the feast
    is something the Æsir won't wish;
    for the Æsir know the kind of person for whom
    they ought to pour at fine feasts.'

Loki said:

9. 'Do you recall, Odin, when long ago
    we two blended together our blood:
    you said you would never partake of ale
    unless it was brought to us both.'

Odin said:

10. 'Up then, Vídar, and let the wolf's father   *wolf's father* Loki
    take a seat at the feast,
    lest Loki speaks of us with reproach
    inside Ægir's halls.'

Then Vídar stood up and poured a drink for Loki. But before
he drank, he toasted the Æsir:

11. 'Hail, gods; hail, goddesses,
    and all the most holy powers,
    except that one god, who sits further in,
    Bragi, at the benches' end.'

Bragi said:

12. 'A steed and a sword will I give from my store,
    and Bragi will requite you with a ring,
    if you don't give the Æsir disfavour:
    don't anger the gods against you!'

Loki said:

13. 'As for horses and arm-rings,
    Bragi, you'll always lack both:
    of the Æsir and elves who are gathered herein,
    you are the wariest of war,
    ever the most shy of shooting.'

Bragi said:

14. 'I know, if only I were outside,
    instead of inside Ægir's hall,
    I'd have your head held in my hand:
    I'll take that payback for your lie.'

Loki said:

15. 'You're a soldier in your seat, but you can't deliver,
    Bragi, pretty-boy on a bench:
    go and get moving if you're upset:
    no hero heeds what's to come.'

Idunn said:

16. 'Bragi, I beg you: do a favour to our family
    and all our adopted kin;
    don't speak of Loki with reproach
    inside Ægir's hall.'

Loki said:

17. 'Shut your mouth, Idunn, I declare that you are
    of all women the maddest for men,
    since you laid your bright-scrubbed arms
    around your brother's butcher.'

Idunn said:

18. 'I'm not speaking to Loki with reproach
    inside Ægir's hall;
    I'm calming down Bragi, flushed with beer,
    I don't want you two furiously to fight.'

Gefjon said:

19. 'Why must the two of you Æsir in here
    wrangle with wounding words?
    Is it not known of Lopt that he likes to give lip
    and that all gods properly appreciate him?'

Loki said:

20. 'Shut your mouth, Gefjon, now I'll mention
    someone who seduced you to sex:
    that white boy who gave you a brooch,
    and you thrust your thighs over him.'

Odin said:

21. 'You're quite mad, Loki, and out of your mind
    to make an enemy of Gefjon:
    I reckon she knows all the fates of the world
    just as clearly as me.'

Loki said:

22. 'Shut your mouth, Odin, you never know how
    to hand out hostilities among men;
    often you've granted to those you should not,
    to weaker warriors, a win.'

Odin said:

23. 'I tell you, if I've granted to those I should not,
    to weaker warriors, a win:
    you spent eight winters under the earth,
    as a milking-cow and a matron,
    and there you bore babies;
    that signals to me a cock-craver.'

Loki said:

24. 'It's said you played the witch on Sámsey,
    beat the drum like a lady-prophet;
    in the guise of a wizard you wandered the world:
    that signals to me a cock-craver.'

Frigg said:

25. 'Your past lives neither of you two
    should ever declare to men,
    what you two Æsir did in ancient days:
    past history is best kept concealed.'

Loki said:

26. 'Shut your mouth, Frigg, you're Fjörgyn's daughter,
    and have always been mad for men,
    while Vidrir's wife, after all, you took   *Vidrir* Odin; *Vili and Vé*
         Vili and Vé,   Odin's brothers
    both of them, into your arms.'

Frigg said:

27. 'I tell you that if I had here in Ægir's hall
    a boy to match my Baldr,
    you'd never escape the Æsir's sons,
    and you'd be fought against in your fury.'

Loki said:

28. 'Frigg, do you still want me to say more
    about my dreadful deeds?
    I brought it about that you'd never see
    Baldr ride back to the hall.'

Freyja said:

29. 'You're quite mad, Loki, when you make mention
    of your hateful and horrible deeds;
    Frigg, I think, knows all our fates,
    though she never speaks of them herself.'

Loki said:

30. 'Shut your mouth, Freyja, I know you full well;
     you're scarcely free from flaws.
     As for each of the Æsir and elves here inside:
     at one time you've been their bitch.'

Freyja said:

31. 'Your tongue is treacherous: I think one day
     it'll gabble you into grief;
     the gods and goddesses are all angry with you,
     you'll go home unhappy.'

Loki said:

32. 'Shut your mouth, Freyja, you're a witch,
     and mixed up with much spite;
     you straddled your brother while glad   *brother* Frey
        gods stood by,
     and then, Freyja, you farted.'

Njörd said:

33. 'It matters little, if a wife takes a lover
     instead of or as well as her man;
     but strange that a cock-craving god can come here
     when he has borne babies himself.'

Loki said:

34. 'Shut your mouth, Njörd, East from here
     you were sent as a hostage to the gods;
     Hymir's daughters took you for a toilet
     which is why they pissed in your mouth.'

Njörd said:

35. 'That is my comfort, when far from here
    I was sent as a hostage to the gods:
    that I sired a son, whom no one hates   *son* Frey
    and is deemed the Æsir's defence.'

Loki said:

36. 'Stop now, Njörd, hold yourself back a bit;
    I won't keep it quiet any more:
    on your own sister you sired that son,
    though that's no worse than we expected.'

Týr said:

37. 'Frey is the best of all bold riders
    within the Æsir's courts:
    he makes no girl cry, nor any man's wife,
    and frees each one from chains.'

Loki said:

38. 'Shut your mouth, Týr, you never know how
    to be even-handed among folk:
    I must just mention that right hand of yours
    that Fenrir ripped away.'

Týr said:

39. 'I miss my hand, you miss Famed Wolf:
    both suffer bitter loss;
    nor is the wolf well, but must in chains
    await the powers' fate.'   *powers' fate* Ragnarök

Loki said:

40. 'Shut your mouth, Týr, your wife just happened
    to have a son by me;
    no cloth nor cash did you ever have
    in recompense, you wretch.'

Frey said:

41. 'I see a wolf lie by a river-mouth,
    until the powers are rent;
    unless you shut up now, you'll lie next to it,
    tied up, mischief-maker!'

Loki said:

42. 'You had Gymir's daughter bought   *Gymir's daughter* Gerd
        with gold,
    and also gave your sword;
    but when Muspell's sons ride over Mirkwood,
    you won't know then, wretch, how to fight.'

Byggvir said:

43. 'I tell you, if I had the fine lineage of Yngvi-Frey,
    and such an splendid estate,
    smaller than marrow I'd pound this spite-crow,
    and break every bone that he has.'

Loki said:

44. 'What's that little thing I see, wagging like a dog,
    snapping and yapping away?
    You're always whispering in Frey's ear,
    twittering under the grindstone.'

Byggvir said:

45. 'My name is Byggvir, and I'm called brisk   *Byggvir* Barley-boy
      by every god and man;
      I'm honoured to be here, where all Hropt's kin   *Hropt* Odin
      are drinking ale together.'

Loki said:

46. 'Shut your mouth, Byggvir, you never know how
      to hand out meals among men;
      you can't be found in the platform-straw
      when warriors set to war.'

Heimdall said:

47. 'You're drunk, Loki, and out of your mind,
      why won't you leave off, Loki?
      Too much to drink makes every man
      not mind how much he speaks.'

Loki said:

48. 'Shut your mouth, Heimdall, in ancient days
      for you was a grim life laid down;
      with muddy back you must ever be
      and watch as the guard of the gods.'

Skadi said:

49. 'You're light-minded, Loki, but not for long
      will you go with your tail playing free;
      since on a sword-point, with the guts of your son,
      ice-cold, the gods shall bind you.'

Loki said:

50. 'I tell you, if on a sword-point with the guts of my son,
    ice-cold, the gods shall bind me:
    first and most final I was at the killing
    when we thrust hands on Thjazi.'   *Thjazi* Skadi's father

Skadi said:

51. 'I tell you, if first and most final you were at the killing
    when you laid hands on Thjazi:
    from my shrines and plains shall always come
    cold counsels as far as you go.'

Loki said:

52. Your words were lighter to Laufey's son,   *Laufey's son* Loki
    when you gave me a bidding to your bed;
    one must mention such things, if we're keeping clear count
    of each thing of which we're ashamed.'

*Then Sif approached, offered Loki mead from a crystal cup
and said:*

53. 'Your health, Loki,
    take this white-topped cup
    full of vintage mead;
    say rather there's one woman,
    among the Æsir's sons,
    who is quite without fault.'

He accepted the horn and drank it down:

54. 'You'd be the one, if only you were
    wary and cautious with men;
    but I know someone, it seems to me,
    who made Hlórridi's wife his whore,   *Hlórridi* Thor
    and that one was vice-wise Loki.'

Beyla said: *Beyla* 'Cow-girl'

55. 'All the mountains shake: I think it must be
    Hlórridi coming from home;
    he'll bring silence to the one who smears everyone here,
    all the gods and men.'

Loki said:

56. 'Shut your mouth, Beyla, you're Byggvir's wife,
    and mixed up with much spite;
    no greater disgrace came among the Æsir's sons:
    you're dripping with shit, dairy-maid!'

Then Thor came up and said:

57. 'Shut your mouth, you cock-craving creature:
    my mighty hammer Mjöllnir
    will cut you off from your cackle;
    the rock of your shoulders I'll strike   *rock of . . . shoulders* head
        from your neck,
    and then your life will be done.'

Loki said:

58. 'Look! The Son of Earth has now entered in: *Son of Earth* Thor
    why, Thor, do you thrash about so?
    You won't be so brave when you must battle the wolf,
    and he swallows Victory-father whole.'   *Victory-father* Odin

Thor said:

59. 'Shut your mouth, you cock-craving creature:
    my mighty hammer Mjöllnir
    will cut you off from your cackle;
    I'll cast you up on the roads to the East:
    then no one will see you again.'

Loki said:

60. 'As for your trips East: those you never
      should ever declare to men,
      since in a glove's thumb you huddled, fine fighter,
      and scarcely did you seem then like Thor.'

Thor said:

61. 'Shut your mouth, you cock-craving creature:
      my mighty hammer Mjöllnir
      will cut you off from your cackle;
      with his right hand Hrungnir's slayer   *Hrungnir's slayer* Thor
         will strike you,
      so that every bone will he broken.'

Loki said:

62. 'I intend to keep living for a long time yet,
      though you wave your hammer at me;
      you thought Skrýmir had tough leather straps,
      and you couldn't get at the food,
      and you starved from hunger, unharmed.'

Thor said:

63. 'Shut your mouth, you cock-craving creature:
      my mighty hammer Mjöllnir
      will cut you off from your cackle;
      Hrungnir's slayer will send you to Hel,
      down below Corpse-gates.'

Loki said:

64. 'I spoke before the Æsir,
    I spoke before the Æsir's sons,
    what my heart spurred me to say;
    but before you alone will I walk out,
    since I know you do throw blows.

65. 'Ale you made, Ægir, but never again
    will you hold a feast after this;
    as for all your possessions which are here inside:
    may flame play over it,
    and burn you behind!'

Frá Loka: About Loki

But after that Loki hid in the waterfall of Fránang in the form of a salmon. The Æsir caught him there. He was tied up with the guts of his son Nari. But Narfi, his other son, turned into a wolf. Skadi took a venomous snake and fastened it over Loki's face. Venom dripped from it. Sigyn, Loki's wife, sat there and held a bowl under the venom. When the bowl was full, she carried off the venom; but in the meantime venom dripped on Loki. Then he had such violent spasms that the whole world shook as a result. These we now call earthquakes.

Thrymskvida: The song of Thrym

1. Ving-Thor was enraged, when he awoke,   *Ving-Thor* Thor
   and felt his hammer gone.
   His beard started to bristle, his locks to toss;
   the son of Earth kept groping about.   *son of Earth* Thor

2. These were the first words he found to say:
    'Listen now, Loki, to what I now tell,
    what no one on earth or heaven knows:
    the god has been robbed of his hammer!'

3. They both set off to Freyja's fair halls,
    and these were the first words he found to say: *he* Loki
    'Freyja, will you lend me your feather-cloak,
    so I can find the hammer's trace?'

Freyja spoke:

4. 'Though it were gold, I should still give it you;
    though it were silver, I should still pass it on.'

5. Then Loki flew, and the feather-cloak whirred,
    until he passed beyond the borders of the gods,
    and passed inside Giants' Domain.

6. Thrym sat on a grave-mound, the lord of ogres,
    clasping golden collars on his bitch-hounds,
    smoothing the manes on his steeds.

Thrym spoke:

7. 'What's with the Æsir? What's with the elves?
    Why come alone into Giants' Domain?'

[*Loki spoke:*]

    'It's bad for the Æsir, [it's bad for the elves;]
    have you hidden Hlórridi's hammer?'   *Hlórridi* Thor

[*Thrym spoke:*]

8. 'I have hidden Hlórridi's hammer
   eight leagues under the earth.
   No one shall have it back again
   unless he brings me Freyja as bride.'

9. Then Loki flew, and the feather-cloak whirred,
   until he passed beyond Giants' Domain,
   and passed inside the borders of the gods;
   he met Thor in the midst of that land,
   and these were the first words he found to say: *he* Thor

10. 'Have you tidings, as well as trouble?
    Give me a full account from on high!
    Often a sitting storyteller lapses,
    or when lying will deal in lies.'

[*Loki spoke:*]

11. 'I have trouble as well as tidings:
    Thrym, lord of ogres, has your hammer.
    No one shall have it back again
    unless he brings him Freyja as bride.'

12. Then they went to visit fair Freyja,
    and these were the first words he found to say: *he* Thor
    'Freyja, put on your bridal veil,
    we two must drive to Giants' Domain.'

13. Freyja was enraged, and gave a snort,
    so that the whole gods' hall trembled,
    and the great Brísings' neck-ring tumbled:
    'You'd think I'd become the maddest for men,
    if I drove with you to Giants' Domain.'

14. At once all the gods were gathered,
    and all the goddesses came to speak,
    the mighty deities made a plan,
    how they might restore Hlórridi's hammer.

15. Then Heimdall spoke, most sparkling of gods:
    he saw far ahead, like the other Vanir.
    'Let us put Thor in the bridal veil,
    let him wear the great Brísings' neck-ring!

16. 'Let us have keys jangling beneath him,
    and women's clothes falling round his knees,
    and broad gem-stones sitting on his chest,
    let us top out his head with style.'

17. Then Thor spoke, the strapping god:
    'The gods will call me a cock-craver,
    if I let myself be put in a bridal veil.'

18. Then Loki spoke, the son of Laufey:
    'Shut your mouth, Thor, and don't say such things;
    Giants will soon dwell within the gods' borders
    unless you have your hammer back.'

19. Then they put Thor into a bridal veil,
    had him wear the great Brísings' neck-ring;
    they had keys jangling beneath him,
    and women's clothes falling round his knees,
    and broad gem-stones sitting on his chest,
    and they topped out his head with style.

20. Then Loki spoke, the son of Laufey:
    'I shall come too, to be your maid,
    we two must drive to Giants' Domain.'

21. At once the goats were driven home,
    hastened to their traces; they had to run well.
    The mountains shattered, the earth was ablaze:
    Odin's son drove to Giants' Domain.   *Odin's Son* Thor

22. Then Thrym spoke, the lord of ogres:
    'Stand up, giants, and spread the benches;
    now they bring me Freyja as bride,
    the daughter of Njörd from Naval-yard.

23. 'Here in my fields wander gold-horned cattle,
    jet-black oxen, a giant's delight;
    I have plenty of treasures, plenty of neck-rings,
    only Freyja seems missing to me.'

24. Evening arrived all too soon,
    and beer was brought forth before the giants.
    One guest ate a whole ox, eight salmon too,   *guest* Thor
    and all of the dainties intended for the women;
    then Sif's husband drank three casks of   *Sif's husband* Thor
        mead.

25. Then Thrym spoke, the lord of ogres:
    'Did you ever see a bride eat more keenly;
    I never saw a bride eat more broadly,
    nor any maiden drink more mead.'

26. The all-cunning handmaid sat ready,   *all-cunning handmaid* Loki
    and found something to say to the giant's speech:
    'Freyja hasn't eaten at all for eight nights,
    she was so desperate for Giants' Domain.'

27. He bent down under the veil, and wished for a kiss;
    and then jumped back the whole length of the hall:
    'Freyja's eyes! Why are they so fierce?
    Fire seemed to me to flare from her eyes.'

28. The all-cunning handmaid sat ready,
    and found something to say to the giant's speech:
    'Freyja hasn't slept at all for eight nights,
    she was so desperate for Giants' Domain.'

29. Then in came the sorry sister of giants;
    she dared to beg for a bridal gift:
    'Offer red rings from your arms and fingers,
    if you wish to secure my love,
    my love, and all my favour.'

30. Then Thrym spoke, the lord of ogres:
    'Bring in the hammer, to hallow the bride,
    lay there Mjöllnir on the maiden's lap,
    hallow us together by the hand of Vár.'   *Vár* oath-goddess, Frigg?

31. The heart of Hlórridi laughed in his chest,
    when the hard-hearted one felt his hammer.
    Thrym, lord of ogres, was the first one he felled,
    before battering all of the giant-race.

32. Then he felled the aged sister of giants;
    who dared to beg for a bridal gift;
    instead of shillings, she took a beating,
    a hammer's blow, instead of many rings.

So Odin's son gained his hammer again.

Völundarkvida: The song of Völund

Frá Völundi: About Völund

*Nídud was the name of a king in Sweden. He had two sons
and one daughter; she was called Bödvild. There were three
brothers, sons of the king of the Finns. One was called
Striking-Finn, the second Egil, the third Völund: they went on*

snowshoes and hunted game. They came to Wolf-dales and made themselves a house there. There is a lake, which is called Wolf-lake. Early one morning they found three women on the lake-shore, spinning flax. Near them were their swan-cloaks: they were valkyries. Two of them were the daughters of King Hlödvér: Hladgud [Swan-white] and Hervör [Strange-creature]; the third was Ölrún, the daughter of Kjár of Valland. They took the women back to the hut with them: Egil took Ölrún, Striking-Finn Swan-white, and Völund Strange-creature. They dwelt there for seven years; then the women went to seek battles, and never returned again. Egil went off on snowshoes to look for Ölrún, and Striking-Finn looked for Swan-white; but Völund sat in Wolf-dales. He was the handiest of men that are known in ancient tales. King Nídud had him seized, as is told of here:

About Völund and Nídud.

1. Maids flew from the south, right through Mirkwood,
    strange young creatures, fulfilling fate;
    beside the lake-shore they settled to rest:
    southern ladies, spinning dear linen.

2. One of them chose Egil to fold in her arms,
    fair maid of men, within her bright bosom;
    the second was Swan-white, wearing swan-feathers,
    and the third of those sisters
    wrapped round Völund's white neck.

3. Then they stayed, for seven years after,
    but the whole of the eighth they yearned to go,
    and in the ninth need made them depart;
    the maids then longed to go through Mirkwood,
    strange young creatures, fulfilling fate.

4. There came from the chase the weather-   *weather-eyed archer*
        eyed archer;   Völund
    Striking-Finn and Egil found the halls empty:
    they walked in and out, and looked all around.
    Egil slid off East after Ölrún;
    south went Striking-Finn after Swan-white.

5. But all alone Völund sat in Wolf-dales;
    hammering red gold on his anvil:
    he closed up all the serpent-rings well;
    so he waited for his radiant wife,
    in case she ever came back.

6. Nídud found out, the lord of the Njárs,
    that all alone Völund sat in Wolf-dales;
    at night fighting-men journeyed, their corselets
        were studded:
    their shields shone in the crescent moon.

7. They stepped down from their saddles at the hall's gable,
    then walked in the whole length of the hall;
    they saw on the bast-rope rings all strung:
    seven hundred all told, that the fighting-man owned.

8. And they took them off, and put them back,
    all except one, which they left off.
    There came from the chase the weather-eyed archer,
    Völund, travelling a very long way.

9. He went to roast a brown she-bear steak,
    the brushwood burned high, the very dry pine,
    the wind-dried firewood in Völund's face.

10. He sat on a bearskin, counting rings,
    the prince of elves; one he missed.
    He thought that Hlödvér's daughter had it,
    strange young creature, that she'd come back.

11. He sat so long he fell to sleeping;
    then he woke, deprived of joys:
    he sensed on his arms heavy bonds,
    and on his legs fetters fast.

12. 'Who are the warriors who've laid on me
    ropes of bast, and bound me up?'

13. Now Nídud called out, lord of the Njárs:
    'Where did you, Völund, leader of elves,
    obtain our gold from in Wolf-dales?'

14. 'That was no gold as on Grani's path:
    I thought our land far from Rhine-fells;
    I remembered that we had more wealth
    when we were a whole household at home.

15. 'Hladgud and Hervor were born to Hlödvér,
    Ölrún, Kjár's daughter, was well-known.'

16. She walked in the whole length of the hall,   *She* Nídud's queen?
    stood on the floor, and spoke low: Bödvild?
    'Not so tame now, the one from the woods.'

*King Nídud gave to Bödvild, his daughter, the gold ring which
he took from Völund's bast-rope. He himself wore Völund's
sword; but the queen said:*

17. 'He bares his teeth, when he's shown the sword,
    or catches sight of Bödvild's ring.
    His gaze is as piercing as a gleaming snake:
    sever him from his sinews' strength,   *sever ... sinews' strength*
    then set him up in Sævarstöd.'   hamstring him

*So it was done: the sinews behind his knees were cut, and he was
set up in an island, near the place called Sævarstöd ['Sea-side
place']. There he forged for the king all kinds of treasure; no one
dared to go to him except only the king. Völund said:*

18. 'On Nídud's belt there shines a sword,
    which I sharpened as best I knew how,
    and I tempered as seemed most fit;
    that gleaming blade has been borne far from me forever,
    I won't see it brought to Völund in the smithy.

19. 'Now Bödvild bears – I expect no recompense for this –
    the red-gold rings of my bride.'

20. He sat, and never slept, but beat away with his hammer,
    creating feats of cunning quite quickly for Nídud.
    Two young men hastened to see the treasure,
    Nídud's sons, in Sævarstöd.

21. They came to the casket, asked for the keys;
    ill intent was evident when they looked in;
    many circlets were inside, which seemed to the boys
    to be red gold and great treasures.

22. 'Come just the two of you, come tomorrow,
    I shall have that gold given to you;
    don't tell the housemaids, nor the household,
    nor anyone, that you're meeting with me.'

23. Early there called one lad to another,
    brother to brother: 'Let's go look at the rings!'
    They came to the casket, asked for the keys;
    ill intent was evident when they looked in.

24. He cut off the heads of those small cubs,
    and in the mud beneath the anvil he laid their limbs;
    the skulls that were left beneath their locks
    he swept round with silver, and gave to Nídud.

25. And out of their eyes he sent gleaming gems
    to that crafty queen of Nídud;
    and from the teeth of those two
    he beat out brooches, sent them to Bödvild.

26. Then Bödvild began
    to praise the ring that she had shattered:
    'I don't dare talk of it, except only to you.'

Völund said:

27. 'I'll repair the rift in the gold
    till it seems fairer to your father,
    much better to your mother
    and the same as before to yourself.'

28. He overbore her with beer, since he knew better,
    so that on the seat she dropped off to sleep.
    'Now I have avenged my grievances,
    all except one, most malicious.

29. 'If only,' said Völund, 'I could get properly on my pins,
    of which Nídud's warriors have deprived me.'
    Laughing, Völund raised himself aloft;
    weeping, Bödvild went from the island:
    she couldn't stand her lover's leaving or her father's wrath.

30. Outside stands the crafty queen of Nídud,
    and she walked in the whole length of the hall;
    but he on the hall's wall settled to rest.   *he* Völund
    'Are you awake, Nídud, lord of the Njárs?'

31. 'I'm always awake, deprived of joys,
    I sleep very little since the death of my sons;
    there's a chill in my head, and your counsels are cold
            to me;
    now I should wish to speak with Völund:

32. 'Tell me then, Völund, leader of elves:
    what happened to my healthy young cubs?'

33. 'First you must swear solemn oaths:
     by a ship's sides and a shield's rim,
     by a steed's shoulder and a sword's edge,
     that your hand will never harm a wife of mine,
     that you will not slaughter Völund's bride,
     though you know well the one I wed,
     and we have a baby born in your halls.

34. 'Go to the smithy that you set up:
     there you'll find bellows spattered with blood;
     I cut off the heads of those small cubs,
     and in the mud beneath the anvil I laid their limbs.

35. 'The skulls that were left beneath their locks
     I swept round with silver, and gave to Nídud.
     And out of their eyes I sent gleaming gems
     to the crafty queen of Nídud.

36. 'And from the teeth of those two
     I beat out brooches, sent them to Bödvild;
     now Bödvild goes expecting a child,
     the only daughter of the two of you!'

37. 'Nothing you'd say could have caused me more grief,
     nor would I wish, Völund, any worse on you;
     no man is so tall as to take you from a horse,
     nor so mighty as to shoot you from below,
     where you hover up there in the clouds.'

38. Laughing, Völund raised himself aloft;
     full of sadness Nídud sat there behind.

39. 'Stir yourself, Thakrád, best of all my servants;
     ask Bödvild, that white-browed maid,
     that bright-robed girl, to come talk to her father.

40. 'Is it true, Bödvild, what I've been told:
    you and Völund, did you two spend time together
        on the island?'

41. 'It's true, Nídud, what he told you:
    Völund and I, we two spent time together on the island,
    a single tide's turn: it should never have been.
    I didn't have the wit to struggle against him;
    I didn't have the strength to struggle against him.'

Alvíssmál: The lay of All-wise

1. 'Now must a bride spread the benches for me,
   and be taken home in a trice;
   it'll seem a rushed match to everyone here:
   but at home no one will rob us of rest.'

2. 'You're what kind of creature, and why so pale-nosed?
   Did you pass the night with a corpse?
   You seem like an ogre to me:
   you're never born for a bride.'

3. 'All-wise I'm called; I live under the earth;
   I have a home under a rock;
   I've come to visit the charioteer: *charioteer* Thor
   let no one break folk's firm pledge!'

4. 'I shall break it, since I'm most concerned,
   since I am the father of the bride;
   I wasn't home when the pledge was made,
   and only I can make that gift among gods.'

5. 'Who's that warrior, who thinks he's involved
   in giving that fair-glowing girl?
   Ragamuffin-man, few will recognize you:
   who's raised you up with rings?'

6. 'I am called Ving-Thor: I'm widely travelled;
    I'm the son of Drooping-moustache;   *Drooping-moustache* Odin
    you won't get the young girl unless I consent,
    and make that marriage-match.'

7. 'Your consent I'd quickly like,
    to make that marriage-match;
    I'd rather have her than live without
    that lass as white as snow.'

8. 'The lass's love from you, wise guest,
    will not happen to be withheld,
    if you can say from every world,
    all that I wish to know.

9. 'Tell me this, All-wise, since, dwarf, I suspect
    you know every creature's whole history:
    what the earth's called, spread before the sons of men,
    in every world there is.'

10. '"Earth" it's called by men, by Æsir "ground",
    the Vanir call it "ways";
    "evergreen" giants, "growing" elves,
    the lofty powers call it "mud".'

11. 'Tell me this, All-wise, since, dwarf, I suspect
    you know every creature's whole history:
    what the heaven is called, familiar to all,
    in every world there is.'

12. '"Heaven" it's called by men, "star-studded" by the gods,
    the Vanir call it "wind-weaver";
    "up-world" giants, "pretty roof" elves,
    the dwarfs "dripping hall".'

13. 'Tell me this, All-wise, since, dwarf, I suspect
   you know every creature's whole history:
   what the moon is called that people see
   in every world there is.'

14. ' "Moon" it's called by men, but "glow-ball" by the gods,
   they call it "spinning wheel" in Hel;
   "speeder" giants, "shining" dwarfs,
   the elves call it "tally of years".'

15. 'Tell me this, All-wise, since, dwarf, I suspect
   you know every creature's whole history:
   what the sun is called, which the sons of men see,
   in every world there is.'

16. ' "Sun" it's called by men, but "sunlight" by the gods,
   the dwarfs call it "Dawdler's deluder";
   "ever-glow" giants, elves "pretty wheel",
   "all-bright" the Æsir's sons.'

17. 'Tell me this, All-wise, since, dwarf, I suspect
   you know every creature's whole history:
   what the clouds are called, that are mingled with showers,
   in every world there is.'

18. ' "Clouds" they're called by men, but "shower-prospect"
         by the gods,
   the Vanir call them "wind-swimmers";
   "drizzle-prospect" giants, elves "weather-might",
   "helm of concealment" they call them in Hel.'

19. 'Tell me this, All-wise, since, dwarf, I suspect
   you know every creature's whole history:
   what the wind is called, which journeys the widest,
   in every world there is.'

20. ' "Wind" it's called by men, but "wanderer" by the gods,
    the great powers call it "neigher";
    "howler" giants, elves "noisy traveller",
    "stormer" they call it in Hel.'

21. 'Tell me this, All-wise, since, dwarf, I suspect
    you know every creature's whole history:
    what the calm is called, which must lie still,
    in every world there is.'

22. ' "Calm" it's called by men, but "still" by the gods,
    the Vanir call it "wind's end";
    "mighty lee" giants, elves "day's ease",
    the dwarfs call it "refuge of day".'

23. 'Tell me this, All-wise, since, dwarf, I suspect
    you know every creature's whole history:
    what the ocean is called, that men row upon,
    in every world there is.'

24. ' "Ocean" it's called by men, but "ever-flat" by the gods,
    the Vanir call it "wave-surge";
    "eel-world" giants, elves "brew-stuff",
    the dwarfs call it "the deep sea".'

25. 'Tell me this, All-wise, since, dwarf, I suspect
    you know every creature's whole history:
    what the fire is called, which burns for the sons
         of men,
    in every world there is.'

26. ' "Fire" it's called by men, but by the Æsir "flame",
    the Vanir call it "warm conflagration";
    "greedy" giants, dwarfs "burner-up",
    they call it "hastener" in Hel.'

27. 'Tell me this, All-wise, since, dwarf, I suspect
    you know every creature's whole history:
    what the wood is called, that grows for men's sons,
    in every world there is.'

28. ' "Wood" it's called by men, but "field's mane" by the
        gods,
    human folk call it "slope-kelp";
    "stuff for burning" giants, elves "pretty-limbed",
    the Vanir call it "wood-stick".'

29. 'Tell me this, All-wise, since, dwarf, I suspect
    you know every creature's whole history:
    what the night is called, born to Nör,
    in every world there is.'

30. ' "Night" she's called by men, but "dark" by the gods,
    the great powers call her "mask";
    "unlight" giants, elves "sleep-joy",
    the dwarfs call her "goddess of dreams".'

31. 'Tell me this, All-wise, since, dwarf, I suspect
    you know every creature's whole history:
    what the seed is called, that the sons of men sow,
    in every world there is.'

32. ' "Barley" it's called by men, but "grain" by the gods,
    the Vanir call it "waxing-growth";
    "scoff" giants, elves "brew-stuff",
    they call it "crestfallen" in Hel.'

33. 'Tell me this, All-wise, since, dwarf, I suspect
    you know every creature's whole history:
    what the ale is called, that the sons of men drink,
    in every world there is.'

34. ' "Ale" it's called by men, but by the Æsir "beer",
      the Vanir call it "wet booze";
      "clear-draught" giants, but in Hel "mead",
      Suttung's sons call it "drinking-feast".'   *Suttung's sons* giants

35. 'In one chest I never saw
      more ancient lore was stored;
      I reckon I've fooled you with plenty of wiles:
      dwarf, your day is up;
      now Sun shines in the hall.'

THE HEROIC POEMS
OF THE CODEX REGIUS

Helgakvida Hundingsbana in fyrri: The earlier song of Helgi, the slayer of Hunding

Here begins the poem about Helgi, the slayer of Hunding, and his men and Hödbrodd. The Völsungs' poem.

1. It was early in ages when eagles screamed,
   holy streams poured down from Heaven-fells;
   at that time Helgi the mighty-hearted,
   was born to Borghild in Brálund.   *Borghild* Sigmund's first wife

2. It was night in the homestead; the norns came,
   those who would shape fate for that noble;
   they said he'd become the most famed of war-lords,
   and be thought the best of princelings.

3. They braided strongly the strands of fate,
   shook up the stronghold in Brálund;
   they arranged the golden threads
   and fixed them in the middle under Moon's   *Moon's hall* sky
      hall.

4. East and west they hid the ends,
   that praiseworthy one owned all lands between;
   Neri's kinswoman cast northwards   *Neri's kinswoman* a norn?
   a single fastening, bid it hold always.

5. One thing caused grief to the Ylfings'   *Ylfings' kinsman* Sigmund,
      kinsman,   Helgi's father
   and to the girl who'd brought forth her beloved:
   raven spoke to raven, sitting on a high tree,
   expecting food: 'I know something.

6. 'There stands in his mailcoat Sigmund's son,
   one day old: now day has come;
   his eyes are as sharp as warriors' are,
   he's a friend to wolves: let's we   *friend to wolves* mighty warrior,
          two be glad.'   and supplier of slain flesh

7. He seemed to the troops to be a hero,
   they said good times had come among men;
   the king himself came from war-turmoil
   to bring a noble leek to the young prince.   *noble leek* sword?

8. He gave him the name Helgi, and Ringstead,
   Sun-fells, Snowfells and Sigar's Plains,
   Ringsteads, Highfields and Heaven-meadow,
   a patterned blood-serpent for Sinfjötli's   *blood-serpent* sword;
          brother.   *Sinfjötli's brother* Helgi

9. Then he began to flourish in the bosom of his friends,
   a high-born elm in the radiance of bliss;   *high-born elm* mighty
   freely he gave and paid gold to his warriors   warrior
   nor did the prince spare blood-stained treasure.

10. He did not wait long, but went to war
    as soon as the war-lord was fifteen years old;
    he brought about tough Hunding's slaughter
    who had long ruled both lands and men.

11. Afterwards, Hunding's sons demanded
    wealth and rings from Sigmund's boy,
    they had to have recompense from the hero
    for much despoiling and their father's death.

12. The princeling would not pay the price,
    nor could the kinsfolk get any compensation;
    he said they might expect a mighty storm   *mighty storm of . . .*
    of grey spears and Odin's wrath.   *spears* battle

13. The chieftains go to a sword-meeting,   *sword-meeting* battle
which was set up at Fire-fells;
Fródi's peace was rent between   *Fródi's peace* proverbial calm
foes,
Vidrir's bitches go corpse-eager   *Vidrir's bitches* Odin's wolves
over the island.

14. The war-lord sat still, once he had slain
Álf and Eyjólf under Eagle-stone,
Hjörvard and Hávard, Hunding's sons;
he overthrew all of that spear-Mímir's   *spear-Mímir* warrior
line.

15. Then a radiance shone from Fire-fells,
and from that radiance lightning-bolts leapt;
then under helmets heading to Heaven-meadow,
[the princeling saw a valkyrie-troop]
their corselets were spattered with blood,
and from their spears light-beams burst.

16. From the wolf's lair, early in the morning,
the hero asked the southern *dísir*,
if they wished to come home that night
along with the warriors; there was a crash   *crash of elms*
of elms.   battle of warriors

17. Then from her horse Högni's daughter   *Högni's daughter* Sigrún
– the shields' din was dimmed –
spoke to the praiseworthy one:
'I think we have other business
than drinking beer with the breaker   *breaker of rings*
of rings.   generous lord

18. 'My father has betrothed his daughter
to the grim son of Granmar;   *son of Granmar* Hödbrodd
but, Helgi, I have called Hödbrodd
a king as courageous as a kitten.

19. 'That war-lord will come within a few nights,
    unless you send him to the battlefield
    or take the maiden from the prince.'

20. 'Have no fear of Ísung's killer,   *Ísung's killer* Hödbrodd
    there'll first be battle's din, or I'll lie dead.'

21. The all-powerful man sent out envoys from there
    through sea and sky, to summon a host,
    Terror's radiance aplenty   *Terror's radiance* gold, if 'Terror' is a river
    he offered fighting-men and their sons.

22. 'Tell them quickly to go to their ships,
    and make themselves ready from Brand-isle!'
    There the king waited until there arrived
    hundreds of men from Hedin's Isle.

23. And from the shores of Stem-ness
    his fleet slid out, decked with gold;
    Helgi asked at that point Hjörleif:
    'Have you inspected these courageous men?'

24. The young king said to the other
    that it would take long to tally from Crane-bank
    the long-stemmed ships with their sailors,
    that put out to sea in Arrow-sound.

25. 'Twelve hundred trusty men,
    and twice as many in Highfields,
    a king's war-band: we can expect a clash.'

26. The captain had the stem-tents dismantled,
    woke up the horde of men;
    the heroes see the break of day,
    and the princes hoisted up the mast,
    the woven sails in Varin's Fjord.

27. There was oars' thrash and weapons' crash,
    shield struck shield, vikings rowed;
    plunging ahead beneath the princes
    the king's fleet fared far from land.

28. There was to be heard when they came together,
    Kólga's sister and the longships,   *Kólga's sister* wave
    a sound as if cliffs and surge should shatter.

29. Helgi had the high sail set higher;
    the crew didn't fail at the breakers' assembly,
    when Ægir's dread daughter   *Ægir's dread daughter* fearsome wave
    wished to overwhelm stay-bridled   *stay-bridled steeds* ships
        steeds.

30. And Sigrún from above, each one of them,
    battle-brave, helped as they fared forth:
    she firmly wrenched out of Rán's grasp   *Rán's grasp* shipwreck
    the king's beast of the deep at Gnipalund.   *beast of the deep* ship

31. So there in the evening at Una-bay,
    the fine-adorned vessels were floating;
    and those men from Svarin's Howe,   *men from Svarin's Howe*
    could inspect the army with anxious hearts.   Hödbrodd's men

32. Thereupon god-born Gudmund asked:
    'Who is the commander who leads this troop
    and brings a threatening troop to the land?'

33. Sinfjötli spoke – up on the yard he hoisted
    his red shield with golden rim;
    he was a sea-sentry who knew how to respond
    and how to bandy words with princes:

34. 'Say this evening, when you're feeding the swine,
    and enticing your bitch-tykes to the swill,
    that the Ylfings have come from the East,
    keen for battle at Gnipalund.

35. 'There Hödbrodd will meet Helgi,
    a fighter slow to flee, in the midst of his fleet;
    one who's often given eagles their fill
    while you were kissing slave-girls beside the grindstone.'

[*Gudmund said:*]

36. 'War-lord, you must recall little of the ancient tales,
    to taunt princes with such untruths;
    It's you who have eaten the delicacies   *delicacies of wolves* carrion
        of wolves,
    and been the bane of your own brother,
    you've often sucked wounds with a cold mouth,
    crawled into a stone-pile, despised   *stone-pile* grave-cairn?
        by all.'

[*Sinfjötli said:*]

37. 'You were a witch on Varin's Isle,
    a scheming woman, full of falsehood,
    you said that you would never have
    any man in a mailcoat but Sinfjötli.

38. 'You were a spiteful sorceress, a valkyrie,
    dread and loathsome to All-father;   *All-father* Odin
    all the Einherjar had to fight,
    self-willed woman, for your sake.

39. 'Nine wolves we pair bred on Sága's headland:
    I was the only father of them all.'

[*Gudmund said:*]

40. 'You weren't father of any of Fenrir's wolves,
      but older than them all as I remember,
      since ogre-girls near Gnipalund
      cut off your balls at Thórsness.

41. 'You were Siggeir's stepson, skulking   *Siggeir's stepson* Sinfjötli
            under the hay-stacks,
      no stranger to wolf-songs out in the woods;
      all kinds of evil occurred at your hands:
      you ripped open your own brother's breast,
      you made yourself famous for wicked deeds.'

[*Sinfjötli said:*]

42. 'You were a bride of Grani's on Brávöll,   *Grani* Sigurd's horse
      gold-bridled, ready to race;
      on many a course I've ridden you to exhaustion,
      skinny under the saddle, a witch downhill.

43. 'You seemed to be an uncouth youth
      when you were milking Gullnir's goats,   *Gullnir* giant?
      and another time you were Imd's daughter,   *Imd* giantess
      dressed in tatters: do you want to talk more?'

[*Gudmund said:*]

44. 'I'd sooner go to Wolf-stone
      and give ravens the fill of your flesh,
      than entice your bitch-tykes to the swill,
      or feed the gelded boars: let fiends deal with you!'

[*Helgi said:*]

45. 'Sinfjötli, it would suit you two better,
    to wage war and gladden eagles
    than to bandy useless words
    whatever bitter hatred the ring-breakers   *ring-breakers*
        share.   generous warriors

46. 'Granmar's sons don't seem so splendid to me,
    but it's proper for a prince to tell the truth:
    they made it plain at Móinsheimar
    that they have the heart to bear blades.'

47. They sent off galloping out of the realm
    Svipud and Sveggjud to Sólheimar   *Svipud and Sveggjud* horses
    over dew-wet dales and dusky slopes,
    Mist's sea trembled as the boys   *Mist's sea* sea of the valkyrie; air
        passed by.

48. They met the prince at the courtyard-gate,
    said in alarm that the prince had come;
    Hödbrodd stood outside, wearing his helmet,
    he pondered the horse-ride of his kinsmen:
    'Why do the Hniflungs wear such anxious expressions?'

49. 'Turning towards this shore are swift ships,
    harts of mast-rings with long yardarms,   *harts of mast-rings*
    many shields and shaven oars,   ships
    a splendid ruler's host, glad Ylfings.

50. 'Fifteen companies have waded ashore;
    out in Sögn are seven thousand more;
    they lie by the harbours near Gnipalund,
    blue-black sea-beasts, decked with gold.   *sea-beasts* ships
    Their greatest number is there by far;
    now Helgi won't hold back from a sword-meeting.'

51. 'Let the bridled steeds gallop to the mighty meeting,
    but send Spur-wolf instead to Sparin's   *Spur-wolf ... Mélnir ...*
         Heath,   *Mýlnir* horses
    Mélnir and Mýlnir to Mirkwood;
    let no one linger long behind
    who knows how to bear wound-flames.   *wound-flames* swords

52. 'Summon Högni and the sons of Hring,
    Atli and Yngvi, and Álf the Old;
    they're always eager to wage war,
    let's give the Völsungs a welcome!'

53. In one fell swoop they came together,
    pale weapon-points at Wolf-stone;
    always was Helgi, the slayer of Hunding,
    foremost in the fray, wherever men fought,
    fiercest in battle, the slowest to flee;
    that warrior had a hard acorn for a heart.

54. There came down from heaven creatures with helmets
    – the din of spears grew – they protected the king;
    then spoke Sigrún – the wound-   *wound-creatures* arrows
         creatures flew,
    the troll-wife's steed ate Hugin's   *troll-wife's steed* wolf;
         food: *Hugin's food* carrion

55. 'Unharmed, prince, shall you get benefit from your men,
    descendant of Yngvi, enjoy your life;
    you have felled a warrior slow to flee,
    one who caused dreadful deaths.

56. 'Also you, princeling, have well deserved
    both red-gold rings and the mighty maid;
    unharmed, princeling, you shall benefit from both
    Högni's daughter and Ringsteads,
    victory and lands: now the battle is done!'

Helgakvida Hjörvardssonar: The song
of Helgi Hjörvardsson

Frá Hjörvardi ok Sigrlinn: About Hjörvard and Sigrlinn

There was a king named Hjörvard; he had four wives. One
was called Álfhild, and their son was called Hedin; the second
was called Særeid, and their son was called Humlung; the
third was called Sinrjód, and their son was called Hymling.
King Hjörvard had sworn a vow, to marry the finest woman
he could find. He learnt that King Sváfnir had the most
beautiful daughter of all, who was called Sigrlinn.

Idmund was the name of [Hjörvard's] earl; Atli was his son,
who went to woo Sigrlinn on behalf of the king. He spent the
whole winter with King Sváfnir. There was an earl called
Fránmar, Sigrlinn's foster-father; his daughter was called Álöf.
The earl decided that the girl was to be denied [to Hjörvard],
and Atli went home.

Atli, the earl's son, stood one day in a certain grove; a bird
sat in the branches above his head, and had heard that men
called the women married to King Hjörvard the finest. The
bird twittered, and Atli paid attention to what it said. It said:

1. 'Have you seen Sigrlinn, Sváfnir's daughter,
    the fairest of maids in Munarheim,   *Munarheim* 'The land of love'
    even if Hjörvard's wives seem lovely
    to the men in Glasir's Grove?'   *Glasir* 'Beamer'

Atli said:

2. 'Wise-hearted bird, will you say more
    to Atli, Idmund's son?'

The bird said:

    'I will, if the princeling will sacrifice to me,
    and I can choose what I like from the king's court.'

Atli said:

3. 'Don't choose Hjörvard or his sons,
    nor the fair brides of the war-lord,
    nor the brides the princeling has:
    let's strike a bargain; that's the mark of friends!'

The bird said:

4. 'A temple I'll choose, and many shrines,
    gold-horned cattle from the chief's estate,
    if Sigrlinn sleeps in his arms,
    and unforced follows the warrior.'

*This was before Atli left, but when he came home and the
king asked him the news, he said:*

5. 'We've had problems, our errand unaccomplished,
    exhausting our horses on the mighty fells,
    then we had to wade the Sæmorn;
    we were denied Sváfnir's daughter,
    decked with rings, whom we wished to have.'

*The king commanded that they should go a second time; he
went along himself. When they came up on the fells, they
looked at Svávaland and saw the land aflame and a huge
dust-plume from horses. The king rode down from the fells
into the land, and lodged for the night by a river. Atli kept
watch and went over the river; he found a house, and a great
bird was sitting on the house guarding it, but it had fallen
asleep. Atli threw a spear at the bird and killed it, and in the
house he found Sigrlinn, the king's daughter, and Álof, the
earl's daughter, and he took them both away with him. Earl
Fránmar had transformed himself into the likeness of an eagle,
and had protected the women from the army with magic.*

*There was a king called Hródmar, a suitor of Sigrlinn; he
had killed the king of Svávaland, and had pillaged and burnt
the land. King Hjörvard married Sigrlinn, and Atli Álof.*

Hjörvard and Sigrlinn had a fine tall son; he was silent, and
no name stuck to him. He sat on a burial-mound and saw nine
valkyries ride by, and one of them was most majestic. She said:

6. 'Not swiftly will you, Helgi, be lord of rings,
    mighty apple-tree of strife, or of Beam-   *apple-tree of strife*
        plains   warrior
    – the eagle shrieked early – if you always stay silent,
    even though, lord, you prove your harsh heart.'

7. 'What will you give with the name Helgi,
    bright-faced woman, since you've something to offer?
    Think well before you make your response!
    I won't accept it unless I have you too.'

8. 'I know where swords lie on Sigar's Isle
    four fewer than fifty,
    one of them is better than all the rest,
    the harm of battle-needles, decked   *battle-needles* swords
        with gold.

9. 'A ring in its hilt, great heart in its midst,
    awe in its point, for the one that acquires it;
    along its edge lies a blood-stained serpent,
    and on its sword-boss a snake bites its tail.'

There was a king called Eylimi; his daughter was called Sváva.
She was a valkyrie and rode across the sea and sky; she gave
Helgi his name, and often afterwards protected him in battles.
Helgi said:

10. 'Hjörvard, you are not a well-counselled king,
    spear-leader of the army, although you are famed;
    you had fire consume the settlements of princes,
    though they did no harm to you.

11. 'But Hródmar shall distribute rings,
      those which our family used to own;
      that war-lord cares the least for his life,
      he expects the inheritance when all are dead.'

*Hjörvard answered, that he would give help to Helgi, if he
wanted to avenge his mother's father. Then Helgi went to look
for the sword to which Sváva had directed him. Then he and
Atli went and killed Hródmar, and performed many heroic
deeds. He killed the giant Hati, where he was sitting on a
certain mountain. Helgi and Atli tethered their ships in Hati's
Fjord. Atli kept watch for the first part of the night;
Hrímgerd, Hati's daughter, said:*

12. 'Who are these warriors in Hati's Fjord?
      Shields are set up along your ships;
      you're behaving boldly: I don't reckon you fear much;
      let me know the name of the king!'

Atli said:

13. 'He's called Helgi, and you'll never be able
      to bring harm to that noble man;
      there are iron plates on the prince's ships:
      no troll-wives can take us.'

14. 'What are you called,' said Hrímgerd, 'mighty hero,
      what name do people give you?
      Your war-lord trusts you, to let you stay
      in the fair prow of the ship.'

15. 'I am called Atli, I'll be "Hateful" to you,
      I'm very grim to giantesses;
      in the damp prow I've often stayed
      and abused women who ride at   *women who ride at evening*
         evening.   valkyries or witches or troll-wives

16. 'What are you called, corpse-greedy witch?
    Ogress, tell me the name of your father!
    Nine leagues down you ought to be,
    with pine-trees growing from your breast.'

17. 'My name is Hrímgerd, my father's name Hati,
    whom I knew as the most mighty of giants,
    many a bride he had snatched from their homes,
    till Helgi hewed him down.'

18. 'Ogress, you were in front of the leader's ships
    and blocked off the mouth of the fjord;
    the prince's men you wanted to give to Rán,   *Rán* 'Plunder'
    if a spiteful man did not spike you.'

19. 'Now you're demented, Atli; I reckon you're dreaming,
    letting eyebrows droop over your lashes;
    my mother lay in front of the prince's ships,
    I drowned Hlödvard's sons in the sea.

20. 'You would neigh, if your balls weren't cut off:
    Hrímgerd tosses her tail;
    I think your heart is in your arse, Atli,
    though you have a stallion's voice.'

21. 'You'd soon learn what a stallion I was
    in strength, if I stepped on shore:
    you'd take a great pasting, if I so wished,
    and, Hrímgerd, you'd lower your tail.'

22. 'Come ashore then, Atli, if you think you're up to it:
    I'll be waiting in Varin's Bay.
    You'll get your ribs crushed, warrior,
    if you come within reach of my claws.'

23. 'I won't come before folk wake,
    and keep watch over the prince;
    it wouldn't be unexpected if there came close
    a witch from up under the ship.'

24. 'Wake up, Helgi, and compensate Hrímgerd,
    since you've had Hati cut down;
    if she could spend but one night by the prince
    she'd have compensation for her griefs.'

25. 'He's called Shaggy, and he'll have you,
    since you're loathsome to men,
    the ogre who lives on Tholley;
    the very wise giant, and worst of rock-dwellers:
    he's a suitable mate for you.'

26. 'She's the one, Helgi, you'd rather have,   *She* Sváva
    who looked out the harbours,
    the other night with the crew;
    the sea-gold girl seemed to me to be strong;
    she came ashore from the sea
    and then tethered your fleet:
    she alone has caused it, that I am unable
    to kill the princeling's men.'

27. 'Listen now, Hrímgerd,
    if I compensate your griefs
    tell the warrior more plainly:
    was it just one creature protecting the prince's ships,
    or did more women travel together?'

28. 'Thrice nine maids, but one rode in front,
    a fair girl wearing a helmet;
    the horses shuddered, and from their manes
    fell dew into the deep dales,
    hail in the high woods;
    from there comes prosperity for men;
    all I looked at was loathsome to me.'

29. 'Look East now, Hrímgerd, since Helgi has
    struck you down with Hel-staves;   *Hel-staves* deadly runes?
    on land and sea the prince's fleet is protected,
    and the chief's men just the same.

30. 'Day's here now, Hrímgerd, Atli's delayed you
    until you have laid down your life;
    as a harbour-marker you'll seem quite a joke,
    as you stand in the likeness of stone.'

*King Helgi was a very great warrior; he came to King Eylimi
and asked for the hand of Sváva, his daughter. Helgi and
Sváva exchanged vows and loved each other very much. Sváva
stayed at home with her father while Helgi was off raiding;
Sváva was a valkyrie as before.*

*Hedin was at home with his father, King Hjörvard, in Nor-
way. Hedin was going home on his own through the woods one
yuletide-eve, when he met a troll-wife; she was riding a wolf
with snakes for reins, and she offered herself as company to
Hedin. 'No,' said Hedin. She said: 'You'll pay for this at the
bragarful.' In the evening they were making vows. A sacrificial
boar was led forward, and men placed their hands on it, and
swore a vow with the bragarful. Hedin swore a vow to have
Sváva, the daughter of Eylimi, although she was the beloved of
Helgi, his brother, and he regretted it so much that went off,
travelling unknown paths south by land until he found Helgi,
his brother. Helgi said:*

31. 'Welcome, Hedin. What news
    can you tell from Norway?
    What has driven you out, prince,
    to travel alone to find me?'

32. 'I have done a dreadful deed:
    [. . .]
    I have chosen the child of a king,
    your own bride, at the *bragarful*.'

33. 'You've done nothing wrong; it may turn out
      that your ale-talk, Hedin, comes true for us both.
      A prince has challenged me to a duel
      in three nights' time, and I must go;
      I doubt I shall return again:
      then let it turn out for the best.'

34. 'Helgi, you have said that Hedin was
      worthy of good will and fine gifts from you;
      it's more seemly for you to redden your sword,
      than to give peace to your foes.'

*Helgi said, that he suspected that he was doomed, and that it
was his fetch that had visited Hedin, when he saw the woman
riding the wolf.*

   *There was a king called Álf, Hródmar's son, and it was he
who had marked out with hazel-wands the duelling-ground at
Sigar's Plains for Helgi three nights later on. Then Helgi said:*

35. 'She rode on a wolf, as it grew dusk,
      a woman, who offered him company,
      she knew that Sigrlinn's son would be   *Sigrlinn's son* Helgi
         killed
      there at Sigar's Plains.'

There was a mighty battle, and Helgi got there his death-wound.

36. Helgi sent Sigar to ride
      after Eylimi's only daughter,
      to tell her quickly to come prepared
      if she wished to find her war-lord alive.

[*Sigar said:*]

37. 'Helgi has sent me here,
      to speak to you, Sváva, yourself;
      the prince said he would see you
      before the noble one loses his life.'

[*Sváva said:*]

38. 'What has happened to Helgi, Hjörvard's son?
    I am summoned to heavy sorrows;
    if the sea took him, or a sword cut him,
    I shall make someone pay.'

[*Sigar said:*]

39. 'He fell this morning at Wolf-stone,
    the best princeling under the sun.
    Álf will win the whole victory;
    would that this time never were!'

40. 'Hail, Sváva, you must steady your heart,
    this will be our last meeting in the world;
    the princeling does bleed below,
    a sword has come close to my heart.

41. 'I ask you, Sváva – bride, don't weep –
    that you will pay heed to my words,
    that you go into Hedin's bed,
    and show the young warrior love.'

42. 'I said in my beloved homeland
    when Helgi picked me with rings,
    that I would not happily, when my war-lord was dead,
    take an untried warrior into my arms.'

43. 'Kiss me, Sváva: I'll not come
    to see Strife-home or Beam-fells,
    before I've avenged Hjörvard's boy,   *Hjörvard's boy* Helgi
    the best princeling under the sun.'

It's said that Helgi and Sváva were born again.

Helgakvida Hundingsbana önnur: The second song of Helgi, the slayer of Hunding

Frá Volsüngum: About the Völsungs

King Sigmund, the son of Völsung, married Borghild of Brálund; they named their son Helgi, after Helgi the son of Hjörvard. Helgi's foster-father was Hagal ['Handy'].

There was a powerful king called Hunding; Hundland is named after him. He was a mighty war-lord, and had many sons who went raiding. There was great animosity and hostility between King Hunding and King Sigmund; each of them killed the other's kin. King Sigmund and his family were called Völsungs or Ylfings.

Helgi went secretly to spy out King Hunding's court. Hæming, King Hunding's son, was at home; when Helgi left, he met a shepherd-boy and said:

1. 'Tell Hæming that Helgi recalls
   someone the warriors felled in his mailcoat;
   you had a grey wolf inside your hall,
   where Hamal was remembered by King Hunding.'

Hamal was the name of Hagal's son. King Hunding sent men to Hamal's home to look for Helgi, and since Helgi couldn't escape any other way, he put on serving-girl's clothes and went grinding. They looked, but they couldn't find Helgi. Then Blind spoke, the mischief-maker:

2. 'Hagal's work-wench has piercing eyes;
   no lackey's child stands at the grindstone:
   the stones crumble, the stand shatters.

3. 'Now the prince has had a harsh turn of fate,
   when a chief must grind foreign barley.
   That hand would hold more fitly
   a sword-haft than a mill-handle.'

Hagal answered and said:

4. 'Little wonder though the mill-stand screams,
    when a king's daughter turns the handle;
    above the clouds she used to sweep,
    she dared to slaughter like a viking,
    before Helgi held her captive;
    she is the sister of Högni and Sigar:
    the Ylfing maid has a dreadful gaze.'

*Helgi got away and went to the warships. He killed King
Hunding and was then called Helgi, the slayer of Hunding.
He stayed with his war-band in Bruna-bay, and there held a
cattle-slaughter on the beach, and ate them raw. There was
a king called Högni, who had a daughter called Sigrún; she
became a valkyrie, and rode across sea and sky: she was Sváva
reborn. Sigrún rode to Helgi's ships and said:*

5. 'Who has brought these ships to anchor by the shore?
    Where, you warriors, do you have a home?
    What are you awaiting in Bruna-bay?
    Where do you wish to set your course?'

6. 'Hamal has brought these ships to anchor by the shore;
    at Hlésey we have a home;
    a wind we're awaiting in Bruna-bay;
    eastwards we wish to set our course.'

7. 'Where have you, prince, begun a battle,
    or fed the goslings of Battle's sister?   *goslings of Battle's sister*
    Why is your mailcoat spattered with   *ravens of a valkyrie*
        blood?
    Why, wearing helmets, must you eat raw meat?'

8. 'Most recently the Ylfings' kinsman fought anew
    west of the sea, if you want to know,
    when I captured bears in Bragalund
    and with weapon-points gave eagles their fill.

9. 'Now I've said, maid, how the conflict occurred,
   and why I'm eating barely-cooked meat by the sea.'

10. 'You're proclaiming a killing, when at Helgi's hands
    King Hunding was made to fall on the field;
    the battle was brought about to avenge dead kin,
    and blood streamed along the edges of blades.'

11. 'How do you know that these are the ones,
    wise-hearted woman, on whom we avenged dead kin?
    There are many keen warrior's sons
    who seem similar to us kinfolk.'

12. 'I was not far away, spear-leader of war,
    yesterday morning, when the warrior died;
    but I reckon that the cunning son of Sigmund
    is telling war-tidings in slaughter-runes.

13. 'I watched you once before on the longships,
    when you stayed on the blood-stained stems,
    and the waves were playing cold and wet;
    now the prince wants to hide himself from me,
    but Högni's girl knows Helgi well.'

*Granmar was the name of a powerful king, who dwelt at
Svarin's Howe. He had many sons: Hödbrodd, then
Gudmund, third Starkad. Hödbrodd went to a meeting of
kings; he betrothed himself to Sigrún, Högni's daughter. But
when she discovered that, she rode with her valkyries across
the sea and sky to look for Helgi.*

*Helgi was at Fire-fells and had fought with King Hunding's
sons; there he killed Álf and Eyjólf, Hjörvard and Hervard,
and was completely exhausted by war, and sat under Eagle-
stone. Sigrún met him there, and flung her arms round his
neck, and kissed him, and told him her errand, just as it says
in the 'The ancient poem of the Völsungs'.*

14. Sigrún visited the cheerful prince,
    at home she took Helgi by the hand;
    she kissed and greeted the king in his helmet,
    the leader's heart turned to the woman.

15. She said she'd loved with all her heart
    Sigmund's son before she'd seen him.

16. 'I've been betrothed among the troop to Hödbrodd,
    but I wish to have another lord;
    war-lord, I fear the wrath of kinsmen,
    I've broken my father's dearest contract.'

17. Högni's girl did not hide her heart,
    she said she should have Helgi's favour.

18. 'Don't pay any heed to Högni's wrath,
    nor the wicked thought of your family;
    young girl, you must live with me:
    fine one, you have no family I fear.'

Helgi gathered a great fleet and went to Wolf-stone, but they
met at sea with a great and life-threatening storm. Then
lightning flashed over them, and beams of light hit the ship.
They looked aloft and saw nine valkyries riding, and
recognized Sigrún. Then the storm died down, and they
reached land safely.

   Granmar's sons were sitting on a cliff, when the ships sailed
towards land; Gudmund leapt on to his horse and rode down
to a rock by the harbour to spy them out. The Völsungs lowered
their sails; then Gudmund said what's written above in 'The
poem of Helgi':

   'Who is the commander who leads this troop
   and brings a threatening troop to the land?'

Gudmund, Granmar's son, said this:

19. 'Who is the prince who steers the ships,
    and puts up golden war-banners at the prow?
    Peace doesn't seem to me at the forefront of your craft,
    a red glow of battle plays over the vikings.'

Sinfjötli said:

20. 'Here can Hödbrodd recognize Helgi,
    slow to flee, in the midst of the fleet;
    he's taken hold of your family's land
    the Fjörsungs' inheritance under his control.'

[*Gudmund said:*]

21. 'Before that at Wolf-stone,
    must men meet and consider the case;
    it's time, Hödbrodd, to take revenge:
    we've long had to bear the lower share.'

[*Sinfjötli said:*]

22. 'Before that, Gudmund, you must herd your goats,
    scramble up steep rocky-clefts,
    holding a hazel switch in your hand:
    for you that's easier than the judgement of blades.'

[*Helgi said:*]

23. 'Sinfjötli, it would suit you better,
    to wage war and gladden eagles,
    than to bandy useless words,
    even though warriors bitter hatred share.

24. 'Granmar's sons don't seem so splendid to me,
    but it's proper for a prince to tell the truth:
    they made it plain at Móinsheimar
    that they have the heart to bear blades;
    the warriors are far too brave.'

*Sinfjötli, Sigmund's son, answered, as has also been written.
Gudmund rode home with news of the army; then Granmar's
sons assembled an army. Many kings came; Högni was there,
Sigrún's father, with his sons Bragi and Dag. There was a
mighty battle, and all Granmar's sons fell together with all
their chieftains, except Dag, Högni's son, who obtained a
truce and swore an oath to the Völsungs.*

*Sigrún went among the slain and found Hödbrodd close to
death; she said:*

25. 'Never will Sigrún from Sefafells,
    King Hödbrodd, sink into your arms;
    your life is done. The troll-wife's grey   *troll-wife's grey
        stud-horse   stud-horse wolf*
    often gets corpses: here, Granmar's sons.'

Then she met Helgi and was overjoyed. He said:

26. 'Strange-creature, not everything worked out for you:
    I reckon it's the norns' doing in part;
    there fell this morning at Wolf-stone,
    Bragi and Högni, and I killed them both.

27. 'And at Steer-clefts, King Starkad;
    and at Hlébjörg, Hrollaug's sons;
    I saw the most grim-hearted king:
    his trunk fought on; his head was gone.

28. 'There lie on the ground almost all
    of your kinsmen, turned into corpses;
    you couldn't stop the battle: you were destined
    to be the cause of strife for mighty men.'

Then Sigrún wept. He said:

29. 'Be consoled, Sigrún: you've been our battle-goddess;
    warriors cannot fight against fate.'
    'Now my choice would be that all these dead should live,
    but I could still enfold you in my embrace.'

*Helgi and Sigrún married and had sons. Helgi did not live to
grow old. Dag, son of Högni, sacrificed to Odin for help in
avenging his father. Odin lent Dag his spear; Dag met Helgi,
his sister's husband, at a place called Fetter-grove: he ran
Helgi through with his spear. Helgi died there. Dag rode to
the fells, and told Sigrún the news:*

30. 'Sister, I am sorry for what I must tell you,
    I never meant to make you cry.
    This morning at Fetter-grove there fell,
    the best of princelings in the world,
    one who put his heel on the necks of kings.'

[*Sigrún said:*]

31. 'May all those oaths bring you to grief
    that you and Helgi have sworn,
    by the shining water of Lightning,
    and the wet-cold stone of Water.

32. 'May that ship not slip onwards, that slips under you,
    though the wished-for wind lies behind;
    may that horse not run onwards, that runs under you,
    though your enemy is hot on your tail.

33. 'May your sword not bite that you brandish,
    unless it's whistling above your own head.
    Helgi's death would be avenged on you,
    though you were a wolf out in the woods,
    lacking wealth and every delight,
    without food but what you guzzle from corpses.'

[*Dag said:*]

34. 'You're insane, sister, and out of your wits,
    to call down such harm on your brother;
    Odin alone caused all the evil,
    for he bore strife-runes among princes.

35. 'Your brother offers you red-gold rings,
    all Vandilsvé and Slaughter-dales;
    ring-adorned woman, have half our homeland,
    to repay the harm done to you and your boys.'

[*Sigrún said:*]

36. 'I shall never sit happy at Sefafells,
    from dawn till night-time I shall loathe my life
    until brightness dawns on that fine one's folk
    where Vígblær gallops beneath the ruler,
    the gold-bitted steed, and I can welcome the warrior.

37. 'So much fear did Helgi incite in the hearts
    of all his foes and their kin,
    as before a wolf, running mad,
    mountain-goats scatter in terror.

38. 'So much did Helgi rise, above heroes
    as the well-formed ash above the thorn,
    or that noble stag dripping with dew,
    who lives higher than all beasts,
    and its horns gleam against the sky itself.'

*A burial-mound was made for Helgi; what is more, when
he came to Slain-hall, Odin bid him govern everything at
his side. Helgi said:*

39. 'You shall, Hunding, for every man
 fetch a foot-bath and kindle the fire,
 tie up the dogs, look after the horses,
 give the pigs slops, before going to bed.'

*One evening Sigrún's maid went close by Helgi's burial-
mound, and saw Helgi riding to the burial mound with many
men. The maid said:*

40. 'Is this some trickery, that I seem to see,
 dead men riding, or Ragnarök?
 Do you spur your horses forward,
 or have heroes been allowed to go home?'

[*Helgi said:*]

41. 'It is no trickery, that you seem to see,
 nor the end of the world, when you look at us,
 though we spur our horses forward,
 nor have heroes been allowed to go home.'

The maid went home and said to Sigrún:

42. 'Go out, Sigrún, from Sefafells,
 if you want to find the army's chief;
 the grave-mound is open, and Helgi has come:
 his battle-traces bleed, and the prince asks you
 to come to staunch dripping wounds.'

Sigrún went into the burial-mound to Helgi and said:

43. 'Now I am as keen for us to meet
 as Odin's hawks, eager to eat,   *Odin's hawks* ravens
 when they scent the slain, the warmth of flesh,
 or, dew-bright, see the glint of the day.

44. 'First I will kiss the lifeless king
    before you cast off your bloody mail.
    Helgi, your hair is heavy with hail;
    wholly is the warrior drenched in   *slaughter-dew* blood
        slaughter-dew,
    ice-cold the arms of Högni's kin.   *Högni's kin* Helgi
    How, princeling, can I make this better?'

45. 'You alone, Sigrún of Sefafells,
    drench Helgi in sorrow's dew;
    with bitter tears you grieve, gold-wrapped girl,
    sun-bright southerner, before you sleep;
    each one drops like blood on the leader's breast,
    ice-cold, searing, heavy with pain.

46. 'Let us drink up costly draughts,
    though we have lost both love and lands;
    no man must make a dirge for me,
    though wounds gape upon my breast,
    now that my bride lies buried in the barrow,
    the longed-for woman at this dead man's side.'

Sigrún prepared a bed in the burial-mound:

47. 'Here, Helgi, I've made a bed ready for you,
    descendant of Ylfings, quite free from pain;
    in your embrace, lord, I'll sleep,
    as I would with the living leader.'

[*Helgi said:*]

48. 'Now I reckon nothing could be beyond hope,
    neither early nor late at Sefafells,
    than that you should sleep in the arms of the dead,
    Högni's daughter, bright in the burial-mound,
    while you are alive, and of royal birth.

49. 'It's time for me to ride the reddened roads,
    let my pale charger tread the paths of flight;
    I must pass west of the rainbow bridge
    before Salgófnir wakes the victory-   *Salgófnir* cockerel at
          host.'   Slain-hall

*Then Helgi and his men rode away, while the women went
home to the house. The next evening Sigrún made the maid
keep watch by the burial-mound. At nightfall, when Sigrún
came to the burial-mound, she said:*

50. 'He would have come now, if he meant to come,
    Sigmund's son, from Odin's halls;
    I reckon hopes of seeing the chief come fade
    when eagles sit on the ash-tree's branches,
    and the whole host heads for the meeting   *meeting of dreams*
          of dreams.'   sleep

51. 'Don't be so insane as to go alone,
    warriors' lady, to the house of the dead,
    they all turn out more powerful at night,
    dead assailants, girl, than in daylight.'

*From grief and sorrow, Sigrún's life was brief. There was a
belief in olden days that people were reborn, though
nowadays that is reckoned an old wives' tale. Helgi and
Sigrún are said to have been reborn. He was then known as
Helgi Haddingjaskadi, and she Kára, Hálfdan's daughter, as is
mentioned in 'Kára's song', and she was a valkyrie.*

Frá dauda Sinfjötla: About Sinfjötli's death

*Sigmund, Völsung's son, was king in Francia. Sinfjötli was his
eldest son, the second Helgi, the third Hámund. Borghild,
Sigmund's wife, had a brother called [. . .] , and Sinfjötli, her
stepson, and [. . .] were both pursuing the same woman, and on*

that account Sinfjötli killed him. When he came home, Borghild told him to go away, but Sigmund offered her compensation, and she had to accept it. But at the funeral-feast Borghild was bearing the ale; she took poison, a great hornful, and bore it to Sinfjötli. But when he looked into the horn, he realized, that there was poison in it, and said to Sigmund: 'The drink is cloudy, papa.' Sigmund took the horn and drank it down. It is said that Sigmund was so tough, that poison couldn't harm him inside or out, but all his sons could only stand poison outside on their skin. Borghild bore a second horn to Sinfjötli, and bid him drink it, and the whole thing happened as before. Yet a third time she bore him a horn, and taunted him with not drinking it. He said the same as before to Sigmund. He said: 'Let your moustache strain it, son!' Sinfjötli drank it and immediately died.

Sigmund carried him in his arms for a long time, and arrived at a long narrow fjord; there was a little boat there, and a man in it. He offered Sigmund a passage over the fjord. But when Sigmund carried the corpse on to the boat, the vessel was fully laden. The old man said that Sigmund would have to walk around the fjord; then the old man pushed out the boat and immediately disappeared.

King Sigmund stayed in Denmark in Borghild's kingdom for a long time, after he married her. Then Sigmund went south to Francia, to the estates that he had there. Then he married Hjördís, the daughter of King Eylimi; their son was Sigurd. King Sigmund fell in battle against Hunding's sons; Hjördís was then given to Álf, King Hjálprek's son: Sigurd grew up there in his youth.

Sigmund and all his sons far surpassed all other men in strength and size and all accomplishments; but Sigurd was the most outstanding, and in the ancient traditions all men call him the noblest and most accomplished of warlike kings.

Grípisspá: Grípir's prophecy

Grípir was the name of Eylimi's son, and the brother of Hjördís; he governed estates and was the wisest of men, and a prophet. Sigurd was riding all alone and came to Grípir's hall;

Sigurd was easy to recognize. He struck up a conversation
with a man outside the hall who was called Geitir; Sigurd
gave him a greeting and asked:

1. 'Who lives here within this fortress,
   what do warriors call that mighty king?'
   'He is called Grípir, that ruler of men,
   who governs the land and the warriors well.'

2. 'Is the wise king at home in the land,
   will that prince come and speak with me?
   An uncrafty man needs to talk,
   I'd like to meet Grípir soon.'

3. 'The gracious king will inquire of Geitir,
   who the man is who seeks to speak with Grípir.'
   'I'm called Sigurd, born to Sigmund,
   and Hjördís is this warrior's mother.'

4. Then Geitir went to speak to Grípir:
   'There's an unknown man arrived outside;
   he is lordly to look at,
   he wants, lord, to meet with you.'

5. The lord of men walks from the halls
   and greets well the warrior who'd come:
   'Welcome here, Sigurd: it would have been better before;
   but Geitir: look after Grani.'   *Grani* Sigurd's horse

6. They began to speak and discuss many things,
   when the warriors wise in counsel met:
   'Tell me, my uncle, if you know,
   how life will turn out for Sigurd.'

7. 'You will be of men the mightiest under the sun,
   the highest born of any prince;
   giving of gold, a stranger to flight,
   glorious to gaze on and wise in words.'

8. 'Say plainly, as I ask, just king,
   wisely to Sigurd what you seem to see:
   how will it first turn out for my fate,
   when I have gone from your court?'

9. 'First, lord, you will avenge your father,
   and requite all Eylimi's grief;
   you will fell Hunding's hard sons
   boldly, and win the victory.'

10. 'Say to me, noble king, kinsman so wise,
    as we speak from our hearts:
    do you see for Sigurd bold deeds ahead,
    soaring highest under heaven's roof?'

11. 'Alone you will kill the shining serpent
    that lies greedy on Gnita-heath;
    you'll end up the killer of them both,
    Regin and Fáfnir: Grípir says what is right.'

12. 'There'll be wealth enough, if I can accomplish
    killing among men, as you know for sure;
    consider my course and say further:
    what else will my life prove?'

13. 'You will find Fáfnir's lair
    and win wonderful wealth,
    load up the gold on Grani's back;
    ride to Gjúki's, warrior gallant in war.'

14. 'Still you must with your words of wisdom
    say more to the lord, high-minded prince;
    I am Gjúki's guest, and I'm off from there:
    what else will my life prove?'

15. 'A prince's daughter sleeps on the fell,
    bright, in a mailcoat, after Helgi's death.
    You shall slice, with your sharp blade,
    cut that mailcoat with Fáfnir's bane.'   *Fáfnir's bane* Sigurd's sword

16. 'The mailcoat is in tatters, the lady begins to speak,
    the woman who's woken from sleep;
    what will that noblewoman say to Sigurd
    that will bring about the prince's fate?'

17. 'She will teach you runes, powerful man,
    all those that men wish to know,
    and how to speak the tongues of all men,
    medicine and healing: live in health, king!'

18. 'Now that's finished, the wisdom is learned,
    and I'm ready to ride away from there;
    consider my course and say further:
    what more will my life prove?'

19. 'You will arrive at Heimir's estates
    and be the mighty king's gracious guest;
    it's already passed, Sigurd, what I knew before,
    you shouldn't ask Grípir any more.'

20. 'Now they give me grief, the words that you say,
    since, lord, you see much further ahead;
    you know of very great sorrow for Sigurd,
    but you, Grípir, won't say plainly.'

21. 'In your life your youth lay before me
    most clearly for me to look on;
    I'm not rightly accounted wise in counsel,
    or a prophet: I've simply said what I know.'

22. 'I know of no man across the earth,
    with greater foresight, Grípir, than you;
    you mustn't hide it, even if it is grim,
    or brings pain into my plight.'

23. 'Your life is not laid out with shame,
    allow that to me, noble prince;
    for there will be remembered, while the world lasts,
    your name, bidder of battle's   *bidder of battle's storm* warrior
        storm.'

24. 'This seems the worst, that we should part
    Sigurd and the lord with things so;
    show me the path – it's all laid before you –
    famed uncle, if you will.'

25. 'Now I shall tell Sigurd plainly:
    the prince has forced me to this;
    you'll know for sure that this is no lie:
    one day death is destined for you.'

26. 'I don't want the wrath of the mighty king:
    I'd rather, Grípir, have good advice;
    now I will know for sure, albeit undesirable:
    what's been seen ahead for Sigurd?'

27. 'There's a lady at Heimir's, fair to behold:
    warriors call her Brynhild,
    the daughter of Budli; but the bold king,
    Heimir, is raising that harsh-hearted girl.'

28. 'What is it to me, though the girl be
    fair to behold, brought up at Heimir's?
    You should tell plainly, Grípir,
    since you see all fate lying ahead.'

29. 'You will be robbed of all delight
    by Heimir's fosterling, fair to behold;
    you will be deprived of sleep and peace,
    care for nothing else, except that girl.'

30. 'What is laid down of comfort to Sigurd?
    Say, Grípir, if you seem to see,
    shall I buy that girl with a bride-price,
    the fair daughter of the lord?'

31. 'The two of you will swear oaths
    most firmly, though few will you keep;
    when you've been Gjúki's guest for a single night,
    you won't remember Heimir's wise fosterling.'

32. 'What's this, Grípir? Tell me now!
    Do you see fickleness in the prince's mind,
    that I am to break faith with that girl
    that I seemed to love with all my heart.'

33. 'Princeling, it'll happen through another's plots,
    Grímhild's counsels will prevail;
    she'll offer you the maid with the shining hair,
    her daughter; she'll deceive the prince.'

34. 'Will I then gain kinship with Gunnar
    to go and marry Gudrún?
    Then this lord would be well wed,
    if regrets did not give me grief.'

35. 'Grímhild will wholly deceive you,
    urge you to woo Brynhild
    on Gunnar's behalf, the lord of the Goths;
    you'll soon promise the trip to the ruler's mother.'

36. 'Harm is at hand: I can well see that;
    Sigurd's plans will wander awry,
    if I must woo that famous maid
    for another, when I loved her well.'

37. 'All of you will swear oaths,
    Gunnar and Högni, and you, prince, third,
    for you'll change forms when you're on the road,
    Gunnar and you: Grípir doesn't lie.'

38. 'What does that mean? Why must we swap
    forms and manner when we're on the road?
    A second deception must follow this first,
    wholly grim: tell me, Grípir!'

39. 'You'll have Gunnar's form and his bearing,
    but your own speech and sense;
    you'll betroth yourself to the high-minded maid,
    Heimir's fosterling: nothing lies in the way.'

40. 'This seems the worst, that I'll be called wicked,
    Sigurd, among soldiers, with things so;
    I wouldn't wish to play any tricks,
    on that well-born bride, that I know to be best.'

41. 'You'll sleep, army-spearhead,
    famed, by the maid, as if she were your mother;
    nation's prince, for that your name
    will be remembered, while the world lasts.

42[43]. 'Both wedding-toasts with be drunk together,
    Sigurd's and Gunnar's, in Gjúki's halls;
    you'll exchange shapes, when you come home,
    each will have his own spirit back.'

43[42]. 'Will Gunnar wed that good woman,
        famed among men – tell me, Grípir –
        though the warrior's bride, bold-hearted,
        has slept three nights by me? That would be a wonder!

44. 'How can it turn out well after that,
    kinship among those folk? Tell me, Grípir!
    Will there be pleasure to be had afterwards
    for Gunnar, or for me?'

45. 'You'll remember your oaths, but be able to keep quiet:
    you want things to turn out well for Gudrún and you;
    but Brynhild will think herself a bride badly given,
    and the lady will trace ways to take her revenge.'

46. 'What kind of compensation will that bride take,
    when we've deceived the woman so?
    The lady will have had from me sworn oaths,
    none fulfilled, and little love.'

47. 'She'll tell Gunnar plainly
    that you didn't keep those oaths pure,
    when the noble king, with all his heart,
    Gjúki's heir, put his faith in the prince.'   *Gjúki's heir* Gunnar

48. 'What then, Grípir? Tell me now!
    Will those tales be proved true of me?
    Or will that glorious lady tell lies about me,
    and herself? Grípir, tell me that!'

49. 'In her wrath against you the powerful woman
    will not act well because of deep grief;
    you'll never harm the good lady,
    though the king's wife plays her tricks.'

50. 'Will wise Gunnar, and Gutthorm and Högni,
    act on her urging afterwards?
    Will Gjúki's sons on me, their kin,
    redden their blades? Grípir, tell me!'

51. 'Gudrún's heart will then turn grim
    when her brothers bring about your death;
    and no delight will come again
    to that wise woman: Grímhild's the cause.

52. 'So you must always consider, army-spearhead,
    what part luck plays in a prince's life:
    no mightier man will walk the earth
    under the sun's dwellings than you, Sigurd, seem.'

53. 'Let's part in peace: one can't fight one's fate;
    now, Grípir, you've done well what I asked;
    you'd soon have said it, if you could,
    if my life would prove prettier!'

Reginsmál: Regin's lay

*Sigurd went to Hjálprek's stud, and from it chose for himself
a horse, and it was called Grani afterwards. Then Regin,
Hreidmar's son, came to Hjálprek's; he was handier than any
man, and a dwarf in height: he was wise, stern and skilled in
magic. Regin offered to foster and teach Sigurd, and loved
him a lot. He told Sigurd about his family background, and
the following events: Odin, Hœnir and Loki had come to
Andvari's Falls; in that waterfall there were a lot of fish. There
was a dwarf called Andvari, who spent much time in the
waterfall in the form of a pike, and got himself food. 'Our
brother's name was Otter,' said Regin, 'and he often went into
the waterfall in the form of an otter. He'd caught a salmon,
and was sitting on the riverbank, eating it with his eyes
closed. Loki hit him with a stone and killed him; the Æsir
thought this was a piece of good luck, and flayed the otter for*

a bag. That same evening they sought to stay the night at Hreidmar's, and showed him their catch. Then we seized hold of them and imposed a ransom on their lives of filling the otter-skin bag with gold, and covering it on the outside with red gold.' They sent Loki off to raise the gold. He went to Rán and got her net, and then went to Andvari's Falls, and cast the net in front of the pike; she jumped into the net. Then Loki said:

1. 'What's that fish that rushes through the flood,
    and can't beware of harm?
    Free your head from mortal peril:
    find some flood-fire for me!'   *flood-fire* gold

2. 'Andvari is my name, Óin was my father's;
    I've travelled through many a falls;
    in ancient days a cruel norn shaped our fate,
    so that I've had to wander the waters.'

3. 'Tell me Andvari,' said Loki, 'if you wish
    to keep your life in men's halls:
    what price do the sons of men pay
    if they wound one another with words?'

4. 'A high price the sons of men pay:
    they must wade through Vadgelmir;
    of untrue words, when one lies about another,
    the consequences last very long.'

Loki saw all the gold that Andvari owned, and when he had handed over the gold, he kept back a ring, but Loki took it from him. The dwarf went into the rock and said:

5. 'Now the gold that belonged to Gust
    shall drive two brothers to their deaths,   *two brothers* Fáfnir and
    push eight princes to killing and strife;   Regin?
    no one wins joy with my wealth.'

*The Æsir handed the wealth over to Hreidmar, and stuffed
the otter-skin bag, and raised it upright. Then the Æsir had
to pile up the gold and cover it. When that was done,
Hreidmar stepped up and saw a whisker, and told them to
cover it; then Odin took out the ring, Andvari's Heirloom,
and covered the hair.*

6. 'Now you've had the gold,' said Loki, 'and the price
         has been paid,
     a high one, for my head;
     it will not seem well-fated to your son,
     and will prove the death of you both!'

[*Hreidmar said:*]

7. 'You gave gifts, but no love-gifts you gave,
     you gave them with no whole heart;
     your lives I should have taken
     if I'd known that danger before.'

8. 'It's still worse, as far as I can tell,
     the scathing strife of kin;
     I think that princes as yet unborn
     have been intended enmity.'

9. 'With red gold,' said Hreidmar, 'I reckon I'll manage,
     for just as long as I live;
     your threats don't bother me a bit:
     now get away back home from here!'

*Fáfnir and Regin claimed a share of the compensation from
Hreidmar for their brother Otter; he said no to that. So Fáfnir
stuck a sword in Hreidmar, his father, while he was asleep.
Hreidmar called out to his daughters:*

10. 'Lyngheid, Lofnheid, look: my life is lost!
     Necessity's a fiercesome force.'

Lyngheid replied:

'Few sisters, though their father is lost,
can avenge a brother's crime.'

Hreidmar said:

11. 'But raise a daughter, wolf-hearted girl,
if you don't get a son by a prince;
get a man for that maid, since there is great need,
then their son will right your wrong!'

Then Hreidmar died, and Fáfnir took all the gold. Then Regin asked for his father's inheritance, but Fáfnir said no to that. Then Regin sought advice from Lyngheid, his sister, as to how he should obtain his father's inheritance. She said:

12. 'You should ask your brother pleasantly
about the inheritance with a friendly heart;
it's not right that with a sword
you should demand treasure from Fáfnir.'

Regin told Sigurd these things. One day when he came to Regin's house, he was warmly welcomed; Regin said:

13. 'Sigmund's issue has come here,
the soldier of bold plans, into our halls;
he has more heart than any mature man:
I expect a snatch from a greedy wolf.

14. 'I shall raise the battle-brave prince
now Yngvi's issue has come to us;   *Yngvi's issue* Sigurd
that lord will prove most powerful under the sun,
his threads of fate spread over all lands.'

Sigurd was with Regin all the time, and he told Sigurd that Fáfnir was lurking on Gnita-heath in the form of a serpent; he had a helmet of dread, which inspired terror in all living creatures.

*Regin made Sigurd a sword, called Gram. It was so sharp,
that he dipped it in the Rhine, and let a tuft of wool drift on the
current, and it cut apart the tuft like water; with that sword
Sigurd sliced apart Regin's anvil.*

Then Regin urged Sigurd to kill Fáfnir. He replied:

15. 'Loud would Hunding's sons laugh,
    who snatched away Eylimi's life,
    if the prince's desires were more inclined
    to red-gold rings than his father's revenge!'

*King Hjálprek gave Sigurd a fleet to avenge his father. They
met a great storm and sought shelter by a rocky promontory;
a man stood on the rocks and said:*

16. 'Who rides there on Rævil's steeds,   *Rævil's steeds* ships
    the towering waves and roaring seas?
    The sail-chargers are drenched in spume,   *sail-chargers* ships
    the wave-steeds won't withstand the wind.'   *wave-steeds* ships

Regin answered:

17. 'Here are Sigurd and I on the trees of the   *trees of the sea* ships
        sea,
    we've caught a wind that'll be our death;
    a steep breaker falls higher than the prows,
    the roller-chargers stumble; who's asking?'   *roller-chargers* ships

18. 'Hnikar they called me, when young Völsung
    gladdened the raven and waged   *gladdened the raven*
        war;   *supplied carrion*
    now you can call me the Old Man of the Mountain,
    Feng or Hider: I'd like a passage.'

*They turned ashore, and the old man came on board; the
storm ceased.*

19. 'Tell me, Hnikar, since you know all things
    in the destiny of gods and men;
    what are the best, when it comes to battle,
    of the omens when swords are swinging?'

Hnikar said:

20. 'Many are good, if a warrior is aware
    of the omens when swords are swinging;
    I reckon that a dark raven's presence
    bodes a sword-tree well.   *sword-tree* warrior

21. 'There's a second, when you step outside,
    about to take a trip,
    if you see stand in your way,
    a pair of men, praise-eager man.

22. 'There's a third, if you hear howl
    a wolf beneath ash-boughs;
    you'll get good luck from helmeted men
    if you see them walking ahead.

23. 'No fighting-man must strive in the face
    of the late-shining sister of Moon;   *sister of Moon* Sun
    they win the struggle, brisk of battle,
    who can see to set up their wedge.

24. 'There's great danger, if you slip up,
    as you stride to war;
    deceitful *dísir* stand on each side
    and wish to see you wounded.

25. 'Combed and washed should be the wise
    and fully fed each morning;
    no one knows what evening brings;
    it's bad to set out before one's set fair.'

Sigurd had a great battle against Lyngvi, the son of Hunding, and his brothers. Lyngvi fell there, along with his three brothers. After the battle Regin said:

26. 'Now is the bloody eagle carved on the back
    of Sigmund's slayer with a sharp sword!
    None is more accomplished than the leader's heir,
    who reddened the ground and gladdened the raven.'

Sigurd went home to Hjálprek's; then Regin urged Sigurd to kill Fáfnir.

Fáfnismál: Fáfnir's lay

Sigurd and Regin went up on to Gnita-heath, and came upon the trail by which Fáfnir slithered to the water. Then Sigurd dug a great pit in the path, and he entered into it. When Fáfnir slithered away from his gold, he spewed poison, which spurted from above on to Sigurd's head. When Fáfnir slithered over the hole, Sigurd pierced him to the heart with his sword. Fáfnir twisted about, flailing with his head and tail. Sigurd jumped out of the pit, and each of them gazed at the other. Fáfnir said:

Concerning the death of Fáfnir:

1. 'A boy, just a boy! From which boy were you born?
   Which man's son are you,
   who reddened on Fáfnir your gleaming blade?
   Your sword stands right at my heart!'

Sigurd hid his name because in olden days it was believed that the words of the dying man had great power, if he cursed his enemy by name. He said:

2.   ' "Noble Beast" I'm called, and I've wandered
     a motherless boy;
     I have no father, like other sons of men;
     I always wander alone.'

[*Fáfnir said:*]

3.   'Do you know, if you've no father, like other sons of men,
     from what wonder you were born?'

[*Sigurd said:*]

4.   'My family I reckon unknown to you,
     and myself the same;
     Sigurd I'm called, Sigmund my father's name,
     I'm the one who's killed you with weapons.'

[*Fáfnir said:*]

5.   'Who urged you on, why let yourself
     be urged to seek my life?
     Boy with piercing eyes, your father was fierce:
     breeding shows in time.'

[*Sigurd said:*]

6.   'My heart urged me, my hands gave help,
     and this sharp sword of mine;
     few are bold when age comes upon them
     that are cowards when they are young.'

[*Fáfnir said:*]

7.   'I know if you'd been able
     to grow up in the bosom of your friends,
     we'd see you fight fiercely;
     now you're a prisoner, captured in war:
     they say a man tied up always trembles.'

[*Sigurd said:*]

8. 'You're taunting me, Fáfnir, since I'm so far
    away from my father's care;
    I'm no prisoner, and even if captured in war,
    you'd find that I live free enough!'

[*Fáfnir said:*]

9. 'Spiteful speech alone you count everything I say,
    but I'll tell you one true thing;
    the jingling gold and red-glowing wealth:
    those rings will deal you your death!'

[*Sigurd said:*]

10. 'Every man ought to govern his goods
    right up to his dying day;
    for only once must each man go
    from here straight down to Hel.'

[*Fáfnir said:*]

11. 'The norns' decree you'll get at the nesses:
    that of a foolish blockhead;
    you'll drown in the water, if you row in the wind:
    all's a danger to the doomed.'

[*Sigurd said:*]

12. 'Tell me, Fáfnir, since they call you wise,
    and you know very much:
    who are the norns, who come to those in need,
    and deliver mothers of children?'

[*Fáfnir said:*]

13. 'Those norns, I say, are born from different kin,
      they don't share a common family;
      some are born of the Æsir, some of the elves,
      some are the daughters of Dawdler.   *Dawdler* dwarf

[*Sigurd said:*]

14. 'Tell me, Fáfnir, since they call you wise,
      and you know very much:
      what that island is called where they'll blend
            sword-sweat,   *sword-sweat* blood
      Surt and the Æsir as one?'

[*Fáfnir said:*]

15. 'Unshaped it's called, where all the gods
      shall play sport with their spears;
      Bilröst will break as they go away   *Bilröst* rainbow-bridge
      and their horses swim in the swell.   to Ásgard

16. 'The helmet of dread I wore for the sons of men,
      while on circlets I lay;
      I thought I alone was strongest of all:
      I didn't find many young heroes.'

[*Sigurd said:*]

17. 'The helmet of dread protects no one
      wherever folk fight fiercely;
      he finds that out who comes among many,
      that no one is boldest of all.'

[*Fáfnir said:*]

18. 'Poison I breathed forth when I lay upon
      the mighty inheritance of my father.'

[*Sigurd said:*]

19. 'Gleaming serpent, you made much hissing:
    and harsh you made your heart;
    more anger is found in the sons of men
    when they don't have that helmet.'

[*Fáfnir said:*]

20. 'Now I advise you, Sigurd, to take this advice,
    and ride home from here!
    The jingling gold and red-glowing wealth,
    those rings will deal you your death!'

[*Sigurd said:*]

21. 'Advice has been advised, but I'll ride to this gold
    where it lies in the heather,
    but you, Fáfnir, lie in your last agony
    and there may Hel take you!'

[*Fáfnir said:*]

22. 'Regin betrayed me, he will betray you,
    he'll prove the killer of us both;
    I reckon that Fáfnir must lose his life;
    now your might has turned out more.'

*Regin had disappeared, while Sigurd slaughtered Fáfnir, and
came back as Sigurd was wiping the blood off his sword.
Regin said:*

23. 'Hail to you now, Sigurd, now you've won victory
    and put an end to Fáfnir;
    of the men now treading the earth
    I reckon you've been brought up least scared.'

[*Sigurd said:*]

24. 'No one knows, when we all come together,
    the sons of the victory-gods,
    who's been brought up least scared;
    many are brave but do not redden
    their sword in the chest of another.'

25. 'You're cheerful now, Sigurd, and glad to have won,
    as you wipe Gram dry on the grass;
    it's my brother you've wounded to death,
    but I'm partly to blame myself.'

[*Sigurd said:*]

26. 'You've advised that I ride
    the holy fells over here;
    both wealth and life that gleaming serpent would keep,
    unless you'd questioned my courage.'

*Then Regin went to Fáfnir and cut his heart out with the
sword which is called Ridil, and then he drank blood from the
wound.*

27. 'Sit now, Sigurd, while I go to sleep,
    and hold Fáfnir's heart in the flame;
    I want to have that heart to eat
    after that drink of gore.'

Sigurd said:

28. 'Far off, you went while in Fáfnir
    I reddened this sharp sword of mine;
    I needed my strength against the serpent's might
    while you hid on the heather.'

[*Regin said:*]

29. 'For long you'd have left that ancient giant
       lying in the heather,
    if you hadn't used the blade that I made myself,
       that sharp sword of yours.'

[*Sigurd said:*]

30. 'Courage is better than a sword's might may prove,
       wherever folk fight fiercely;
    for I've seen a brave man fighting hard,
       who wins with a blunted sword.

31. 'Bravery is better than not being brave
       wherever war-play occurs;
    cheerfulness is better than losing heart,
       whatever comes to hand.'

*Sigurd took Fáfnir's heart and roasted it on a stick; when he
thought that it was fully cooked, and juice was exuding from
the heart, he touched it with his finger to test if it was fully
cooked. He burnt his finger and stuck it in his mouth. But as
soon as the blood from Fáfnir's heart hit his tongue, he
understood the speech of birds; he heard nuthatches in the
undergrowth. One nuthatch said:*

32. 'There sits Sigurd, spattered with blood,
       roasting Fáfnir's heart in the flames;
    wise to me would the ring-breaker   *ring-breaker* generous
          seem,   warrior
    if he ate the gleaming life-muscle.'   *life-muscle* heart

33. 'There lies Regin, planning for himself:
       he wants to deceive the boy who trusts him;
    in his anger he's brought false words together,
       that evil-worker wants to avenge his brother.'

34. 'A head shorter he should let the grey sage   *grey sage* Regin
    go off from here to Hel;
    then he alone can control all the gold,
    the pile that lay under Fáfnir.'

35. 'Smart he'd seem to me, if only he recognized
    much useful advice from you sisters;
    he's thought of himself and gladdened   *gladdened the raven*
        the raven;   *supplied carrion*
    I expect a wolf, seeing his ears.'

36. 'That battle-tree is not so smart,   *battle-tree* warrior
    as I'd have thought an army-protector should be,
    if he lets one brother get away,
    when he's ended the life of the other.'

37. 'He's very unwise if he still spares
    the soldier-scathing foe;
    there lies Regin, who's plotted against him,
    he can't beware such a thing.'

38. 'A head shorter he should have the ice-   *ice-cold giant* Regin
        cold giant
    do without the rings;
    then the wealth that Fáfnir controlled
    would be in one man's power.'

[*Sigurd said:*]

39. 'Fate won't prove so mighty that Regin shall
    pronounce a death-sentence on me;
    for both those brothers shortly shall
    go off from here to Hel.'

Sigurd cut off Regin's head, then ate Fáfnir's heart and drank the blood of them both, Regin and Fáfnir. Then Sigurd heard what the nuthatches said:

40. 'Sigurd, bind up the red rings;
    it is not princely to mourn very much;
    I know a maid, the fairest by far,   *maid* Gudrún
    decked with gold, if you can gain her.

41. 'Green paths lead to Gjúki's home,
    fates point forward for a brave warrior;
    the rich king there has raised a daughter,
    she can be bought for a dowry, Sigurd.

42. 'A high hall stands on Hind's Fell,
    entirely fenced in with flame;
    wise men have made it
    from the undark radiance of   *radiance of Terror* gold, if
        Terror.   'Terror' is a river

43. 'I know that a valkyrie sleeps on the fell,
    and there plays over her the peril of wood;   *peril of wood* fire
    Dread stabbed her with a thorn: that   *flax-goddess* woman
        flax-goddess
    slew another man than he had wished.

44. 'You can see, lad, that helmeted maid,
    who rode from battle on Vingskornir;   *Vingskornir* her horse
    you cannot rouse Sigrdrífa from sleep,
    child of princes, in the face of the norns' decree.'

Sigurd rode along Fáfnir's trail to his lair, and found it open, with doors and door-frames of iron; all the house-beams were also iron, buried at the base in the earth. Sigurd found a vast amount of gold there, and filled up two chests. He took the helmet of dread, a gold corselet and the sword Hrotti, along with many valuable items, and loaded it in Grani's packs; but the horse wouldn't set off until Sigurd mounted on to his back.

Sigrdrífumál: Sigrdrífa's lay

Sigurd rode up on to Hind's Fell and headed south towards the land of the Franks. On the fell he saw a great light, as if fire was burning, and it beamed up to the sky; when he reached it, there was a shield-fortress standing there, with a banner flying over it. Sigurd went into the shield-fortress and saw that someone was lying there sleeping in full armour. He first took off the helmet and saw that it was a woman. The corselet was close-fitting, as if it had grown round the flesh. He cut the corselet from the neck down with Gram, and along both arms; then he took the corselet off her, and she woke up, sat up, saw Sigurd and said:

1. 'What cut my corselet? Why was I woken?
    Who's freed me from pale constraints?'

He answered:

    'Sigmund's son and Sigurd's sword,
    that recently sliced flesh for the raven.'

2. 'Long I've slept; long I've slumbered;
    long are the misfortunes of men.
    Odin is the cause why I could not
    break the sleeping-charms.'   *sleeping-charms* runes of sleep

Sigurd sat down and asked her name; she took a horn full of mead, and gave him a memory-drink.

3. 'Hail, Day, hail, Day's sons,
    hail, Night and her kin!
    Look on us here with kindly eyes
    and grant victory to those sitting here!

4.   'Hail, gods, greetings, goddesses   *goddesses* female Æsir
     greetings, this bounteous earth!
     Grant speech and sense to us famous pair
     and healing hands, while we live!'

*She called herself Sigrdrífa, and was a valkyrie; she said that
two kings had been fighting: one of them was called Helm-
Gunnar, who was old and the greatest of warriors, and it was
to him that Odin had pledged the victory, but:*

     'the other was called Agnar, Auda's brother,
     whom no one wanted to help.'

*Sigrdrífa felled Helm-Gunnar in the battle, but Odin stuck
her with a sleep-thorn in revenge for this, saying that she
should never again gain victory in battle, and saying that she
must be married. 'But I told him that I'd taken a vow against
marrying any man who knew fear.' He [Sigurd] spoke up and
asked her to teach him wisdom, since she had news from
every world. Sigrdrífa said:*

5.   'Beer I bring you, apple-tree of conflict,   *apple-tree of*
     blended with might and powerful glory;   *conflict* warrior
     it's full of spells and healing charms,
     fine incantations and runes of delight.

6.   'Victory-runes you must know if you want to have victory,
     and cut them on the hilt of your sword;
     some on the sword-rings, some on the sword-plates,
     and twice invoke Týr's name.

7.   'Ale-runes you must know if you want not to be beguiled
     by another's wife that you trust;
     one must cut them on a horn and the back of the hand,
     marking "Need" on the nail.   *Need* N-rune

8.   'The cup must be signed to guard against ill,
     and leek cast into the liquid;
     but I know that for you there never shall be
     mead blended with malice.

9.   'Protection-runes you must know if you want to protect
     and release children from women's wombs;
     one must cut them on the palm and clasp them on
          the limbs,
     and then ask the *dísir* for help.

10. 'Sea-runes you must make, if you want to keep safe
     sail-steeds out on the waves;   *sail-steeds* ships
     one must cut them on the prow and the rudder's blade
     and pass fire over the oars;
     no breaker is so steep, nor waves so blue,
     that you won't come home from the ocean.

11. 'Limb-runes you must know if you want to be a leech
     and know how to investigate wounds;
     one must cut them on the bark and the wood of that tree
     whose branches bend to the East.

12. 'Speech-runes you must know if you want no one
     to pay you back harm with hate;
     one winds them around, one weaves them around,
     one sets them all together,
     at the meeting where men must
     go to full-blown courts.

13. 'Thought-runes you must know if you want to be
     more strong-minded than any man;
     he read them, and he cut them,
     and he thought them up: Hropt,   *Hropt* Odin
     from the liquid, which had leaked
     from Heiddraupnir's skull
     and Hoddrofnir's horn.

14. 'On a cliff he stood with Brimir's blade: *he* Odin
he had a helmet on his head.
Then Mím's head spoke
the first word wisely
and said a true speech:

He said:

15. ' "On the shield they should be cut,   *they* runes
that stands before the bright god,   *bright god* Sun
on Early-waker's ears and the hoof of All-swift,
on the wheel turning under Hrungnir's chariot,
on Sleipnir's teeth, and on the straps   *Sleipnir* Odin's horse
    of sledges,

16. ' "on a bear's paw, and on Bragi's tongue,   *Bragi* god of poetry
on a wolf's claws, and on an eagle's beak,
on bloody wings, and on the end of a bridge,
on a deliverer's hand, and on a healer's trail,

17. ' "on glass and on gold, and on men's amulets,
in wine and unfermented beer, and on a comfortable seat,
on Gungnir's point, and on Grani's   *Gungnir* Odin's spear; *Grani*
    breast,   Sigurd's horse
on the nail of a norn, and on the beak of an owl."

18. 'All were shaved off, those that were cut in,
and mixed with the holy mead,
and sent on wide wanderings:
they are with the Æsir, they are with the elves,
some with the wise Vanir,
and humankind has some.

19. 'There are the book-runes,
    there are the protection-runes,
    also all the ale-runes,
    and the splendid power-runes;
    for those who can, unblemished and unspoiled,
    have them on their amulets;
    use them, if you've learnt them,
    until the powers are rent.

20. 'Now you must choose, since a choice is offered you,
    maple-tree of keen weapons,   *maple-tree of keen weapons* warrior
    speech or silence: decide for yourself;
    all wrongs are already measured.'

21. 'I won't flee from it, though I find out I'm fey: *fey* doomed
    I wasn't born to be a coward;
    I want to have all your useful advice,
    as long as my life lasts.'

22. 'I advise you first, that towards your family
    you should be without fault;
    take no revenge, though they give you cause,
    they say that helps the dead.

23. 'I advise you second, that you don't swear an oath,
    unless that swearing turns out true;
    terrible threads bind the breaker of faith,
    pitiful is the violator of vows.

24. 'I advise you third, that at a meeting
    you don't quarrel with a stupid man;
    for an unwise man often lets himself say
    worse words than he realizes.

25. 'Everything's up if you're lost for a reply,
    then you seem born to be a coward,
    or what was said was true:
    home gossip is dangerous
    unless the gossip is good.
    Next day have him breathe his last,
    and so pay back public lies!

26. 'I advise you fourth, if there lives a witch,
    full of faults, upon your way:
    better go on than be her guest,
    even though nightfall catch you.

27. 'Far-seeing eyes the sons of men need,
    wherever they must fiercely fight;
    often mischievous wise women sit by the roads,
    who blunt both swords and spirits.

28. 'I advise you fifth, though you see
    fair females on the benches:
    don't let silver-decked ladies govern your dreams;
    don't seduce women into kissing you!

29. 'I advise you sixth, though it happens among men
    that speech over ale turns ugly:
    don't argue with a warrior when you are drunk;
    wine steals from many their wits.

30. 'Singing and ale have often been
    a cause of grief for many men;
    death for some, misfortune for some:
    there is much that grieves men.

31. 'I advise you seventh, if you are quarrelling
    with courageous men:
    better to fight than be burnt at home
    inside by other men.

32. 'I advise you eighth, that you must look out for evil,
    and avoid wanton ways;
    don't seduce girls or another man's wife,
    or urge excessive delight!

33. 'I advise you ninth, that you take care of corpses
    wherever on earth you find them,
    whether they died of sickness or of the sea,
    or else are weapon-dead men.

34. 'A bath should be made for the ones passed away,
    their heads and hands should be washed;
    they should be combed and dried before going
         into the casket,
    and prayed for to sleep in peace.

35. 'I advise you tenth, that you never trust
    the oaths of an enemy's offspring;
    whether you were his brother's butcher,
    or have felled his father:
    the wolf still lurks in the young son,
    though he be gladdened by gold.

36. 'Quarrels and strife should never be thought put to sleep,
    no, nor sorrow either;
    wits and weapons are what a prince needs to get,
    to be most outstanding among men.

37. 'I advise you eleventh, that you look out for evil
    in every way you can;
    I don't think the praiseworthy one will live long,
    great discord has come about.'

Brot af Sigurdarkvidu: A fragment
of the song of Sigurd

1.   . . . 'Whatever harm has Sigurd caused,
     that you want to rob the bold man of his life?'

2.   'Sigurd has given oaths to me,
     given oaths, and all broken;
     he has deceived me, when he ought to have been
     totally trustworthy in all oaths.'

3.   'Brynhild has brought you into strife,
     urged enmity, causing harm;
     she begrudges Gudrún her happy match,
     and her own attachment to you.'

4.   Some roasted wolf, some sliced serpent,
     some gave Gutthorm wolf-meat to eat,
     before they were able, eager for harm,
     to lay hands on that wise hero.

5.   Sigurd was close to death south of the Rhine;
     a raven called out loud from a tree:
     'Atli will redden his blades in you:
     oaths will destroy you warriors.'

6.   Outside stood Gudrún, Gjúki's daughter,
     and these were the first words she found to say:
     'Where now is Sigurd, the soldiers' lord,
     since my kinsmen are riding in front?'

7.   Högni alone gave a reply:
     'We've cut Sigurd apart with a sword,
     the grey steed ever bows its head over the   *grey steed* Grani
         dead prince.'

8. Then spoke Brynhild, Budli's daughter:
    'Now you'll enjoy weapons and lands,
    all that Sigurd alone would have ruled,
    if only he'd held on to his life a little longer.

9. 'It wouldn't have been fitting that he'd have ruled
    Gjúki's inheritance and troops of Goths,
    when he'd already had five sons,
    keen warriors, to govern the people.'

10. Then Brynhild laughed – the whole bower resounded –
    a single time, with all of her heart:
    'Long should you enjoy lands and retainers,
    now you've had the bold prince felled.'

11. Then spoke Gudrún, Gjúki's daughter:
    'You've said many dreadful things;
    may the fiends take Gunnar, who set Sigurd to die:
    wicked thoughts shall end up avenged.'

12. It was late in the evening, the drinking had been heavy,
    every kind of friendly word had been said;
    everyone went to their beds and slept,
    but Gunnar lay awake long after the rest.

13. His foot started to twitch, his lips started to mutter,
    the troop-wrecker began to ponder
    what was the meaning of that pair in the wood,
    a raven and eagle, as they rode home.

14. Brynhild awoke, Budli's daughter,
    Skjöldung's lady, a little before day:
    'Spur me on or stop me – the harm is done –
    there is sorrow to be told or let pass!'

15. Everyone was silent after that speech;
    few could fathom the conduct of women,
    when, weeping, she began to say
    what, laughing, she'd told the warriors.

16. 'I thought, Gunnar, I was having a grim dream:
    it was all cool in the hall, and I had a cold bed;
    and you, prince, were riding, deprived of joy,
    shackled with fetters among a troop of foes.
    So from all of you family of Niflungs
    the power will pass: you are oath-breakers.

17. 'You plainly did not remember, Gunnar,
    when you both had your blood run into a trench;
    now you've paid him back badly for all that,
    when he wished to make himself best.

18. 'He proved that when he had ridden,
    the brave one, rode up to ask for my hand,
    how the army-destroyer had before   *army-destroyer* Sigurd
    kept his oaths with the young prince.   *young prince* Gunnar

19. 'He laid a wound-wand, inlaid with gold,   *wound-wand* sword
    the magnificent king, between us;
    the outer edges were hardened in fire,
    and patterned with venom-drops within.'

Frá dauda Sigurdar: About Sigurd's death

*It is said here in this poem about the death of Sigurd, and
here it indicates, that he was killed outdoors. But some say
that they killed him indoors, sleeping in his bed. And
Germans say that they killed him in a forest. It says in 'The
ancient song of Gudrún', that Sigurd and the sons of Gjúki
were riding to a meeting, when he was killed; but everyone
agrees that they tricked him with cunning, and slew him
unawares when he was lying down.*

Gudrúnarkvida in fyrsta: The first song of Gudrún

Gudrún sat over the dead Sigurd; she did not weep like other women, but she was on the verge of breaking down with grief. Both men and women approached to comfort her, but that was not easy to do. People say that Gudrún had eaten of Fáfnir's heart, and understood the speech of birds. This is also said of Gudrún:

1. In ancient days it was, when Gudrún made to die,
   as she sat full of sorrow over Sigurd:
   she didn't howl or beat her hands
   or keen like other women.

2. Noblemen stepped up, all-knowing,
   to ease her harshness of heart;
   yet Gudrún was unable to weep:
   so heart-full she was about to burst.

3. The stately wives of the noblemen sat
   decked in gold before Gudrún;
   each of them told their own great grief,
   the bitterest they'd had to bear.

4. Then spoke Gjaflaug, Gjúki's sister:
   'I think myself the world's most loveless:
   I've felt the loss of five husbands,
   three daughters, three sisters,
   eight brothers; but I live on alone.'

5. Yet Gudrún was unable to weep,
   she was so fervent about the dead youth
   and hard-hearted over the prince's corpse.

6. Then spoke Herborg, queen of Hunland:
    'I have a still greater grief to tell:
    in the south of the land, my seven sons,
    my husband the eighth, all fell slain;

7. 'Likewise father and mother, my four brothers,
    when the wind got up on the sea,
    were all wave-battered inside their boats.

8. 'I had to lay them out myself, I had to bury them myself,
    I had to handle their trip to Hel myself;
    I went through all this in a single season,
    and no one could ever bring me joy.

9. 'Then I was caught and taken captive
    the same season after that happened;
    I had to dress and bind the shoes
    of my master's wife every morning.

10. 'She hated me from jealousy,
    and beat me with heavy blows;
    I never knew a better master,
    or a mistress who was worse.'

11. Yet Gudrún was unable to weep,
    she was so fervent about the dead youth
    and hard-hearted over the prince's corpse.

12. Then spoke Gullrönd, Gjúki's daughter: *Gullrönd* Gudrún's
    'You know little, foster-mother, wise as you are   sister
    how to answer a wife who's young.'
    She told them not to keep the prince's corpse covered.

13. She swept back the bed-clothes from Sigurd
    and puffed the pillow upon his wife's knees:
    'Look on your loved one, put your mouth to his
        moustache,
    as you used to embrace the warrior unwounded.'

14. Gudrún gave a single glance:
    she saw the prince's hair drip blood,
    the warrior's keen eyes dimmed,
    the chieftain's mighty chest sword-scored.

15. Leaning, Gudrún bent low to the pillow;
    her hair came loose, her cheeks grew red,
    rain-drop tears ran down her knees.

16. Then Gudrún, Gjúki's daughter, grieved
    and tears streamed through her tresses;
    out in the yard, the geese began honking,
    those famous fowl the lady owned.

17. Then spoke Gullrönd, Gjúki's daughter:
    'I know that your love was greater
    than any man's or woman's in the world;
    you were never happy outside or in,
    my sister, except by Sigurd.'

[*Gudrún spoke:*]

18. 'Next to Gjúki's sons, my Sigurd towered
    like a leek that stands among grass,
    or a dazzling gem on a string of beads,
    a precious jewel among princes.

19. 'My lord's retainers once honoured me
    more than any of Odin's maids;   *Odin's maids* valkyries
    now I am as little as a winter-leaf
    that clings to a willow, now the prince is dead.

20. 'I miss in his seat, and also in bed,
    his friendly words to me: Gjúki's kin have caused it!
    Gjúki's kin have caused my grief
    and their sister's bitter tears.

21. 'May all the land be laid waste because of you,
     because of the oaths that you swore;
     Gunnar, you'll never enjoy that gold:
     those rings will prove the death of you,
     since to Sigurd you swore oaths.

22. 'Often in the meadow there was greater joy
     when my Sigurd saddled Grani,
     and they went to woo Brynhild,
     vile creature, because of bad fate.'

23. Then spoke Brynhild, Budli's daughter:
     'Let that creature lack husband and children
     who caused you, Gudrún, to grieve,
     and gave you speech-runes in the morning.'

24. Then spoke Gullrönd, Gjúki's daughter:
     'Shut your mouth, you hateful bitch, and
          don't say such words!
     You have always proved poisonous to princes:
     the whole world sees you steeped in wickedness,
     a source of sorrow for seven kings,
     a mighty widow-maker of wives.'

25. Then spoke Brynhild, Budli's daughter:
     'Atli alone caused all the grief,
     my brother, born to Budli;

26. 'For in the hall of the Hunnish people
     we saw on the prince the serpent-bed's   *serpent-bed's fire* gold
          fire;
     I've paid for this trip ever since:
     those sights I never stop seeing.'

27. She stood by the standing-beam, summoned her strength:
     her eyes blazed fire, she snorted venom,
     Brynhild, Budli's daughter,
     when she gazed on Sigurd's wounds.

*Gudrún went away from there to the woods of the wasteland,
and travelled all the way to Denmark, and stayed there for
seven seasons with Thóra, Hákon's daughter.*

*Brynhild didn't want to live after Sigurd; she had eight slaves
and five slave-girls killed, then she killed herself with a sword,
just as it says in 'The short song of Sigurd'.*

Sigurdarkvida in skamma: The short song of Sigurd

1. It was in ancient days that Sigurd came to Gjúki's home,
   the young Völsung, who'd accomplished killing;
   he accepted the pledges of both brothers: *brothers* Gunnar
   they gave oaths to each other, valiant men.   and Högni

2. They offered him the girl and a wealth of treasures,
   young Gudrún, Gjúki's daughter;
   they drank and discussed for many days,
   young Sigurd and Gjúki's sons.

3. Until they went to woo Brynhild
   with Sigurd riding in their retinue,
   the young Völsung, and he knew the way;
   he would have had her if he could.

4. The southern soldier laid a naked sword,   *southern soldier*
   an inlaid blade between them;   Sigurd
   nor did he make to kiss the woman,
   nor did the Hunnish king take her in his arms;   *Hunnish king*
   that fresh young girl he granted Gjúki's son.   Sigurd

5. In her whole life, she'd known no wrong,
   and in her span no harm,
   there was no flaw, imagined or real:
   the cruel fates came between.

6. Alone she sat outside one evening,
    she began to tell herself quite openly:
    'I must have Sigurd – or else die –
    the fresh young boy in my arms.

7. 'Now I've spoken words I shall later repent;
    his wife is Gudrún, and I am Gunnar's;
    contrary norns have pitched us long yearning.'

8. Often she goes out, filled with hostility,
    with ice-floes and glaciers every evening,
    while he and Gudrún go to bed,
    and Sigurd sweeps her up in the linen,
    the Hunnish king making love to his wife.

9. 'I go deprived of both joys and husband,
    I have to delight myself with dark thoughts.'

10. She began in hate to urge herself to killing:
    'You must, Gunnar, completely give up
    both my land and myself;
    I'll never be happy with you, prince.

11. 'I'll go back where I was before,
    among my close-born kinsmen;
    there I'll sit and sleep my life away,
    unless you have Sigurd slain,
    and become greater than other lords.

12. 'Let the son go along with his father:
    one shouldn't raise a young wolf for long;
    for whom does revenge prove easier
    as later settlement than when a son is alive?'

13. Angry was Gunnar and quite downcast,
    he turned things over in his heart and sat the whole day;
    he didn't know at all clearly,
    what for him would be most fit to do,
    what for him would be best to do,
    since he felt himself robbed of the Völsung,
    and in Sigurd he felt a great loss.

14. He pondered variously for long stretches at a time;
    it was not customary in those days
    for wives to abandon their royal position;
    he summoned Högni for a private talk:
    in him he had one he could trust completely.

15. 'To me Brynhild alone is better than all others,
    born to Budli, she's the foremost of women;
    I should rather forsake my life
    than lose the treasures of that girl.

16. 'For wealth will you betray the prince for us?
    It's good to govern the Rhine's metal,   *Rhine's metal* gold
    and happily to control those riches,
    and, sitting easy, benefit from joy.'

17. Högni answered with this alone:
    'It's not seemly for us to do such a deed,
    to sunder with the sword-sworn oaths,
    oaths sworn, avowed pledges.

18. 'We know on earth no men more fortunate,
    while we four govern the people,   *four* Sigurd, Gunnar, Högni
    and that Hunnish war-prince lives,   and Guthorm
    nor a worthier folk on earth,
    if we five should at length raise sons,   *five* including Gudrún?
    and increase our noble line.

19. 'I know clearly from where these roads come:
    these are Brynhild's overweening demands.'

20. 'Let's prepare Guthorm for the killing,   *Guthorm* Gjúki's stepson
    our younger brother, less experienced;
    he wasn't involved in the sworn oaths,
    sworn oaths, avowed pledges.'

21. Easy it was to urge the intrepid one on:
    [. . .]
    a sword stood in Sigurd's heart.

22. The war-eager man thought of vengeance   *war-eager man*
                in the chamber,   Sigurd
    and flung back at the intrepid one;
    there flew firmly at Guthorm
    Gram's fine-bright iron from the king's hand.

23. His enemy sank down in two pieces:
    arms and head sank down one way,
    and the legs' part fell right back.

24. Gudrún was asleep in bed,
    free of sorrows at Sigurd's side,
    but she awoke, far from joy,
    as she bathed in Frey's friend's blood.   *Frey's friend* Sigurd

25. She clapped together heavy hands
    so that the stout-hearted one rose up on the bed:
    'Weep not, Gudrún, so bitterly;
    fresh young bride: your brothers live.

26. 'I have too young an heir,   *heir* Sigmund
    he cannot decamp from the enemy court;
    they've thought up, dark and dire,
    and almost accomplished, new-fangled schemes.

27. 'There will never ride, though you raise seven,
    a sister's son like him to the Thing;
    I see quite clearly what brought this about:
    Brynhild alone causes every ill.

28. 'That girl loves me above every man,
    but against Gunnar I did no harm;
    I spared our kinship, our sworn oaths,
    so I shouldn't be called his wife's lover.'

29. The lady cast away a sigh, the king his life;
    she clapped together heavy hands
    so that there echoed the cups in the corner:
    out in the yard, the geese began honking.

30. Then Brynhild, Budli's daughter, laughed
    a single time, with all her heart,
    when she could hear from bed
    the shrill weeping of Gjúki's daughter.

31. Then spoke Gunnar, prince of warriors:
    'You do not laugh, spiteful lady,
    merry on the floor, because this brings you joy.
    Why do you lose your bright appearance,
    bringer of evils? I reckon you're fey.

32. 'You deserve most of all women
    that in front of your eyes we should strike Atli,
    that you'd see on your brother bleeding wounds,
    dripping cuts for you to bind.'

33. 'No man will taunt you, Gunnar, you've fought enough;
    Atli fears little your enmity:
    between you two his breath will last longer,
    he'll always have the greater strength.

34. 'I'll tell you, Gunnar, what you know yourself full well,
    how you from the start were embroiled in spite;
    I wasn't too young, nor too constrained,
    well-endowed with wealth in my brother's hall.

35. 'Nor did I wish to have a husband
    before you sons of Gjúki rode to the court,
    three mighty kings on horseback:
    their journey should never have been.

36. 'And Atli said to me in secret
    that he would never share possessions,
    gold or territories, unless I let myself be married,
    nor any part of the wealth did he bestow,
    the property he gave me when I was very young,
    the wealth he called mine when I was very young.

37. 'Then my heart was in doubt about that:
    whether I should fight and fell the slain,
    bold in my mailcoat for my brother's sake;
    that would become well-known among nations,
    be for many a man affliction of mind.

38. 'We let an agreement settle between us;
    it pleased my heart more to accept the treasures,
    the red-gold rings of Sigmund's son,
    nor did I want another man's wealth.

39. 'I betrothed myself to him
    who sat with gold on Grani's back;
    he wasn't like you in his eyes
    nor in any part of his appearance:
    though you thought yourselves mighty kings.

40. 'I loved but one man, not many:
    this circlet-valkyrie had no changeable heart;   *circlet-valkyrie*
    all this will Atli find out after,   woman
    when he learns that murderous journey is made;

41. 'Never shall this faint-hearted woman
    accompany another's husband alive;
    there will be vengeance for my griefs.'

42. Up rose Gunnar, the warrior of the retinue,
    and put his arms around his wife's neck;
    folk of all kinds approached,
    to dissuade her with all their hearts.

43. Briskly she flung from her shoulders everyone's embraces,
    let no one dissuade her from the long journey.

44. He began to urge Högni to speak with him in secret:
    'I want all the soldiers to go into the hall,
    yours and mine – now there's great need –
    to see if we can stop my wife's murderous journey,
    in case harm should come of it;
    so let us of necessity think up a plan.'

45. Högni answered with this alone:
    'Let no one dissuade her from the long journey,
    from where she'll never be reborn!
    She came uncouth from her mother's knees,
    ever born for lack of joy,
    for grief of heart for many a man.'

46. He turned dejected from their talking,   *He* Gunnar
    to where the circlets'-land dealt out   *circlets'-land* woman
        treasures.

47. She looked over all her possessions,
    slave-girls slain and serving-women;
    she donned her gold corselet, no good thought
        in her heart,
    before she pierced herself with the blade's edge.

48. She sank on the bolster back on one side,
    and, sword-wounded, pondered what to do:

49. 'Now they should step forward who want to take
    gold and lesser treasures from me;
    I'll give to every woman a decorated gem,
    embroidered coverlets, bright-coloured clothes.'

50. Everyone was silent, pondered what to do,
    all together they gave an answer:
    'Women enough have been slain: we still want to live;
    serving-women should act well.'

51. Until, still brooding, the linen-clad lady,
    young in age, spoke words in reply:
    'I want no one reluctant or hard to persuade
    to lose their life for my sake.

52. 'But there will burn upon your bones,
    fewer coins, when you journey forth
    – none of Menja's goods –   *Menja's goods* golden treasures
        visiting me.

53. 'Sit down, Gunnar: I'll tell you,
    your bright bride has no hope of life;
    your vessel will not be fully floated,
    though I have given up my breath.

54. 'You and Gudrún will be reconciled quicker than
        you think;
    the wise woman will have alongside a king,   *king* Atli
    sad memories of her dead husband.

55. 'A girl will be born: her mother will raise her;
    she will be brighter than the dazzling day,
    Svanhild, brighter than a sun-beam.

56. 'You'll give Gudrún to one fine man,
    to a marksman, the destoyer of many men,
    willingly she will not be given, happily married;
    Atli will come to take her as his wife,
    the one born of Budli, my own brother.

57. 'I have much to remember, how they went against me,
    when you had betrayed me as I grieved;
    I was shorn of pleasure as long as I lived.

58. 'You'll want to have Oddrún as your wife,
    but Atli will never allow that to you;
    you two will turn togcther in secret:
    she will love you as I should have done
    if our fates had turned out fair.

59. 'Atli will act badly towards you:
    you'll be laid in a tight-cramped snake-pit.

60. 'And not long afterwards it shall happen
    that Atli will breathe his last,
    his happiness and his sons' lives;
    for Gudrún will smear him with blood in bed,
    by a sharp blade, because of a bitter heart.

61. 'More seemly would it be for Gudrún, our sister,
    to follow her first dead husband,
    if she'd been given proper advice,
    or had a heart like mine.

62. 'Now I speak without speed, but she will not
    lose her life for our sake;
    high waves will carry her
    to Jónakr's family realms.

63. 'With care will be raised Jónakr's sons;
    she'll send Svanhild out of the land,
    her own daughter and Sigurd's.

64. 'Bikki's counsels will wound her well,
    since Jörmunrekk lives to wreak havoc;
    then the whole line of Sigurd will be destroyed,
    Gudrún's weeping the greater.

65. 'I will make you but one request,
    it will be my last request in the world:
    have such a broad pyre raised on the plain
    that under it will be equal space for us all,
    who have died alongside Sigurd.

66. 'Let the pyre there be hung with hangings and shields,
    well-dyed foreign cloth and a host of foreign slaves;
    let the southern king burn beside me.

67. 'Burn on the southern king's other side
    my servants, circlet-adorned,
    two at the head, and two hawks;
    then everything will be properly arranged.

68. 'Let there lie between us the ring-adorned blade,
    the keen-edged iron, laid once again,
    as when we both climbed into one bed,
    and had the name of husband and wife.

69. 'Then there won't fall with a crash on his heels
    the bright hall's doors, decorated with a ring,
    if my entourage follows him hence;
    our passing will be far from pitiful.

70. 'For five slave-girls will follow him there,
    eight servants of fine family,
    the slaves who grew up with me, my father's bequest,
    what Budli gave to his girl.

71. 'Much have I said; I would say more
    if fate gave me more space for speech;
    my voice fails, my wounds swell,
    I've said but the truth, and so must stop.'

Helreid Brynhildar: Brynhild's Hel-ride

*After Brynhild's death two pyres were prepared, one for
Sigurd, which burned first, and Brynhild was burned on the
other; and she was in a wagon, hung with valuable cloths. It
was said, that Brynhild drove in her wagon along the road to
Hel, and went past an enclosure, where a certain ogress lived.
The giantess said:*

(Brynhildr reid helveg: Brynhild rode the path to Hel)

1. 'You must not pass through
    my courtyards paved with stone;
    it would suit you better to be at your weaving,
    rather than visit another's husband.

2. 'Why should you visit from Valland,
    scatter-brain, my dwelling?
    You have, gold-goddess, if you want   *gold-goddess* woman
        to know,
    gentle lady, washed a man's blood from your hands.'

Then Brynhild said:

3. 'Don't taunt me, woman from out of a rock,
    though I have been off with the vikings;
    I'll be thought nobler than you,
    wherever folk know our descent.'

The giantess said:

4. 'Brynhild, you were Budli's daughter,
    born to the worst luck in the world;
    you have ruined Gjúki's children,
    destroyed their splendid homes.'

Brynhild said:

5. 'I, the wise one in the wagon, will tell you,
    who are totally witless, if you want to know,
    how Gjúki's heirs acted towards me,
    loveless and breaking their oaths.

6. 'The courageous king had the feather-cloaks
    of us eight sisters placed under an oak;
    I was twelve years old, if you want to know,
    when I swore oaths to the young prince.

7. 'Everyone who knew me in Din-dales
    called me War-maiden wearing a   *War-maiden wearing a*
         helmet.   *helmet* valkyrie

8. 'Then I let the old man of the Goths,
    Helm-Gunnar, go straight off to Hel;
    I gave the victory to Auda's young brother;
    Odin became very angry with me for that.

9. 'He surrounded me with shields in Skata-grove,
    red and white, and bucklers touching;
    he bade someone to end my sleep,
    one who never knew any fear.

10. 'He caused around the south of my hall,
    wood's enemy to blaze up high;   *wood's enemy* fire
    he bade a warrior ride over it,
    who brought me the gold that lay under Fáfnir.

11. 'The fine gold-giver rode Grani   *gold-giver* warrior, here Sigurd
    where my foster-father governed his halls;
    he alone seemed better than all the rest,
    a Danish viking among the retinue.

12. 'We slept and were happy in but one bed,
    as if he'd been born my brother;
    not at all for the space of eight nights
    did we lay one arm over another.

13. 'But Gudrún taunted me, Gjúki's daughter,
    that I slept in Sigurd's arms;
    then I found out, what I never wanted:
    that they'd tricked me into taking a husband.

14. 'They must all too long in the face of great strife
    men and women be born and raised;
    we two shall never be torn apart,
    Sigurd and I together: sink yourself, giantess-spawn!'

Dráp Niflunga: The killing of the Niflungs

*Gunnar and Högni took all the gold, Fáfnir's inheritance.
There was a feud between Gjúki's family and Atli; he
reckoned Gjúki's family were to blame for Brynhild's death. A
settlement was reached, that they should give him Gudrún in
marriage, and they gave her a potion of forgetfulness to drink,
before she would agree to be married to Atli. Atli's sons were
Erp and Eitil, but Svanhild was the daughter of Sigurd and
Gudrún.*

   *King Atli invited Gunnar and Högni to his home, and sent
Vingi or Knéfröd [as his messenger]. Gudrún recognized his
scheming and sent word in runes that they should not come,
and as a token she sent Högni the ring Andvaranaut, and
wrapped a wolf's hair around it.*

   Gunnar had asked for the hand of Oddrún, Atli's sister, but

didn't get her; he married Glaumvör, and Högni married
Kostbera; their sons were Sólar and Snævar and Gjúki. When
the Gjúkungs came to Atli's, Gudrún asked her sons to plead
for the lives of her brothers, but they wouldn't. Högni's heart
was sliced out, and Gunnar was put in a snake-pit. He played
the harp and put the snakes to sleep, but an adder stung him
in his liver.

Gudrúnarkvida in forna: The ancient song of Gudrún

King Thjódrek was with Atli, and had lost almost all his men.
Thjódrek and Gudrún swapped the stories of their sorrows.
She spoke to him and said:

1. 'I was the maid among maids: my mother brought me up
   bright in the bower; I adored my brothers;
   until Gjúki showered gold on me,
   showered gold and gave me to Sigurd.

2. 'So Sigurd was beside Gjúki's sons
   like a green leek grown in the grass,
   or a high-pointed hart beside fallow deer,
   or gold red-glowing beside grey silver.

3. 'Until my brothers begrudged it to me
   to have a husband more splendid than all;
   they couldn't sleep or pass any judgements,
   before they'd brought Sigurd to his death.

4. 'Grani galloped back from the meeting: *Grani* Sigurd's horse
        a stir could be heard,
   but Sigurd himself never came.
   The saddle-horses were all dark with sweat;
   they'd had hard work, carrying killers.

5. 'I went in tears to talk to Grani;
   I asked the horse, weeping, what occurred.
   Grani looked down then, dropped his head to the grass;
   the horse knew its master was gone.

6. 'Long I pondered, long I considered,
   before I asked the people's ruler about the prince.

7. 'Gunnar looked down; Högni told me
   about Sigurd's sorry death:
   "He lies, cut down, by the river side,
   Gutthorm's killer, given to wolves.   *Gutthorm's killer* Sigurd

8. ' "Seek out Sigurd on the road to the south:
   you'll hear the ravens screech,
   the eagles screech, content with their carrion,
   wolves howl around your husband."

9. ' "How, Högni, can you tell such terrible harm
   to me, bereft of joys?
   May ravens slice apart your heart,
   across wider lands than you know."

10. 'Högni answered a single time,
    slow to be kind, from great grief:
    "Gudrún, you'd have more to bewail,
    once ravens sliced apart my heart."

11. 'I turned away alone from that exchange,
    to the wood, to gather what wolves had left;
    I didn't howl or beat my hands
    or keen like other women,
    when I sat half-dead over Sigurd.

12. 'The night seemed to me pitch-black,
    when I sat sorrowfully over Sigurd;
    as for the wolves, it seemed better to me
    if they caused me to lose my life
    or burnt me like dry birch.

13. 'I travelled from the fell, for five days all told,
    until I spotted the high hall of Hálf.

14. 'I sat with Thóra for seven seasons,
    Hákon's daughter, in Denmark;
    to give me joy she embroidered in gold
    southern halls and Danish swans.

15. 'We two portrayed the play of warriors,
    the leader's troops with delicate toil,
    red shields, and ranks of Huns,
    a sword-band, a helm-band, a leader's train.

16. 'Sigmund's ships, slipped from shore,
    with gilded beaks and graven stems;
    on the cloth we embroidered the battle
    of Sigar and Siggeir, south at Fjón.

17. 'Then Grímhild found out, queen of the Goths,   *Grímhild*
    in what frame of mind I was: Gunnar's mother
    she threw down her embroidery, fetched her sons,
    with eagerness she asked
    who would compensate their sister for her son,
    or pay for her slaughtered husband.

18. 'Gunnar said that he was keen to offer gold
    to settle the case, and Högni the same;
    she asked that everyone willing to go
    should saddle a steed, harness a wagon,
    ride a horse, fly a hawk,
    shoot arrows from a yew-bow.

19. 'Valdar and the Danes, with Jarisleif,
    Eymód third, with Jariskár;
    they entered in, the image of princes,
    Lombard troops wearing red cloaks,
    splendid corselets, pointed helmets,
    girt with short swords, chestnut-haired.

20. 'Everyone wanted to choose treasures for me,
    to choose treasures and speak softly,
    to see if they could soothe through trust
    my many griefs: I couldn't trust them.

21. 'Grímhild brought me a beaker to drink,
    cool and bitter: I forgot my wrong;
    it was enhanced by the power of fate,
    the sea cooled chill and sacrificial boar's blood.

22. 'There were on the horn all sorts of runes
    cut and reddened – I couldn't read them –
    a long heather-fish and an uncut grain   *heather-fish* snake
    from Haddings' land, the innards of   *Haddings' land* sea
        animals.

23. 'In that ale was every kind of evil,
    the roots of every tree and a burnt acorn,
    dew from around the hearth, sacrificed entrails,
    pig's liver boiled, and with it she deadened the wrong.

24. 'And then there faded what had been remembered,
    the whole death of the prince in the chamber;
    three kings came on bended knee,
    before she herself began to address me: *she* Grímhild

25. ' "Gudrún, I will give you gold,
    a great fortune from your dead father,
    red-gold rings from Hlödvér's hall,
    all the bed-curtains, for the fallen prince;

26. ' "Hunnish girls for tablet-weaving
      working fair gold as your heart desires;
      alone you shall govern Budli's treasure,
      decked in gold and given to Atli."

27. ' "I don't want to have a husband
      nor to marry Brynhild's brother;
      it's unseemly for me with the son of Budli   *son of Budli* Atli
      to have children or to live in joy."

28. ' "Don't pay back the men for bad deeds done,
      that we were the cause of before;
      it'll seem to you as if they both live,
      Sigurd and Sigmund, if you have sons."

29. ' "Grímhild, I cannot plunge into pleasure,
      nor think there's any hope for the warrior,
      since sorely Sigurd's heart-blood they sipped
      together, the corpse-beast and the raven."   *corpse-beast* wolf

30. ' "I've found the one of noblest blood,
      the ruler by far the finest;
      him you'll have, or old age will find you,
      without a husband, unless you'll have him."

31. ' "Don't offer me with eagerness
      such a wicked family!
      He'll do Gunnar harm
      and slice out Högni's heart;
      and I won't cease until I deprive
      the brisk urger of sword-play of   *urger of sword-play* warrior
          his life."

32. 'Weeping, Grímhild clutched at the words
      which pointed to evil for her sons
      and great damage to her boys.

33. ' "I'll give you lands and retinues of men,
 Vínbjörg, Valbjörg, if you'll take them;
 have and enjoy them your whole life, daughter!"

34. ' "I'll choose him from among the kings,
 forced by my family to have him;
 he won't prove a husband to give me joy,
 nor my brothers' pain shelter my sons."

35. 'At once every man was shown to his horse,
 the southern women placed in the wagons;
 for a whole week we rode over the cool ground,
 and for another week churned up the waves,
 in the third week we crossed dry land.

36. 'The gate-keepers of the high fortress
 opened the gates, and we rode into the courtyard.

37. 'Atli awoke me, for I seemed to be
 full of foreboding for the deaths of kin.

38. ' "So just now the norns awoke me"
 – he wished me to read the grim prophecy –
 "I thought that you, Gudrún, Gjúki's daughter,
 speared me with a harm-blended sword."

39. ' "It means fire, when one dreams of iron,
 secrecy and deception, when of a woman's wrath;
 I'll come and cauterize your wounds,
 soothe and heal, though it's loathsome to me."

40. ' "I thought that here in the meadow shoots fell,
 that I would have wished to let grow,
 ripped up by the roots, reddened with blood,
 brought to the bench, offered me to eat.

41. ' "I thought that out of my hand hawks flew
    without food to evil buildings;
    their hearts I thought I chewed up with honey,
    troubled in mind, swollen with blood.

42. ' "I thought that out of my hand pups were freed,
    lacking joy: both of them howled;
    their flesh I thought turned into carrion,
    and I was forced to eat their dead flesh."

43. ' "So soldiers will be considering the sacrifice,
    cutting the heads off white beasts;
    they will, doomed to die within a few nights,
    just before day be eaten by the host."

44. 'Then I lay awake, not wishing to sleep,
    defiant in my bed of grief: I remember it well.'

Gudrúnarkvida in thridja: The third
song of Gudrún

*Herkja was the name of one of Atli's slave-girls; she had been
his mistress. She told Atli that she had seen Thjódrek and
Gudrún together. Atli was very unhappy; then Gudrún said:*

1. 'What ails you Atli? Always, Budli's son,
    your heart seems heavy; why never laugh?
    To your noblemen it would seem better
    to talk to folk, and look at me.'

2. 'I am grieved, Gudrún, Gjúki's daughter:
    in my hall Herkja told me,
    that you and Thjódrek had slept under sheets,
    and lightly lingered under linen.'

3. 'I shall swear the most solemn oaths,
   on the white and holy stone,
   I never did so with Thjódmar's son,
   what man and woman might do.

4. 'I only embraced the leader of hosts,
   the warrior brave, a single time;
   our conversations were otherwise
   when we two sank sadly into solitary talk.

5. 'Thjódrek came here with thirty men,
   of all those thirty not one yet lives:
   you robbed me of brothers and mail-clad men,
   you robbed me of every close kin.

6. 'Send for Saxi, the southern prince:
   he knows about the sacred boiling pot!'

7. Seven hundred men strode into the hall,
   before the king's wife placed her hands in the pot.

8. 'Gunnar won't come now, I can't call for Högni,
   I'll never see my sweet brothers again.
   With a sword would Högni have avenged such a slur;
   now I have to purge myself of this charge.'

9. She plunged her bright hand down to the bottom
   and there snatched up the precious stones:
   'See here, soldiers – I'm quite cleared
   in the holy way – how the cauldron boils.'

10. Then Atli's heart laughed in his breast,
    when he saw Gudrún's hands unharmed:
    'Now must Herkja go to the cauldron,
    since she intended Gudrún ill.'

11. They looked on wretchedly, those who looked on,
     seeing how Herkja's hands were scalded;
     they led the girl off to a stinking bog:
     thus Gudrún purged her wrongs.

Oddrúnargrátr: Oddrún's lament

Frá Borgnýju ok Oddrúnu: About Borgný and Oddrún

There was a king called Heidrek; his daughter was called Borgný. Vilmund was the name of her lover. She was unable to give birth until Oddrún, Atli's sister, came; she [Oddrún] had been the beloved of Gunnar, Gjúki's son. About this tale it is said as follows:

1. I heard tell in ancient tales,
    how there came a girl to Mornaland;
    no one across the whole earth was able
    to give Heidrek's daughter help.

2. Oddrún learned, Atli's sister,
    that the girl had mighty pains;
    she took from the stall a well-bridled steed
    and saddled up the black horse.

3. She let the horse run over smooth earth-tracks,
    till she came to a high-standing hall,
    and she walked in the whole length of the hall,
    swept off the saddle from the worn horse,
    and these were the first words she found to say:

4. 'What's most noteworthy in this land,
    or what's most celebrated in Hunland?'
    'Here lies Borgný, overcome with pain,
    your friend, Oddrún: help if you can!'

5. 'What warrior has brought about this disgrace?
    Why has Borgný got these sudden pains?'

6. 'Vilmund is the name of the valiant lover,
    who kept the maid in a warm bed
    for five years, and her father never knew.'

7. I think they did not speak much more:
    the kind lady went to sit at the girl's knee,
    strongly Oddrún chanted, firmly Oddrún chanted,
    bitter spells to help Borgný.

8. A boy and a girl to tread the earth-tracks,
    happy children for Högni's killer;   *Högni's killer* Vilmund?
    then the seriously-sick girl began to speak,
    though she'd said not a word before:

9. 'May the kindly powers help you:
    Frigg and Freyja and more of the gods;
    since you kept danger from me with your hands.'

10. 'I didn't stoop to help you
    because you ever deserved it;
    I made a vow and kept it: that I'd come here,
    that I ought to help everyone
    who shared the prince's inheritance.'

11. 'You're insane, Oddrún, and out of your wits,
    to speak all these harsh words to me;
    I used to accompany you on the earth,
    as if we were born of two brothers.'

12. 'I recall what you said one evening,
    when I was making up Gunnar's drink;
    you said that such a thing should never be seen
    of any maid, but only of me.'

13. Then the troubled woman sat down,   *troubled woman* Oddrún
    to recount her sorrows from great grief:

14. 'I was raised in the princes' hall
    – most folk rejoiced – on men's advice.
    I enjoyed my life and my father's goods   *father* Budli
    for just five years, while my father lived.

15. 'He began to speak of the loftiest matters,
    the proud king, before he died:
    he said he'd deck me with red gold,
    and give me away to the south to Grímhild's   *Grímhild's*
        son.   *son* Gunnar

16. 'He asked that a helmet be obtained for Brynhild,
    said that she would become a wish-maid;   *wish-maid* valkyrie
    said that she'd be raised the noblest
    maid in the world, unless fate spoiled things.

17. 'In the bower Brynhild was weaving,
    she had lands and men beneath her,
    the earth trembled, and heaven above,
    when Fáfnir's killer found the fortress.   *Fáfnir's killer* Sigurd

18. 'Then warfare was waged with a foreign sword,
    the fortress breached, that Brynhild owned;
    it wasn't long after, woefully little,
    until she knew all the plotting.

19. 'Then she had harsh vengeance brought about,
    of which we have all had experience enough;
    it will travel around all men's lands,
    that she slew herself alongside Sigurd.

20. 'And I came to love Gunnar,
    giver of rings, as Brynhild should have done.

21. 'They offered Atli red-gold rings
    and no small compensation to my brothers;
    he offered fifteen farms for me,
    Grani's pack-load, if he'd have it.   *Grani's pack-load* gold

22. 'But Atli said that he would never
    want a dowry from Gjúki's kin;
    we couldn't withstand our love,
    so I laid my head against the
          ring-breaker.   *ring-breaker* prince; here Gunnar

23. 'Many of my kinsmen spoke
    and said we'd both been together,
    but Atli said that I would not
    be guilty or commit any wrong.

24. 'But one should never deny such a thing,
    one man to another, when love's concerned!

25. 'Atli sent out his envoys
    through Mirkwood to try me out;
    and they came where they shouldn't have come:
    where we'd spread out a single bed-cover.

26. 'We offered the retainers red-gold rings,
    to tell nothing to Atli;
    but in great excitement they did tell Atli,
    swiftly scurrying home.

27. 'But they wholly hid from Gudrún
    what she properly should have known.

28. There was a din to be heard of golden hoofs,
    when Gjúki's heirs rode into the courtyard;
    they cut the heart from out of Högni
    and placed the other in the snake-pit.

29. 'I'd just gone that single time
    to prepare the drink for Geirmund;
    the brave king began to pluck the harp,   *brave king* Gunnar
    for the king of mighty family thought   *king of mighty family*
    I'd come and give him help.   Gunnar

30. 'I got to hear at Hlésey,
    how the strings were speaking of strife;
    I told my maids to make ready:
    I wanted to rescue the lord.

31. 'We had the boat floating across the straits
    until I saw all of Atli's courts.

32. 'Then came the wretched lady slithering out,
    Atli's mother: she ought to shrivel up!
    She bit Gunnar to the heart,
    so I could not rescue the famed man.

33. 'I often wonder how ever afterwards,
    pillow-goddess, I can carry on living,   *pillow-goddess* woman,
    when I seemed to love the battle-brisk man,   here Borgný
    the swordsman, as much as myself.

34. 'You've sat and listened while I told you
    much evil of my fate and theirs;
    each man lives the way he wants;
    now is ended Oddrún's lament.'

Atlakvida: Atli's song

Daudi Atla: The death of Atli

*Gudrún, Gjúki's daughter, avenged her brothers, as is well
known: first she killed Atli's sons, then she killed Atli and set
fire to his hall and all his court. This poem was composed
about these things:*

1. Atli sent an envoy to Gunnar,
   a famous rider; he was called Knéfröd.
   He came to Gjúki's courts and Gunnar's hall,
   to benches close around the hearth, and to
        sweet-tasting beer.

2. The warrior-band were drinking, concealing thoughts
        in silence,
   wine in the fine hall: they looked out for the Huns' wrath.
   Then Knéfröd called out in a cold voice,
   the southern warrior, where he sat on the high bench:

3. 'Atli sent me here, riding on an errand,
   on a horse bit-champing over Mirkwood untracked,
   to ask you two, Gunnar, to come to   *two* Gunnar and Högni
        our benches
   with helmets close around the hearth, to visit Atli's home.

4. 'There you both can choose shields and shaved ash-spears,
   red-gold helmets and a host of Huns,
   silver-gilt saddle-cloths, fine red tunics,
   pennons and lances, bit-champing chargers.

5. 'He said he'd also grant the plain of wide
        Gnita-heath,   *Gnita-heath* where Sigurd met Fáfnir
   with screaming spears and gilded prows,
   mighty treasures and estates on the Dneiper,
   the far-famed forest that men call Mirkwood.'

6. Then Gunnar turned his head and spoke to Högni:
   'What do you advise, young warrior, when we hear
        such things?
   I didn't know that there was any gold on Gnita-heath,
   that the two of us didn't own the same again.

7. 'We two own seven buildings full of swords;
    and every one has a hilt of gold.
    I know my mount's the best, my blade the keenest;
    bows grace my benches and mailcoats of gold,
    the brightest helmets and shields, brought from
        Kjár's hall;   *Kjár* king of Valland
    one of mine's better than those of all the Huns.'

8. 'What do you think the lady meant, sending us a ring,
    wrapped in the heath-dweller's coat?   *heath-dweller* wolf
    I reckon she was trying to warn us;
    I found a heath-dweller's hair wreathed round the red ring:
    our way is wolfish, riding on this errand.'

9. No kinsman pushed Gunnar on, nor any near-relation,
    no counsellor, nor confidant, nor any noble.
    But Gunnar spoke, as a king should,
    magnificent in the mead-hall, out of mighty spirit:

10. 'Rise up now, Fjörnir, make the golden cups   *Fjörnir* Gunnar's
        of warriors,   cupbearer
    flow around the platform in the hands of men.

11. 'The wolf shall possess the Niflung inheritance,
    old guardians in grey, if Gunnar disappears.
    Black-coated bears shall chew with fiercesome fangs,
    delight the dog-stud, if Gunnar doesn't return.'

12. They led the land-ruler, the inciter to war,
    folk unafraid, grieving, from the young cubs' courts;
    then said the young heir of Högni:
    'Go safe and wise, where your heart urges!'

13. The brave men let speed at full gallop, over the fells,
    the bit-champing steeds, over Mirkwood untracked:
    all Hun-country shook as they passed by, determined,
    driving whip-shy creatures over plains all-green.

14. Atli's land they saw, with its deep-set watchtowers,
    Bikki's men standing on the high fortress;   *Bikki's men* Huns
    a hall over southerners surrounded with stout benches,
    with well-bound bucklers and shining shields,
    pennons, lances: there Atli drank
    wine in the fine hall; the guards were set outside,
    to keep a watch for Gunnar's men, in case they came
        visiting
    with screaming spears, to stir their lord to war.

15. Their sister met them first, when they entered the hall,
    both of her brothers; she had drunk little beer:
    'Now, Gunnar, you have been tricked: mighty man,
        what'll you do
    against the Huns' cunning harm? Quick, get out of
        the hall!

16. 'You'd have done better, brother, to come in your corselets,
    with helmets close around the hearth, to seek Atli's home;
    to sit in the saddle through sun-bright days,
    making norns weep at corpses made pale,
    making Huns' shield-maids get to know the harrow,
    making Atli himself go into a snake-pit:
    now that snake-pit's destined for the pair of you.'

17. 'Too late now, sister, to summon the Niflungs,
    a long time to look for a company of men,
    warriors unafraid from the Rhine's red hills.'

18. They seized Gunnar, and set him in fetters,
    the friend of Burgundians, and bound him fast.

19. Högni cut down seven with his keen sword,
    and an eighth he hurled into hot flames;
    so should a brave man guard himself against foes,
    as Högni guarded both Gunnar and himself.

20. They asked the brave man, the lord of the   *lord of the Goths*
        Goths,   Gunnar
    if he would buy back his own life with gold.

21. 'Högni's heart must lie in my hand,
    bleeding and cut from the bold rider's breast,
    from the ruler's son, with a cruel-biting knife.'

22. They cut out the heart from Hjalli's chest;   *Hjalli* Atli's servant
    bleeding, they bore it to Gunnar on a plate.

23. Then said Gunnar, lord of men:
    'Here I have the heart of Hjalli the craven,
    unlike the heart of Högni the bold:
    it quivers much as it lies on the plate;
    it quivered twice as much when it lay in his chest.'

24. Then Högni laughed, when they sliced to his heart,
    still living, the wound-smith; least of all   *wound-smith* warrior
        did he reckon to sob;
    bleeding, they bore it to Gunnar on a plate.

25. Famed Gunnar spoke, the spear-Niflung:
    'Here I hold the heart of Högni the bold,
    unlike the heart of Hjalli the craven;
    it quivers little as it lies on the plate:
    it quivered still less when it lay in his chest.

26. 'You, Atli, shall be as far from my eyes,
    as you shall be from my treasures;
    in me alone does the secret lie
    of the Niflings' hoard, now Högni lives not.

27. 'I always had doubt while we two lived,
    now I have none, while I live alone;
    the Rhine shall rule the strife-metal of men,   *strife-metal* gold
    that Æsir-sprung stream, the Niflung inheritance.
    In surging waters the fine rings shall shine,
    before gold will gleam on the arms of young Huns.'

28. 'Bring out the wagon: now the captive is caught!'

29. Mighty Atli rode a horse with jingling mane,
    their brother-in-law, surrounded by
        battle-thorns;   *battle-thorns* spears
    Gudrún the sister of those godlike heroes,
    bereft, held back her tears, in the din-filled hall.

30. 'May it go with you, Atli, according to those oaths
    you often swore to Gunnar, and invoked long ago:
    by the sun in the south and by Victory-   *Victory-god* Odin
        god's rock;
    by the horse of sleep's bedding   *horse of sleep's bedding* bedstead
        and by Ull's ring.'

31. And on from there the bit-shaker   *bit-shaker* horse
    dragged the treasure-warden,   *treasure-warden* Gunnar
    the prince of strife, on to his death.   *prince of strife* Gunnar

32. The living prince a band of warriors
    laid in a pit which was slithering
    inside with serpents; and alone Gunnar,
    angry-hearted, struck away at his harp with his hand.
    The strings sounded: so must a brave ring-giver
    guard his gold against men.

33. Atli turned towards his lands
    his gravel-treading steed, back from murder;
    there was a din in the courtyard, a crowding of chargers,
    a weapon-song of men: they'd returned from the heath.

34. Then Gudrún walked out to meet Atli
    with a gilded goblet, to give the warrior his reward:
    'Lord, you should get gladly from Gudrún in your
          own hall,
    tender cuts from creatures gone to
          Niflheim.'   *Niflheim* land of the dead

35. Atli's ale-cups rang, wine-heavy,
    as together in the hall the Huns assembled;
    broad-whiskered men briskly walked in.

36. Bright-faced she darted, bringing them drink,
    terrifying lady, for the warriors; she picked out
          ale-dainties,
    revolted, for drunkards, then told Atli in spite:

37. 'Spreader of swords, it is your own   *Spreader of swords* Atli
          sons'
    corpse-bloody hearts you've chewed up with honey;
    proud man, you've consumed dead men's meat,
    eating it as ale-dainties, sending it to the high seat.

38. 'Never again will you call to your knee
    Erp or Eitil, an ale-merry pair;
    never again will you see in the platform's midst
    those givers of gold putting shafts to spears,
    trimming manes or trotting mounts.'

39. A groaning grew on the benches, a dreadful dirge of men;
    a crying under rich cloaks: the Huns' children grieved,
    all except Gudrún, who never grieved,
    for her bearish brothers, for her sweet little sons,
    so young, so fresh, whom she had borne to Atli.

40. Shining-cheeked, she scattered gold,
    showered the servants with red-gold rings.
    She brought events to a head, she poured out bright metal;
    little did the lady pay the temple-treasuries heed.

41. Unsuspecting, Atli had drunk himself to a stop;
    he had no weapons, he did not shy from Gudrún;
    often sport was sweeter, when with many a kind kiss
    they often embraced in front of the nobles.

42. With the point of a blade she gave the bed a bloody drink,
    with a Hel-keen hand, and set the dogs free;
    she woke the servants, and in front of the hall-door
    she flung a burning brand: she paid them back for her
        brothers.

43. To the fire she gave everyone who was inside,
    who'd come from Myrkheim after murdering Gunnar and
        his men;
    the ancient timbers fell, the temples smoked,
    the buildings burned of Budli's kin, and the shield-maids
        inside;
    their lives stemmed, sinking into hot flames.

44. The whole story has been told: nor ever since
    has any corseleted bride avenged her brothers;
    she brought destruction on three mighty kings,
    shining woman, before she perished.

The tale is told more clearly in the Greenlandic 'Lay of Atli'.

Atlamál in grœnlenzku: The Greenlandic lay of Atli

1. Folk have heard of the strife when long ago
   warriors held a meeting that helped very few;
   they spoke together in private, then terror overwhelmed
       them,
   as well as Gjúki's sons, who were wholly betrayed.

2.   They brought about the princes' fate – they should not
          have been fey –
     Atli was badly counselled, although he was no fool;
     he brought down mighty pillars, harmed himself harshly;
     he sent a hasty message for his in-laws to come quick.

3.   The lady of the house was shrewd, made   *lady of the house*
          use of her wits,   Gudrún
     caught the drift of the words that they spoke in secret;
     the wise woman was perplexed: she wanted to help them,
     they had to sail across the sea and she couldn't reach
          them herself.

4.   She took to cutting runes; Vingi ruined them
     – he was making mischief – before he passed them on;
     afterwards they went off, Atli's envoys,
     over Limfjord, to where brave folk dwelt.

5.   They were very affable and kindled fires,
     thought of no plotting from those who had come:
     they took the presents the fair lady had sent them,
     hung them on a pillar, thought them unimportant.

6.   Then Kostbera came – she was Högni's wife,
     a highly sensitive lady – and greeted them both;
     glad too was Glaumvör, whom Gunnar had married:
     the wise woman lacked no courtesy; she looked to her
          guests' needs.

7.   They invited home Högni, to see if he'd come too;
     the duplicity was obvious, if they'd only been on guard;
     Gunnar agreed, if Högni was willing;
     Högni did not gainsay whatever Gunnar suggested.

8.   Fine ladies brought mead, the feast was quite splendid,
     many a horn passed around, till all had drunk their fill.

9. Husband and wife got ready for bed as seemed best to
         them;
     Kostbera was learned, she could read the runes,
     she spelt out the word-staves by the firelight;
     she had to hold her tongue, choke back speech:
     they were so spoilt it was hard to read.

10. Afterwards they went to bed, Högni and his wife;
     the courtly woman dreamed, and did not hide it,
     wisely she told her lord as soon as she awoke.

11. 'You're intending to leave home, Högni; take some advice
     – few folk have mastery of runes – go another time!
     I've read the runes your sister cut:
     the lovely lady hasn't invited you this time.

12. 'One thing makes me most surprised – I still can't
         understand –
     what brought it about that the wise woman's cutting
         was so spoilt;
     what seemed to be indicated underneath
     was that both of you were to die, if you went there soon;
     the lady missed out a stave, or others did.'

13. 'All women are suspicious,' said Högni, 'but I am not;
     I won't look for trouble unless we get trouble in return;
     that lord will please us with glowing-red gold;
     I'll never be frightened, whatever horrors we hear.'

14. 'You'll take a tumble if you head off there:
     there'll be no warm welcome this time.
     I had a dream, Högni, I make no mistake:
     things will go wrong for you, or else I'm too filled
         with fear.

15. 'I thought your bed-clothes were all ablaze;
     the flame leapt high throughout my house.'

16. 'There's linen here you little like:
    it'll soon be burnt, like the bed-clothes you saw.'

17. 'I thought a bear had entered, broke up the boards,
    swiped with its paws and made us scared.
    Its jaws had many of us, and we were powerless;
    its stomping tread did not sound soft.'

18. 'The weather will change; it'll soon be dawn.
    You imagined a white bear: there'll be snow from the
          East.'

19. 'I thought an eagle had flown in, the whole length of
          the hall;
    there'll be a mighty pay-off for us: it spattered us all
          with blood.
    I thought from its threats it was Atli's form.'

20. 'Soon we put beasts to slaughter; then we'll see blood.
    It often means oxen, a dream of eagles.
    Atli's sound of spirit, whatever dreams you dream.'
    That's where they left it; every talk comes to an end.

21. The ones well-born also awoke; they had the same
          experience;
    Glaumvör was worried that there were dread things in
          her dreams;
    Gunnar said they could be read two ways.

22. 'It seemed I saw a gallows prepared for you; you went
          to be hanged,
    worms ate you, I lost you still alive:
    Ragnarök had come. Work out what that was!

24. 'I thought I saw a bloody sword pulled from your shirt:
    dreadful to tell a dream like that to a husband so close.
    I thought I saw a spear stand right through your middle;
    wolves bayed on each end of the spear.'

25. 'It must be dogs running, howling loud;
    often dogs' barking signals the flight of spears.'

26. 'I thought I saw a river running in the whole length of
        the house;
    it crashed with its current, swelled over the benches,
    broke the legs here of both you brothers:
    the water wouldn't stop: it must stand for something.

28. 'I thought I saw dead women come here in the night:
    they weren't badly dressed. They wanted to pick you,
    quickly called you to their benches;
    I reckon your *dísir* have been torn apart.'

29. 'It is too late to talk: it's all settled now;
    I cannot get away from fate, since going is decided;
    many things seem to point to our being short-lived.'

30. They saw that day was dawning, said that they were keen,
    every one, to get up; others would have kept them back.
    They travelled, five all told, and twice as many more
    retainers could have gone: it was badly thought-out;
    Snævar and Sólar, who were Högni's sons;
    they called him Orkning, their other companion:
    a happy shield-tree, the brother of Högni's   *shield-tree* warrior
        wife.

31. Fair-adorned, the ladies went, until the fjord separated
        them,
    the fine women kept on urging caution, but they would
        not be told.

32. Glaumvör said a word, Gunnar's wife;
    she spoke to Vingi about what she thought fit:
    'I don't know that you'll repay us suitably, as we
        would want.
    A guest's arrival is wicked if anything arises from it.'

33. Then Vingi took a vow; he scarcely spared himself:
    'Let giants take the man that tells you a lie;
    let the gallows have him wholly if he plots about your
        peace.'

34. Bera spoke up, happy in her heart: *Bera* Kostbera
    'Sail safe and achieve the victory;
    let it go as I foretell, and let no one gainsay it!'

35. Högni answered – he felt kindly towards his family –
    'Cheer yourselves up, wise women, however it turns out;
    many say – though it misses the mark –
    that it matters little to many, how a man's escorted
        from home.'

36. Then they looked at each other, before turning away;
    I reckon then their fates were sealed: their paths were
        sundered.

37. They began to row mightily, almost ruptured the keel,
    leant back and pulled, made themselves quite enraged;
    the oar-thongs tore, the thole-pins smashed,
    they didn't tie the vessel up before they turned away.

38. A little later – I'll tell the tale to the end –
    the buildings they saw standing that Budli had owned;
    loud creaked the gate when Högni struck it.

39. Then Vingi said something that should have been unsaid:
    'Get away from this house: it's perilous to approach!
    Soon I'll have destroyed you, in a short time you'll be
        cut down
    – I extended a fine invitation, but a peril lurked
        underneath –
    otherwise, wait here, while I cut you a gallows!'

40. Högni said something – he felt little urge to yield –
    wary of nothing, as was to be tested:
    'Don't bother trying to scare us, don't say another thing:
    if you keep on talking, you'll make your bad luck worse.'

41. They shoved Vingi away; sent him to Hel,
    laid at him with axes while he struggled for breath.

42. Atli and his men mustered, they put on their mailcoats,
    and walked when they were ready, to the rampart that lay
        between;
    they hurled insults, and were all soon enraged:
    'For a while we've been determined to deprive you of
        your lives.'

43. 'It's not too clear that such has been your intention:
    you're still unready, while we have killed a man,
    beaten him to death: he was one of your number.'

44. They became furious when they heard those words,
    moved their fingers and felt their spear-loops,
    shot sharply, protecting themselves with shields.

45. Inside was reported what outside was endured,
    loud in front of the hall: they heard a slave tell.

46. Gudrún was grim when she heard that grief;
    burdened with necklaces, she cast them all off,
    she flung away the silver so the rings burst asunder.

47. Then she walked out, flung wide the doors,
    unafraid, she stepped forward and welcomed the visitors;
    turned to the Niflungs – it was their last greeting –
    she was quite sincere, and she said much more:

48. 'I sought to save you by keeping you from leaving home:
    none can escape fate, and you have had to come here.'
    She spoke with sense, hoping there could be a settlement;
    they would not be agreed: everyone said no.

49. The high-born woman saw that they were playing harshly,
    her heart turned harder, and she cast off her cloak;
    she took a naked sword and defended the lives of her kin;
    she was skilful in the fray, wherever she set her hands.

50. Gjúki's daughter caused two fighters   *Gjúki's daughter* Gudrún
        to fall:
    she struck at Atli's brother – he had to be carried after –
    she acted in the fighting so that she slashed his leg away.

51. She managed to strike a second man so that he didn't get
        up again;
    she sent him to Hel, and her hands did not tremble.

52. They held a conflict there that was made famous;
    it surpassed every other deed, what Gjúki's children did;
    so they said that the Niflungs, as long as they lived,
    shaped an assault with swords: corselets were cut off;
    helmets hewed, while their courage endured.

53. They fought for most of the morning until it was past
        midday,
    through the dawn to the late morning;
    before the fighting was finished, the whole field was
        flooded with blood;
    eighteen they ended, before they fell,
    Kostbera's two boys, and her brother.

54. The brave one broke into speech, though he   *brave one* Atli
        was enraged:
    'It's awful to look around, and you are to blame:
    we were thirty formidable warriors;
    eleven still live, but we are destroyed.

55. 'We were four brothers, when we lost Budli:
    now Hel has half; two lie slain.

56. 'I have powerful marriage-kin – I can't hide it –
    a harmful wife: I've had no benefit from it.
    We've hardly had any peace since you came into our
        hands:
    you've robbed me of kin, often swindled me of wealth,
    sent my sister to Hel: that's what I count the   *sister* Brynhild
        most.'

57. 'You mention this, Atli? You did it first:
    you took my mother, murdered her for her treasures,
    you starved to death my wise cousin in a cave;
    laughable I think it that you recount your griefs,
    I thank the gods when things go ill for you.'

58. 'I urge you, noblemen, to add to the great grief
    of this remarkable woman: I want to look at it;
    use all your might to make Gudrún cry:
    I could certainly bear to see her bereft of joy.

59. 'Grab hold of Högni and slice his flesh with a knife,
    cut out his heart: you ought to be ready for this;
    grim-hearted Gunnar string up on a gallows,
    press on with that deed then, and summon the snakes!'

Hogni said:

60. 'Do what you like: I'll gladly take it,
    boldly will I be tested by you: I've known sterner tests
        before.
    You had some resistance while we were unscathed:
    now we are wounded you can do what you like.'

61. Beiti spoke – he was Atli's steward –
    'Let's grab Hjalli, and let's spare Högni;
    let's complete a task half-done: he's ripe for death.
    However long he lives, he'll always be called a clot.'

62. The saucepan-keeper panicked; he didn't   *saucepan-keeper*
        hang around: Hjalli
    he knew how to blub, and climbed into every cranny.
    He called himself a victim of their war, repaying all his
        effort:
    it was a sad day for him, to die and leave the pigs,
    all the resources which he'd owned before.

63. They grabbed hold of Budli's braising-boy and pulled
        out a knife;
    the bad slave squealed before he felt the point,
    said he'd be only too glad to spread shit on all the fields,
    do the filthiest work, if that would square it;
    he'd be so happy, said Hjalli, if he could but keep his life.

64. Högni took it upon himself – very few act like that –
    to see that the slave should make his escape:
    'I swear that it's less pain for me to play out this game;
    why would we want to hear all that screeching in here?'

65. They seized hold of the excellent man; there was no option
    for the stout fighters to put off their plan any longer;
    Högni laughed then – the day-workers heard –
    he knew how to prove himself a hero, he bore the
        torture well.

66. Gunnar took a harp, strummed it with
        foot-twigs;   *foot-twigs* toes
    he knew how to play, so that women wept,
    and men sobbed, who could hear it quite clearly.
    He announced the affair to the powerful lady: the rafters
        burst apart.

67. The dear ones died; it was rather early in the day:
    at the last they left their prowess living.

68. Atli thought himself a big man: he'd had the better of
        them both;
    he spoke to the wise woman of her grief, began to taunt
        her a bit:
    'Now it's morning, Gudrún – you've lost men true
        to you –
    it's partly your own doing that things have turned out so.'

69. 'You're content, Atli, proclaiming killings,
    regret will come upon you, when you go through it all;
    this will be your legacy – I can tell you –
    it'll go ill for you always, unless I die too.'

70. 'I can't contradict what you say, but I see another course,
    twice as apt – we often turn our backs on benefits –
    I'll cheer you up with jewels, splendid treasures,
    snow-white silver, just as you yourself desire.'

71. 'There's no hope of that, I shall refuse them:
    I've broken other bargains with less cause;
    I seemed wild before, that'll now be increased,
    I could put up with anything while Högni lived.

72. 'We were raised together in the same house,
    played many a game and grew up in the grove,
    Grímhild provided us with gold and necklaces;
    you will never make good the killing of my brothers
    nor ever achieve contentment for me.

73. 'Men's overbearing kills women's choice,
    the trunk sinks down if the twigs diminish,
    a tree begins to tumble if the root is cut away;
    now you alone, Atli, can wield all power here.'

74. His shallowness was sufficient that the prince believed it;
    the duplicity was obvious, if he'd only been on guard.
    Gudrún was inscrutable, she knew how to dissemble,
    she made herself cheerful, played a double game.

75. She made a great ale-feast in memory of her brothers;
    Atli said the same should be done for his men.

76. That's where they left it; the drink was brewed;
    that was a meeting which brought great upheaval;
    the strong woman was mighty-hearted, brought harm
        on Budli's line,
    she wished to bring upon her husband a dreadful revenge.

77. She lured her little ones and placed them by the beam;
    the stern ones lost heart, but did not cry,
    they went to their mother's arms, and asked what was up.

78. 'Don't ask any more: I mean to harm you both;
    I've long wanted to cure you of old age.'
    'Sacrifice, if you will, your children, no one will stop you;
    a rest from anger will be brief, if you bring this about.'

79. The formidable lady stole the childhood of the brothers,
    she arranged things aright: cut both their throats.
    Atli kept asking, where they'd gone,
    the boys, off playing, since he couldn't see them at all.

80. 'I plan to go over to tell it to Atli,
    I, Grímhild's daughter, won't keep anything from you.
    It won't cheer you much, Atli, when you find out;
    you provoked great affliction when you slew my brothers.

81. 'I've slept very seldom since they fell,
    I promised you harshness, now I've reminded you;
    you told me it was morning – I remember it well –
    now it's evening: you have like news to hear.

82. 'You've lost your boys, as you shouldn't have done;
     their skulls, you know, you have used as ale-cups:
     I fixed your drink by blending in their blood.

83. 'I took their hearts and roasted them on a spit,
     I gave them to you afterwards, and said that it was calf;
     you finished it off alone, and you left no remnants,
     you chewed ravenously, relying on your grinders.

84. 'Now you know of your children – few would ask for
          worse –
     I played my part, but I'm not proud of it.'

85. 'Grim you were, Gudrún, that you could do this,
     to blend me a drink with the blood of your children;
     you've wiped out your blood-kin, as you oughtn't have
          done;
     and grant me little space between the grim deeds.'

86. 'My one remaining wish is to kill you,
     few things are bad enough for such a prince to suffer;
     previously you've perpetrated unparalleled deeds
     of foolishness and cruelty in this world;
     now you have surpassed what we'd learnt before:
     snatched at a great atrocity, made your own funeral feast.'

87. 'You'll be burnt on a pyre, but first beaten with rocks:
     then you'll have achieved what you always wanted.'
     'Tell yourself such sorrows early in the morning:
     I'll be going to another world by a more pleasing death.'

88. They sat under the same roof, sending out hostile
          thoughts;
     hurling harsh words back and forth: neither one was
          happy.
     Harshness grew in Hniflung, he thought   *Hniflung* Högni's son
          ambitiously,
     mentioned to Gudrún that he felt grim towards Atli.

89. There came into her heart how Högni was handled,
    she reckoned it his good fortune if wrought revenge;
    then Atli was slain: there was little time to wait,
    Högni's son struck, as did Gudrún herself.

90. The bold man began to speak, started from his sleep,
    soon sensed he was wounded, said there was no need of
        bandages:
    'Tell me most truly, who's killed Budli's son?
    I've not been played a little trick: I reckon there's no
        hope of life.'

91. 'I, Grímhild's daughter, won't keep anything from you;
    I declare that I caused it, and partly Högni's son,
    that your life is gone, that wounds weaken you.'

92. 'You've waded in slaughter, though that was not right;
    it's wicked to defraud a friend, who puts his faith in you.

93. 'Reluctantly I left home, to woo you, Gudrún;
    you were an admired widow, they called you ambitious,
    that expectation was no lie, as we have found out;
    you came home here, an army of men followed us,
    everything was wonderful in our way of life.

94. 'Every single honour there was for men of rank,
    cattle were plentiful, we benefited greatly;
    there was wealth enough: many received it.

95. 'I paid the dowry for a famed bride, to gain a deal of
        treasure,
    thirty slaves, seven splendid maids;
    there was honour in such things, though the silver
        was more.

96. 'You said that to you all this seemed as nothing,
    while those lands lay by that Budli left me;
    you undermined me, and received your share,
    you often left your mother-in-law to sit in tears,
    I never found our family in good heart again.'

97. 'Now you're lying, Atli, though I pay that little heed;
    I seldom kept myself in check, but yourself you puffed
        up hugely;
    you young brothers battled among yourselves, slandered
        each other:
    half your household went to Hel.
    Everything faltered that should have proved a boon.

98. 'We were three siblings, we thought ourselves unassailable,
    we left our lands and followed Sigurd;
    each steered a ship and made it speed,
    we wandered where fate led, until we came East.

99. 'We killed a king first, chose land there;
    lords submitted to our hands, showing their fear;
    we battled out of outlawry those we wanted cleared,
    set up in affluence those who had nothing.

100. 'The man from the south died: my   *man from the south* Sigurd
        prospects quickly perished;
    it was a heavy grief for a young girl to bear the name
        of widow,
    it seemed torture to one left alive to enter Atli's house;
    before, I'd married a champion: his loss was hard.

101. 'You never came back from a meeting, as far as we
        heard,
    where you'd fought a case or caused another's to collapse;
    you were always willing to give way, never to stand your
        ground,
    but quietly to acquiesce.'

102. 'Now you're lying, Gudrún, that won't better much
      either of our lots: we've all had our losses;
      do now, Gudrún, out of your goodness,
      what is fitting for our honour, when they carry me out.'

103. 'I'll buy a boat and a painted casket,
      wax the winding-sheet well, to wrap your corpse,
      consider every requirement, as if we were agreed.'

104. A corpse then was Atli, his kin's grief greatened;
      the well-born one brought about all that she'd promised.
      Gudrún, who had seen much, wished to do away with
          herself,
      the delay stretched for days: she died another time.

105. Happy is anyone afterwards, who can raise
      offspring as outstanding as Gjúki sired;
      after them will live in every land,
      their bravado, wherever folk hear of it.

Gudrúnarhvöt: Gudrún's inciting

Frá Gudrúnu: About Gudrún

*Gudrún walked to the sea, when she had killed Atli; she
waded out into the sea, and wanted to do away with herself;
but she couldn't sink. She drifted over the fjord to King
Jónakr's land: he married her.*

*Their sons were Sörli and Erp and Hamdir; Svanhild,
Sigurd's daughter, was raised there. She was betrothed to the
mighty Jörmunrekk. Bikki was with him; he advised that
Randvér, the king's son, should have her. Then Bikki told the
king. The king had Randvér hanged, and Svanhild trampled
under horses' hooves. When Gudrún heard of this, she spoke
to her sons:*

1. Then I heard accusations of the most vicious kind,
   a reluctant speech, spoken from great grief,
   when hard-hearted Gudrún incited her sons
   to war by using grim words.

2. 'Why are you sitting and sleeping away your life?
   Why aren't you grieved to talk of happiness?
   When Jörmunrekk had your sister,
   young in age, trampled with his steeds,
   white and black on the high road,
   with the grey and gait-tame horses of the Goths.

3. 'You have not turned out like Gunnar and his men,
   still less as brave-hearted as Högni was;
   you'd have looked to avenge her,
   if you had my brothers' spirits,
   or the hard heart of the Hunnish kings.'

4. Then said Hamdir the stout-hearted:
   'Little, once, did you praise Högni's deeds,
   when they awakened Sigurd from sleep;
   your blue-white cloth coverlets,
   were reddened with your husband's blood, drenched
         in corpse-gore.

5. 'Avenging your brothers turned out for you
   cruel and painful, when you murdered your sons;
   we could all with one mind
   have avenged our sister upon Jörmunrekk.

6. 'Bring out the treasures of the Hunnish kings:
   You have incited us to a meeting of swords!'

7. Laughing, Gudrún turned to the storeroom,
   picked out from the chests the panoply of kings,
   broad corselets, and brought them to her sons:
   bravely they mounted their steeds.

8. Then said Hamdir the stout-hearted:
   'So shall return again to visit his mother,
   a spear-prince fallen in the land of the Goths,   *spear-prince*
   so that you'd drink the funeral ale for us all,   great warrior
   both for Svanhild and your sons.'

9. Gudrún, weeping, Gjúki's daughter,
   went with grief to sit on the threshold
   and to recount, with cheeks tear-stained,
   grief-filled tales, many a time:

10. 'Three fires I've known, three hearths I've known,
    to three husbands' houses I've been brought;
    Sigurd alone to me was better than them all,
    the one whom my brothers put to death.

11. 'A more heavy wound I haven't seen or felt:
    they meant to cause me more pain
    when the princes gave me to Atli.

12. 'My brisk young cubs I called to speak to me in secret;
    I could get no cure for my griefs,
    until I'd cut off the heads of the Hniflungs.   *Hniflungs* Niflungs

13. 'I went to the sea-shore, I was angry with the norns,
    I wanted to rid myself of their painful plans:
    high waves lifted me, didn't drown me;
    I climbed up on to the land, since I had to live.

14. 'I went to the bed – I planned something better
         for myself –
    for a third time of a mighty king;
    I bore children, lawful heirs,
    lawful heirs, Jónakr's sons.

15. 'All round Svanhild sat serving-maids,
    she it was I loved best of all my bairns.
    Such was Svanhild in my chamber:
    like a glorious gleam of the sun.

16. 'I decked her with gold and gorgeous gowns,
    before I gave her away to the Goths.
    For me the hardest of all my griefs
    is that the fair head of Svanhild,
    they trod in the mud under horses' hooves.

17. 'That was the sorest, when my Sigurd,
    robbed of victory, they slew in my bed;
    and that was the grimmest, when towards Gunnar,
    the glistening serpents slithered deadly;
    and that was the sharpest, when to the heart
    the uncowardly king they cut still   *uncowardly king* Högni
        living.

18. 'Many are the griefs I remember . . .
    Bridle, Sigurd, the dusky horse,
    the swift-paced stallion, let it gallop here!
    Here there sits no daughter or daughter-in-law
    who might give to Gudrún precious gifts.

19. 'Do you remember, Sigurd, what we said,
    when we both lay in bed together,
    that you, proud warrior, would visit me
    from Hel, and I you from this world?

20. 'Nobles, pile up the oaken pyre:
    let it be the highest under heaven;
    let fire burn my grief-filled chest,
    forced from my heart, let sorrows melt.'

21. For all fighters: may their lot grow lighter;
    for all ladies: may their griefs grow less;
    as this series of sorrows has been told.

Hamdismál: Hamdir's lay

1. There sprung up on the walkway grievous deeds,
    elves' weeping, hindered in joy;
    early in the morning all afflictions
    of human pain kindle sorrow.

2. It was not now, nor yesterday,
    a long time has passed since then,
    – few things are so ancient that this was not twice so –
    when Gudrún, born to Gjúki, urged
    her young sons to avenge Svanhild.

3. 'Your sister was called Svanhild,
    whom Jörmunrekk trampled with his steeds,
    white and black on the high road,
    with the grey and gait-tame horses of the Goths.

4. 'You've been forced back, you mighty kings,
    of the strands of my line only you still live.

5. 'Solitary I stand as an aspen in a wood,
    bereft of kin as a pine-tree of branches,
    shorn of pleasure as a tree of leaves,
    when that branch-stripping girl passes   *branch-stripping girl* fire
         one warm day.'

6. Then said Hamdir the stout-hearted:
    'Little once, Gudrún, would you praise Högni's deeds,
    when they awakened Sigurd from sleep;
    you sat up in the bed, and the slayers laughed.

7. 'Your blue-white cloth coverlets,
    woven by craftsmen, were soaked in your husband's
         blood;
    then Sigurd died, you sat over the dead man,
    you cared not for happiness: it's what Gunnar wanted.

8. 'You meant to harm Atli with Erp's murder
    and Eitil's death: it was worse still for you;
    everyone should bring about death for another
    with a wound-biting sword, without getting hurt.'

9. Then said Sörli; he had a shrewd mind:
    'I won't bandy words with my mother;
    each of you thinks more needs to be said:
    what do you want now, Gudrún, that you won't
         get with weeping?

10. 'Weep for your brothers and sweet sons,
    your close-born kin, brought near to strife;
    for both of us also, Gudrún, you must weep,
    sitting here doomed on our horses, we who'll die far away.'

11. They went from the court, ready to rage;
    the young men travelled over damp fells,
    on Hunnish horses, avenging murder.

12[13.] They met on the road one planning great deeds:
    'How will a chestnut midget give us help?'

13[14.] The one with another mother answered, said he'd give
    help to his kinsmen like one leg to another.
    'How can a leg give help to a leg,
    or one flesh-grown arm to another?'

14[12.] Then Erp spoke a single time,
    as on horseback splendid he pranced:
    'It's no good showing a coward the way.'
    They said the bastard was very hard.

15. They drew from their sheaths the sheathed iron,
    the sword's edges, to the joy of the ogress;
    their strength they shrunk by a third,
    made the young lad sink to the earth.

16. They shook their wool-cloaks, fastened on their blades,
    the god-born heroes donned their fine clothes.

17. The road lay ahead; they found the woe-paths,
    and their sister's son wounded on a   *sister's son* Randvér
        branch;
    a wolf-tree wind-cold west of the   *wolf-tree* gallows
        homestead:
    the cranes' bait kept swinging; it wasn't   *cranes' bait* corpse
        sweet to linger.

18. There was celebration in the hall, warriors ale-happy,
    and they did not hear the sound of horses,
    until a brave warrior blew his horn.

19. They went to tell Jörmunrekk
    that soldiers under helmets had been seen:
    'Consider a plan; powerful princes are here:
    you trampled a maid of mighty men!'

20. Then Jörmunrekk laughed, and smoothed his moustaches,
    he stirred himself to struggle, made war-keen by wine;
    he shook out his chestnut locks, glanced at his white
        shield,
    held waving in his hand a golden goblet.

21. 'Happy I'd think myself, if I could see,
    Hamdir and Sörli here in my hall;
    I'd bind up those boys with bow-strings,
    tie the good sons of Gjúki to the gallows.'

22. Then spoke a fame-glad girl, stood on the threshold;
    she said, slender-fingered, to a young lad:
    'Now they promise what they cannot achieve;
    can only two men fight ten hundred Goths,
    fight and bind them in the high fortress?'

23. A stirring occurred in the hall: ale-cups crashed,
    men lay in blood shed from the Goths' breasts.

24. Then said Hamdir the stout-hearted:
    'You longed, Jörmunrekk, for our arrival,
    brothers born of the same mother, inside your fortress.
    You see your own legs, you see your arms,
    Jörmunrekk, flung into hot flames.'

25. Then growled the man powerful in magic,
    the mailcoated warrior, as a bear would growl:
    'Stone the men, since spears won't bite,
    neither edges nor iron, Jónakr's sons.'

[*Then said Sörli; he had a shrewd mind:*]

26. 'You've caused harm, brother, opening up that bag:
    often from a bag bold counsels come.

27. 'What a heart you'd have, Hamdir, if it was a wise one:
    a man lacks much who has no sense.

28. 'Now the head would be off, if Erp were alive,
    our battle-bold brother, whom we slew on the road,
    a man brave in conflict – the *dísir* urged me on –
    a warrior blessed in battle – they made me kill.

29. 'I think it's not for us, the wolves' example,
    to fight among each other,
    like the norns' curs, reared ravenous,
    away in the wilderness.

30. 'Great glory we have gained
    though we die now or tomorrow;
    no man survives a single dusk
    beyond the norns' decree.'

31. There Sörli fell at the hall's gable;
    and Hamdir slumped at the rear of the house.

This is called the ancient 'Lay of Hamdir'.

APPENDIX

Some Eddic Poems Not Contained in the Codex Regius

Rígsthula: Ríg's list

People say that in the ancient tales one of the Æsir, who was called Heimdall, went in his travels along a certain sea-shore; he came to a farmstead and called himself Ríg. About that story this poem was made:

1. In ancient times, they said, there wandered on green paths
   a mighty and ancient and much-crafty god,
   vigorous and vibrant, Ríg, striding along.

2. Next thing, he wandered in the middle of the path;
   he came to a building, with its door on the latch,
   and stepped right in: there was a fire on the floor;
   a couple sat there, grey-haired at the hearth,
   Great-grandpa and Great-grandma, with her old
       head-dress.

3. Ríg was able to give them advice;
   next thing, he sat in the middle of the bench,
   and on either side the household couple.

4. Then Great-grandma took a rough loaf,
   thick and heavy, packed with grain;
   next thing, she brought it in the middle of the platter,
   broth was in the bowl, that she set on the table,
   [boiled calf-meat, the best of dainties;]
   he got up from there and got ready for bed.

5. Ríg was able to give them advice;
   next thing, he laid in the middle of the bed,
   and on either side the household couple.

6. He was there for three nights together:
   next thing, he wandered in the middle of the path;
   next thing, nine months passed.

7. Great-grandma had a child; they sprinkled it with water,
    the swarthy boy they called Slave.

8. He began growing and gathering strength;
    on his hands the skin was wrinkled,
    knuckles gnarled, [crooked nails,]
    fingers fat, face repulsive,
    back bowed, heels long.

9. Next thing, he began to try his strength,
    binding bast, making bundles:
    he brought home brushwood all day long.

10. There came to the courtyard a gangly girl;
    there was mud on her soles, sun-burnt arms,
    her nose was turned down, her name was Wench.

11. In the middle of the bench, next thing, she sat,
    next to her sat the son of the house;
    they talked and told secrets, made up a bed,
    Slave and Wench, through well-packed days.

12. They had children, lived and loved;
    I think their names were Big-mouth and Byre-boy,
    Stomp and Stick-boy, Shagger and Stink,
    Stumpy and Fatso, Backward and Grizzled,
    Bent-back and Brawny; they set up farms,
    shovelled shit on the fields, worked with pigs,
    guarded goats and dug the turf.

13. Their daughters were Dumpy and Frumpy,
    Swollen-calves and Crooked-nose,
    Screamer and Serving-girl, Chatterbox,
    Tatty-coat and Crane-legs;
    from them have come the generations of slaves.

14. Ríg then wandered by straight paths;
    he came to a house, with its door ajar,
    and stepped right in: there was a fire on the floor;
    a couple sat there, and kept on working.

15. The man there was carving wood for a loom-beam;
    his beard was trimmed, his fringe across his forehead,
    his shirt close-fitting; a box was on the floor.

16. There sat the woman, twirling her spindle,
    spreading her arms, ready to make cloth.
    On her head a head-dress, a smock over her bosom,
    around her neck a kerchief, dwarf-pins   *dwarf-pins* brooch-
        on each shoulder: ornaments?
    Grandpa and Grandma owned that house.

17. Ríg was able to give them advice;
    [next thing, he sat in the middle of the bench,
    and on either side the household couple.]

[18]. [Grandma offered well-ground bread,
    fine and filling, fairly spread;
    next thing, she put in the middle of the platter,
    proper portions of soup and meat;
    all was ample, aptly tasty,
    he got up from there and got ready for bed.]

19. [Ríg was able to give them advice;]
    he got up from the table and got ready for bed.
    next thing, he laid in the middle of the bed,
    and on either side the household couple.

20. He was there for three nights together:
    [next thing, he wandered in the middle of the path;]
    next thing, nine months passed.

21. Grandma had a child; they sprinkled it with water,
    called him Carl; the woman wrapped him in linen
    red-haired and ruddy, with roaming eyes.

22. He began growing and gathering strength:
    began taming oxen, making a plough-share,
    building houses, assembling barns,
    making carts and driving the plough.

23. Then they drove home a girl with dangling keys
    and a goat-skin long-coat, and gave her to Carl;
    she was called Daughter-in-law: she settled under the veil,
    the couple lived together and exchanged rings,
    spread the coverlets and made a home.

24. They had children, lived and loved;
    one was called Fellow, another Chap;
    there was Bloke, Thegn and Smith,
    Stout, Farmer, Neat-beard,
    Owner and Householder, Short-beard and Guy.

25. But there were called by different names:
    Lass, Bride, Damsel, Dame, Miss,
    Lady, Madam and Wife, Shy-girl, Lively;
    from them have come the generations of carls.

26. Ríg then wandered along straight paths;
    he came to a hall, with its doors facing south,
    the door was half-open, with a ring on the latch.

27. He stepped in at that: the floor was spread with straw;
    a couple were sitting, gazing softly at each other,
    Father and Mother, with fingers entwined.

28. The householder sat, twisting a bow-string,
    bending an elm-bow, making arrow-shafts;
    but the lady of the house was looking at her arms,
    stroking the linen, smoothing the sleeves.

29. She arranged her head-dress; there was a coin-brooch
      on her bosom,
    a trailing dress, and blue-dyed tunic;
    she had a brighter brow and lighter breast,
    a whiter neck than fresh-fallen snow.

30. Ríg was able to give them advice;
    next thing, he sat in the middle of the bench,
    and on either side the household couple.

31. Then Mother took a decorated cloth,
    white and flaxen, covered the table;
    then she took some dainty loaves,
    white and wheaten, and covered the cloth.

32. She set out full platters,
    mounted with silver, set them on the table,
    streaky bacon, pork and roast fowl;
    there was wine in a tankard and mounted goblets;
    they drank and chatted, and the day was done.

33. Ríg was able to give them advice;
    then Ríg rose, and got ready for bed;
    he was there for three nights together:
    next thing, he wandered in the middle of the path;
    next thing, nine months passed.

34. Mother had a boy; she wrapped him in silk,
    sprinkled him with water, had him named Earl;
    blond was his hair, bright his cheeks,
    fierce were his eyes like a little snake's.

35. Then there grew up Earl by the benches,
    began brandishing shields, fitting bow-strings,
    bending elm-bows, making arrow-shafts,
    casting javelins, shaking spears,
    riding horses, hunting hounds,
    swinging swords, practising swimming.

36. There came from the thicket Ríg wandering;
    Ríg wandering taught him runes,
    gave him his own name, said he had a son;
    told him to obtain ancestral property,
    ancestral property, ancient estates.

37. He rode from there next thing, through Mirkwood,
    frost-covered fells, till he came to a hall;
    he began to shake his spear-shaft, he brandished his shield,
    he galloped his horse, he drew his blade;
    he began to rouse war, began to redden the plain,
    began to fell the slaughtered, won himself lands.

38. Then he alone ruled eighteen estates;
    he began to hand out wealth, offer to everyone
    treasures and riches, slim-flanked steeds;
    he showered circlets, cut apart arm-rings.

39. Messengers drove over dripping paths,
    came to the hall where Leader lived;
    [they met] a maid with slim fingers,
    white-skinned and wise: her name was Brisk.

40. They asked for her hand and then drove home,
    married her to Earl: she went under the veil;
    they lived together and loved each other,
    they increased their family and enjoyed their lives.

41. Born was the eldest and Bairn the second,
    Child and Well-born, Heir, Offspring,
    Kindred and Kinsman, Son and Boy,
    – they learnt to play, swimming and board games –
    one was called Breed, Kin the youngest.

42. Then there grew up the boys born to Earl,
    tamed horses, curved shields,
    shaved shafts, shook ash-spears.

43. But young Kin knew about runes,
    life-runes and living-runes;
    moreover he knew how to protect men
    by blunting blades and calming waters.

44. He learned bird-song, how to quench fires,
    soothe seas, calm sorrows;
    [he had] the strength and vigour of eight men.

45. He contended in runes with the Earl Ríg,
    he baited him with cunning and knew better than he;
    then he won and gained the right
    to be called Ríg and know about runes.

46. Young Kin rode through brush and woodland,
    let fly bolts, and silenced birds.

47. Then said a crow – it sat alone on a twig –
    'Why must you, young Kin, silence the birds?
    You might rather ride on horses,
    [draw your blade] and destroy an army.

48. 'Dan and Danp own costly halls,
    finer property than you have;
    they know well how to make ships run,
    make a blade felt, make a wound run red.'

Baldrs draumar: Baldr's dreams

1. All at once the gods were gathered,
   and all the goddesses came to speak,
   the mighty deities had a discussion,
   why Baldr's dreams were foreboding.

2. Odin rose up, the ancient sacrifice,
    and on to Sleipnir placed a saddle;
    he rode down from there to Niflhel,
    and met a whelp that came from Hel.   *whelp* Garm?

3. It was bloody on the front of its chest,
    and barked for long at the father of spells;   *father of spells* Odin
    Odin rode on, the highway resounded,
    he came up to the high hall of Hel.

4. Then Odin rode East of the door,
    where he knew the seeress was buried;
    the cunning one began to recite a corpse-spell,
    until she rose reluctant, and spoke the words of the dead:

5. 'What man is that, unknown to me,
    who has made me take a troublesome trip?
    I've been covered with snow, battered with rain,
    drenched with dew: I've been long dead.'

6. 'Way-tamer I'm called, Slain-tamer's son;
    tell me tidings from Hel – I know about the world –
    for whom are the benches strewn with rings,
    the platform fairly flooded with gold?'

7. 'Here stands mead brewed for Baldr,
    the shining liquor, a shield hangs above,
    and the Æsir-folk are in despair.
    Reluctant I told you, now I'll be still.'

8. 'Don't shut up, seeress, I want to question you
    until all is known, and I still wish to know:
    who will turn out to be Baldr's killer,
    and snatch the life from Odin's son?'

9. 'Höd will send off the lofty glory-tree;   *glory-tree* warrior?
   he will turn out to be Baldr's killer
   and snatch the life from Odin's son.
   Reluctant I told you, now I'll be still.'

10. 'Don't be still, seeress, I wish to question you
    until all is known, and I still wish to know:
    who will bring vengeance on Höd for his wickedness,
    and put Baldr's killer to the funeral pyre?'

11. 'Rind will bear Váli in the western halls,
    that son of Odin will kill, one night old;
    he won't wash his hands or comb his head,
    till he puts to the pyre Baldr's opponent.
    Reluctant I told you, now I'll be still.'

12. 'Don't be still, seeress, I wish to question you
    until all is known, and I still wish to know:
    who are those maidens who weep as they will,
    and fling their cloth-flaps up to the sky?'

13. 'You are not Way-tamer, as I suspected,
    rather are you Odin, the ancient sacrifice.'
    'You are not a seeress or a wise woman,
    rather are you the mother of three ogres.'

14. 'Ride home, Odin, and be proud:
    may no one else come back to visit me,
    till Loki slips loose from his bonds,
    and there comes the powers' fate, destructive.'

Hyndluljód: Hyndla's poem

Here begins 'Hyndluljód', recited about Óttar the Simple.

1. 'Wake up, lass of lasses, wake up, my friend,
   Hyndla, sister, who lives in a cave.
   Now is the twilight of twilights: let's ride
   to Slain-hall, to the sacred sanctuary.

2. 'Let's ask the Host-father to sit in good   *Host-father* Odin
         cheer;
   he grants and gives out gold to the worthy;
   he gave Hermód a helmet and corselet,
   and to Sigmund a sword to keep.

3. 'He gives victory to some, to some wealth,
   eloquence to many, and sense to men;
   a fair wind he gives to sailors, and fine words to skalds;
   he gives manliness to many a fighter.

4. 'She must sacrifice to Thor, she must ask for this:
   that he always act well towards you,
   though he has little time for giant-brides.

5. 'Now take one of your wolves from the stall,
   let him run alongside my boar.'
   'Slow is your hog to tread the paths of the gods,
   I don't want to overtax my splendid steed.

6. 'You're being dishonest, Freyja, testing me out,
   casting your eyes on me so,
   since you're taking your lover off to Slain-hall:
   young Óttar, Innstein's son.'

7. 'You're being silly, Hyndla, I think you're dreaming,
   when you say my lover's off to Slain-hall;
   when my hog is gleaming, with golden bristles,
   Battle-swine, that those skilful ones made for me,
   two dwarfs, Dead-one and Nabbi.

8. 'Let's dismount and dispute this, let's sit down
   and discuss the blood-lines of princes,
   those men who have come from the gods.

9. 'They've made a wager with foreign gold,
   young Óttar and Angantýr;
   I'm obliged to help the young warrior
   get his inheritance from his family.

10. 'He made me a high altar of heaped-up stones:
    the gathered rocks have turned to glass,
    and he reddened them anew with fresh cattle-blood;
    Óttar has always had faith in goddesses.

11. 'Now make a tally of their ancient ancestors
    and the blood-lines born of those men:
    which are Skjöldungs, which are Skilfings,
    which are Ödlings, which are Ylfings,
    which are farm-born, which are fair-born,
    the best selection of men in the world?'

12. 'You, Óttar, were born to Innstein,
    and Innstein to Álf the Old;
    Álf to Úlf, Úlf to Sæfari,
    and Sæfari to Svan the Red.

13. 'Your father had a mother decked with necklets,
    I think she was called Hlédís the Priestess;
    Fródi was her father, and Frjaut her mother:
    that whole blood-line was reckoned among the best.

14. 'Áli had been the mightiest of men,
     before Hálfdan the highest of the Skjöldungs;
     famed were the battles the brave ones waged,
     his deeds seemed to spread to the ends of the earth.

15. 'He made a match with Eymund, noblest of men,
     and slew Sigtrygg with cold steel;
     he went and married Álmveig, noblest of women,
     they had and brought up eighteen sons.

16. 'From there came the Skjöldungs, from there came
          the Skilfings,
     from there came Ödlings, from there came Ynlgings,
     from there came the farm-born, from there came the
          fair-born,
     the best selection of men in the world;
     that's your whole blood-line, Óttar the Simple.

17. 'Hildigunn was her mother,   *her mother* Álmveig's mother?
     the child of Sváva and Sækonung;
     that's your whole blood-line, Óttar the Simple.
     It's important to know it: do you want still more?

18. 'Dag married Thóra, mother of heroes;
     there sprang from that blood-line the noblest champions:
     Fradmar and Gyrd and both the Freki's,
     Ám and Jösurmar, Álf the Old.
     It's important to know it: do you want still more?

19. 'Ketil was their friend, the heir of Klypp,
     he was the father of your mother's mother;
     then Fródi came before Kári:
     the eldest-born son was Álf.

20. 'Nanna came next, Nökkvi's daughter,
    her son was related by marriage to your father;
    that kinship's forgotten, but I can still tally more:
    I know of both Brodd and Hörvir;
    that's your whole blood-line, Óttar the Simple.

21. 'Ísólf and Ásólf, Ölmód's sons,
    and of Skúrhild, Skekkil's daughter:
    you must include among many men;
    that's your whole blood-line, Óttar the Simple.

22. 'Gunnar the Side-wall, Grím the Hard-shaver,
    Thórir Iron-shield, Úlf the Gaper;

23. 'Búi and Brámi, Barri and Reifnir,
    Tind and Tyrfing, and the two Haddings;
    that's your whole blood-line, Óttar the Simple.

24. 'Áni and Ómi were both born,
    the sons of Arngrím and Eyfura;
    berserks' clamour of various afflictions
    swept like flame over land and sea;
    that's your whole blood-line, Óttar the Simple.

25. 'I knew both Brodd and Hörvir,
    they were in the troop of Hrólf the Old,
    all descended from Jörmunrekk,
    the marriage-kin of Sigurd (hear my tale),
    the grim fighter who slew Fáfnir.

26. 'That prince was descended from Völsung,
    and Hjördís from Hraudung,
    and Eylimi from the Ödlings;
    that's your whole blood-line, Óttar the Simple.

27. 'Gunnar and Högni, Gjúki's heirs,
and likewise Gudrún, their sister;
Gutthorm was not of Gjúki's blood-line,
though he was brother of them both;
that's your whole blood-line, Óttar the Simple.

28. 'Harald War-tooth was born to Hrœrek,
the flinger of rings, he was Aud's son;   *flinger of rings*
Aud the Deep-minded, daughter of Ívar,   generous one
but Rádbard was Randvér's father:
they were men dedicated to the gods;
that's your whole blood-line, Óttar the Simple.

[The shorter 'Prophecy of the seeress']

29. 'There were eleven Æsir reckoned up:
when Baldr sank against the death-hummock;
Váli was born to avenge his brother's loss,
he slew the one whose hand had killed;
that's your whole blood-line, Óttar the Simple.

30. 'Baldr's father was Bur's heir,   *Baldr's father ... Bur's heir* Odin
Frey married Gerd, she was the daughter of Gymir,
of the giant-race, and of Aurboda;
their kinsman was Thjazi,
the cover-keen giant: his daughter was Skadi.

31. 'We're telling you much, and will tell more,
we think this should be known: do you want still more?

32. 'Haki was by far the best of Hvædna's sons,
and Hvædna's father was Hjörvard;
Brightness and Horse-thief were Hrímnir's children.

33. 'All seeresses are descended from Forest-wolf,
all wizards from Wish-giver,
and those who practise *seid* from Swarthy-head,
all giants are descended from Ymir.

34. 'We're telling you much, and will tell more,
    we think this should be known: do you want still more?

35. 'One was born in ancient days,
    much imbued with strength, of the race of gods;
    nine bore him, a spear-glorious man,
    giant's maids, on the edge of the earth.

36. 'We're telling you much, and will tell more,
    we think this should be known: do you want still more?

37. 'Gjálp bore him, Greip bore him,
    Eistla bore him, and Eyrgjafa.
    Úlfrún bore him, and Angeyja,
    Imd and Atla, and Járnsaxa.

38. 'He was imbued with the strength of the earth,
    with the chill-cold sea, and the blood of a boar.

39. 'We're telling you much, and will tell more,
    we think this should be known: do you want still more?

40. 'Loki sired the wolf on Strife-bidder
    and bore Sleipnir to Svadilfœri;
    one mighty witch most wicked of all
    was born of Býleist's brother.   *Býleist's brother* Loki

41. 'Loki ate from a heart, burnt with linden,
    a half-charred woman's mind-stone he'd   *mind-stone* heart
        found;
    from that wicked woman Lopt came with child,   *Lopt* Loki
    thence in the world every ogress sprang.

42. 'The sea heaves with squalls against heaven itself,
    floods over the lands, as the sky gives way;
    from there come snows and mighty winds;
    then it is decreed that rain should cease.

43. 'One was born, greater than all,
    he was imbued with the strength of the earth;
    they say that he is a very rich prince,
    related kin to every great house.

44. 'Then will come another, mightier still,
    though I dare not speak his name;
    few see now any further on,
    than when Odin will meet the wolf.'

45. 'Bring memory-ale to my boar,   *boar* warrior, Óttar
    so that he will recount every word
    of this discussion on the third morning,
    when he and Angantýr trace their blood-lines.'

46. 'Turn away from here: I want to sleep;
    you'll get little from me of promising prospects;
    you scamper off, concubine, out into the night,
    just as Heidrún goes among the he-goats.

47. 'You frolicked with Ód, ever yearning,
    many have shoved themselves up the front of your skirt;
    you scamper off, concubine, out into the night,
    just as Heidrún goes among the he-goats.'

48. 'I'll fling fire over the ogress,
    so that you'll never get away from here.'

49. 'A flame I see burning, the earth ablaze;
    most have to suffer an end to their life;
    bring this beer to Óttar's hand,
    blended with much venom for his ill luck.'

50. 'Your spell will not succeed,
    though, giant's bride, you summon harm;
    he shall drink precious draughts,
    I ask that all gods are good to Óttar.'

Grottasöngr: Grotti's chanting

'Why is gold called Fródi's mill?' About this there is the
following story, that there was a son of Odin called Skjöld
('Shield'), from whom the Skjöldungs descend. He lived and
ruled over the land, which is now called Denmark, but was
then called Gotland. Skjöld had a son called Fridleif, who
ruled the land after him. The son of Fridleif was called Fródi,
and he took over the kingship after his father at the time
when the Emperor Augustus pacified the whole world; at that
time Christ was born. Since Fródi was the most powerful king
in the lands of the north, peace was attributed to him in the
whole Norse-speaking area, and the Norse people call it
Fródi's peace. No one harmed another, even when he had in
front of him the killer of his father or brother, bound or free.
There were at that time also no thieves or robbers, so that a
gold ring lay for a long time on Jelling Heath. King Fródi
accepted an invitation to visit Sweden from the king who was
called Fjölnir, and he bought back two maidservants who
were called Fenja and Menja; they were big and strong. At
that time there were in Denmark two millstones that were so
big, that no one was so strong that he could stir them; but the
mill had the property that it milled whatever the miller
wanted: the mill was called Grotti. Hengikjöpt is the name of
the one who gave the mill to King Fródi. King Fródi had the
maidservants led to the mill and told them to mill gold and
peace and happiness for him. Then he gave them no more
peace or sleep than for as long as a cuckoo was silent or for
as long as it took to sing a song. It is said that there they sang
the song that is called Grottasöngr; and before the song came
to an end, they milled an army against Fródi, and that night
the sea-king called Mýsing came there, and killed Fródi: he
carried off a bundle of booty. Then Fródi's peace ceased.
Mýsing took Grotti with him and also Fenja and Menja and
told them to mill salt, and around midnight they asked if
Mýsing was not sick of salt; but he asked them to mill more.
They milled for a short time before the ship was overwhelmed

and sank, and a whirlpool formed in the sea, where it spins
into the eye of the millstone. Then the sea became salty.

1. Now there have come to the king's buildings
   two prescient women, Fenja and Menja;
   they were with Fródi, Fridleif's son,
   mighty maidens, to be made his slaves.

2. They were led off to the mill-stand,
   and set the grey stones in motion;
   he promised the pair neither pause nor pleasure,
   before he heard the slave-girls' clamour.

3. They made the never-silent mill scream:
   'Let's set down the stand, let's lift the stones!'
   Still he ordered the maids that they must grind on.

4. They sang and set moving the quick-spinning stone,
   while most of Fródi's maids went to sleep;
   then said Menja, who'd come for milling:

5. 'Let's grind out cash for Fródi, let's grind and make
         him wholly happy,
   let's grind lots of wealth on the marvellous mill!
   Let him sit on his cash, let him sleep on eider-down,
   let him wake to his wishes: then it's well-ground!

6. 'Here shall no one harm another,
   plan any evil or plot any death,
   or strike with a sharp sword,
   though he finds his brother's butcher bound.'

7. He did not speak any words before these: *He* Fródi
   'You two shan't sleep any more than a cuckoo
         over the hall,
   any longer than I can sing a single song.'

8. 'Fródi, you weren't wise enough for yourself,
   speech-friend of men, when you bought your slaves;
   you chose from strength and from appearance,
   but never asked about their provenance.

9. 'Hrungnir was hard, as was his father,
   but Thjazi was mightier than them;
   Idi and Aurnir, our relations,
   rock-giants' brothers: we were born from them.

10. 'Grotti would not come from the grey fell,
    nor the hard slab from the earth,
    nor the rock-giants' girls grind so,
    if we didn't know some wisdom.

11. 'For nine winters we were playmates,
    mighty, brought up under the earth;
    slaves who were suited to powerful deeds,
    we shifted the flat rock ourselves from its place.

12. 'We set the stone rolling from the giants' court,
    so that the earth shuddered beneath;
    we set moving the quick-spinning stone,
    the heavy slab, so that men took it.

13. 'Then afterwards, in the land of Sweden,
    two prescient women, we went to war;
    we baited bearish warriors, we broke up shields,
    we went right through the grey-mailed troop.

14. 'We overthrew one prince and propped up another,
    we gave support to Gutthorm's good troop;
    there was no sitting still, before Knúi fell.

15. 'We carried on for several seasons,
    until we were recognized for our exploits;
    there we scored with sharp spears
    blood from wounds and reddened blades.

16. 'Now we have come to the king's buildings,
    without mercy, to be had as slave-girls;
    mud gnaws at our soles, and chills above,
    we haul the strife-settler; it's dreary at   *strife-settler* Grotti
        Fródi's.

17. 'Hands must rest, the slab must stand still,
    for myself I have ground my share.'
    'We cannot well give rest to our hands
    until it seems full-ground to Fródi.'

18. 'Hands must handle hard shafts,
    slaughter-stained weapons: Fródi, awake!
    Fródi, awake, if you wish to hear
    our songs and ancient tales.

19. 'I see a fire burning East of the fortress,
    war-tidings wakening, a beacon must be ordered;
    an army will come here in a short time
    to burn the dwelling in the face of the prince.

20. 'You won't keep hold of the throne of Lejre,
    the red-gold rings or the mighty slab.
    Let's grab the mill-handle, girl, with more force:
    we aren't yet warm in corpse-blood.

21. 'My father's girl ground forcefully,
    since she saw the doom of a great many men;
    the thick supports tore loose from the stand,
    iron-clad: let's still grind on!

22. 'Let's still grind on: since Yrsa's son
    will avenge Fródi on the Half-Danes;
    he will become known as her son
    and her brother: we both know about that.'

23. The girls ground on and tried their strength,
the youngsters were in a giant-rage;
the shaped wood shook, the stand collapsed,
the heavy slab shattered in two.

24. And the rock-giant's bride spoke these words:
'We have ground, Fródi, until we must stop,
the ladies have stood long enough at the milling.'

Abbreviations of Texts
in the Notes and Index

PrAt	Prose *Daudi Atla*: The death of Atli
PrBorg	Prose *Frá Borgnýju ok Oddrúnu*: About Borgný and Oddrún
PrBryn	Prose *Brynhildr reid helveg*: Brynhild rides the way to Hel
PrDráp	Prose *Dráp Niflunga*: The killing of the Niflungs
PrFáf	Prose *Frá dauda Fáfnis*: About Fáfnir's death
PrGud	Prose *Frá Gudrúnu*: About Gudrún
PrHj	Prose *Frá Hjörvardi ok Sigrlinn*: About Hjörvard and Sigrlinn
PrLok	Prose *Frá Loka*: About Loki
PrSig	Prose *Frá dauda Sigurdar*: About Sigurd's death
PrSin	Prose *Frá dauda Sinfjötla*: About Sinfjötli's death
PrVöls	Prose *Frá Völsungum*: About the Völsungs
PrVölund	Prose *Frá Völundi*: About Völund
Reg	*Reginsmál*: Regin's lay
Ríg	*Rígsthula*: Ríg's list
Sigrd	*Sigrdrífumál*: Sigrdrifa's lay
Sigsk	*Sigurdarkvida in skamma*: The short song of Sigurd
Skáld	Snorri Sturluson, *Skáldskaparmál*
Skírn	*För Skírnis*: Skírnir's journey
Thrym	*Thrymskvida*: The song of Thrym
Vaf	*Vafthrúdnismál*: The lay of Vafthrúdnir
Vkv	*Völundarkvida*: The song of Völund
Vsaga	*Völsunga saga*: The saga of the Völsungs
Vsp	*Völuspá*: The prophecy of the seeress
Yngsaga	Snorri Sturluson, *Ynglinga saga*

Notes

Below, 'pr' refers to the prose associated with the poem.

Völuspá: The prophecy of the seeress

Völuspá is an extraordinarily powerful poem, a fit opening for CR (folios 1r–3r), given that it spans the history of the world, from its mysterious beginnings in icy silence to its fiery end in the mighty fighting that will surround Ragnarök ('The fate, or doom, of the powers'), when the world will be submerged in the sea; and then, we learn, reborn. The apocalyptic ending is a theme in several of the poems, but in none is the description so dramatic or so immediate. In *Vsp* we are invited to contemplate events outside of time – and outside of normal human experience.

The poem is clearly a composite piece, produced in *fornyrðislag* ('old poetry metre'), but with expansions and interpolations, notably the *Dvergatal* ('The tally of dwarfs') in stanzas 9–16, that make the structure and original form difficult to determine. Apparently, the god Odin, addressed as 'Corpse-father' (1), has awoken a dead and unknowably ancient seeress, who tells her own history (2), the beginnings of the earth, sky and timekeeping itself (3–6), followed by a brief golden age for the gods, the Æsir (7–8). As in other medieval verse, especially in the Old English *Beowulf*, which has other affinities with the texts of CR, the poet signals a change of mood by the word 'until' (8), introducing the arrival of 'three ogres' daughters'. The interpolation of the tally or catalogue of dwarfs obscures the structure, but *Vsp* begins again at 17 with 'until' and describes the wanderings of three Æsir, who form a male counterweight to the three giantesses of 8, and who create mankind from two kinds of driftwood (17–18); at that point fate is introduced in the form of three norns, who live under the World-tree (19–20). The first war in the world is described in allusive terms (21–4), and seems to be the result of bad faith on the part of the Æsir, who first attempt to kill the mysterious Gold-draught (perhaps one of the giantesses, although she has also been identified with the goddess Freyja), who will go on to spread feminine magic (*seið*: see note to 22); and then they debate about whether they are liable to have to pay for their actions. The Vanir, a rival group of gods, defeat the Æsir on the battlefield and overrun Ásgard, the home of the Æsir (24). The account of rebuilding its walls alludes to the myth of the 'Master-builder', where again the Æsir are treacherous (25–6). A transition stanza (27) reveals more of the seeress's hidden knowledge, and then the major theme of Odin consulting with a prophetess is repeated, now in the present (28–30) – perhaps the beginning of a different poem.

The rest of *Vsp* focuses on a prophecy about Ragnarök, beginning with the death of Baldr and the binding of Loki (31–5), the ominous mustering of hostile forces and the announcement of the end in all the worlds, as Loki and Fenrir the wolf break free (36–49). Then the opposing forces come face to face (50–52), and we learn of the deaths of Frey, Odin and Thor on the side of the Æsir, and Surt (presumably), Fenrir and the World-serpent on that of the giants (53–6). The old world is destroyed by fire and flood (57–8), only to rise again and see the return of certain Æsir, including Baldr and Höd, both back from the dead, as well as Hœnir and others, including the 'Virtuous folk'; all will live together in happiness (59–64). Stanza 65, not in CR but supplied from the fourteenth-century Hauksbók, only underlines the Christian flavour that permeates the poem. The ominous final stanza describes the dragon Spite-striker carrying off corpses (66).

The successive focus on past, present and future; the 'three ogres' daughters'; the odd switches between the first person and the third person ('she') by the seeress; Odin's consultation with the decapitated head of Mímir (or Mím, if they are not the same) under the roots of the World-tree, Yggdrasil (46); and, according to Snorri, the norns or 'fates', three maidens who lived under the roots of Yggdrasil (see headnote to *HH I*) – all make it attractive to suppose that Odin is consulting the norns, but of all the poems in CR, *Vsp* is perhaps the hardest to fathom. The fact that it survives in other versions, including Hauksbók and different recensions of Snorri's Edda – some certainly more Christian than others – makes clear its allure to Icelanders. In several of the other mythical poems of CR, Odin also consults a wise source about his fate and that of the world. As in *Vaf*, what is given is both ancient lore and prophecy; the seeress speaking in the first person and the third preserves, albeit somewhat confusingly, the distinction between past and present knowledge and future prediction, a contrast echoed in the observation: 'much lore she knows, I see further ahead' (44, 49, 58).

There is much lore, delivered with a sense of urgency, that seeks to explain the sweep of history: our created world is born from the blood and bones of a murdered giant who, elsewhere in CR (see *Vaf*), had himself emerged only slowly from primeval ice. Bloodshed begins and ends our world, alongside a greed for gold, a breaking of vows, and an essential enmity and deep disparity between beings: in the world of *Vsp*, gods and giants are simply born, while men and dwarfs are made. There are different kinds of beings, who might coexist and consult but are not the same, and there are different kinds of gods, who wage war. The Æsir loss and Vanir victory are not found in the other texts, where the Vanir seem subordinate, or simply subsumed.

But stranger still is the ongoing enmity between gods and giants: the gods, Odin and his brothers, murder the first giant Ymir, the father of them all, and then all the gods are attacked by the giants at the end of the world. We are evidently not supposed to sympathize with the giants, and we are seldom given their perspective; they are apparently all killed (but see 66). Moreover, while Christianity has influenced the text and the thought-world of *Vsp*, it is not a Christian poem; the level of Christianity implied is casual and a late addition by a poet on the very cusp of becoming Christian (but not yet having fully embraced it). This accounts in an elegant way for the oddly nostalgic and deferential view of the pagan gods, even as their amoral behaviour and culpable role in their own downfall are emphasized.

The earliest reference to *Vsp* occurs in the skaldic poetry of the devoutly Christian poet Arnórr jarlaskáld (d. after 1073), who, in a series of poems composed 1046–65, refers to pagan gods in a literary and untroubled acknowledgement of ancient history. In one, perhaps composed *c.* 1065, Arnórr apparently draws disparate elements of *Vsp* together to praise his dead lord (*Þorfinnsdrápa*: Thorfinn's poem 22):

> The bright sun will turn black,
> earth will sink into the dark sea,
> the burden of East will break,
> the whole ocean crash on to the mountains,
> before in the Isles a chieftain
> (may God help that keeper
> of his retinue) finer
> than Thorfinn will be born.

This combines the apocalypticism of *Vsp* 57 and 41 with the world being supported on the shoulders of four dwarfs called North, South, East and West (11). It has also been suggested that the use of the valkyrie-name 'Spear-brandisher' (*Geirskögul*) (30) is a misunderstanding of stanza 12 of *Hákonarmál*, which is dated to 961. If both of these links are accepted, then we can date at least one version of *Vsp* to between 961 and 1065. Because several aspects of the description of Ragnarök match with observations of a volcanic eruption (41), *Vsp* is generally considered an Icelandic composition: the activity that created Eldgjá ('Fire-gorge') in South Central Iceland, the largest volcanic gorge in the world, erupted as early as 934. Another interesting suggestion would connect *Vsp* with the acceptance of Christianity at the Althing (national assembly) of 999 or 1000. Attempts to place its composition in Norway or locate in the Anglo-Scandinavian Danelaw are largely unconvincing.

Vsp is found in a variant form in Hauksbók (AM 544 4to), which supplies some of the deficiencies of the CR scribe; his performance here, which can be checked with this early witness and includes the botching of the opening line, does not inspire confidence. It is conventional to attribute all 66 stanzas to *Vsp*, but 34, 54 and 65 are entirely missing in CR, along with parts of 47 and 60; while Hauksbók lacks 28–33, the first half of 35 and 36–7, as well as having a very different, confused sequence for 21–44. Most commentators agree that the 'Tally of dwarfs' is interpolated but disagree about whether stanzas 9–16 or just 11–16 have been added.

As far as attempting to ascertain the earliest form of *Vsp* is concerned, its dream-like structure makes it unlikely that the 'original' can be constructed from the surviving witnesses. The seeress stands (or rather sits (28)) outside time, a living presence perched atop the past and singing songs of the future, not unlike the giant 'happy Eggthér' sitting on a grave-mound and plucking his harp (42). The poem is in its somewhat confused and confusing form a microcosm of CR as a whole, an enlightening and entertaining if fractured overview that seeks, sometimes unsuccessfully, to justify the ways of gods (and heroes) to later mortal men. We might argue that the gods are in the wrong from the start, when Odin and his brothers kill Ymir, so that when the giants attack at Ragnarök they are simply fulfilling blood-revenge for their kin. Certainly, from the Christian perspective of the scribes, the Æsir were fallen, and were bound to fail. Likewise, we, as modern readers, looking backwards to the source and meaning of this text, can find ourselves in the opposite situation from Odin; *Vsp* reminds us of the limitations of individual knowledge.

1   For Heimdall as the progenitor of the different classes of mankind, see the headnote to *Ríg*; 'holy offspring' refers to the supernatural beings described in, e.g., *Alv*. For Odin as father of the slain, cf. 27–8 and *Grím* 48.

2   See *Vaf* 28–35, where the wise giant Vafthrúdnir relies on his long memory to answer Odin's questions about the first beings in the world. The word translated as 'wood-dwelling witches' (*íviðjur*) might perhaps be rendered as 'wooden supports'; the seeress may be alluding either to the position of the different worlds within the World-tree, Yggdrasil, or to nine wood-dwelling ogresses. According to Snorri, Heimdall is the son of nine mothers, and the seeress may be claiming knowledge of them (*Skáld* 8); see too *Hynd* 35–7.

3   For Ymir, see *Vaf* 21 and *Grím* 40–41.

4   According to Snorri (*Gylf* 6), Bur's father, Búri, was licked out of the primaeval ice by the cow Audhumla, who fed Ymir from her udders; Snorri then describes how Odin and his brothers killed Ymir and fashioned from his corpse the world we know (*Gylf* 7).

8   The Norse game of *hnefatafl* is a board-game somewhat like 'Fox and geese', evidently played with pleasure by both men and gods. It is unclear who these mysterious giant women may be; some commentators equate them with the norns (20).

9–16 Brimir ('Sea') and Bláin ('The Blue One') may be alternative names for Ymir. Snorri quotes this verse when he describes the origins of the dwarfs (*Gylf* 14): 'The dwarfs had first acquired form and life in the flesh of Ymir, and were at that time maggots, but through a decision of the Æsir they acquired consciousness and wit and had the appearance of men, although they live in the ground and in rocks.' The interpolated catalogue of dwarfs was – given, e.g., the opening formula at the beginning of 14; the closing formulas at the end of 12 and 16; as well as the repetition, e.g., 'Oaken-shield' (13, 16) and Durin (10) – likely culled from disparate sources. These two names, with Wand-elf (in the original form Gandálf), supplied J. R. R. Tolkien with the names of three characters from Middle Earth.

17 These three Æsir form a parallel with the 'three ogres' daughters' (8). The first humans, fashioned from driftwood, are called Ash and Embla (perhaps cognate with the Greek word for 'vine'; perhaps a form of 'elm'): that fire can be produced by rapidly rotating a pointed stick of hard wood (such as ash) in a groove of some softer wood (elm or vine-wood) provides evidence for an ancient origin for the myth (the psycho-sexual imagery is obvious); their initials are the same as those of Adam and Eve.

In his retelling of the story, Snorri substitutes the names of Odin's brothers Vili and Vé (*Gylf* 9).

18   Little is known from other sources about either Hœnir or Lódur, although the former reappears after Ragnarök (63).

19   Yggdrasil, a common name for the World-tree, means 'Horse of Ygg', while Ygg ('Dread') is a name for Odin (see, e.g., *Vaf* 5; *Grím* 53, 54; *Hym* 2; *Fáf* 43). The idea seems to be that Odin 'rode' the tree by hanging himself from it; see further *Háv* 138. Cf. the explanation for the origin of dew in *Vaf* 14.

20   Another description of the coming of three individuals (see 8 and 17); these supernatural wise-women, generally known as the norns, may be associated with the giant-born 'maidens who pass over the sea' in *Vaf* 48–9; the clearest description of their activities as determiners of destiny is found in *HH I* 2–4; see also next note below. (There is confusion over the precise roles of the norns, *dísir* and valkyries in CR and the other manuscripts.) Line 4 presumably refers to runic inscriptions, perhaps for casting lots; cf. *Hym* 1.

21   Note the change to third person: the seeress drifts between 'I' and 'she' throughout the rest of the poem. She seems here to identify herself with the strife-sowing women Gold-draught (*Gullveig*) and Brightness (*Heiðr* (22)). If the 'three ogres' daughters' (8) are indeed norns (20), both are linked with gold. Gold-draught may be associated with the Vanir goddess Freyja, who is well-known for her vast sexual appetites (which would put a different meaning to the Æsir 'stabbed at [her] with many spears'), as well as her link both with gold and with *seid* (see next note), and if so, the Vanir going to war on her account (24) makes sense. The epithet for Odin 'High One' (*Hár*) might etymologically also derive from a word meaning 'blind', 'one-eyed' (see also note to 27).

22   This form of magic, *seid* (see further *Hynd* 33), is associated both with witches and Odin. *Seid* seems to be a particularly feminine form of magic, to the point where male practitioners might be accused of *ergi* (see headnote to *Lok*).

24   Odin dedicated a host to himself in the account of the Battle of Fýrisvellir in the 980s between the Swedish King Eirík and Styrbjörn the Mighty in *Styrbjarnar þáttr Svíakappa* ('The tale of Styrbjörn the Swedish champion'), where we are told that Eirík worshipped the god Odin, and Styrbjörn the god Thor:

> Eirík dedicated himself to [Odin] in exchange for victory, and pledged to die in ten years' time. He had already made many sacrifices, since

it seemed likely that he would come off worst. Shortly afterwards, he saw a tall man with a hood over his face [presumably Odin]. He gave Eirík a thin stick, and told him to cast it over Styrbjörn's host, and to say: 'Let Odin take you all.' But when he had thrown it, it seemed to him like a javelin in flight, and it soared over Styrbjörn's host. Instantly a blindness fell over Styrbjörn's men, and then over Styrbjörn himself. Then a great miracle occurred, because an avalanche took hold on the mountain, and collapsed on to Styrbjörn's host, and all his men were killed.

The Flateyjarbók manuscript was written 400 years later. This passage from *Vsp* is the only account of the war between the Æsir and the Vanir, as a result of which Njörd, Frey and Freyja, as well as the giantess Skadi, who married Njörd, came to Ásgard (cf. *Gylf* 22–5).

25   Snorri (*Gylf* 41) described how after the victory of the Vanir, a giant offered to rebuild the walls of Ásgard in three seasons (eighteen months), and make them impregnable; in return he wanted Freyja as his wife, and the sun and the moon. The Æsir agreed, insisting that he do so without the help of humans and complete it in a single winter; the giant asked that he be allowed the assistance of his stallion, Svadilfœri; and strong oaths were sworn to seal the deal. Just when it looked like the giant would finish, the stallion was lured away by a mare. The giant complained angrily, and Thor killed him. Some months later Loki, who had apparently been the mare in disguise, gave birth to the eight-legged horse Sleipnir, which became Odin's favoured mount. (Loki is chided for having given birth in *Lok* 33: see also headnote to *Lok*.)

27   Both Odin and Heimdall suffered loss: Odin is supposed to have pledged his eye in exchange for wisdom (28), hence his depiction as a one-eyed god, and Heimdall his hearing. This is the first occurrence of a refrain that grows in intensity as *Vsp* moves towards a description of Ragnarök.

30   The valkyries, literally 'choosers of the slain', are Odin's maidens, who select the Einherjar, so that they can join him in Valhöll ('Slain-hall'): see also note to *Vaf* 41. A rousing catalogue of valkyries is given in *Grím* 36, and their activities are described by Snorri (*Gylf* 36). The formulaic ending of this stanza echoes that of 12. The phrase 'people of the gods' could also be 'people of the Goths', though that seems unlikely here.

32   Snorri (*Gylf* 49) tells how after Baldr, the son of Odin and Frigg, had foreboding dreams (see *Bdr*), Frigg made all harmful things

take an oath not to harm the boy but omitted the feeble-seeming
mistletoe. Loki found this out and when all the gods were throw-
ing weapons at Baldr for sport (since he could not be harmed),
Loki sharpened and hardened a shaft of mistletoe, and gave it to
Baldr's blind brother, Höd, who, with Loki's assistance, killed
Baldr. Loki's punishment is described in the prose at the end of
Lok. 'Baldr's brother' here is usually identified as Váli, apparently
fathered by Odin on the giantess Rind for the purpose of aveng-
ing Baldr. According to the tenth-century Icelandic poet Kormák
Ögmundarson, Odin bewitched Rind by using *seid* (see note to
22). Váli appears in 34 as the name of Loki's son, whose guts
were used to bind his father (but in the *Lok* pr, it is Loki's son
Nari whose guts were used).

33 For Valhöll, see note to 30. For a full description, see *Vaf* 41;
Grím 8–10, 18, 23.

36 The East is the direction of Giants' Domain (*Jötunheim*); when
Thor goes giant-slaying, he heads East, and returns from the East
to Ásgard (*Hár* and *Lok*).

37 As in 9, Brimir appears as a generic giant-name. Snorri seems to
misinterpret this verse, giving Brimir as a beer-hall where folk
will feast after Ragnarök (*Gylf* 52); elsewhere, in the Epilogue to
Skáld, he identifies it with the palace of King Priam of Troy!

38 Like the East (see note to 36), the North was associated with bad
luck; cf. *Ríg* 26.

40 The giantess is perhaps Angrboda ('Strife-bidder'); Fenrir's brood
is perhaps Garm (see note to 44), Spite and Hate, who will swal-
low the sun and moon at the end of the world. See further *Grím*
39; *Hynd* 12, 40.

41 Cf. *Vaf* 44.

42 The giant Thrym adopts a similar position outside his own home
in *Thrym* 6.

43 Presumably Valhöll, see note to 30.

44 The Æsir described as 'victory-gods' in this context is somewhat
pointed: their victory is pyrrhic. According to Snorri, Garm, who
guards the underworld, is a hell-hound, rather like the classical Cer-
berus; he will fight against the god Týr at Ragnarök (*Gylf* 51; see
further *Bdr* 2). *Grím* 44 names Garm as the 'finest . . . of hounds'.

47 Presumably a reference to the World-tree: see note to 19, and
Grím 29, 30–35, 44.

50 Snorri's explanation that Nail-boat is made from the uncut nails
of the dead seems overly glib (*Gylf* 51).

53 'Frigg's beloved' is ambiguous: assuming that Hlín ('Protectress')

is an alternative name for Frigg, she may be mourning either for
Odin or for Frey.

56   In l. 2, CR reads 'wolf', presumably imported from 53, while
Hauksbók and later paper manuscripts have 'serpent'. Loki
taunts Thor with a failure of courage when he faces the wolf at
Ragnarök in *Lok* 58; as Odin's son he would have the first duty
of vengeance, although it is also true that *Lok* may be building on
the same tradition as *Vsp* recorded here.

61   Refers back to 8.

63   Presumably Hœnir will act as chief lot-caster of the gods in the
new world. Cf. *Hym* 1.

66   The dead seeress also sinks, presumably back into the grave, in
Bdr, *Hynd* and *Grógaldr*, on all of which *Vsp* is a certain or likely
influence. An alternative explanation is that the final phrase refers
to Spite-striker carrying corpses: in the reborn world, there will
be no need for dragons or death.

Hávamál: The lay of the High One

After the lofty mysticism and long perspectives of *Vsp*, *Hávamál*, the
longest poem in CR (folios 3r–7v), comes as something of an earthy
and playful comedown. There are several reasons why *Háv* has been
thought to be a composite work, with up to six different contribu-
tors. Large initials, of the sort used in CR to indicate the start of a
new poem, are found at the beginning of stanzas 111 and 138, and
seventeenth-century manuscripts of *Háv* actually give titles to these
sections: *Loddfáfnismál* ('Loddfáfnir's lay') and *Rúnatalsþáttr* ('The
episode of the tally of runes'); the last can be subdivided into *Rúnatal*
('The tally of runes'), 138–45, and *Ljóðatal* ('The tally of spells'),
146–63. Other more-or-less self-contained sections are the accounts
of Odin's seductions of Billing's girl, 95–102, and Gunnlöd, 104–10.
The gnomic wisdom of 103, enjoining the host to do his duty, seems
an unsuitable bridge between these two accounts of Odin's adventur-
ing, and it is directed more at the hapless hosts upon whom Odin as
guest presses himself; in tone and sense, 103 accords much better with
the earlier folk wisdom and sensible words that characterize 1–79.
Stanza 80 opens portentously, but the link settles down to the kind of
cautious advice a viking might welcome, especially given the increas-
ing emphasis on the fickleness of women and untrustworthiness of
men in matters of love; of the fifteen stanzas that comprise this link
(81–95), only five (83, 85, 87–9) lack any kind of love-interest at all.
Having succeeded with Gunnlöd, and so winning the Mead of Poetry,

Odin declaims with some majesty the rest of the poem, with advice and a sense of his magical powers.

What connects all of these putative sections is the character of Odin himself, who appears to speak at various stages. Also an attempt has been made by one compiler, likely before *Háv*'s inclusion in CR, to knit the sections together; the concluding stanza gives the poem its name (164). The appeal for good luck to those who recite and those who know the verses of *Háv*, as well as an injunction to make good use of their knowledge, which is also presumably linked to the wish for further good luck to the audience, links back to the beginning of stanza 2, which sets the scene: 'Good luck to those giving; a guest has entered'. Such a plea has been, of course, the opening gambit of wandering travellers and poets throughout the ages, and the fact that the word for 'guest' (*gestr*) is also one of Odin's names adds piquancy, especially given the continuing focus on the best way to treat guests (7, 31, 32, 35, 103, 132, 135). Likewise, it seems significant that the next two poems, *Vaf* and *Grím*, both concern Odin's undercover travels to a hostile hall to gain and impart wisdom, and contain puns on the identity of the 'guest' as Gest/Odin (*Vaf* 9, 19; *Grím* 9), while *Alv*, a poem that inverts many expectations, but seems based at least in part on *Vaf*, makes a similar point about a 'wise guest' engaging in a battle of wits (8). The process of accretion, rearrangement, rewriting and assimilation that has given us the text of *Háv* in CR is in many ways analogous to the composition of the manuscript as a whole. Given its heavily gnomic and proverbial content, there are many apparent echoes of and parallels to *Háv* in both Norse and other literatures; so, e.g., the opening stanza is quoted near the beginning of Snorri's *Gylf* 2, while the end of 84 is quoted in chapter 21 of the fourteenth-century *Fóstbræðra saga*.

2   Cf. *Vaf* 6–10, where Odin visits a strange hall.

13   The otherwise unknown Gunnlöd might be linked to the giantess daughter of Suttung, who guards the Mead of Poetry, and whose seduction by Odin is described in 104–10 and by Snorri in *Skáld* 5–6; the reference to 'Much-wise' in 14 would then be another name for Suttung, and indeed it is attested as a giant-name in, e.g., *Hár* 26. To support this: first, because Odin stole the mead by drinking it, a reference to drunkenness seems warranted; second, in Norse literature the heron is proverbially associated with vomiting (presumably because of its feeding habits), and, according to Snorri, Odin disgorges the stolen mead by spewing it into vats in Ásgard.

14   Two different characters called 'Much-wise' (*Fjalarr*) appear in
      Vsp 16 (a dwarf) and 42 (a bright-red cock who announces Rag-
      narök); also a name of the giant Skrýmir in *Hár* 26. Here, the
      name seems to be an alternative to Suttung ('Sup-heavy'?), which
      seems just as appropriate as Much-wise for a guardian of intoxi-
      cating mead. See also note to 13.

25   The Norse law-assemblies were called 'Thing' (*Althing*), and met
      regularly at the district and the national level (see *Sigrd* 12, 24;
      Sigsk 27; *Gkv II* 4; *Atm* 101), and even the gods seem to have
      had such assemblies (cf. 61 and 114; *Vsp* 48; *Grím* 49; *Skírn* 38;
      Hym 39; *Thrym* 14; *Bdr* 1).

49   It is not clear what these carved wooden statues are, and whether
      they represent local idols or simply scarecrows; like Ash and
      Embla (*Vsp* 17), they can presumably be imbued with life. There
      are several examples in Norse literature, often associated with
      cultic practice: in Flateyjarbók, Saint Óláf speaks of a wooden
      carved image of Frey worshipped by pagans, while the Arab
      traveller Ibn Fadlān notes that the Swedish vikings (Rūs) that he
      met on the Volga in 921–2 worshipped a tall wooden statue with
      the face of a man.

62   An obscure verse, not least because it is extremely unclear what
      the eagle is doing, and why.

64   Cf. *Fáf* 17.

65   The stanza is evidently missing some lines.

73   Another short stanza, with a sudden change of metre: the meaning
      is obscure, but is presumably cautioning about how fine appear-
      ances can be deceptive: 'the hand' here may be about to strike.

76–7 These stanzas have a close parallel in the Old English poem *The
      Wanderer*, preserved in the Exeter Book, written *c.* 1000; lines
      108–10 read: 'Here property is fleeting, here a friend is fleeting,
      here oneself is fleeting, here a kinsman is fleeting: all this founda-
      tion of earth comes to nothing' (*Her biþ feoh læne, her biþ freond
      læne, / her biþ mon læne, her biþ mæg læne / eat þis eorþan gesteal
      idel weorþeð*). There, however, an apparently secular and heroic
      notion in *Háv* has been transmuted into an argument for the fra-
      gility of the earthly life, as opposed to the heavenly life (as the poet
      goes on to make clear).

78   Fitjung's sons are otherwise unknown; presumably, an example
      of how a family can lose or squander inherited wealth.

80   On the staining of runes, see also 142 and 144.

81   Perhaps a reference to the Norse practice of wives burning on the
      funeral-pyre of their dead husbands; see further *HH II* 46.

84   This apparently proverbial expression, drawn from the practice
     of potters, also appears in *Fóstbræðra saga* 21.

86   Presumably the necessary caution springs from the practice of
     young noblemen ('king') to promise future wealth to potential
     retainers ('young boy'), when such hopes are often thwarted.

96   The link with the preceding stanzas seems extremely slight.

97   Billing's girl is otherwise unknown, although the name Billing
     ('Twin'?) belongs to a dwarf in *Skáld* 47; this young woman is
     more likely the daughter of a giant, given that dwarfs and giants
     often share names. For once, Odin's lust is thwarted; the bitch in
     101 is intentionally insulting. Odin's craving for Billing's girl
     seems simply a desire for recreational sex; cf. his boasts in, e.g.,
     Hár 16, 18, 20, 30, 32.

104 A return to the story of the seduction of Gunnlöd and the Mead
     of Poetry, mentioned in 13–14.

106 According to Snorri (*Gylf* 58), Rati ('Gimlet') is the mythical
     auger used to pierce the rock to penetrate the chamber where
     Gunnlöd was guarding the Mead of Poetry.

107 Frenzy-stirrer (*Óðrerir*) is suitable for the Mead of Poetry; Snorri
     (*Gylf* 58) says the name refers to just one of the three vats guarded
     by Gunnlöd.

110 The story is remarkably similar to that of Völund's revenge on
     Níðud through his daughter Böðvild, in *Vkv*, where the element
     of oath-swearing is also present (*Vkv* 33), though there it is
     Völund who demands the oaths. Swearing on a ring was a com-
     mon and sacred undertaking, and need not mean a marriage
     ceremony; Odin's oath-breaking is serious and highly reprehen-
     sible. Ring-oaths are found in the sagas and the *Anglo-Saxon
     Chronicle* for 876, where King Alfred has a defeated viking army
     at Wareham swear 'on the sacred ring'; see also *Atk* 30. A large
     iron ring (43cm in diameter), carved with around 250 runes in a
     style of *c.* 800, is preserved at the church of Forsa in Hälsing-
     land, northern Sweden, and has been identified as an oath-ring.

112 The verbs 'take' and 'learn' are interchangeable in Norse; Loddfáf-
     nir (who is not attested outside *Háv* and here is a travelling poet)
     is being urged both to follow what is being said, and to assimi-
     late its wisdom.

129 The phenomenon of looking up in battle and going mad is well
     attested, and can be traced to Irish sources, most famously in the
     tale of *Suibne geilt* ('Wild Sweeney') at the Battle of Magh Rátha.
     Geilt seems to have influenced the Norse word *gjalti*, used here
     uniquely in the surviving poetry. The same notion is explicit in

the Norse *Konungs skuggsjá* ('King's mirror'), a Norwegian text of about 1250, describing the ideal conduct of a prince.

134 A 'shrivelled bag' is obscure, although the resemblance of a withered mouth to the opening of a skin-bag is clear enough: see *Ham* 27.

137 This kind of folk medicine leads on to the discussion of runic spells.

138 Odin as a god hanged on a tree with roots unknown, pierced by a spear, and self-sacrificing, has led to comparisons with Christ; Christian influence is possible here, even though many of Odin's titles in clearly pagan poems refer to him as the god of the hanged or the hanging god, and the practice of sacrificing to Germanic gods by hanging is attested as early as Tacitus in the first century AD. Odin is also specifically associated with dedication by a spear in pre-conversion poetry; a later prose account in *Gautreks saga* 7 includes both stabbing with a spear and hanging. On the World-tree as a horse, see *Vsp* 19 and note.

140 The unnamed 'son of Bölthor' (given in other manuscripts as 'Bölthorn' ('Bale-thorn')) would have been Odin's maternal uncle; the relationship between a mother's brother and her son was held to be particularly close in Germanic society, and these uncles often offer wisdom and advice that has a special resonance, e.g. the human hero Sigurd seeks out his maternal uncle Grípir in *Gríp*. The 'nine mighty songs' seem to refer to the eighteen spells in 146–63, although nine healing elements are enumerated in 137.

141 Cf. *Grettis saga* 79, where an old woman carves baleful runes on a 'tree-root' (*rótartré*).

142 Cf. 80.

143 Translating *Alsviðr* ('All-wise') instead of the CR form *Ásviðr*; the giant Vafthrúdnir is described as *alsviðr* in *Vaf* 1, 5, 6, 34, 42. 'Dead-one' and 'Dawdler' appear as harts in *Grím* 33.

144 It is possible that the staining was done with blood, though surviving rune-stones seem to have been painted.

146 Several noble women are credited with runic knowledge in CR, including the valkyrie Sigrdrífa, and Gjúki's queen Grímhild and his daughter Gudrún. The spells here correlate well with the list of Odin's powers in Snorri's *Yngsaga* (2, 6).

149 Cf. the story of Imma in Bede's *Historia ecclesiastica* IV.22, completed in 731, where an Anglo-Saxon captive is freed from bondage through the use of *litteras solutorias* ('freeing letters').

151 For a bewitching tree (presumably a reference to poison), cf. the Icelandic outlaw Grettir Ásmundarson, who, after a bewitched tree-trunk fetches up at his island retreat of Drangey, lames

himself trying to chop it; his injury becomes disastrously infected and so speeds his death (*Grettis saga* 81). For 'right-strong' wood, cf. *Skírn* 32.

155   On depriving supernatural women of their 'skins', cf. *Vkv* pr.

158   Presumably the heathen name-giving ceremony; cf. *Ríg* 7. The same kind of baptism of pagan infants is also described in *Egils saga* 31 and *Laxdæla saga* 25.

160   Delling also appears in *Vaf* 25 as the father of Day; it is unclear whether this is the same character.

163   *Vaf* also concludes (54) with a piece of knowledge known to Odin alone. Odin has no sister.

Vafthrúdnismál: The lay of Vafthrúdnir

Like *Grím*, which immediately follows it in the CR, *Vafthrúdnismál* (folios 7v–8v) is a display of lore between Odin and the antagonistic owner of a hostile hall. In both, Odin's very life is at stake, although since we know from other sources (including *Vsp*) that his fate is to die after being swallowed by the wolf Fenrir at Ragnarök, the threat may seem somewhat empty. Yet in the opening sequence (stanzas 1–4), spoken between Odin and his wife Frigg (who in *Lok* is credited with a full knowledge of fate), she seems genuinely concerned that he may not come back, and in his final comment to her (3), he utters the refrain that he will use six more times at the height of his wisdom-contest with Vafthrúdnir: 'Much have I travelled, much have I tried, / much have I tested the powers', as he asks about the world after Ragnarök, and then again (54) when he asks an unanswerable question. A similarly underhand trick is used by Odin, calling himself Gestumblindi ('Blind Guest'), to win a riddle-contest in *Heidreks saga* 9.

The framing stanzas are economical, but still very full; there is even a transitional stanza to mark Odin's journey (5). The preliminary skirmishes from the hall-floor begin immediately he enters, with a rather aggressive opening: 'The first thing I'll know is whether you're wise, / or really all-wise, giant' (6), and conclude with Odin apparently pleading reticence, but in fact also warning Vafthrúdnir against talking too much (10), which could have come straight out of the opening section of *Háv* (7). The contest proper is a highly choreographed affair, with Vafthrúdnir (whose name seems to signify 'Mighty Weaver' or some such, which highlights his role as a spider-like creature in whose web Odin may be caught) asking the first four questions (11–18). All of them involve simply naming different mythological items, and are little different from the naming tasks that Thor sets Alvíss in *Alv*, a poem that seems to draws on *Vaf* in part (indeed the variant form of its name, *Alsvinnsmál*, is reminiscent of the use of 'all-wise' (*alsvinnr* or *alsviðr*) to describe Vafthrúdnir (1, 5, 6, 34, 42)). After Odin answers the questions correctly, Vafthrúdnir raises the stakes, and invites Odin to join him on the bench, making it clear that this is a contest in which his life is on the line.

The next twelve questions are all asked by Odin, and break down into groups of four. The first set concerns the origins of matched pairs: earth/heaven, moon/sun, day/night, winter/summer (20–27). The next four focus on the time before the creation of the world and the ancestry of the primeval giant Ymir (28–35), although the last might be ruled out of order as being simply personal, since it concerns how Vafthrúdnir comes to have this knowledge. His answer (35) is important in establishing his extreme age, by using a phrase 'the first I remember' (*þat ek fyrst of man*) that is almost identical to the opening words of the resurrected prophetess in *Vsp* 1 (*þau er fremst of man*), and in endorsing questions arising from personal experience, which will allow Odin to win. The last four questions are again about general mythological lore before and (for the Einherjar) leading up to Ragnarök (36–43), and again conclude with a personal question about Vafthrúdnir's wanderings. His answer, namely that he (like Odin) has access to the wisdom of the dead, seems to spark off the final six exchanges (44–55), all of which begin with Odin's refrain about his travels in search of wisdom.

Here again, the first four questions are of a piece, concerning events *after* Ragnarök and focusing on its survivors. Apparently satisfied, Odin asks his last two questions (52, 54), which skip backwards in time and concern personal details of his life, to match the two questions about Vafthrúdnir posed previously (34, 42). Of his own death, Odin is well aware, but it causes him to curtail the contest by asking the unanswerable. Vafthrúdnir's answer is dignified in defeat, switching to the second person to acknowledge his opponent for the first time (55).

Like *Vsp*, *Vaf* concerns Odin's quest for knowledge about the past (20–35), present (36–43) and future, specifically about Ragnarök (44–54). Part of *Vaf* (20.2–55) is also found in the eddic manuscript AM 748 Ia 4to, written around 1300. The final two lines of 31 come from manuscripts of *Gylf*; 40, from a suggestion by Sophus. Bugge; the first two lines of 41 from AM 748 Ia 4to.

1   Odin dissimulates here, since only half of the contest is about 'ancient lore': it appears that he wants to know about his own future, after which he abruptly ends the contest.

5   This is a rare example of *ljóðaháttr* ('song metre') being used to convey narrative movement, and the stanza may be an interpolation.

9   Odin is invited to the scat again in 19. 'Guest' is a pun, apparently
     inadvertent on Vafthrúdnir's part: one of the disguised Odin's names
     is *Gest* ('Guest'). Vafthrúdnir refers to himself as 'the ancient sage';
     on a similar term, 'Mighty Sage', see *Grim* note to 27.

10   This gnomic stanza is very similar in sentiment to many at the
     beginning of *Háv*, e.g., 19, 27.

13   It is surprising, given the unending antipathy of gods and giants,
     that Vafthrúdnir should use such positive terms; presumably the
     poet has intruded his own voice; cf. 17.

14   For the dew dropping from supernatural horses, see *HHj* 28. Cf.
     Vsp 19.

17   Cf. *Vsp* 52; cf. 13.

18   Beginning here, the abbreviations *o.q.* ('*Odin said*') and *v.q.*
     ('*Vafthrúdnir said*') appear in the margin of CR, to signify the
     speaker. Similar extra-metrical marginal attributions are found
     in CR for *Skírn, Hár* and *Lok*. For a dramatization of the con-
     flict, citing this stanza, cf. *Gylf* 51. Vígríd is the place also called
     'Unshaped' in *Fáf* 15.

19   Immediately preceding the speaker-attribution for 20, the scribe
     adds: '*Capitulum*' (Latin; Chapter); the word also precedes the
     prose following *Reg* 25 and following *GKv* III 44.

20   Odin pointedly throws back the adjective 'wise' that Vafthrúdnir
     used of him (19).

21   This stanza is almost the same as *Grím* 40, and may indeed draw
     on it. See too *Vsp* 3, which offers a rather different account of
     the creation of the world. Snorri (*Gylf* 4–8) combines many of
     the details of these three poems in his version. Cf. *Grím* 40–41.

25   Cf. *Vsp* 6, 11 where 'New-moon' and 'Moon-wane' are the names
     of dwarfs.

29   Aurgelmir is only attested in *Vaf*; according to Snorri (*Gylf* 5),
     perhaps extrapolating from this stanza, it is the name given to
     Ymir by the frost-giants.

34   Echoes in part *Vsp* 1.

35   The word translated as 'cradle' (*lúðr*) is obscure, and seems to
     signify a kind of wooden frame. It has therefore also been ren-
     dered as 'coffin' depending on the antiquity of Vafthrúdnir, who
     would then be a witness to Bergelmir's death, rather than his
     birth. In *Gylf* 7, Snorri implies that Bergelmir is a type of Noah,
     and that his *lúðr* is an ark, but that seems his own interpretation.
     The same word appears in *Grott* 2 (translated as 'mill-stand'),
     where it seems to mean the cradle in which the mill-stone sits.

38   The usual Ragnarök ('The fate of the powers') varied and 'fate

of the gods' (*tíva rök*), found only here and 42. There are metrical problems with this stanza, part of which may have been interpolated.

39   *Vaf* is the only source that claims that Njörd will return to Vanaheim after the end of the world.

41   The Einherjar ('Sole champions') are the cream of slain warriors, chosen for Odin by the valkyries ('Choosers of the slain') to fight at Ragnarök; note here that the Einherjar themselves are given a role in the choice. They will fight on behalf of the Æsir at Ragnarök, and practise their martial talents every day – and enjoy continuous feasting.

43   For the nine worlds, see *Vsp* 2 and note.

44   Odin matches Vafthrúdnir's boast in 43 about his extensive travels as a repeated and enigmatic opening to his last set of questions; up to 54, the lines could be taken as flattering Vafthrúdnir that Odin has never met his like, but 54 confirms that Vafthrúdnir has met his match. The 'Great Winter' (*Fimbulvetr*) also features in *Vsp* 45 and *Hynd* 42.

45   Given the link between Mímir and the World-tree in *Vsp* 28 and 46, Hoddmímir's wood may be another name for the World-tree. If so, this stanza offers the only evidence as to what happens to it after Ragnarök. The 'morning-dew', repeated along with this stanza in *Gylf* 53, is seen as an allusion to the manna from heaven that sustained the wandering Israelites in Exodus 16:13–16.

47   Elf-disk is also used for the sun in *Skírn* 4; other names are found in *Alv* 16.

48–9 Who these maidens are is obscure, although we might connect them to the 'three ogres' daughters' of *Vsp* 8, who also seem to bring on Ragnarök. See further *Vsp* 20 and note and *Fáf* 13.

52   For 'when the powers are rent', referring to Ragnarök, see *Grím* 4; *Lok* 41; *Sigrd* 19.

54   Cf. the injunction to keep back a piece of wisdom for oneself in *Háv* 163. Presumably Odin promises his son resurrection: see *Vsp* 62.

55   Vafthrúdnir echoes Odin's words about 'ancient lore', but adds ruefully that he has also spoken of Ragnarök. Since the head was widely recognized as the seat of wisdom, Vafthrúdnir's final words have a chilling ring: he has surrendered his head to Odin.

Grímnismál: The lay of Grímnir

There is something Homeric or perhaps biblical (that is, likely imported) about the way in which Odin and his wife Frigg gaze loftily down, in the introductory pr to *Grímnismál* (folios 8v–11r in CR) and blithely define the fates of mortal men. Like Zeus and Hera squabbling over the lives of hapless heroes outside Troy, or Jehovah and the Devil lightly bargaining about the sufferings of the stoic Job, Odin and Frigg settle their personal scores by proxy. Also the Norse gods walking among mankind is widespread in the poems in CR, and it is in the guise of an elderly couple that Frigg and Odin first interfere in the lives of King Hraudung's young sons. Odin starts it, favouring the younger, Geirröd, and Frigg's Agnar is abandoned to the destiny of other solitary wanderers, a sexual liaison with a giantess beyond the realms of men (see also *HHj* and *Skírn*). *Grím* offers in many ways the purest form of Norse myth, which can come across as a kind of stream of consciousness, working by association, and focused on identification through naming of the wider tradition.

Most of *Grím* is in song metre (*ljóðaháttr*), with old poetry metre (*fornyrðislag*) scattered throughout.

Grím is a display of arcane lore on a level with *Vaf* and even, in its delight in the multiplicity of names and in lists, with *Alv*. Certainly, all three poems are of great use in assessing the older poetic traditions, yet also are ultimately mean-spirited poems: while the gods acquire and reaffirm their wisdom (Odin and Thor), other beings pay the fatal price for their imperfect knowledge (a giant in *Vaf*, a 'pale-nosed' dwarf in *Alv* (2) and a man in *Grím*). Given the range and depth of the lore in *Grím*, beginning appropriately, in the setting in Geirröd's hall, with a list of gods and their dwelling-places (stanzas 4–17), focusing in particular on Slain-hall (Valhöll) and the activities of the Einherjar, it is the kind of text that invites embellishment, including the (likely interpolated) lists of names of rivers (27–9), horses (30) and valkyries (36), before building up to a climax with the names and titles of Odin (46–50). Snorri, evidently recognizing and relishing this store of myth, quotes twenty-two stanzas, whole or in part, in his Prose Edda, and appears to paraphrase half a dozen more, while the Icelandic grammarian Óláfr Þórðarson (active *c.* 1210–59) in the *Third Grammatical Treatise* quotes part of 47 for linguistic purposes. *Grím* is found in the eddic manuscript AM 748 Ia 4to, written around 1300, which also has the prose introduction. Some versions of *Grím*, or at least parts of it, had a fairly broad circulation.

Some readers have seen aspects of Odin's torture as a kind of shamanism, where the extremes of deprivation and pain lead to a higher degree of knowledge (see note to 42). But more intriguing in the light of potential rivalry between Odin and Frigg is the extraordinary Latin text known as the *Origo gentis Langobardorum* (*Origin of the Lombard people*), a source perhaps used by Paul the Deacon for his *Historia*

Langobardorum (*History of the Lombards*), written 787–95/6. In *Origo*, Frigg (called 'Frea', which accords better with Freyja) tricks her husband Odin ('Godan') into giving a name to the Lombards, and therefore a traditional name-giving gift (a victory in battle). Such an early witness only underlines the antiquity of and potential for confusion and conflation in *Grím*.

pr   Hlidskjálf ('Gate-tower'?) is Odin's vantage-point into the worlds; see *Skírn* introductory pr and *Atk* 14 and note. Snorri describes Fulla (*Gylf* 35): 'She is a virgin, who goes about with flowing hair untied, and wears a golden band about her head. She carries Frigg's basket, and takes care of her footwear, and is privy to her secrets.' *Blár*, translated here as 'blue', can also be 'blue-black'; when characters in sagas wear cloaks of such a colour, bloodshed almost always follows swiftly. Note that Agnar is the same age as his namesake uncle was when his adventure began.

5   Ull is the archer god, and most bows were made of yew, so his homestead is appropriately named. Snorri says (*Gylf* 31): 'He is such a fine archer and skier that no one can match him; he is also handsome in appearance, with the talents of a warrior: he is good to pray to in single combat.' Children were given a tooth-gift when their first teeth came out; the reference to Frey's childhood is rare among the gods (repeated in *Skírn* 5, 7), and possibly matched only by the giant Bergelmir's infancy in *Vaf* 35 (Váli is a special case in *Vsp* 32–3).

6   It is unclear as to who this god is: Váli might seem the most obvious option, although he was born only after Baldr's slaying; Snorri (*Gylf* 17) thinks it is Odin.

7   It may be that 'Sunken-bank' (*Sökkvabekkr*) is another name for 'Fen-halls' (*Fensalir*), where Frigg weeps for Baldr (*Vsp* 33). Sága is an otherwise unknown goddess, according to Snorri (*Gylf* 35), who simply paraphrases this stanza, but it is likely another name for Frigg.

8   Cf. *Vaf* 40–41.

10   The phrasing is ambiguous, but aligns Slain-hall with the carrion beasts, the eagle and the wolf. The reference to hanging may be a parallel with the great pagan rites held at Uppsala every nine years, described by Adam of Bremen, writing shortly after 1066:

> nine males of every living creature are offered up, and it is custom-
> ary to placate the gods with their blood: their corpses are hanged in

the grove beside the temple. That grove is so sacred to the heathens that every single tree is considered to be divine, thanks to the death or rotting carcass of the sacrificed creatures; they hang dogs and horses there alongside men. One Christian told me that he had seen seventy-two corpses of various kinds hanging there.

11 How the giant Thjazi abducted the goddess Idunn and was killed by Thor, while his daughter Skadi demanded compensation from the gods and was granted Njörd as a husband, is told in detail by Snorri (*Gylf* 23, 56). See too *Hár* 19 and *Lok* 50. '[T]hat gigantic giant' is used of Gymir, the father of Gerd, in *Skírn* 10.

15 Forseti ('President') is another god about whom little is known; Snorri claims he is Baldr's son.

17 Etymological wordplay between 'wood' (*viðr*) and Vídar.

18 For the Einherjar, see *Vaf* 41 and note. According to Snorri (*Gylf* 38), Andhrímnir is the cook, Eldhrímnir the pot, and Sæhrímnir a boar eaten every day and reborn every night.

19 Snorri (*Gylf* 38) explains that Geri and Freki are Odin's pet wolves, hand fed by their master.

20 Snorri (*Gylf* 38) explains that Hugin ('Thought') and Munin ('Memory') are Odin's ravens. It is, of course, ironic that the aged Odin worries more about losing the latter one.

21 A very obscure stanza: Thund elsewhere (*Háv* 145; *Grím* 46, 54) is a name of Odin, but it might be a river; 'Mighty Wolf's fish' may refer to the Midgard-serpent, if 'Mighty Wolf' (*Þjóðvitnir*) is a name for Fenrir (cf. 'Famed Wolf' (*Hróðvitnir*) in 39 and *Lok* 39).

23 Not clear whether this is the so-called 'long hundred,' i.e. 120; the building may have either 540 or 640 doors.

24 Snorri (*Gylf* 21) explains that Bilskírnir ('Lightning-crack'?) belongs to Thor.

25 See Snorri (*Gylf* 39).

27–9 The list of river-names contains some genuinely historical ones (e.g. the Rhine and the Dvina).

27 'Mighty Sage' is apparently applied to Odin in *Háv* 80 and 142; that rivers might share names with Odin is perhaps explicable in terms of the etymology of his name: 'The Frenzied One'. See too the note on 21.

28 For a river called Lightning, see *HH II* 31.

32 Spite-striker (*Níðhöggr*) also appears in *Vsp* 39 and 66, notably at the rebirth of the new world. More information is given by Snorri (*Gylf* 10), perhaps based on an earlier version of *Grím*.

33 'Dead-one' and 'Dawdler' are given as the names of an elf and a dwarf, respectively, in *Háv* 143.

36 The names of the valkyries seem highly anti-romantic in tone. For valkyries, see note to *Vsp* 30.

37 Apparently the names of the horses that pull Sun through the sky (see also *Sigrd* 15); cf. Snorri's account (*Gylf* 36).

39 Cf. the note to 21. See further Snorri (*Gylf* 12).

40–41 Cf. *Vaf* 21 and note.

42 The meaning is unclear; perhaps a shamanistic ritual, involving a combination of heat and steam, which enables the adept to see into other worlds. The parallel with Odin (disguised as Grímnir) bound between flames and starved seems deliberate.

43 For Ívaldi's sons, described as dwarfs and skilled craftsmen, see Snorri (*Gylf* 42), who appears in part to be embellishing this apparently interpolated stanza.

44 Another seemingly interpolated stanza, evidently mnemonic.

45 Ægir, evidently a sea-giant, is the host of the fateful banquet that is the scene for *Lok*.

46 The catalogue of Odin-names is an impressive illustration of his multi-faceted nature. For a similar list, drawing partly on this, see Snorri (*Gylf* 3, 20).

49 For Grey-beard, see *Hár*.

50 An obscure reference: Midvitnir is the third unidentified character in *Grím* to bear a name ending in *-vitnir*. The other two, Mighty Wolf (21) and Famed Wolf (39), are plausibly references to Fenrir the wolf. If this too is the same being, it implies that Odin (acting in the persona of 'Calmer' and 'Cooler') has tamed Hate (39), who, according to Snorri (*Gylf* 13), is ultimately set to devour the sun.

53 The *dísir* ('ladies') appear in other CR poems (*HH I* 16; *HH II* 46, 51; *Reg* 11, 24; *Sigrd* 9; *Gkv I* 19; *Brot* 18; *Atk* 35; *Atm* 28; *Ham* 28), and seem to be conflated with both valkyries and norns as fateful female figures of power; can be used metaphorically of humans. Here, they simply signal the fact that Geirröd is doomed.

54 For the names Ofnir and Sváfnir, given here as Odin's, see 34, where they are names of serpents biting the branches of the World-tree.

För Skírnis: Skírnir's journey

För Skírnis is a taut and beautifully characterized drama, in which even the sparse stage directions may seem superfluous, and what is unsaid is often of great weight. Given the compact text (folios 11r–12r of CR), much cultural and mythological material is covered. Stanzas 1–27 are also found in the later eddic manuscript AM 748 Ia 4to, written around 1300, where the poem is known as *Skírnismál* ('The lay of Skírnir'); presumably this title aligns it with the versions of the similar dialogue-poems *Vaf* and *Grím* in the same manuscript. Snorri also summarizes *Skírn* (*Gylf* 37), including a slightly variant version of the final stanza. The action begins (perhaps with a dumbshow), according to the introductory pr, when Lord Frey of the Vanir, depicted as a great warrior sitting on the lofty vantage-point of Hlidskjálf – an activity usually associated with Odin or, as in *Grím*, Odin and Frigg – catches sight of Gerd, the daughter of the sea-giant Gymir (evidently an Ægir by another name), and is entranced by her coral-bright arms. His subsequent brooding is taken for wrath, and his doting parents, Njörd and Skadi (herself once ensnared by the sight of her husband's bright legs), dispatch Frey's page Skírnir to find out more. Though in purely mythological terms the proposed union between the god Frey and the giantess Gerd has been read as a 'sacred marriage' (*hieros gamos*), the wooing is earthy and direct: the suitor sending a proxy to traverse a wall of fiery flame to woo and win him a wife is a parallel to the mighty hero Sigurd seducing Brynhild on behalf of his blood-brother Gunnar, and is a central scene of the tragedy of the Völsungs, Gjúkungs and Niflungs in the heroic poems in CR; see further *Gylf* 27–51.

If in *Skírn* the gods do even less to evoke our sympathy than in the preceding poems, there is a distinctly down-to-earth aspect to the main actor. Although Frey and Skadi speak in lofty aristocratic tones, Skírnir, who often repeats the words of his betters, is refreshingly blunt, taking on his mission with some relish. There are six speaking parts: three male (Skírnir, Frey and the giant herdsman) and three female (Skadi, Gerd and her maid). But the male characters have more than three-quarters of the stanzas, with Skírnir uttering 25 of the 42 stanzas, so reducing Gerd (8) and particularly Frey (6) to bit-part players. The focus of *Skírn* is the elaborate threatened curse Skírnir delivers to a silent and presumably stunned Gerd (25–36), which, beyond the more general threats of violence and sex, condemns Gerd to a passive parody of Frey's passionate affliction: just as he stared out from Hlidskjálf, anxious, longing and caring little for food or sleep, so too she will be a spectacle to all. A particular feature of Skírnir's curse is the reference to the thistle (31), for which there are parallels outside the Norse tradition: Gerd, with only joyless sex and evil company, will end up as a withered husk. Rhymes increase with the curse, which is appropriately enough in 'spell metre' (*galdralag*), as opposed to the 'song metre' (*ljóðaháttr*) elsewhere: the use of regular metre at the more tranquil

beginning and end of *Skírn*, with more ragged usage in the confronta-
tion between Skírnir and Gerd, is artful. As befits a poem of pining, the
gods are young, and this may well reflect that it is the only poem in CR
dealing exclusively with the Vanir; the gifts granted and promised,
including a sword, a stallion, a ring and apples are potent symbols of
fecundity; in *Skírn* (as in *Alv*) what is at stake is not wisdom, but a wife.

pr   See the introductory pr to *Grím* and its note on Hlidskjálf and
      Fulla's function. Skadi, the giantess, is Njörd's wife, and there-
      fore Frey's stepmother; see further *Grím* 11 and note.

4   For 'Elf-disk', see *Vaf* 47 and note.

6   The identification of the giant Gymir with the sea-giant Ægir is
      explicit in the introductory pr to *Lok*; Snorri (*Skáld* 25) accepts
      the attribution.

7   There seems to be a stanza missing here, where Frey would actu-
      ally ask Skírnir to carry out his mission; Snorri (*Gylf* 36–7)
      includes the request.

8   Gerd is guarded by a ring of fire, as is the valkyrie Sigrdrífa (*Fáf* 43;
      see too the introductory pr to *Sigrd*), and Brynhild too, in versions
      that identify her with Sigrdrífa (*Vsaga* 21, 29). Snorri (*Gylf* 36–7)
      omits the fire, but includes it in the wooing of Brynhild (*Skáld* 41).

9   Loki taunts Frey about the loss of this sword in *Lok* 42.

10   Cf. Gudrún's conversation with Grani, Sigurd's horse, after Sigurd
      has been killed (*Gkv II* 5). '[T]hat gigantic giant' is used for Thjazi
      in *Grím* 11.

12   The stanza is evidently defective, although no one has suggested
      a reasonable reconstruction.

13   A suitably gnomic and heroic opening that again aligns this
      poem with several of the heroic poems in CR.

16   The reference to 'my brother's butcher' is more intriguing if we
      suppose that Frey has killed Gerd's brother (perhaps Beli?),
      which would account for her reluctance to sleep with him; Loki
      uses almost the same accusation to the goddess Idunn (*Lok* 17).
      Gerd does not appear in *Lok*, but may be (like Idunn) associated
      with apples that can cure old age; see the next note. For another
      connection between *Skírn* and *Lok*, see the note to 37. For
      'much-famed mead', cf. *Lok* 6.

19   'Apples against old age' (*epli ellilyfs*) is not in CR, which has
      'eleven apples' (*epli ellifu*). Snorri wrote of the goddess Idunn hav-
      ing such apples, and, basing his account on the poem *Haustlöng*
      by the skald Þjóðólfr of Hvinir, composed *c.* 885–*c.* 920, describes
      how the giant Thjazi had Loki abduct Idunn, and how in reclaim-
      ing her he was killed by the gods, notably Thor when he chased

Idunn back to Ásgard in the form of a bird. (*Gylf* 25, 56; *Skáld* 21). See also the preceding note.

21   Probably the ring Draupnir ('Dripper'), to which Snorri (*Gylf* 49; *Skáld* 32) gives these magical properties, and which was placed by Odin on the pyre of his son Baldr, but then returned to him from Hel. *Vsp* 15, in 'The tally of dwarfs', includes 'Dripper' (*Draupnir*), and when the word appears in numerous kennings for gold, it is hard to decide whether dwarf or ring is intended; it is possible that they have been conflated.

28   The rhyming effect (glare . . . stare) is also in the original (*hari* . . . *stari*).

32   For 'right-strong' wood, cf. *Háv* 151.

35   Cf. Thor's final threat to Loki (*Lok* 63): 'Hrungnir's slayer will send you to Hel, / down below Corpse-gates.' The punishment for women of doubtful reputation by being imprisoned under the roots of a tree is found for the norns (*Vsp* 20), Hel, the keeper of the underworld (*Grím* 31), and the giantess Hrímgerd, berated as 'corpse-greedy witch . . . / Nine leagues down you ought to be, / with pine-trees growing from your breast' (*HHj* 16). Cf. the variant text of *Hel* 6 in Flateyjarbók, where Brynhild's father, instead of hiding her feather-cloak and those of her sisters under an oak, as in CR, instead banishes Brynhild herself, and has her 'dwell under an oak' (*undir æik búa*). The Old English poem *The Wife's Lament* has its female protagonist bemoan being forced to dwell 'under an oak-tree, in that scraping of earth' (*under actreo in þam eorðscræfe*); it has been suggested that this is a punishment for adultery. The notion of drinking goats' piss is presumably introduced to contrast Gerd's unhappy lot with that of the Einherjar in Valhöll (see *Grím* 25).

36   The import of this runic magic is transparent: Gerd will become insatiably filled with lust for continuous sex with ogres, as payback for her refusal to sleep with the god. For the notion of 'cock-craving', see headnote to *Lok*. On the removal of runes, see *Sigrd* 18.

37   Repeated practically verbatim in *Lok* 53.

39   As she capitulates, Gerd can only refer to herself in the third person, and name Frey obliquely, through his patronymic.

Hárbardsljód: Grey-beard's poem

Hárbardsljód (folios 12r–13v of CR) is a curious text, combining rather choppy bits of interpolated prose (in the poem itself) and verse of an uneven metre. Whereas most of the CR dialogue-poems concern exchanges between the gods and different kinds of beings – the dead (*Vsp*), giants (*Vaf*, *Skírn* and *Thrym*), men (*Grím*) or dwarfs (*Alv*) – both *Hár* and *Lok*, which resembles *Hár* in many respects, are poems of invective: a 'flyting' (*senna*) between gods (see headnote to *Lok*). The frame-tale is simple: Thor is returning to Ásgard after an adventure in the East, presumably including the slaying of giants. He is evidently alone, and wishes to cross a sound, but is thwarted by the ferryman, Grey-beard, one of Odin's aliases (*Grím* 49). The ensuing battle of words is characterized as a conflict between the popular, muscular Thor and the aristocratic, cerebral Odin. Thor threatens, while Odin demurs. Thor boasts of battles and slayings, Odin of seductions and recreational sex (cf. *Háv* 95–102, 104–10). The same characteristics are played out throughout CR, but nowhere more pointedly (see stanza 24). Odin openly taunts Thor about his success with the ladies (some distinctly unladylike) in 18, 20, 30; the last takes place 'in the East', so presumably she is a giantess, and this is the only occasion on which Thor shows any interest, as the two gods banter about having 'to hold down that linen-bright lady' (32). Here distinctions of class and rank seem to operate: Thor is happy to offer his services, but only Odin gets to service the lady. The direct comparison between them is set against each bragging about his own activities and then asking the other, 'What did you do meantime?' (15–39, addressed five times to each). Such clear verbal cues set off stanzas 15–46 (when the question raised in 39 is finally settled, notwithstanding some coarse innuendo) as an example of a formal 'comparison between men' (*mannjafnaðr*), with 1–14 comprising a formal *senna*, and the last section (47–60) describing how a humbled Thor extracts himself from the situation, with Odin's final curse (60) distinctly reminiscent of that uttered by his protégé Geirröd in the introductory pr to *Grím* ('*Get off now, where the trolls can take you!*'). Stanzas 19.4–60 are also in the later eddic manuscript AM 748 Ia 4to, written around 1300.

pr   Thor's travels East usually involve giant-slaying; see also *Hym*, *Lok* and *Thrym*. Odin also appears as a ferryman in *PrSin*.

2   Both Thor and the ferryman (Odin) use derogatory opening forms of address that immediately intensify the conflict: by calling the ferryman 'lad of lads', Thor attempts to assert his social superiority, while the ferryman flings the insult back in his face. The irony is that the younger Thor is in this contest the 'lad', while the ferryman, as Odin, is referred to as an 'old man' or 'gramps' (*karl*) elsewhere, in the *PrSig*; see too *Reg* 18 and pr following. See also note to 10.

3   Thor's proposed diet is scarcely aristocratic, and supports Odin's

later assertions (e.g. 24) about Thor's associations with the common people.

5   Given that Thor's mother Fjörgyn (56) is 'Earth', the point is well made, especially as both gods are still anonymous (see also *Vsp* 56).

6   According to *Grím and Snorri*, Thor owns 'Strength-home' (*Þrúðheimr*) and Bilskírnir (4, 24.); no third home is identified, unless we count Snorri's naming of 'Strength Plains' (*Þrúðvangar*; *Gylf* 21).

8   The names and epithets here are all suitably Odinic, but are otherwise unknown; *Gylf* 21 Odin tricks Thor and lures him in 9 into identifying himself.

9   Thor introduces himself with four resounding kennings clearly designed to impress. Odin, the god of poetry, is entirely unmoved.

10   The name 'Grey-beard' (*Hárbarðr*) is used by Odin of himself in CR only in *Hár* and *Grím* 49, where he pointedly says that he is called 'Grey-beard among gods'. That he rarely conceals his name is of course a lie, but Thor still doesn't get it.

14   The story of Thor's combat with the giant Hrungnir ('Brawler') is a mock-heroic one, told by Snorri (*Skáld* 17) with relish, and involves a horse-race against Odin in which Hrungnir is defeated, and a consolation drink back at Ásgard in which Hrungnir turns nasty, threatens to smash up the place and carry off the more attractive goddesses (Freyja and Sif, Thor's wife), at which point Thor shows up and ejects him. Hrungnir immediately challenges him to a duel. Thor throws his hammer, and Hrungnir's weapon (a whetstone) and his head (also made of stone) are both smashed, and he falls down dead. Unfortunately, a piece of the whetstone lodges itself in Thor's head, and he is trapped by Hrungnir's leg. None of the Æsir can free him, till his own three-year-old son Magni ('The Strong') manages it. A later attempt to dislodge the whetstone through magic is only partially successful, and Thor presumably still bears the wound and the pain. Hrungnir is also named in *Hym* 16; *Lok* 61, 63; *Sigrd* 15.

16   A pattern is established here: Thor fights mighty giants, albeit often compromising his dignity, while Odin plays favourites in indiscriminate battles, uses magic to gain his ends and engages in a good deal of recreational sex.

18   Presumably the 'ropes from sand' refers to the sandy ripple-effect left by the retreating tide, just as the following line suggests erosion by the waves. It seems to mean that Odin slept with sea-giantesses, perhaps in a further search for wisdom. In *Skírn* the beautiful Gerd is described as the daughter of Gymir, another name for the sea-giant Ægir.

19   For Thjazi, see *Grím* 11 and note and *Lok* 50. Snorri elaborates
      in *Skáld* 22 (see also note to *Skírn* 19), while in *Gylf* 56 he gives
      the credit for transforming Thjazi's eyes into stars to Odin,
      rather than Thor.

20   A 'wand of power' is used by Skírnir to subdue Gerd in *Skírn* 32.

22   An otherwise unknown proverb, much like those in the first part
      of *Háv*.

24   Odin has given away his identity here, after which the whole con-
      versation goes downhill.

25   In other words, Odin would be truly supreme among the Æsir if
      he had it all his own way. The implication is that he still needs the
      likes of Thor to kill giants. As far as we know, Odin kills none,
      after he and his brothers dispatched the primordial giant Ymir.

26   Also mocked by Loki (*Lok* 60, 62). Snorri recounts (*Gylf* 45)
      that during a visit to the Giants' Domain, and in the company of
      a giant Snorri names as Skrýmir, Thor is duped, cowed and liter-
      ally belittled when he spends the night in a vast and empty hall
      while loud and terrible rumblings are heard outside. In the morn-
      ing, Thor and his companions discover they have been in
      Skrýmir's glove while he lay snoring nearby. The giant's name is
      changed to 'Much-wise' here (see the note to *Háv* 14).

27   On the inflammatory escalation involved in using the term 'cock-
      craver' here, see headnote to *Lok*.

29   According to *Vaf* 16, the river that divides the land of the giants
      from that of the gods is called Ífing. Svárang's sons are otherwise
      unknown, but given that Thor fights them 'in the East', they are
      likely to be giants.

30   On 'East' conquest, see headnote.

34   Cf. *Háv* 110; Odin is the one who cannot be trusted.

37–9 Berserks ('bear-shirts' or 'bare-shirts') were generally male warri-
      ors, associated with Odin; Snorri says in *Yngsaga* (6):

> Odin could make his enemies in battle blind, or deaf, or panic-
> struck, and their weapons so blunt that they could cut no better
> than a willow-wand; but his own men dashed forward without
> armour, and became as frenzied as dogs or wolves. They chewed
> their shield-rims, and became as strong as bears or bulls, and
> slaughtered people at a single stroke, but neither fire nor iron could
> touch them. It was called 'going berserk'.

The island of Hlésey (modern Læssø) lies north-east of Jutland,
and was named for Hlér ('Roarer'), which Snorri (*Skáld* 1)

explains is another name for Ægir, the sea-giant; the 'berserk' – women – would then be the waves a buffeting sailors. But a more intriguing possibility of these women as 'bewitched' and 'wolf-bitches' is with the sirens of Graeco-Roman legend, which several sources describe as having the bellies of she-wolves.

42 Odin's words, which on one level can be interpreted as a form of monetary compensation, are perhaps intended to be accompanied by an insulting gesture that would make plain that Odin, after Thor's 'cock-craver' gibe (27), is implying that it is Thor who should be sexually penetrated, perhaps even by some form of fisting.

44 Evidently 'the woods at home' is a kenning for burial-mounds (45). Odin communes with the dead to gain knowledge: see *Háv* 157.

48 Loki claims to have been Sif's lover in *Lok* 54.

52 The word translated as 'ferryman' here is more strictly 'herdsman' (*féhirði*), and is so rendered in *Skírn* 10 pr.

56 Fjörgyn is not yet dead, despite Odin's claim in 4. But if the trip is taking place at the end of winter (note 'thaw' in 58), the 'Earth' could indeed be said to be both dead and ready to meet her son. Odin calls the home of the gods 'Odin's lands', presumably to remind Thor who is in charge.

Hymiskvida: The song of Hymir

Hymiskvida (folios 13v–15r of CR) leads on logically from *Hár*, in that its subject is another of Thor's trips to the East, ostensibly to bring back a vast cauldron, or brew-kettle, from the mighty giant Hymir (the disastrous drinking-party that follows its success is described in grim detail in *Lok*). Although in terms of the wider structure of CR, Thor's winning of the giant's cauldron is a crucial part of the narrative, *Hym* is a crucial witness to Thor's other interactions with the giant-world. Other accounts of Thor's exploits among the giants have many parallels of structure to *Hym*, including trials of strength and courage, and a series of challenges. The longest is by Snorri (*Gylf* 44–7), who tells how Thor and his companions Loki and Thjalfi were bested in competitions in the hall of the giant with the suggestive name Útgarda Loki ('Loki of the Lands Beyond', presumably a reference to the Giants' domain). In *Hym* these exploits include Thor concealing himself from Hymir's wrath behind a pillar (stanza 12), demonstrating his enormous appetite (15) as well as displaying his vast strength (19, 27, 31, 34). Little wonder that in the finale he smashes all the pursuing giants (36). While the tale of how Thor acquired his two servants, Thjálfi and Röskva, seems to have been inserted almost as an afterthought (7 and 37–8), the undoubted centre-piece is his encounter with the World-serpent (20–24). This is widely depicted in poetry and stonework: in Bragi Boddason's *Ragnarsdrápa* (*c.* 850) and in Úlfr Uggason's *Húsdrápa* (*c.* 985), and on several viking-age pictorial stones, Ardre VIII (eighth century), Hørdum (eighth to eleventh centuries), Gosforth (tenth century) and Altuna (early eleventh century).

Like *Skírn* and *Thrym*, *Hym* gives a fully-formed quest-narrative. Of all the poems in CR, *Hym* contains by far the greatest density of kennings, and its language is highly allusive; it contains very little direct speech. The poet also uses other poetic forms, *heiti*, for the protagonist Thor: Hlórridi (4, 16, 27, 29, 37) and Véur (11, 17, 21). The name Thor is only given twice (23, 28); by contrast, Hymir is named eleven times in all. I count some thirty-two kennings in the thirty-nine stanzas; thirteen concern Thor, who is described in eleven different ways, and the others demonstrate considerable consistency of subject. For example, the heads of Hymir's ox, the World-serpent and Hymir are all the subject of kennings (19, 23, 31), as is Hymir's boat (20, 26, 27). An individual giant is described as a 'cliff-dweller', 'Hrungnir's hoary friend', 'offspring of apes' or 'lava-dweller' (2, 16, 20, 38), and giants as a group as 'rock-Danes', 'rock-monsters' or 'lava-whales' (17, 24, 36); a head is a 'lofty . . . pasture of . . . horns', a 'hair-summit' or a 'helmet-stump' (19, 23, 31), a beard is a 'cheek-forest' (10); and a ship is a 'roller-steed', 'floating-goat', 'sea-steed' or 'basin' (20, 26, 27). Thor is described as 'son of Dread' (one of Odin's many names), 'Sif's husband', 'Hród's adversary', 'griever of giantesses', 'breaker of rock-Danes', 'lord of goats', 'Odin's kin', 'protector of men', 'serpent's sole slayer', 'Módi's father', 'Odin's son', 'strength-mighty one' (2, 3, 11, 14, 15, 17, 20, 21, 22 (twice), 31, 34 (twice), 35, 39).

In short, *Hym* is designed to appeal to those already familiar with ancient lore, beginning with the first word, *Ár* ('Long ago'): see note to stanza 1. In stanza 38 there is a rare address to the audience, as well as an appeal to other poets ('But you have heard – someone more aware / of the lore of the gods can tell better'), that again marks out *Hym* as a poem for those already well-versed (as it were). It is a rather self-conscious poem that is almost a kind of collection of kennings like that Snorri assembled in the *Skáldskaparmál* ('Treatise on the art of poetry') section of his Prose Edda. *Skáld* 4 directly addresses the different ways to speak of Thor:

How shall Thor be referred to in kennings? By calling him the son of Odin and Earth, father of Magni and Módi and Thrúd, husband of Sif,

stepfather of Ull, ruler and owner of Mjöllnir and the girdle might, of
Bilskírnir, defender of Ásgard (and) Midgard, enemy and slayer of giants
and troll-wives, killer of Hrungnir, Geirröd, Thrívaldi, lord of Thjálfi
and Röskva, enemy of the Midgard serpent, foster-son of Vingnir and
Hlóra.

Snorri then cites seventeen skaldic extracts to illustrate; the overlap
with the names in *Hym* is striking. By contrast, the one explicit reference
to Loki occurs in what looks like a random and perhaps interpolated
pair of stanzas (37–8), giving information that is distinctly out of
place about Thor's goat with the broken leg, and how Thor gained his
servants (also told by Snorri in *Gylf* 44, as a precursor to Thor's trip to
the land of Útgarda-Loki (*Gylf* 45–7), immediately before his account
of Thor's fishing-trip with Hymir). The goats also appear in 7, and of
course Thor is called 'lord of goats' (20, 31).

Just as Odin travels alone and as one of three, Thor travels alone
(as in *Hár*) or alongside one or more of the Æsir. Loki is his compan-
ion in *Thrym*, just as (according to Snorri) he was when Thor travelled
to the court of the giant Útgarda-Loki, whose very name and tricky
dealings with Thor seem to reveal him as Loki's alter ego. Other trans-
lations and interpretations have assumed that in *Hym* Thor is
accompanied by Týr, and that Hymir is Týr's father, although there is
no evidence for either identification. The word *týr* does indeed occur
in stanza 4 (see note), but while it may signify the god's name (as it
clearly does in, e.g., *Lok* 38, 40), it can also simply mean 'god' and,
given the allusive nature of the language of *Hym* as a whole, one
might find the latter more likely. This god, in offering 'welcome
advice', tells us that he has the 'hugely-wise' and 'fierce' giant Hymir
for a father (5), and when Thor asks if Hymir's cauldron can be
obtained, answers laconically: 'If, friend, we two do it with cunning'
(6). He then accompanies Thor on his journey, where they first leave
the goats that pull Thor's chariot with Egil (7), presumably the 'lava-
dweller' (giant) who has to give up two of his children as recompense
for damaging one of the goats (37, 38). But the god who is described
elsewhere as possessing cunning, offering advice, having a giant for a
father, accompanying Thor on expeditions to the Giants' Domain, and
being present when Egil was forced to offer Thor his children is Loki.
And the laming of Thor's goat is explicitly attributed to him in 37
('vice-wise Loki had caused it'); Loki is 'vice-wise' (*lævíss*) in *Lok* 54.
The argument in *Lok* that he deliberately provokes the gods at the
feast in order to bring Ragnarök closer gains a particular poignancy if
he is also responsible for bringing in the cauldron.

Hym is also found in the later eddic manuscript AM 748 Ia 4to, written around 1300, and although the episode of the cauldron does not feature in the Prose Edda, the tale of Thor fishing for the World-serpent is in *Gylf* 48, where Snorri insists: '[Thor] set out on his trip so quickly that he took with him no chariot, no goats and no companions.'

1   *Ár* (translated here as 'Long ago') comes at or near the beginning of four other poems in CR (*Vsp* 2, 3; *HH I* 1; *Gkv I* 1; *Sigsk* 1), and perhaps a fifth (the meaning in *Atk* 1 is disputed), as well as in several other eddic poems not in CR (*Ríg* 1); it was presumably a traditional opening. For the general scenario, cf. *Lok* 3, 4, 7, 8, 10, 65. There is perhaps a pun on the interchangeable forms *saðir / sannir* ('sated' or 'full' / 'true'), since the latter is connected etymologically with *senna* ('invective', 'flyting') that defines *Lok*. For the practice of casting lots, presumably inscribed with runes that could be read and interpreted, cf. *Vsp* 20, 63. The sea-giant Ægir as chief brewer for the gods appears in the skaldic poem *Sonatorrek*, composed *c.* 980 by the celebrated Icelandic poet Egill Skallagrímsson, who mourns the loss of his son at sea and blames the 'ale-smith' (*ölsmiðr*, stanza 8).

2   Perhaps contains an echo of *Vsp* 28.

4   The word translated 'one' here is usually taken to be the god Týr, but I follow other commentators in preferring the reading *týr* ('a god'), here tentatively identified with Loki: see also headnote and note to 6. For Hlórridi as a name for Thor, see headnote and also *Lok* 54, 55; *Thrym* 7, 8, 14, 31.

5   For Thor's trips to the East, see too 35; and for other poems in CR, see *Hár* 23; *Lok* 60, and their introductory pr. For Élivágar, see *Vaf* 31, and 'heaven's edge' is also mentioned in *Vaf* 37.

6   The form *Veiztu* ('Do you know?') here, the response to Hymir's son, is used emphatically and repeatedly in *Lok*, generally in the variant sense of 'I tell you' (*Lok* 4, 5, 23, 27, 42, 43, 50, 51), but always by or to Loki, and this may offer further evidence that he is the god (*týr*) referred to in 4. The dual form ('we two') is also used in 9 and 11, as it is in *Thrym* 20, where it refers to Loki and Thor.

7   Elsewhere in CR, Ásgard is only named in *Thrym* 18. The role of the giant Egil, who eventually gives up his two children to be Thor's servants (37–8), is told by Snorri (*Gylf* 44, 47–8).

11   To the extent that the kenning 'Hród's adversary' is Thor, Hród must be an otherwise unknown giant, although it is worth noting that Fenrir the wolf is called Hródvitnir ('Famed Wolf') in *Grím* 39 (and see note to *Grím* 21), and in CR *Vsp* 56 appears to note that Thor battles Fenrir; cf. *Lok* 39.

12 The word translated as 'pillar-beam' (*áss*) also signifies one of the Æsir. Since Thor is an Æsir, some pun seems likely.

15 For 'shorter by a head', see too *Fáf* 34, 38; Thor's vast appetite also features in *Thrym* 24.

16 On Thor's battle with Hrungnir, see *Hár* note to 14.

17 For a parallel kenning, also referring to Thor, see Þjóðólfr of Hvinir, *Haustlöng* 18.

18 Cf. *Hár* 1–2, where the poet presents Thor as a lad (*sveinn*). Similarly coloured oxen are found in *Thrym* 23.

19 The gap can be supplied from Snorri's account (*Gylf* 48), where Thor uses the giant ox-head as fishing-bait. Hymir says he is worried to be heading out towards the deep waters where the World-serpent lives, but Thor, who probably planned to fish for it all along, is unperturbed.

20 The menagerie implied by the combination of kennings is striking, and presumably deliberate, so adding to the comic effect.

22 See further *Vsp* 54–5.

23 Loki sired both Fenrir the wolf and the World-serpent on Strife-bidder. See further *Vsp* 51 and *Hynd* 40.

24 The rhyme (groaned . . . thundered) is in the original (*hrutu . . . þutu*). The general disturbance among 'rock-monsters', whether they are giants or dwarfs, resembles the apocalyptic disquiet in *Vsp* 48. The gap can again be supplied from Snorri's account, which describes the terror felt by Hymir on seeing the World-serpent, and his immediate decision to cut the line (*Gylf* 48).

26 This unusual kenning presumably refers to Thor's usual mode of transport, a goat-drawn chariot: see 7; cf. Thor as 'lord of goats' in 20, 31.

31 Cf. the kenning 'hair-summit' in stanza 23. For the giant as an 'old' man, see 10 and 32, while Thor as a young man is contrasted in 18. Also cf. the opening stanzas of *Hár*.

34 Thor's foot sinking into the floor with the effort of lifting the cauldron is echoed vividly in many of the pictorial stones (see headnote), with scenes of his trying to land the World-serpent; a foot is often seen piercing the floor of the boat.

38 See the note to 7.

Lokasenna: Loki's home-truths

Lokasenna is the most knowing and allusive of the mythological poems in CR (folios 15r–17r). The *senna* ('invective', 'flyting'), found also in *Hár* and the Helgi-lays (*HH I*, *HHj* and *HH II*), is related in form to the practice of *mannjafnaðr* ('comparison between men'); both aim at one-upmanship and the exposure of the opponent's personal weaknesses or shameful activities. Obviously, the force of the invective increases exponentially with the accuracy and disgracefulness of the charge, and etymologically *senna* seems to be related to the Old English *sōð* ('true', 'truth') and the Old Norse *saðr*, *sannr* ('true'); such a contest would have no point if it were simply lies.

The framing of *Lok* leads on smoothly from the hunt for a giant cauldron in *Hym*, gaining added point if Thor's companion was Loki. Indeed, Loki's parting shot to Ægir (stanza 65), the unwitting and unwilling host of the Æsir, seems to damn Ægir to the same fate as his newly acquired cauldron. And a similarly apocalyptic fate of destruction through fire and water awaits the world itself after Ragnarök (*Vsp* 57–8).

Fate, and specifically that leading up to Ragnarök, is a concept central to *Lok*, as it is indeed a thread in the other wisdom-poems, notably *Vsp* and *Vaf*, both of which seem to have been familiar to the poet of *Lok*, who plays on the concept of shared and shocking knowledge. Loki knows that he will be bound (49, 50), and he responds to Frey's taunting about the binding of Loki's son, Fenrir the wolf (41), by reminding Frey of his own future (42). At the height of his taunts (58), Loki even baits Thor, returning from his giant-slaying feats, with cowardice after Fenrir consumes Odin, here grimly described as 'Victory-father' to remind Thor that Ragnarök will be no victory for him or the father he should avenge. The spiteful description of Odin at his death is Loki's response to Odin's equally loaded, if perhaps more rueful, description of Loki as 'the wolf's father', when Odin permits him to return to the feast after Loki reminds him of their blood-brotherhood (10). Vídar, the son Odin asks to give up his seat, will avenge him against Fenrir, and by referring to Loki as the father of the wolf that will kill him, Odin reminds Loki of his own shameful past, as the father of monsters, as well as the fate that binds them all. Odin's provocative opening contradicts his hope that Loki will moderate his words: Loki is clearly bent on provocation himself.

Unlike the other mythological poems, the timing of *Lok* is more precise: the war between the Æsir and the Vanir is over (Loki taunts Njörd with his former hostage-status (34–5)); Fenrir is bound (Loki taunts Týr with the hand he lost (38–9)); and Baldr is dead (27–8). The only remaining events fated to occur before Ragnarök, as given in *Vsp*, are the binding of Loki, the freeing of Fenrir and the unbinding of Loki (*Vsp* 35, 44, 51). Loki's purpose in *Lok* is then plain: to provoke his own binding and so hasten Ragnarök, and to remind the gods of how degenerate they are; none escapes whipping. The prose ending shows how successful Loki was; the parallel passage in Snorri's Prose Edda (*Gylf* 50) relates Loki's capture immediately after the death of Baldr (*Gylf* 50), which itself follows the account of Thor's fishing-expedition with Hymir (*Gylf* 48). In his account of the fishing-expedition, however, no mention is made of the search for a cauldron nor of Loki's provocation, although Snorri does quote a verse (*Gylf* 20), put into the mouth of Odin and reproaching him for attacking Frigg, that combines aspects of *Lok* 21 (Odin on Gefjon) and 29 (Freyja on Frigg).

Lok therefore represents a quite different kind of truth-seeking. Loki is the unwelcome visitor to the halls of the gods, bringing equally unwelcome truths. But just as Odin's dialogues with hostile hosts have a higher purpose in eliciting or exhibiting knowledge, so too Loki draws out information about the future. The language is shockingly crude, and deliberately so: the fucking, shitting, pissing and farting deliciously undercut the decorum of the feast. The introductory pr, which has details not corroborated in the poem, is evidently a later addition produced to attach *Lok* to *Hym*, its immediate predecessor in CR: despite having brought home the cauldron at the end of *Hym* for the feast, Thor apparently departs again to the East – since he cannot appear until the end. The introductory pr emphasizes the married couples at the feast: Odin and Frigg, Bragi and Idunn, Njörd and Skadi; presumably Frey and Freyja are to be seen in the same light, as are Frey's servants. This focus is all the more intriguing because the three poems that follow in CR (*Thrym*, *Vkv* and *Alv*) all concern thwarted or failed marriages; given that the focus of Loki's attacks are to depict the males as cowards or effeminate and the women as unfaithful or promiscuous, it is clear that the martial and marital failings of the gods are dissected along gender lines.

Loki is accused of being 'mad' (21 and 29), 'drunk' (47) and 'out of [his] mind' (21, 47), but it is clear that he alone keeps his cool, even in the face of Thor's naked aggression, the only one apart from Loki to use the crude 'Shut your mouth' form (*Þegi þú*) repeatedly (57ff.), which only emphasizes his linguistic and imaginative poverty. Loki uses the phrase a dozen times (from 17), but outside *Lok*, it occurs only twice more in CR (*Gkv I* 24 and *Thrym* 18). Loki says it to Thor in *Thrym*, so a connection between *Thrym* and *Lok* seems a possibility, the more so in that they are the only CR poems to use *vergjörn* ('mad for men'): by Loki of Idunn and Frigg (*Lok* 17, 26), by Freyja of herself in *Thrym* 13, in response to a request to go to Giants' Domain. Verbal connections link *Lok* to other CR poems, and some are strong enough to suggest that the poet of *Lok* is using them carefully and with great skill.

Some parallels can of course be discounted as commonplace; it is hard to see any point, for example, in the shared 'Hail, gods; hail, goddesses' that open *Lok* 11 and a similar greeting in *Sigrd* 4, except that in both the speakers have just been offered a drink. But there are more specific links between *Lok* and *Háv*: Loki's warning comment to Eldir (5) about talking too much seems ironic given Loki's subsequent garrulous behaviour, and this has a number of verbal parallels with *Háv* 27. Loki's jibe at Freyja (30) that she is 'scarcely free from flaws' seems ironic, given the warning of *Háv* 22: 'he doesn't know what he ought to know: that he's not free from flaws'. Freyja's response to Loki (31) that 'Your tongue is treacherous: I think one day / it'll gabble you into grief' has a close parallel in the same section of *Háv* (29): 'a fast-talking tongue, unless held by its owner, often gabbles itself into grief'. There are other minor parallels (e.g., cf. *Lok* 13 and *Háv* 16; *Lok* 23, 24 and *Háv* 103), including that it is Loki, not Odin, who comes into a hostile hall for a contest of wits.

Moreover, just as Odin when entering Vafthrúdnir's hall (*Vaf* 8) immediately declares himself 'thirsty', so too does Loki (*Lok* 6). Although the pr interlude after stanza 10 says that Vídar poured a drink for Loki, and he is accused of being drunk (47), we are told he spoke *before* drinking, so that it is left to Sif, in a late attempt to make peace, to offer Loki a drink (53). Rather ominously, her words echo closely those spoken by Gerd in *Skírn* 37, where they signify her capitulation. Once again, the arch fitness of the parallel strongly suggests that the poet of *Lok* knows exactly what he is doing.

Further confirmation of this poet's skill at echoing deliberately other mythological poems in CR can be found in the final exchanges between Loki and Thor. Given their hostility, we might perhaps expect some resemblance to *Hár*, and indeed Thor's repetitive and ultimately impotent invective is similar. Specifically, in the mythological CR poems the most explosive charge that can be brought against a male god is that he is a 'cock-craver' (adjectival form: *argr* or *ragr*; *ergi* is the noun ('cock-craving'); *Hár* uses the metathesized form *ragr*, but the sense is the same); legally and in the human sphere, a man could kill another with impunity for calling him this without substantive cause. (In *Thrym* 17, Thor complains that the plan to dress him up as Freyja would lay him open to the charge.) It is only vocalized, to the man's face, three times about Odin and six about Loki: neither troubles to dispute the allegation, and with good reason: several poems show that both had played a woman's part (albeit with more gusto by Loki). The first time the word is used of Odin in *Hár* 27, Thor says: 'Grey-beard, you cock-craver, I'd smash you into Hel', and the last time Thor speaks in *Lok*, he makes much the same empty threat (63): he 'will send you to Hel, down below Corpse-gates'. The poet of *Lok* seems also to be alluding to Skírnir's threatened curse which condemns Gerd to insatiable 'cock-craving' (*ergi*) with only hideous giants to satisfy her lust 'down below Corpse-gates' (*fyr nágrindr neðan* (*Skírn* 35–6)).

More impressive still is the insult in *Lok* 60 that Odin throws at Thor, alluding to *Hár* 26, when Thor spent the night in a giant's glove; Odin taunts Thor: 'since in a glove's thumb you huddled, fine fighter, and scarcely did you seem then like Thor'. The word translated as 'fine fighter' (*einheri*) is an allusion to the Einherjar, the dead heroic warriors who will fight alongside the Æsir at Ragnarök, but it also refers to Loki's complaint to Odin that he sometimes lets the weaker warriors win (22–3; Odin does not deny it), presumably so that the slaughtered and unfairly defeated stronger warriors will be available to fight for him on that fateful day. But this form is not found elsewhere, and in the context of the charge of cowardice, has also been interpreted as 'solitary hare', a creature widely renowned for its timidity. Loki is here responding to Thor's initial threat (59): 'I'll cast you up on the roads to the East: / then no one will see you again', which draws on a boast that Thor makes in *Hár* 19, when he talks of how he made Thjazi famous:

> 'I slew Thjazi, the great-hearted giant,
> and cast up the eyes of Allvaldi's son
> into the shining sky . . .'

Indeed, Loki's skill as a playful word-twister is enshrined in his name, to judge by Gefjon's question (19): 'Is it not known of Lopt [= Loki] that he likes to play [*leikinn*] / and that all gods properly appreciate him?'

Frigg expresses the futile hope that all the home-truths that Loki utters should be kept decently hidden (25): 'past history is best kept concealed'. But 'past history' (*forn rök*) introduces 'fate' (*rök*), Loki's central concern, especially with regard to Ragnarök. Frey's 'until the powers are rent' (41) echoes the prophetic language of *Vsp*, but also *Grím* 4 and *Sigrd* 19, where this phrase appears. It is perhaps surprising that *Lok* does not make more explicit use of *Vsp*, but Loki's last words to Thor (64): 'since I know you do throw blows', may allude to Thor acting against the giant master-builder, after others have sworn solemn oaths in *Vsp* 26: 'Thor alone threw blows there.' Even as he leaves, Loki is on the offensive.

pr For Ægir and Gymir, see note to *Skírn* 6. Given the focus on married couples, it is possible that this was a wedding-feast for Frey and Gerd, although there is no evidence to support this. The hall as '*a great place of sanctuary*' simply indicates that no weapons were to be carried.

6   For 'much-famed mead', cf. *Skírn* 16.

9   Loki appears as a travelling companion to both Odin and Thor; here he pulls rank by asserting his rights as a blood-brother to the one presiding. On the ceremony of blood-brotherhood, see note to *Brot* 17.

10 Odin's response to Loki is hardly friendly; in describing him as 'the wolf's father', he condemns Loki as a father of monsters and reminds him that his son lies bound by the gods (see further *Vsp* 35; *Hynd* 40–41). Odin's claim that the gods should tolerate their unwelcome guest is disingenuous, given his knowledge of the workings of fate.

16 '[A]dopted kin' is perhaps intended as a sign that neither Bragi nor Idunn was born Æsir.

17 On 'brother's butcher', see note to *Skírn* 16.

20 Snorri (*Gylf* 35) states that Gefjon was a virgin, and was attended by all who died virgins, but this is totally at odds with this stanza and with *Gylf* 1, where Gefjon, 'a certain wandering woman', was granted Zealand by King Gylfi as a reward 'for his entertainment'. Being granted a jewel in exchange for sex with 'that white boy' (Heimdall?) sounds very like Freyja's acquisition of the *Brísingamen* (see *Thrym* 13 and note).

22 For the 'weaker warriors', see the headnote. In *Eiríksmál* 7, Odin says that he needs them for his battle with the Wolf (Fenrir) at Ragnarök.

24 Sámsey is an island in Denmark, north of Fyn.

26 Fjörgyn is more usually the mother of Thor (see too *Vsp* 56 and *Hár* 56).

28 See further *Vsp* 32; Snorri elaborates further (*Gylf* 49).

32 For Loki's description of Freyja as a 'witch' (*fordæða*; also in *Sigrd* 26), see further *Vsp* 22, and *Vsp* notes to 21 and 22. The Vanir accepted marriage between brother and sister: see also 36. In the heroic poems of CR, the only case of sibling incest recorded is the hero Sigmund and Signý, producing Sinfjötli. It is odd that Frey does not respond here.

34 On Njörd's role as a hostage, see further *Vaf* 39.

36 The word translated as 'expected' (*ván*) is a pun on Vanir.

38   Snorri elaborates vividly on the tale of the binding of Fenrir (*Gylf* 25, 34).

40   Nothing more is known of this lurid tale, which is well in keeping with Loki's boasts.

41   Snorri (*Gylf* 32) adds that the river, which he calls 'Wanting' (*Ván*), presumably punning again on Vanir, is formed from the slavering jaws of the bound wolf. The language recalls *Vsp*, and points to Ragnarök and the events that lead up to it; cf. 49 and 58.

42   According to *Skírn* 8–9, Frey gave Skírnir his magical sword, one that fights 'of itself'. Muspell's sons will ride over Mirkwood at Ragnarök (*Vsp* 51).

44   This and 46 play on Byggvir's name: 'Barley'.

47   Heimdall's comments on Loki's supposed drunkenness (which come directly after the intervention of Byggvir (Barley)) have general parallels with the gnomic injunctions of *Háv* 11–14, 27–9; *Vaf* 10.

48   It is clear from *Vsp* 19 and 27 that the World-tree (a fair translation of Heimdall's name) is covered in white mud.

49   Presumably the 'tail' is an allusion to Loki's role as the mother of Odin's eight-legged horse Sleipnir, after Loki in the guise of a mare lured away the giant stallion Svadilfœri: see note to *Vsp* 25. Loki's role makes the charge of 'cock-craving' (*ergi*) stick. Further horse-related insults of a similar kind are found in the flyting in *HHj* 20–21. For Loki's punishment, cf. *Vsp* 34–5. For Thjazi, see notes to *Grím* 11 and *Skírn* 19. For the binding of Loki, see pr ending to *Lok*.

51   Skadi's 'cold counsels' seems to hint at a proverbial expression that 'cold are the counsels of women'; on which see headnote to *Vkv*.

52   Loki as Skadi's lover is nowhere else attested, although the odd description of her as 'bright bride of the gods' (*Grím* 11) might at a stretch be held to imply promiscuity. Snorri describes how Loki made Skadi laugh, one of the conditions of her settlement with the gods (*Gylf* 56): 'So Loki tied a piece of string around the beard of a nanny-goat, and the other end around his balls, and they tugged each other to and fro, squealing loud. Then Loki collapsed into Skadi's lap, and she laughed.' The obvious sexual imagery, together with Loki, perhaps naked, collapsing 'into Skadi's lap', may lie behind his innuendo here.

53   Almost the same stanza is found in *Skírn* 37.

54   Odin taunts Thor with his wife's infidelity in *Hár* 48, while

Snorri describes when Loki got close enough to Sif to cut off all her hair (*Skáld* 35). Loki, by mentioning the title Hlórridi (unique to *Lok*), seems to prompt Thor's immediate appearance.

57   On Thor's repeated opening, see headnote.

58   For Thor fighting the wolf, see note to *Vsp* 56.

59   On Thor's threat to Loki to 'cast you up', see headnote.

60   On Skrýmir (62) and his glove, see headnote and the note to *Hár* 26.

61   On Thor's battle with Hrungnir, see note to *Hár* 14.

pr   Snorri explains that Narfi, in the shape of a wolf, rips his brother Nari apart (*Gylf* 50). See further *Vsp* 34 (and note to *Vsp* 32). A parallel to Loki's punishment, being buried underground and causing earthquakes, has been suggested with Typhoeus (Ovid, *Metamorphoses* V.346–8); the late-thirteenth-century *Banda-manna saga* (*The saga of the bonded men*) 12 also has a slight parallel with the end of outlaw Óspakr Glúmsson.

Thrymskvida: The song of Thrym

Thrymskvida, like *Lok* and *Hym*, is among the most overtly comic of eddic poems. The story itself (folios 17r–18r of CR), describing the theft and recovery of Thor's hammer Mjöllnir (named in stanza 30), the gods' chief defence against the giants, is serious, but the brisk and collo-quial manner of its telling undercuts any more profound purpose and provides instead a spirited romp through an otherwise-unattested epi-sode of mythical history. The ballad-like repetition and simple style belie a deep sense of the absurd, and the poem inverts a whole range of stereotypes for humorous effect. So Thor, usually the most aggressively masculine of all the gods, is depicted in a bridal gown, after the sexu-ally voracious Freyja indignantly refuses the role. That the idea for Thor's disguise should come from Heimdall, the taciturn watchman of the gods, and that Thor's helpful assistant on his trip should be Loki, the sworn enemy of both Heimdall and Thor, only underlines the topsy-turvy logic. In contrast with the impetuous god Thor, the giant Thrym ('Crash') is an unusually dignified and sympathetic figure, fond of dogs and horses, rich and eager for a well-born wife. Such an essentially simple soul, quite unlike the wise giant of *Vaf*, is wholly perplexed at the outrageous behaviour and forbidding appearance of his bride-to-be, and the reader surely sympathizes at least a little with his sudden demise.

Thrym appears to have borrowed a substantial proportion of its imagery and phrasing from other eddic poems, and is therefore often considered among the last to have been composed. So, e.g., compare

Thrym 14 with *Bdr* 1, or the repeated phrasing of *Thrym* 2, 3, 9, 12 with *Brot* 6 or *Odd* 3 (also cf. *Thrym* 27). There are other parallels with *Vsp* and *Lok*, as well as with the skaldic poetry of Úlfr Uggason (an Icelander who flourished at the end of the tenth century), and between *Thrym* 24 and *Hym* 15, where the remarkable capacity of 'Sif's husband' (Thor, named pointedly so at his 'bridal' feast) to consume vast amounts is also an issue. Some similarities have also been noted between *Thrym* 22 and *Eiríksmál* 1, composed in 954 in honour of Eirík Bloodaxe, with the customary reversal of roles. A further general analogue can be found in *Skírn*, with the same inversion of a god yearning for a giantess, as well as in the myth of the giant masterbuilder, thwarted by the Æsir, specifically Loki, and slain by Thor's hammer (*Gylf* 42).

It is particularly striking that Snorri does not mention the loss of Thor's hammer in his Prose Edda; and this has led to the suggestion that *Thrym* was Snorri's own composition. Few of *Thrym*'s elements can be traced with any confidence back to the pagan era; the most significant perhaps is the hallowing of a wedding by the goddess Vár. Certain metrical features have been used to suggest a very early date, while on the other hand the use of end-rhyme and repetition, as well as its almost complete lack of kennings, point in the opposite direction: see also note to 3. Several of the words and metrical patterns in *Thrym* are better matched in the Anglo-Saxon tradition than in Old Norse, and so Anglo-Saxon influence or even composition in a Norse-dominated part of Anglo-Saxon England has been suggested (a similar, much stronger argument has been made for *Vkv*, which immediately follows *Thrym*). It seems possible that what we have in CR is a polished version of the twelfth century or later.

Sexual humour is implicit throughout *Thrym*, for example in the parallelism of Thor's response when he discovers the loss of his phallic hammer in stanza 1 ('Ving-Thor was enraged, when he awoke') with that of Freyja in 13 when it is suggested that she offer herself sexually to Thrym ('Freya was enraged . . .'). Likewise, Loki's keenness for cross-dressing contrasts sharply with the disdain felt by Thor for the necessity of the deception, since he is worried that he will be thought a 'cock-craver' (*argr*): see headnote to *Lok*. This is clearly an issue for Thor, as he seeks to redeem his lost manhood.

Analogues are found widely elsewhere, but whether they come from long-held belief among Scandinavian peoples or are much later borrowings is disputed. The story of *Thrym* was retold in ballads and *rímur* (rhyming song-cycles popular from the late medieval period) from all parts of Scandinavia, including the Faroe Islands and Iceland.

3   For Loki's use of the feather-cloak of Freyja (or, perhaps, Frigg), cf. Snorri's Edda about the giants Thjazi and Geirröd (*Gylf* 56, 58). Further parallels are a promise to the giant Thjazi that he will have a goddess as his bride, and an undertaking by Loki to Geirröd that he will accompany Thor into the Giants' Domain without his hammer. These all support the suggestion that *Thrym* is a late composition drawing on familiar motifs.

7   The opening line is identical to *Vsp* 48.

13   The 'great Brísings' neck-ring' (*Brísingamen*) is only found in *Thrym* (also 15, 19), and the identity of the 'Brísings' is a mystery. The neck-ring is apparently alluded to in *Beo* 1199, and was a payment to Freyja for sleeping with each of the dwarf-artisans in turn (cf. *Lok* 20), so Freyja's protest is presumably ironic here. Snorri describes how when Loki steals the necklace, Heimdall recovers it after fighting with him when both are transformed into seals (*Skáld* 8). For the background, cf. *Sörla þáttr*, preserved in the late-fourteenth-century manuscript Flateyjarbók. On 'maddest', see headnote to *Lok*.

15   On the Vanir, see note to *Vsp* 24–5. The twin implications that Heimdall is one of the Vanir, and that they are noted for their prophetic powers, are unattested elsewhere.

16   Cf. *Ríg* 23. The key is a common enough phallic symbol in medieval verse (e.g. the late-tenth-century Exeter Book *Riddles* or the *Cambridge Songs*) to make such an implication likely, given the tone of the poem.

18   Note the same rude refrain in *Lok* 17, etc.

20   In the Norse, the word for 'two' is given in the form for a couple consisting of a man and a woman, repeating its use for Thor and Freyja in 12. Loki is presumably making a joke here at Thor's expense, or his own, given his propensity for cross-dressing (see *Lok* 23, 33; *Hynd* 40).

21   Thor's goats are well-witnessed elsewhere (e.g. *Hym* 37), and it has been suggested that the portentous description of Thor's journey here draws on stanzas 14, 15 in the *Haustlöng* of Þjóðólfr of Hvínir.

22   For spreading the benches, see, e.g., *Alv* 1; *Bdr* 6; *Eiríksmál* 1. On Njörd, see further *Grím* 16.

23   The giant Hymir also owns jet-black oxen (*Hym* 18).

24   On Thor as 'Sif's husband', see headnote. On Thor's vast appetite, see *Hym* 15.

26   Cf. the nine nights at the end of *Skírn*, representing the length of time Frey will have to wait for his beloved Gerd (*Skírn* 39, 41).

30   There is little evidence for the use of a hammer or hammer-sign
     to hallow weddings, although the sheer number of surviving
     hammer-amulets does not preclude it. Vár ('Oath') seems little
     more than a cipher for Frigg; see Snorri's *Gylf* 35.
31   The original puns on 'laughed' (*hló*) and 'Hlórridi'; usually in
     Norse texts, laughter prefigures a killing.

Völundarkvida: The song of Völund

The dark tale of loss, betrayal and vengeance told in *Völundarkvida*
(folios 18r–19v) looks forward to the heroic poems of CR that tell the
litany of woes that afflicted the Völsungs and Gjúkungs, and indeed
some editors assume the scribe made a mistake in not placing *Vkv* as
the first of that section. Völund, the dark and mysterious smith whose
triumphs and disasters punctuate *Vkv*, is described as 'prince of elves'
and 'leader of elves' (stanzas 10, 13, 32), and this may account for the
location between *Thrym* (which features the giant Thrym) and *Alv*
(the dwarf Alvíss), producing a sequence that deals with mythological
creatures who are not gods. We can also note that both *Thrym* and
Vkv show the unmanning of their eponymous heroes by the loss of
phallic symbols (hammer and sword, respectively), as well as the dam-
age to female sexuality symbolized by a fractured ring (*Thrym* 13;
Vkv 26–7); in both, feather-cloaks feature (*Thrym* 3–5, 7; cf. intro-
ductory pr to *Vkv*). For a connection with *Alv*, it is notable that Alvíss
means 'All-wise', and *vísi álfa* (translated in *Vkv* as 'leader of elves')
could also mean 'wise one of the elves'.

   In the Old English translation of Boethius there are three references
(not in the original Latin) to the bones of the legendary smith Weland,
who is described as *wisa*, which could mean 'wise' or 'leader', and this
is important, since there are several oddities of language and metre
that link *Vkv* more closely with Anglo-Saxon England than with
Scandinavia, including the repeated phrase *alvitr unga(r)* ('strange
young creature(s)'; 1, 3, 10). The Old Norse form *alvitr* occurs only in
Vkv and in *HH II* 26, where it is also used of a valkyrie (and which
may derive from *Vkv*). It seems that the author of the introductory pr
to *Vkv* misunderstood the term, perhaps as 'All-wise' (another link to
Alv). But '-*vit*-' may be related to the Old English word *wiht* ('crea-
ture'); the Old Norse equivalent would be *vættr*. And the equivalent
compound *ælwhit* ('strange creature', 'alien creature') is attested in
Beo, where it refers to the beings who inhabit Grendel's mere. *Ørlög
drýgja*, which alliterates with *alvitr ungar* (1, 3), appears in Old Eng-
lish (*orleg dreogan*) in the sense (as here) 'fulfil fate'; the pr-author

seems to have misinterpreted it as 'to choose (for others) fate', and makes the South Germanic swan-maidens into Norse valkyries (in the pr only). An impressive number of details of vocabulary and metre appear to place *Vkv* firmly within an Anglo-Saxon (or more properly Anglo-Scandinavian) ambit, e.g. scenes from the tale of the smith Weland occur widely in Anglo-Saxon England, including on the famous eighth-century Franks Casket, as well as in both *Beo* and *Waldhere*. Weland appears also in the Old English poem *Deor* and possibly in *Wulf and Eadwacer*, which immediately follows it (both precede the first cluster of *Riddles*) in the late-tenth-century Exeter Book, and which some have seen as an enigmatic lament by Bödvild (OE Beaduhild) for her lost lover (these two poems are among the few poems surviving in Old English to use a loose stanzaic structure). Thus it has been suggested that *Vkv*, albeit in an earlier form, was produced in an area of Anglo-Saxon England under Scandinavian influence: tentatively, tenth- or early-eleventh-century Yorkshire.

The story in *Vkv* combines two motifs found widely elsewhere: the otherworldly swan-maiden who marries and then abandons her mortal husband (particularly common in Southern European traditions), and a maimed smith who avenges himself on his captors. Such German elements have been noted in *Vkv*, but may come from a very early stage of transmission. Given such international background, it is not surprising that the derivation of Völund's name is disputed, but the poet of *Vkv* seems to associate the first syllable with *vél* ('skill', 'cunning'), since he consciously plays on it when describing Völund 'creating feats of cunning [or craftsmanship]' (20). There is an element of thoughtful planning even in Völund's failure to pursue his swan-maiden bride, as his brothers do, which prepares us for his plans of revenge. His sword and ring are obvious symbols of male and female fertility, respectively, and his revenge reflects this: he gives Bödvild the wifely role, symbolized by the broken ring she wears and wishes whole again, and while he never recovers his lost sword, he unmans Nídud entirely, depriving him of his beloved sons and his right to arrange his daughter's marriage.

Vkv progresses in a loose form of *fornyrðislag* ('old poetry metre'), with stanzas of differing lengths. It is through repetition of scenes, themes and phrases that the poet makes his point. The gruesome description of Völund's creation of gems and trinkets from the bodies of the murdered sons is repeated almost verbatim later (24–5 and 34–6), just as their greedy temptation is (21 and 23). Likewise, the way in which the heartlessly laughing Völund abandons Bödvild (29) is echoed by his cruel crowing to Nídud (38). Similarly, Völund's own moment of realization that he has been betrayed comes when 'he woke, deprived of joys' (11), while Nídud complains that 'I'm always awake, deprived of joys' (31).

In this topsy-turvy world of parallels and repetitions, the hunter becomes the hunted, the persecuted the persecutor. So, for example, Völund, captured after returning from a hunt and cooking the steak of a she-bear, is depicted as an animal not so much tamed by capture as made wild (16–17); he returns to his hunter-status by killing Nídud's sons, who are described as '(bear-)cubs' (24, 32, 34). In a similar fashion, Nídud's greed for treasure is ultimately rewarded by treasures made from the skulls of those he treasured most. Moreover, the women are depicted in an oddly unsympathetic manner. The three swan-maidens are the protagonists of the opening stanzas of *Vkv*, and they make the conscious choice both to select and to abandon their husbands (note, however, that the pr reverses this), who seem curiously passive as a group, especially Völund. But Nídud's wife is consistently described as 'crafty' (*kunnig*), which may hint at magic (25, 30, 35), and her glee at Völund's capture is unseemly, to say the least (16–17): she is the one who apparently decrees his hamstringing, and his imprisonment at Sævarstöd ('Sea-side Place'), evidently an island. Even her husband seems exasperated as he wearily states that 'your counsels are cold to me' (31), echoing a familiar Norse proverb that 'cold are the counsels of women' (*eru köld kvenna ráð*; found in *Lok* 51; *Njáls saga* 116; *Gísla saga* 19).

Parallels of theme and situation are also found in *Háv*. Völund's seduction of the hapless Bödvild by exchanging beer for sex after she has come to him asking for a favour is a curious reversal of the myth of the Mead of Poetry in *Háv*; in both, the sexual aggressor flies off, leaving the woman behind to lament (*Vkv* 29; *Háv* 110). But while in *Háv* Odin takes the mead with him, Völund leaves behind the real prize (his unborn son, who will grow to be a mighty hero). The irony, of course, is that Völund abandons Bödvild by flying away in much the same way as Hervör abandoned him. No one emerges with much credit in this savage tale.

The opening lines of the introductory pr are also found in the later eddic manuscript AM 748 Ia 4to, written around 1300. Aspects of the background story are found in *Þiðreks saga* 73, perhaps composed as early as the late twelfth century and written by 1250/51.

pr   For the hiding of feather-cloaks to make supernatural women human, see *Hel* 7.

12   The phrase translated here as 'ropes of bast' is a notorious crux, connected possibly to the Old English poem *Deor*.

14   Presumably an allusion to the heroic poems of CR, where Grani
      is the horse of the dragon-slaying hero Sigurd, who gains much
      gold thereby, and is mentioned in ten CR poems.

17 pr The best-known example of the maimed smith is probably the
      Graeco-Roman Hephaestus; see also headnote.

26   The poem elides the mechanics of Bödvild's visit to Völund.

28   The climax of Völund's revenge, namely his seduction or rape of
      the naive Bödvild, occurs offstage.

30   Presumably the final line is spoken by Nídud's queen (on 31, see
      headnote); it is clear from 36 that she is present throughout the
      conversation between Völund and Nídud.

33   The oaths are all sworn on the edges of the most important ele-
      ments of the viking life: ship, shield, sword and steed. Most of the
      oaths mentioned in CR seem to have been broken, both by gods
      and men, but few poems give such specific terms as here (but see
      HH II 31; *Gkv III* 3; *Atk* 30).

Alvíssmál: The lay of All-wise

Alvíssmál (folios 19v–20r in CR) is a dialogue-poem and test of wisdom
between creatures from different worlds: a pale-nosed dwarf called
'All-wise' (*Alvíss*) and the mighty Thor of the Æsir, who, although he
contends verbally with Odin in *Hár* (where, ironically in view of his
stalling tactics here, he complains of having been 'delayed' (*Hár* 51))
and with Loki in *Lok*, is not otherwise known for his brains. Just as
Odin outwits the wise giant Vafthrúdnir in *Vaf* by extracting all the
wisdom he can get before curtailing the contest with an unfair ques-
tion, so too Thor, making the same sudden return home that we see in
Lok, delays his opponent until sunrise. Comparison with *Vaf* is appro-
priate, since only in *Alv* 29 and *Vaf* 25 is Night described as born of
Nör, and Odin's first four questions, all with a common structure ask-
ing from where certain things first came, concern pairings – earth/
heaven, moon/sun, day/night and summer/winter (*Vaf* 20–27) – which
are paralleled in *Alv* 9–16, 29–30 – in the first group we find the pair-
ings of earth/heaven and moon/sun, and in the second simply night,
surely implying the day that turns the dwarf to stone. Moreover, the
reference to 'ancient lore' (*fornir stafir*) in the final stanza of *Alv* can
only be matched in CR in the first and last stanzas of *Vaf*. It is likely
that *Alv* borrowed from *Vaf*.

   But if the frame, set up in the first eight stanzas and in the last, is
broadly familiar, some of the details are not: Thor's daughter, the unwit-
ting and, given the unfortunate connotations of Æsir- or dwarf-sex

elsewhere, likely unwilling 'prize', is otherwise unknown, although the
Æsir were somewhat cavalier about promising away their womenfolk,
as in *Thrym* and the tale of the master-builder told by Snorri (*Gylf* 42).
Within that frame, Thor asks for the names of thirteen things 'in every
world there is', and while thirteen being unlucky is not known before
the conversion, it certainly is for All-wise, whose paleness is emblematic
of his nocturnal and subterranean existence. The dwarf is detained past
daybreak and presumably turns to stone, like the giantess Hrímgerd
at the end of a ritual exchange of insults in *HHj* 12–30. All-wise
clearly knows that such danger applies to him, since he tells Thor that
their name for the sun is 'Dawdler's deluder' (*Alv* 16), invoking the
name of a prominent dwarf (see *Vsp* 14; *Háv* 143; *Fáf* 13). As in *Vaf*,
however, wisdom is no match for cunning.

The precise status of the names supplied by All-wise is hard to
determine; the poem as a whole may simply be an exercise in ingenuity,
as well as a useful storehouse of alternative poetic terms for common
items, but another view is that it gives taboo terms or circumlocutions
to ward off evil. The more positive assessment is supported by two
stanzas of *Alv* (20, 30), which are quoted with slight variations, in
manuscripts of Snorri's *Skáld* (59, 63), where they come from a ver-
sion called *Alsvinnsmál*. (The name Alsvinnr ('All-wise') was an
alternative to Alvíss ('All-wise')). Snorri also attributes to *Alsvinnsmál*
a stanza listing heroes and their horses, which does not fit *Alv* in CR,
and may reflect a different tradition. Certainly, the creatures who live
'in every world there is' are a motley crew: men (who also appear as
'human folk' (28)), gods (presumably the Æsir, although in 16, 'the
Æsir's sons'), the Vanir (who may also be 'the great powers' (20, 30)),
giants (as well as 'Suttung's sons' (34)), elves, dwarfs and those who
live in Hel. There even is an attempt by the poet to characterize the
creatures in their own languages, although the exigencies of metre and
alliteration cause some oddities: for the Vanir every name begins with
'v' (an effect I have tried to replicate with translations beginning with
'w'). Likewise, the elves are given rather naive and wide-eyed words
('pretty roof', 'pretty wheel', 'pretty-limbed'), while by contrast dwarves
and giants seem more practical, if unimaginative ('heaven' is a 'dripping
hall', while 'barley' is 'scoff', respectively), and the inhabitants of Hel
are apparently suitably depressed ('barley' is 'crestfallen', presumably
from the bent-over stalks). In this way, the poet of *Alv* pre-empts Tolk-
ien, and his notion of the essential difference in outlook of various kinds
of beings, by some eight centuries or more.

The sequence of the first ten items is linked pairs, but the following
four stanzas (31–4), covering 'barley' and 'ale', are either displaced or

added later, which is perhaps more likely, given that eddic poems in general and catalogues or wisdom-poems in particular were often augmented with later material. Indeed 'barley' breaks the usual pattern of the generic word in the question being the form used by men: here Thor asks about 'seed', and All-wise makes the intuitive leap to 'barley', so prompting an exchange on 'ale' to complete the pair. Ale alludes to the myth of the Mead of Poetry, and together these stanzas (perhaps also the pairing fire/wood, which are also outside the cosmological scheme) may represent additions made in a performance in a mead-hall, where such associations would have been natural. The final stanza makes best sense if we assume that it should follow immediately after the exchange on 'night', given that Thor triumphantly uses the form 'day': the fourth line in stanza 35 should perhaps read: 'dwarf, you are totally dayed up', using a unique past participle form 'dayed' (*dagaðr*). The final line, which changes the metre of stanza 35 from 'song metre' (*ljóðaháttr*), used in the rest of *Alv*, to 'spell metre' (*galdralag*) then acts as a suitable threatening end (the same technique is used in *Skírn*).

Since *Alv* is an unusual poem, this may explain its placement in CR, the last of the mythological wisdom-poems and the final mythological poem. We might expect it to follow *Thrym*, which also features Thor in customarily combative mode attempting to prevent a goddess from being married to another kind of creature, but like the intervening *Vkv Alv* shows victory through deception rather than force of arms. It is striking that the subject of all three poems is thwarted marriage, and since they all demonstrate different kinds of double-dealing, they carry the same kind of warning implicit in all the CR mythological poems: it is tough to trust outsiders, and intermarriage between different worlds is problematic unless, apparently, you are a (male) god. While gods have sex with giantesses, the giants and dwarfs (no female dwarfs appear) seem condemned to lonely bachelorhood; in that sense, Thor's opening salvo to All-wise is no more than the truth: 'you're never born for a bride' (2).

1   For bench-strewing, see also *Bdr* 6 and *Thrym* 22.
3   The meaning of the original text is obscure.
6   The by-name Ving-Thor is also found in *Thrym* 1.
16 By alluding to the sun catching Dawdler out, All-wise predicts his own demise. Dawdler is among the best-known of the dwarfs; see headnote.
24 The same word (*lagastaf*) is used in 32, and so is part of the elves' vocabulary for both 'ocean' and 'barley': 'brew-stuff' is a compromise, since ale is composed of both barley and water.

32 See note to 24.

34 On the giant Suttung, who is part of the myth of the Mead of
     Poetry, see *Háv* 104–10 and notes. This reference immediately
     after we are told that the name of 'ale' in Hel is 'mead' seems to
     be a form of association, as we have already heard the giants'
     term. 'Suttung's sons' to signify giants is also found in *Skírn* 34.

Helgakvida Hundingsbana in fyrri: The earlier song of Helgi, the slayer of Hunding

Helgakvida Hundingsbana in fyrri is the first of the Helgi-lays in CR
(folios 20r–22r) – the others are *HHj* and *HH II* – and the densest in
structure and style, since it contains a high proportion of kennings
and poetic periphrases. The first word starts with a large capital,
which marks the change from mythological to heroic material, and
that first word (*Ár*, literally 'early', in context 'in days of yore'), the
first word of in several poems in both sections of CR, only adds weight
to the perhaps self-conscious antiquarianism of *HH I*. The retrospect-
ive heroic tone is established in the lofty language of the opening
stanzas, which focus on the role of the mysterious norns in determin-
ing Helgi's fate, and ensuring that, like his half-brother Sigurd, he
would grow up to a life of fame and glory. Snorri explains the role of
the norns (*Gylf* 15):

> There stands a fair hall under the ash, by the well, and out of this hall
> there come three maidens, who are called Urd ('Destiny'), Verdandi
> ('Becoming') and Skuld ('Shall-be'). These maidens shape the lives of
> men; we call them norns. But there are other norns who visit every child
> that is born, to shape its life, and they are descended from the Æsir;
> others still are descended from elves; and a third kind from the race of
> dwarfs . . . [G]ood norns, from a noble line, shape good lives, but wicked
> norns are to blame for those whose lives are miserable.

Stanza 6 highlights Helgi's precocious maturity: like Váli, Odin's son
(*Bdr* 11), he is ready to fight from birth, and, as elsewhere in CR (*Fáf*
32–44), talking birds salute this young prince, who receives consider-
able estates as a naming-gift from his father. Helgi's youthful
generosity to his warriors is applauded, just as such conduct is recom-
mended in the Anglo-Saxon poem *Beo* 20–24a: 'So ought a young
man to ensure by his generosity, by ready gifts, while in his father's
care, that close companions will in turn stand by him in his later years,
his men be loyal when war comes.' Helgi avenges his father's death at

the hands of Hunding when he is only fifteen (10), and then refuses compensation to Hunding's sons.

For such an epic project, many of the place names in *HH I* seem suitably portentous: 'Heaven-fells', 'Fire-fells', 'Eagle-stone', 'Brand-isle', 'Stem-ness', 'Arrow-sound' and 'Wolf-stone'; similar use of specific, transparent place names also marks out the ending of *Beo*, where the dead bodies of Beowulf and the dragon are laid out side by side at 'Eagles' Bluff', Beowulf is buried on 'Whale's Bluff' and the Swedish King Ongentheow kills the Geatish Prince Hæthcyn at a place in Sweden called 'Ravens' Wood' or 'Raven's Holt'. In both poems, the purpose of these names is to heighten the martial and heroic flavour.

The language of *HH I* is rather more allusive than most of the CR mythological poems, with the kennings (especially for warriors and war) adding to the skaldic flavour. The flyting that takes place between Helgi's half-brother, Sinfjötli, and his enemy Gudmund (34–44) is demarcated by an envelope-pattern in which first one, then the other, accuses his opponent of 'enticing [his] bitch-tykes to the swill'. The flyting itself has echoes of the abuse found in the mythological poems, especially *Hár* and *Lok*, and focuses on allegations of unnatural sex with animals, giants and each other; of cowardice; and, above all, of subservience. If we are to believe the accounts of Sinfjötli's life in *Vsaga*, where he is described as being the product of an incestuous union, and as spending time with his father (who is his mother's brother) as a were-wolf in the forest, several of Gudmund's taunts seem close to the mark.

Borghild is not a common name in Norse myth and legend, and the very mention in stanza 1 evokes the Völsung Sigmund and his still more famous son Sigurd, who features heavily throughout the CR heroic poems. References to Sigmund focus almost exclusively on his relationship to his son, and *PrSin* spells out his story, elucidated in *Vsaga* (especially 8–9) and in Snorri's *Skáld* (40, 42).

1   'Early in ages' is found in *Vsp* 3; see also note to *Hym* 1.

3   The original text is corrupt: the translation is simply a guess, as are 15 and 19. The formulation 'moon's hall' resembles other terms for heaven in *Alv* 12.

5   The claim to specialized knowledge is widespread in CR (cf. the refrain 'do you know yet, or what?' in *Vsp* 27ff.).

8   As elsewhere in Norse texts, a naming-gift follows the giving of a name. For Sinfjötli, see *Vsaga* 8.

16   The description of these mysterious women as 'southern' lends them an exotic flavour (cf. *Vkv* 1; *HH II* 45; *Sigsk* 4; *Atk* 2; *Ghv II* 14). For 'elm' as warrior, cf. 9.

21 Cf. the river-names in *Grím* 27–9.

27 Such set-piece rhyming and rhythmical descriptions of battles are found in Old English, notably in Cynewulf's *Elene* 114–15.

30 Rán ('Plunder') is a sea-giantess, perhaps the wife of Ægir, and the mother of the waves, who drags down lost sailors and takes them to her.

34 See headnote.

35 For 'slow to flee', cf. 53, 55 (and *HH II* 20).

40 A similar taunt of unmanliness is found in the parallel flyting in *HHj* 20.

43 In other words, Gudmund has consorted with male and female giants, and has been used and abused at will.

53 That the brave have small, hard, firm and bloodless hearts recurs, e.g. *Atk* 21–5; *Atm* 60–64.

54 For Hugin ('Thought') as one of Odin's ravens, see further *Grím* 20.

Helgakvida Hjörvardssonar: The song of Helgi Hjörvardsson

Helgakvida Hjörvardssonar is out of chronological sequence in CR (folios 22r–24r), dealing with the hero Helgi Hjörvardsson and his valkyrie beloved Sváva, who died before the birth of Helgi Sigmundsson Hundingsbani, celebrated in *HH I*; as the prose at the end of *HHj* makes clear, Helgi Sigmundsson Hundingsbani and Sigrún are to be understood as Helgi Hjörvardsson and Sváva reborn. *HHj* is an odd mixture of prose and verse in different metres with three distinct sections.

The introductory pr describes the legendary King Hjörvard, who has four wives, having vowed to marry the fairest of women. In a scene strongly reminiscent of *Fáf* 40–44, where talking birds reveal the existence and whereabouts of the valkyrie Sigrdrífa to the hero Sigurd, the beauty of a woman called Sigrlinn is celebrated by a bird, and Atli Idmundsson overhears it and presumably tells Hjörvard. In a further echo of the story of Sigurd the Völsung that forms the backbone of the heroic poems of CR, Hjörvard has Atli woo Sigrlinn for him by proxy: see *Vsaga* 28–9; and cf. *Skírn*); both Atli and Hjörvard end up with the wives of their choice (stanzas 1–5 pr). With Sigrlinn, Hjörvard produces a splendid son who happens one day to be sitting on a grave-mound (cf. *Vsp* 42 and *Thrym* 6), when he sees nine valkyries riding past, one of whom, Sváva, gives him the name Helgi ('Holy'), tells him about a special sword and takes care of him and his victories (6–11).

The next section (12–30) focuses on a flyting that Atli, acting as Helgi's proxy, has with a giantess Hrímgerd, whose father, Hati, Helgi had apparently slain; in recompense she wants to have sex with Helgi for one night. This has echoes of the compensation the giantess Skadi seeks from the Æsir for the slaying of her father (see *Grím* 11; *Hár* 19; *Lok* 50–51; *Hynd* 30: see also note 52 to *Lok*). The course of the flyting between Atli and Hrímgerd matches in its harsh use of innuendo those in *Hár* and *Lok*, while the unpleasant sexual imagery (25) echoes the threatened curse to the giantess Gerd in *Skírn* 35. Atli, using the same tactics that Thor employed against Alvíss in *Alv*, simply delays Hrímgerd till dawn, when she turns to stone.

The final section the poem (31–43) focuses on the love between Helgi and Sváva. A prose passage describes how they exchange vows, but then tells how one Yuletide evening (the time when supernatural meetings traditionally occur in Norse texts) Hedin, Helgi's brother, has an encounter with a troll-wife, who offers to sleep with Hedin, and when he refuses she promises revenge. The curse comes true when Hedin, presumably in his cups, vows to have Sváva, Helgi's beloved. Hedin admits this to his brother, who takes the news calmly, seeing in it a prophecy of his impending death in battle, and with his dying breath, he asks his bride to accept his brother. The reincarnation in the final sentence serves to connect *HHj* with the other Helgi-lays (*HH I* and *HH II*).

The structure of *HHj* is relatively clear, although the CR version seems to be a compilation of earlier material, with the pr rather awkwardly bridging the gaps, and stanzas occasionally out of sequence.

4   Golden-horned cattle are found elsewhere in CR, e.g. *Thrym* 23.

6   For eagles screaming early in anticipation of feasting on dead flesh, see *HH I* 1.

7   The giving of a name in Norse culture was followed by a name-gift, so the valkyrie must give Helgi a gift. See further the headnote to *Grím*.

9   Presumably a highly-prized 'pattern-welded' or 'damascened' sword, in which the lamination of different grades of steel causes a tell-tale wavy pattern on the blade.

13   Troll-wives threatening to cause harm to ships, even though they are protected by iron plates, presumably refers to the women being caught out in the daylight and turned to stone. See further note on 29, and the headnote to *Alv*.

14   To be the lead-man in the prow of a warship (*stafnbúi*) was a mark of great respect; and he naturally engaged the enemy first, both verbally and physically.

15   'Hateful' is a pun on the name Atli (*Atli . . . atall*).

16   On women being forced to live under trees, see note to *Skírn* 35.

20   Presumably a stanza is missing here, where Atli suggested that he is the stallion to serve Hrímgerd as mare.

25   Similar kinds of curses are found elsewhere in CR, e.g. *Skírn* 25–36.

28   Lines 3–7 seem to have been interpolated from some general description of valkyries; cf. *Vsp* 30. For dew dropping from supernatural horses, see *Vaf* 14.

29   'Look East': look to the rising sun, which turns dwarfs and trolls to stone.

30 pr For another troll-wife riding on a wolf, see *Hynd* 5. The *bragar-ful* was the passing of the ceremonial drinking-cup at Yuletide, when solemn vows took place; a vow was not to be broken without great loss of face.

33   The word translated 'duel', literally, an 'island-going' (*holm-gang*), was a man-to-man battle with strict rules of reciprocity.

34 pr The family or personal fetch (*fylgja*) was powerful in Norse tradition, as a fetch was a kind of external soul that returned to its twin at death. While it often took animal form, it could also be in the guise of an otherworldly woman, so Helgi's conviction that the troll-woman is his fetch is tantamount to accepting that he will die in the upcoming battle. (In Modern Icelandic, the word means 'after-birth', that which literally follows (*fylgja* as a verb) every child.) Sites of formal combat, including for duels, were marked out with hazel-wands.

Helgakvida Hundingsbana önnur: The second song of Helgi, the slayer of Hunding

Helgakvida Hundingsbana önnur (folios 24r–26v of CR) is notable for the choppily interspersed prose passages and for its clear refer-ences to other poems. Several stanzas from 'The ancient poem of the Völsungs' (*Völsungakviða in forna*) appear after stanza 13; two lines of *HH I* (called 'The poem of Helgi' (*Helgakviða*)) are quoted, appar-ently from memory, after 18; the concluding prose mentions a now-lost '*Kára's song*' (*Káruljóð*), in which the lovers Helgi Hund-ingsbani and Sigrún, reincarnations of Helgi Hjörvardsson and Sváva, are reborn. That the love of Helgi and Sigrún was the focus of the ori-ginal *HH II* seems clear, once the extraneous stanzas, presumably drawn from other poems that have not survived, are ignored. So, e.g., stanzas 1–4 speak of Helgi's youth when he hid disguised as a girl, an episode suspiciously reminiscent of the Classical legend of Achilles hiding out at the court of Lycomedes (also Lycurgos) of Skyros; stanzas 19–24 (which appear in CR after 29) are an abridged and bowdlerized adaptation of the flyting in *HH I* 32–46. The problematic stanza 29 may also be an interpolation, and likewise the mean-spirited, vengeful stanza 39 seems out of place and possibly attributed to the wrong speaker. The use of 'Strange-creature' (*Alvitr*) as a simple designation for a valkyrie (26) seems to suggest that the poet knew *Vkv* (see headnote).

4 pr A *'cattle-slaughter on the beach'* is rare in Norse, although relatively common in Ancient Greek and Medieval Irish heroic literature. The alliterative *'sea and sky'* (*lopt ok lög*) is also found in *Skírn* 6 and *HH I* 6. CR has 'thus was she reborn' (*hún var svá endrborin*), which I have emended to follow later paper manuscripts that make the connection with Sváva explicit: 'she was Sváva reborn' (*hún var Sváva endrborin*).

15 That a woman could fall in love with a man based on his reputation alone is common in Irish sagas; e.g. the beautiful Findabair, daughter of Ailill and Medb, falls in love with the hero Fráech before she sees him in *Táin bó Fraích*.

18 pr For the description of flying valkyries, cf. *HHj* 6 pr. The lines are identical with *HH I* 32.

19–24 See headnote. The foreboding blood-red glow (19) is mentioned in, e.g., *Darraðarljóð* ('The song of the spear'), a poem often associated with eddic verse because of its metre and style, and is apparently chanted by troll-women in a dream, in *Njáls saga* 157, before the Battle of Clontarf (1014); see further headnote to *Grott*. Stanzas 23–4 are nearly the same as *HH I* 45–6.

19 For 'slow to flee', cf. *HH I* 35, 53, 55.

26 On norns, see headnote to *HH I*.

29 pr Tacitus (AD 56–117), in his *Germania* 39, speaks of a sacred grove in the land of the Semnones, where it is said that 'no one can enter unless fettered'. According to *Vsaga* 11, Helgi's father Sigmund is also dispatched by Odin's spear.

31 The River 'Lightning' (*Leiptr*) is listed in *Grím* 28 in a catalogue. Such formal oaths are found elsewhere in CR: see further note to *Vkv* 33.

34 The first line is repeated almost verbatim in *Odd* 11; see also 'out of [one's] mind' (*ørvita*) in *Lok* 21, 47.

38 Sigrún's praise of the pre-eminence of Helgi recalls the mighty stag Oak-antlered, which sits on top of Slain-hall (*Grím* 26); see also *Gkv I* 18; *Gkv II* 2.

39   The speech would be at least as appropriate in the mouth of Odin;
      the stanza may be an interpolation. Cf. the quasi-eddic poems
      Eiríksmál and *Hákonarmál*, in which Odin welcomes Eirík Blood-
      axe (d. 954) and Hákon the Good (d. 961, fighting against Eirík's
      sons) into Slain-hall; the latter poem is composed by Eyvíndr
      Finnsson skáldaspillir, whose nickname may mean 'plagiarist'.

45   For 'southerner', see the note to *HH I* 16.

46   The practice of wives following their husbands into the grave or
      on to the funeral-pyre is described in several Norse sources; e.g.
      Snorri (*Gylf* 49) tells about Nanna, the wife of Baldr, dying of
      grief and being placed on his pyre; see also *Vsaga* 8; in *Njáls saga*
      129, Bergthóra refuses to abandon her beloved husband Njál
      when he is burned inside their house. See also *Sigsk* 65–71; cf.
      Vsaga 33.

49   Just as the giants live in the East, so Ásgard and Slain-hall are
      placed in the West.

51 pr *Kára's song* is cited in the late *Hrómundar saga Greipssonar*,
      preserved in post-medieval paper manuscripts.

Frá dauda Sinfjötla: About Sinfjötli's death

Much of the material in this transitional prose piece is found, using
the same language, in *Vsaga* 8, 10–13; Sinfjötli plays a leading role in
the flyting of *HH I* 33–44. The CR (folios 26v–27r) twice leaves a gap
for the name of Borghild's brother. The *'old man'* (*karl*) in the ferry is
presumably Odin in his role as psychopomp; cf. *Hár*. Here we are pre-
sumably to infer that Odin has come to take Sinfjötli to Valhöll
himself. In *Vsaga* Hjálprek is described as the King of Denmark,
although his name is cognate with that of Chilperic, King of Neustria
(West Francia), 539–84. As for the superlative qualities of Sigurd, see
HH II 38 and note.

Grípisspá: Grípir's prophecy

Grípisspá, also known in later manuscripts as *Sigurdarkvida Fáfnis-
bana in fyrsta* ('The first song of Sigurd, the slayer of Fáfnir'), is the
first in CR (folios 27r–28v) of a series of poems dealing with the life
of the legendary hero Sigurd. *Gríp* seems to be a late poem that echoes
others in CR; it was used with *Vsp* by Gunnlaugr Leifsson (d. 1218/19),
who translated Geoffrey of Monmouth's enormously popular *Prophe-
tia Merlini* ('Prophecy of Merlin') into Icelandic as *Merlínusspá*; a
date in the twelfth century seems likely, and the *Gríp* author was

familiar with other eddic verse. Snorri recounts part of the same tale in *Skáld* 39, and it is very briefly told in *Vsaga* 16.

Grípir is the brother of Hjördís, Sigurd's mother, and as his maternal uncle has a particular role to play in his education. Sigurd's highly stylized entry into Grípir's presence, announced by a lackey who is impressed by his appearance, and evidently recognized immediately by his uncle, has a parallel in the approach by the young Beowulf (who will also turn out to be a formidable dragon-slayer) to the Danish court where his father had taken refuge. Grípir's opening words (stanza 7) are all that a budding champion might wish to hear, and we can compare what the Danish King Hrothgar said to Beowulf: 'you are strong in might, and mature in mind, wise in speaking words' (*Beo* 1844–5a). Grípir is happy to begin by foretelling how Sigurd will do all that a young hero should: avenge his father against an experienced warrior, refuse requests for monetary compensation and build up loyalty among his young peers by proving himself a generous lord; such are the staple attainments of the good Germanic prince.

Yet as the prophecy unfolds, it becomes clear that Sigurd will not have a tranquil life; Grípir expressly warns him against further inquiry (19), and only after much goading does he continue (27), when he introduces the femme fatale Brynhild. Her description (29) predicts for Sigurd the same kind of hapless longing and sleeplessness experienced by the god Frey in *Skírn*. But it is clear that Sigurd's somewhat myopic concern is with his own reputation, and whether he will truly betray his vows. The number of first-person references that he makes is striking, and he is depicted in a somewhat different light from other CR poems. When Grípir concludes his grim prophecy with an account of Sigurd's death (52), he explicitly echoes the hopeful words he had used at the beginning. In using such an envelope-pattern, the poet highlights the essential tragedy of the heroic tradition: luck or fate (the two are not distinguished) can cut down the greatest of heroes, and even the seemingly greatest of them all (the word 'seem' in 52 appears deliberate) is more a figure to be admired than to be emulated. In that sense, Sigurd emerges with his heroic credentials intact, and in the final stanza (53) forgives Grípir for simply saying what he must, before going on regardless to do what he must: face his own fate. Like the god Odin, who likewise asks others often about the manner of his death, Sigurd represents the kind of ironic fatalism that the vikings so much admired, and which colours his final words to his maternal uncle.

When Sigurd presses the reluctant Grípir for information, he repeats the question 'what else will my life prove?' (12, 14, 18), but his refrains towards the end of the poem become increasingly desperate and terse: 'tell me, Grípir!' (38, 43, 44); 'Grípir, tell me that!' (48); and 'Grípir, tell me!' (50). Sigurd's determined quest for knowledge of his own fate echoes Odin's; for in neither can the outcome be called pretty.

pr   On the special relationship between a mother's brother and her son in Germanic society, see note to *Háv* 140. To judge from his name, Geitir is a goat-herd. Cf. Skírnir's interrogation by the giant herdsman in *Skírn* 11–12.

6   The word translated in (24) as 'uncle' (*moðurbróðir*) literally means 'mother-brother': see introductory pr.

9   The prophecy about Sigurd's vengeance against Hunding's sons is played out in *Reg* 15–26; see too *Vsaga* 11–12.

11   See *Fáf*.

15–18 See *Sigrd*. The reference to Helgi (15) is ambiguous, but serves to connect this sequence of poems with the Helgi-lays.

24   See note to 6.

37   See *Brot*.

41   See *Brot* and *Sigsk*, where it is emphasized that a sword separated the sleeping couple.

42–43 The numbering in brackets reflects the order in CR, where apparently the stanzas have been transposed.

48   See *Brot*, *Sigsk* and *Gkv II*.

50   Gutthorm is the only one of the brothers who has not sworn oaths to Sigurd; see further *Brot* 4; *Gkv II* 7.

53   Sigurd's cool acceptance of his fate foreshadows Gunnar and Högni in *Atk* and *Atm*, and Hamdir and Sörli in *Ham*.

Reginsmál: Regin's lay

Reginsmál (folios 28v–30v in CR) begins and ends with a wisdom-dialogue, so aligning it with many of the other poems in CR, particularly the mythological ones; the tale is paraphrased in *Vsaga* 13–14. *Reg* is closely associated with *Fáf*, which immediately follows it, and it seems likely that they were originally intended to be read together; they offer detailed accounts of how Sigurd came to slay the dragon Fáfnir at the instigation of his foster-father, Regin, who was Fáfnir's brother. The introductory pr to *Reg* describes how in his youth Sigurd selected his famous steed, Grani, and was fostered by Regin, who was a dwarf or elsewhere a giant. Stanzas 1–12 give the back-history of the cursed treasure-hoard guarded by Fáfnir, who had transformed himself into a dragon, with vivid exchanges between Loki and the dwarf Andvari. When asked to kill Fáfnir, Sigurd vows first to avenge his dead father, Sigmund, and does so, having had an encounter with the god Odin in disguise, who offers advice to his favourite (20–25) which has the same practical grounding as the gnomic stanzas of *Háv*.

pr   *Vsaga* 13 credits Odin with the gift of Grani, who was descended from Sleipnir, Odin's eight-legged steed (see note to *Vsp* 25). Regin is described as a giant in *Fáf* 38, just as he describes his brother (*Fáf* 29). Hœnir is also a companion to Odin and (perhaps) Loki in *Vsp* 18. Andvari changes himself into a pike (*gedda*), a word which is grammatically feminine, an unusual change of sex here; cf. note to *Vsp* 25. Otter eats as if in a satisfied doze but *Vsaga* 14 explains his eyes are half-closed because he could not stand to see his food grow less. For Rán, see further note to *HH I* 30 and also *HHj* 18.

1   A grim pun on Andvari's name, with *varask*, which has the broad sense 'beware'.

2   For the norns, see headnote to *HH I*.

4 pr   Snorri (*Gylf* 46) connects this ring with Odin's fabled ring Draupnir ('Dripper'), which replenishes itself; see further *Skírn* 21 and note.

5   There are so many deaths associated with the hoard that it is impossible to keep count: the eight may include Sigurd; his three slayers Gunnar, Högni and Gutthorm; Atli; and Gudrún's three sons by Jónakr. This tally ignores (e.g.) such collateral damage as Erp and Eitil, Gudrún's sons by Atli. There are several candidates for the 'two brothers': Fáfnir and Regin, Gunnar and Högni, or Erp and Eitil.

9   Hreidmar's confidence is misplaced, though he does indeed control the gold as long as he lives.

11   An odd stanza, perhaps from another poem entirely? The duty of vengeance devolving upon Lyngheid or Lofnheid or their sons (or grandsons) would work out very well if either of them or a daughter were married to Eylimi, as has been suggested, but such a link is not witnessed in any source.

11 pr   Both Snorri's *Skáld* 38 and *Vsaga* 14 specify that after killing his father and acquiring the doomed gold, Fáfnir became a dragon.

13   The comment about a 'greedy wolf' seems proverbial.

14   For 'threads of fate', cf. *HH I* 3–4.

15   *PrSin* makes it clear that it is Sigmund, rather than Eylimi, who fell in this battle.

15 pr *Nornagests þáttr* 6 clarifies that the 'great storm' was magically
       raised by Hunding's sons.

18   Hnikar and Hider (Fjölnir) are attested as Odin-names in *Grím* 47;
       for Odin as an old man, see note to *Hár* 2. See also *Vsaga* 17.

18 pr In *Háv* 154, Odin claims to know spells for calming storms.

23   The battle-wedge was thought to be Odin's tactical invention,
       imparted only to selected heroes.

24   On the *dísir*, see note to *Grím* 53.

26   This is the only description of 'carving a blood-eagle' in eddic
       poetry, although there are gruesome depictions in the sagas. In
       the late-twelfth- or early-thirteenth-century *Orkneyinga saga* 8,
       when Jarl Torf-Einarad discovers his enemy, Hálfdan Long-leg:
       'There they found Halfdan Long-leg, and Einar his ribs sliced
       from his spine with a sword, and his lungs drawn out through
       the slits in his back; he gave the victim to Odin as a victory-
       offering.' Several scholars doubt the historicity of the practice.

Fáfnismál: Fáfnir's lay

Fáfnismál (folios 30r–31v in CR), together with *Reg*, offers the fullest
account of sigurd's slaying the dragon Fáfnir. *Fáf* deals with the killing
itself and its immediate aftermath; much of stanzas 1–22 is taken up
with a conversation, in which Fáfnir first attempts to discover the
identity of his killer, according to the introductory pr, in order to curse
him. Then there is an odd set of exchanges, part wisdom-contest, part
fatherly advice, in which Fáfnir warns Sigurd against Regin, the
brother he had himself defrauded of their father's (ill-gotten) inherit-
ance. After the killing, Regin duly cuts out Fáfnir's heart and drinks
his blood, but when Sigurd, obediently roasting the heart for Regin,
sucks his thumb and suddenly realizes that he can understand the
language of birds – all of them warning him against Regin – he finally
acts, and kills him too. The birds then send him to the court of King
Gjúki in possession of the dragon's hoard, via a detour that takes in
an encounter with the valkyrie Brynhild, which is more fully described
in *Sigrd*, which immediately follows *Fáf*.

    Both *Fáf* and *Reg* contain a mixture of prose and verse in various
metres, predominantly *ljóðaháttr* ('song metre') and *fornyrðislag* ('old
poetry metre'). The combination of wisdom-poetry and prophecy in
Fáf offers comparison with *Háv*, *Vaf* and *Grím* in CR, and with *Bdr*.

1   Note the suitably serpentine sibilance in the original: '*Sveinn ok
       sveinn, hverjum ertu sveini um borinn*' (line 1).

2   On 'Noble beast', cf. *HH II* 38. That Sigurd 'always wander[s] alone' appears to contradict his being fostered at the court of King Hjálprek (*PrSin*); but cf. traces of a variant version in *Þiðreks saga* 168.

7   See *Vsaga* 12 for Hjördís and her maid being enslaved.

9   After the utterances by Loki and Andvari, this is the third curse.

12   Cf. *Vaf* 26.

13   The variant lineages of norns helps to explain the difference between the kind of fairy-godmothers depicted here and in *HH I* 2–4, with those in *Vsp* 20. See also *Gylf* 15.

15   Cf. *Vaf* 18, where the same place is called Vígríd ('Battle-field').

17   For the 'helmet of dread', cf. *Reg* 14 pr; the second half of the stanza echoes *Háv* 64.

18   Something is evidently missing here: see *Vsaga* 18.

20   The opening line recalls *Háv* 112ff.

31   A similar sentiment is expressed in *Háv* 15.

31 pr There is a close parallel in the Irish story of Fionn mac Cumhaill in *Macgnímartha Finn* ('The boyhood deeds of Fionn'). While cooking the salmon of wisdom on behalf of the leprechaun-like druid and poet Finn Eces, who matches Regin's role here, Fionn sucks his thumb, and gains access to the knowledge of the salmon of wisdom.

42   The same kenning is found in *HH I* 21 (and note).

43   Cf. the prose and verse passage after *Sigrd* 4, and also *Hel* 8–10.

44 pr Iron houses also occur in Irish and Welsh sources, notably in the (twelfth-century?) Welsh *Branwen*, the second of the *Four Branches of the Mabinogi*. The name Hrotti is cognate with that of the mighty sword Hrunting in *Beo*.

Sigrdrífumál: Sigrdrífa's lay

There is no formal break separating *Sigrdrífumál* from *Fáf*, and in the style and wisdom-dialogues, there is much to connect them. *Sigrd* (folios 31v–32v in CR) breaks off in the middle of stanza 29; while the gap (end of 29–37) can be filled from post-medieval manuscripts, there may also be entire poems lost. The story is retold in *Vsaga* and in Snorri's *Skáld* 41–2. See Introduction, pp. xxiii–xxiv.

The poem opens as the sleeping woman awakes and asks who has woken her. While Sigurd identifies himself in stanza 1, it is in the pr following stanza 4 that she is named as the valkyrie Sigrdrífa. In the same pr she says she has vowed never to marry any man who knows the meaning of fear, a motif repeated in *Hel* 8–9 with respect to Brynhild; it is a key moment in the identification of the two that appears elsewhere in CR and in the *Vsaga*. In *Sigrd*, Sigurd simply asks the valkyrie to teach him the wisdom she has acquired. She offers him a drink to help him remember, before embarking on a lengthy exposition of runes, charms and advice, not unlike the *Loddfáfnismál* and *Rúnatalsþattr* sections of *Háv* (111–63).

1   The 'pale constraints' are the bonds of sleep, and, more literally, the mailcoat. It is possible that the eroticized slicing of the latter represents a misunderstanding of an unusual kenning.

2 pr Cf. the 'memory-ale' of *Hynd* 45.

4   Looks forward to stanza 5, where the teaching of runic magic and lore begins.

9   In *Fáf* 12, the norns fulfil this function.

12   On 'speech-runes', cf. *Gkv I* 23.

13   Heiddraupnir and Hoddrofnir are otherwise unknown; perhaps a reference to Mímir. See too *Vsp* 27, 38.

14   Brimir appears in *Vsp* 9, 37, as either a generic giant-name or an alternative to Ymir. Odin is here armed with the sword of the primordial giant that he and his brothers slew when the world was formed. Assuming that Mím is Mímir, in *Vsp* 46 a head with whom Odin consults, he is a figure of great wisdom and authority. Snorri elaborates (*Yngsaga* 4): just as Njörd was sent as a Vanir hostage to the Æsir (*Vaf* 39), so Mímir went as an Æsir hostage to the Vanir, who beheaded him and sent him back. Odin treated the disembodied head with herbs, and consulted it at times of crisis.

15   According to *Grím* 38, this shield is called 'Chill' (*Svalinn*). 'Early-waker' and 'All-swift' are the horses of the sun; cf. *Grím* 37. Hrungnir is the giant slain by Thor; it is possible that this should read: 'Hrungnir's killer's chariot'. For the sledge, cf. *Grím* 49.

20   Sigurd seems to be offered the chance to make a vow, presumably to bind him to Sigrdrífa.

21   Cf. 37, and see *Vsaga* 21.

25   Good advice on how to deal with slander, a flyting or a *senna*.

26   Cf. *HHj* 30 pr.

31   Such burnings-in are well documented: see *Njáls saga* 129; *Vsaga*; and *Atk* and *Atm*: see also note to *HH II* 46. It has been estimated that around a hundred deaths by arson are recorded in Old Norse–Icelandic literature.

34   Reflects the Christian custom of burial, rather than usual cremation rites of pagans; perhaps the stanza has been interpolated.

35   The message is that revenge remains a duty and a temptation, even after a financial settlement.

Brot af Sigurdarkvidu: A fragment of the song of Sigurd

Brot begins in midstream in CR (folios 33r–33v), after the great lacuna (see Introduction, pp. xxiii–xxiv), with the loss of the end of *Sigrd* and the beginning of *Brat* (and perhaps complete poems). Presumably the first speaker is Högni, responding to Gunnar's request to kill Sigurd. Sigurd's death probably happens offstage between stanzas 4 and 5 (cf. Bödvild's seduction or rape in *Vkv*). The fragment concludes with a particularly bitter exchange between Gunnar and his wife Brynhild, whose tragic passion for Sigurd is depicted in the poems that follow. *Brot* ends with a brief transitional prose passage, recounting several traditions concerning Sigurd's death.

2   Sigurd's supposed lack of trustworthiness aligns him with the notorious Odin (cf. *Háv* 110). Gunnar's main complaint must be that he feels deceived by Sigurd over the wooing of Brynhild, a situation she aggravates.

4   There is rare rhyme in the original: '*Sumir úlf svíðu, sumir orm sniðu*' ('Some roasted ... serpent'). See further *Sigsk* 20–21. Gutthorm, the brother of Gunnar, Högni and Gudrún, did not swear an oath of blood-brotherhood (see 17) with Sigurd, and is therefore a perfect candidate to slay him. Gutthorm is fed the wolf and the snake to steel him for his treachery in killing his sister's husband.

6   On Gudrún standing outside, cf. *Vkv* 30; 'and these were the first words she said' is repeated in *Thrym* 2, 3, 9; *Odd* 3.

7   For Grani's grief, cf. *Gkv II* 5.

9   There are problems about the number of sons specified here, but Brynhild claims that in time Sigurd would have displaced the Gjúkungs entirely.

16   Cf. Gunnar's binding in *Atk* 31.

17   The ceremony of blood-brotherhood is described in detail in the mid- or late-thirteenth-century *Gísla saga* 6. By raising an arc of turf from the ground, crawling under it and mixing their blood in the earth, participants symbolized rebirth from the same womb, here the earth.

19 pr Paralleled in *Sigsk* 22–4; *Ghv* 4; *Ham* 6–7. Several details are apparently drawn from *Gkv II*, which is named here (cf. particularly *Gkv II* 4 and 7).

Gudrúnarkvida in fyrsta: The first song of Gudrún

Gudrúnarkvida in fyrsta is the first of the three Gudrún-lays in CR
(folios 33v–34v), a brief and elegiac poem containing several remark-
able passages, beginning with a poignant description of Gudrún
sitting silent and motionless over the corpse of her beloved Sigurd,
transfixed by grief, but unable to weep. In a curious catalogue of the
sorry lot of various noblewomen (otherwise unknown) in this secular
heroic world, they give graphic accounts of their woes, presumably in
an attempt to goad Gudrún to show her grief. The climax comes when
the winding-sheet is swept off Sigurd's bloody corpse with dramatic
effect (stanza 15). Gudrún's lament is both lyrical and restrained,
demonstrating beautifully the extent to which Sigurd's downfall is
also her own (18–19): 'My lord's retainers once honoured me /
more than any of Odin's maids' – a reference to the reverence in which
valkyries were held. Her rival, Brynhild, is in many versions a for-
mer valkyrie herself, and her attempt to comfort Gudrún is roundly
rejected, leaving her seething almost dragon-like in her scorned and
reviled solitude (27).

Alfred Lord Tennyson, apparently influenced by Gkv I, produced
'Home they Brought her Warrior Dead', as part of Canto V of The
Princess (1847), which begins: 'Home they brought her warrior dead: /
She nor swooned, nor uttered cry: / All her maidens, watching, said, /
"She must weep or she will die."' As the succeeding poems of CR
amply demonstrate, Gudrún weeps and others die.

pr   The assertion that Gudrún, like Sigurd in Fáf, has eaten part of
      Fáfnir's heart and so understands the speech of birds, is only
      found here, and seems out of keeping with the rest of Gkv I.
      Implicit in 'This is also said of Gudrún' is that there was more
      than one poem about her.

10   The jealous mistress motif is widespread in Old Norse–Icelandic
      literature: cf., e.g., the mid-thirteenth-century Laxdæla saga 12.

16   For honking geese, see also Sigsk 29.

18   For similar comparisons of their dead husbands, see HH II 38
      and Gkv II 2.

19   For the rather lyrical forest-image of loneliness, cf. Háv 50 and
      Ham 5 (and note).

23   Given her key role in Sigurd's death, Brynhild's words seem deeply
      disingenuous; of course, she is self-cursed: her suicide deprives
      her of both husband and children. On 'speech-runes', see further

Sigrd 12; presumably here they unblock Gudrún's inability to speak and grieve.

24   It is hard to identify the seven kings; cf. *Hel* 2 and 4.

Sigurdarkvida in skamma: The short song of Sigurd

Despite its title, *Sigurdarkvida in skamma* is one of the longer poems in CR (folios 34v–36r). It offers a general survey of the events surrounding the Völsung cycle, with a particular focus on the character and motivation of the tragic heroine Brynhild, whose love for Sigurd leads to their deaths. Stanzas 51–71 are Brynhild's prophecy of the grim events that are to overtake Gudrún, Sigurd's widow, their daughter, Svanhild, and her brothers, Gunnar and Högni Gjúkason. Although *Sigsk* has some mundane verse, it also contains memorable vignettes, not least that of the blood-spattered Gudrún woken from sleep at her murdered husband's side (repeated in *Atk* and *Atm*). After the poem closes, Brynhild perishes on Sigurd's pyre.

4   On the sword that lay between Brynhild and Sigurd, see *Brot* 19.
7   On the role of the norns, see headnote to *HH I*.
8   The ice-floes and glaciers are unrealistic, given the Rhineland setting, but doubtless reflect Brynhild's chilled and chilling interior landscape.
12   For a similar injunction to beware the son of someone you kill, see *Sigrd* 35; here the added frisson is that they are being encouraged to kill their sister's son, a family connection of great significance (see note to *Hav* 140).
15–16 Gunnar's lack of romantic feeling, as well as his greed for gold, are exhibited here (see also 10, 36, 39, 52).
19   Something is lost here: see *Vsaga* 30.
20   For more on Gutthorm, see *Hynd* 27.
21   The narrative gap is filled in *Vsaga* 30.
24   On the god Frey (Yngri) as the progenitor of kings, see *HH I* 55.
25   Rather a bitter complaint: when married to Atli, Gudrún chooses her brothers above her husband (see *Atk* and *Atm*).
26   *Vsaga* 31 states that Sigmund was only three years old when his father was slain.
27   In other words, however many sons Gudrún will have in future marriages, none will match the one that they have had.
29   For the honking geese, see also *Gkv I* 16.
40   This fairly regular women-kenning (circlet-valkyrie) strongly implies that Brynhild is here not considered a real valkyrie.

41   Cf. this heroic resolution with the adulterous offer in *Vsaga* 29.

47   Presumably these maids and serving-women have committed suicide so that they can join their mistress in death; for the reluctant ones, see 50.

52   For Menja, see also *Grott.*

53   Perhaps an allusion to the drink of forgetfulness administered by Grímhild; see further *Vsaga* 31.

55   For Svanhild, see introductory pr to *Ghv* and *Ghv* 15.

58   The story is told more fully in *Odd.*

60   In other words, once again Gudrún will find herself in bed with a husband bleeding to death; but see *Atk* and *Atm.*

62   See also *Ghv* and *Ham.*

64   For Bikki, see headnote to *Ghv*; see also *Ham* and *Skáld* 42.

69   That is, Brynhild's death will follow close on Sigurd's, although it is not clear which hall of death will hold them.

Helreid Brynhildar: Brynhild's Hel-ride

Just like *Sigsk, Helreid Brynhildar* (folios 36r–37v of CR) offers the chance for Brynhild, so often the villain in these heroic poems, to state her case. The introductory pr describes how after she died of grief at the death of her beloved Sigurd, two pyres were built for them; hers contained a chariot and costly cloth (rather in the manner of the famous early-ninth-century Oseberg burial). Brynhild is berated by a giantess for the misfortunes of Gjúki's sons and is reproached for pursuing Sigurd (stanzas 1–4). In reply, Brynhild describes her youth and early life as a valkyrie, and entirely identifies her fate with that of Sigrdrífa; e.g. Brynhild, echoing *Sigrd* 4 pr, explains how she was punished by the god Odin for granting victory to the wrong side in battle (8), and describes how (in a forerunner to the Sleeping Beauty story) she was put into an enchanted sleep, protected by a ring of flame, just waiting for a hero to claim her. When Sigurd did so, she says, they spent eight chaste nights together; it was only when Gunnar, as her husband, had accused her of sleeping with Sigurd that she came to realize that she had been tricked into marrying him. The closing stanza underlines her grim determination (14).

Hel is also found virtually complete, but with textual variants, in *Nornagests þáttr*, which was composed in the fourteenth century.

2   Valland contains a multiple pun: *val-* signifies the dead, the exotic and the simply foreign, with a twist on the first syllable of Völsung.

6   For the hiding of feather-cloaks, see the introductory pr to *Vkv*
       and note; for burial under a tree, cf. note to *Skírn* 35.

7   Something is missing: see *Odd* 13. In *Vsaga* 27, 'Din-dale' is the
       home of Heimir, where Sigurd first falls in love (*Gríp* 19, 29, 31).

11   Sigurd's alleged Danish background is odd, as he is usually called
       a 'southern' king (on the implications of 'southern', see note to
       HH I 16).

14   Cf. the sinking of the prophetess in *Vsp* 66.

Dráp Niflunga: The killing of the Niflungs

Another linking passage that combines elements from the poems that
follow. For the '*potion of forgetfulness*', see *Gkv II* 21–4. The double
use of runes and a gold ring wrapped in a wolf's hair (see *Reg* 4 pr and
Vsaga 28) conflates details found in *Atk* and *Atm*. The first elements
of Sólar and Snævar signify 'sun' and 'snow', respectively; see further
Atm 30.

Gudrúnarkvida in forna: The ancient song of Gudrún

Gudrúnarkvida in forna, also known as *Gudrúnarkvida önnur* ('The
second song of Gudrún') is separated in CR (folios 37r–38r) from *Gkv
I* by several other poems. *Gkv II* is a monologue by Gudrún, giving a
detailed account of what happened to her after Sigurd's death. With the
deep antipathy between Gudrún and Brynhild, the arrival of messengers
from the court of King Atli, Brynhild's brother, bringing an offer of
marriage, naturally evokes fierce rejection, overcome only by Grím-
hild's use of magic. The mixture of extraordinary ingredients in the
potion of forgetfulness (stanzas 21–4) is apparently effective. Gudrún
foresees both the killing of her brothers, Gunnar and Högni, by Atli,
and her subsequent revenge on him (see *Atk* and *Atm*). In a scene that
reverses the foreboding dreams in *Atm* in particular, Gudrún describes
her soothing pillow-talk to Atli, who is distressed by his dreams, por-
tents of his death and that of their sons at her hands. Gudrún's bland
dismissal is made all the more chilling by the disturbing final stanza (44).

pr   Thjódrek is usually identified with Theodoric, king of the
       Ostrogoths (454–526).

2   For similarly romantic laments for lost husbands, see *Gkv I* 18
       and *HH II* 38.

4   CR says Grani galloped 'to' a meeting; the emendation ('back
       from') reflects the prose at the end of *Brot*: one account states

Sigurd was killed as he and the sons of Gjúki were riding to an
assembly, and from which Grani is now presumably returning.

7   For the details of the slaying, cf. *Sigsk* 23.

11 Cf. *Gkv I*, which seems to be an extended dramatization of this
    stanza.

17 For Grímhild, see also *Gríp* 33.

18 The last half of this stanza is likely an interpolation (it would not
    seem out of place in *Ríg*).

19 Presumably this is an embassy to ask for Gudrún's hand in marriage.

21–4 Cf. the memory-drinks in *Sigrd* and *Hynd* 45. It is unclear what 'an
    uncut grain from [the sea]' (22) would be: some form of seaweed?

25 Presumably the Hlödvér mentioned in the introductory pr to *Vkv*.

28 Sigmund is either Sigurd's father or Sigurd's son by Gudrún.

37–43 Contrast with *Vsaga* 35, where Gudrún calmly explains Atli's
    dreams.

40 Presumably a stanza of interpretation is missing here.

44 The poem ends abruptly; maybe something has been lost.

Gudrúnarkvida in thridja: The third song of Gudrún

Gudrúnarkvida in thridja (folios 38r–38v of CR) expands the story of
the doomed Völsungs, by describing a peripheral episode, in which
the slave-girl Herkja accuses Gudrún of adultery. Gudrún defiantly
offers to undertake an ordeal by boiling water to clear her name, and
does so successfully; her accuser, however, is badly scalded and 'exiled'
to a 'stinking bog'.

pr For Thjódrek, see note to *Gkv II* introductory pr.

3   See a similar oath in *HH II* 31.

4   See also introductory pr to *Gkv II*.

11 Tacitus (AD 56–117), *Germania* 12, described the punishments of
    the Germanic peoples of his day: 'Traitors and deserters they hang
    on trees, cowards and those unfit for war, and those impure in
    body, they plunge into a swampy bog, with a lattice-hurdle placed
    on top of them.' He explained the distinction between making an
    exhibition of a criminal and burying him from public sight.

Oddrúnargrátr: Oddrún's lament

Oddrúnargrátr is a slight poem (folios 38v–39v), less weighty than
others in CR. It seems to be a self-conscious attempt at archaizing,
with its reference to spells (stanza 7) and invocations of Frigg and

Freyja (9). Its purpose is to offer a different perspective on the tragic cycle of the Völsungs, Gjúkungs and Niflungs, from the viewpoint of Oddrún, the sister (or perhaps half-sister) of Atli Budlason, Gudrún's second husband, and Brynhild. (Oddrún also appears in *Sigsk* 58.) As befits a sister of Atli and Brynhild, Oddrún is evidently a witch, who travels to help Borgný, the daughter of King Heidrek, give birth. Extra details are that Oddrún had been Gunnar's mistress, apparently after the death of Brynhild, while Borgný's lover (and the father of the child to be born) is Vilmund (see also note to 8). *Odd* is in effect an extended lament for Gunnar, who shortly followed Högni in death (see *Atk* and *Atm*).

pr   See further *Sigsk* 58 and *PrDráp*.

3   Travelling 'the whole length of the hall' is formulaic: cf. *Thrym* 27; *Vkv* 7, 16, 30.

7   For the use of runes and chants to help women give birth, see *Sigrd* 9.

8   Högni's killer is only here specified as Vilmund, if that is the gist of the allusion.

9   Presumably Frigg is invoked as goddess of marital love, and Freyja as goddess of fertility and sex; see further *Vsp* 33 and *Thrym* 3.

11   The first line is repeated almost verbatim in *HH II* 34; see also 'out of [one's] mind' (*ørvita*) in *Lok* 21, 47.

12   Presumably in preparing Gunnar's drink, Oddrún demonstrates the intimate nature of her relationship with him.

16   Budli giving Brynhild to the life of a valkyrie is not dissimilar from early medieval families dedicating younger children to a life in the Church. '[U]nless fate spoiled things' might stand as a motto for much of the tragedy of the Völsungs.

18   A pun on 'foreign' (*völsku*), and Sigurd the Völsung, who accomplished the deed.

21   On Grani's pack-load, see further *Gríp* 13.

25   For the language of the opening lines, cf. especially *Atk* 3 (and note), 5, 13.

32   Atli's mother acts here apparently in the form of a snake; the venomous condemnation of the mother is striking, since she is also the mother (or perhaps stepmother) of Oddrún. See further *Skáld* 42; *Vsaga* 39.

33   The language of the kenning is unclear, and here I read *línvengis Bil* (literally 'linen-pillow goddess') after CR; other texts have *linn-vengis Bil* (literally 'snake-pillow goddess'). Given that the 'pillow of a serpent' is a kenning for gold, and that 'gold-goddess' is a common kenning for 'woman', the readings amount to the same thing.

34   Note the title is mentioned, as at the end of *Háv*.

Atlakvida: Atli's song

Atlakvida is often considered to be one of earliest of the poems in CR (folios 39v–41r), although the extended title in CR suggests it derived from Greenland, which was not settled until around 985; most commentators consider a date of composition around 900 is more likely. Some attribute it to Þorbjörn hornklofi ('horn-clawed'), a late-ninth-century poet of the Norwegian King Harald Fairhair, since there are parallels of style and diction that connect it with his work, specifically a poem in praise of Harald now known as *Hrafnsmál* ('The raven's lay'). *Atk* has a stark quality of grim vengeance, and seems to have influenced *Atm*, which follows it in CR; the Greenlandic credentials of the latter are stronger.

The narrative is briskly told: Atli (Attila), the lord of the Huns and husband of Gudrún – whose sorry series of marriages link the CR heroic poems – sends an invitation to his Burgundian brothers-in-law Gunnar and Högni, to visit and receive rich gifts; Högni points out that their sister has sent them a warning of Atli's impending treachery: a ring wrapped round with a wolf's hair. Gunnar notes that they are not in need of Atli's offerings, but takes up the challenge. On arrival, and after a further warning from Gudrún, the brothers are seized, Högni after great resistance. Atli offers Gunnar his life in exchange for the Niflung treasure, but Gunnar refuses so long as Högni lives, and demands his brother's heart. Atli's men try to trick him, but Gunnar is not fooled; and later he recognizes Högni's heart. Gunnar shows his own mettle when he states he is the last to know where the hoard is hidden and refuses to tell, and Atli promptly has him thrown into a snake-pit to die. Gudrún demonstrates the extent to which birth-ties trump those of the marriage-bed by killing her sons by Atli, and feeding them to their father, before stabbing him, and setting fire to his hall. She survives to wed another day.

Atk is predominantly composed in *fornyrðislag* ('old poetry metre'), although there are some oddly variant lines; likewise, some parts of the text are obscure, and include problematic kennings and *heiti*.

1   The word translated as 'envoy' (*ár*) is a homograph with the word for 'early', 'long ago', which commonly opens CR poems (see note to *Hym* 1).

2   Knéfröd's cold voice is presumably supposed to convey menace or betoken doom; see headnote to *Vkv* on women's cold counsels.

3   On Mirkwood (also 5, 13), see further *Lok* 42; *Vkv* 1, 3; *HH I* 51. It is odd that Mirkwood should be both 'unknown' here and

'far-famed' (5); presumably it is celebrated precisely for being so mysterious and untracked.

7   Kjár is perhaps the king named in the introductory pr to *Vkv*.

8   The sign seems relatively transparent: Gudrún is presumably signalling that a wolf (Atli) is planning to take over their gold (11).

10   Presumably there is something missing; cf. *Vsaga* 35.

14   The word translated as 'watchtowers' (*liðskjálfar*) is cognate with Hlidskjálf, the watchtower of the gods; see introductory pr to *Grím* and *Skírn*. Bikki appears in *Ghv* introductory pr as the wicked counsel or of King Jörmunrekk; it may be that Budli, Atli's father, was meant. '[W]ith screaming spears' (*með geiri gjallanda*) has parallels in Old English; '*giellende gar*' appears in *Widsith* 128, a heroic poem with links to *Beo*.

26   Gunnar seems to be alluding to his own death, and hinting at Atli's fate.

29   Just as Gudrún cannot cry over Sigurd's corpse (see introductory pr to *Gkv I*), so too she retains her reserve here and in 39.

30   Cf. other oaths in CR, especially *HH II* 31. On Ull, see further *Grím* 5.

32   *Vsaga* 37 specifies Gudrún gave Gunnar the harp; cf. *Odd* 29–30.

34   'Niflheim' highlights the association with the doomed family of the Niflungs.

37   The 'high seat' may mask an allusion to the toilet, where the dead flesh will end up.

40   The word translated 'Shining-cheeked' (*gaglbjartr*) is often given as 'gosling-cheeked', building on Gudrún's association with geese (see *Gkv I* 17; *Sigsk* 29). Cf. Old English *ceafl*, *geaflas* (jaws) 'jowls' in Modern English.

44   As often in the final poems of CR, the closing lines acknowledge the audience and the wider legendary tradition.

Atlamál in grœnlenzku: The Greenlandic lay of Atli

The note in CR at the end of *Atk* says that '*The tale is told more clearly in the Greenlandic "Lay of Atli"*', and indeed *Atlamál in grœnlenzku* (folios 41r–44r) tells the same story with considerable expansion: the taut and stark stanzas of *Atk* are spun to more than twice as many (105 as against 44), but many commentators consider the later *Atm* (perhaps twelfth century) a much less accomplished piece. Where *Atk* is bluntly gruesome, *Atm* is often bizarre: if in *Atk* Gunnar playing a harp in the snake-pit seems an extreme of the heroic ideal (see *Háv* 15), the poet of *Atm*, tied up (as it were) with the practicalities, has

Gunnar play the harp with his toes instead (stanza 66). Likewise, in place of the enigmatic wolf's hair wrapped round a ring in *Atk*, which Gudrún uses in vain to warn her brothers, in *Atm* she literally spells it out in runes that are ruined by the wicked Vingi. When it comes time to fight, Gudrún even takes up arms. The attribution of *Atm* to Greenland has support in its text with the dream of a white bear (18).

The distinctly low-brow kenning 'foot-twigs' is one of only two (the other is 'shield-tree' (30)), so the language of *Atm* is unusually transparent, and it has the most sustained use of *málaháttr* ('speech metre') in CR.

1   The opening line, with its invocation of a shared oral tradition, is unparalleled in eddic poetry, although there are examples in Old English (*Beo* 1–2: 'Listen, we have heard of the might of the Spear-Danes in days of yore'); cf. *Ghv* 1.

3   The journey is across water, as opposed to land in *Atk* 13.

6   Atli sends two messengers here, but one in *Atk*.

18   There were no brown bears in Iceland (a starving white one might come on an iceberg from Greenland).

20   Cf. Atli's dream in *Gkv II* 43.

22   Ragnarök (*rök ragna*; 'doom of the powers'): one of the rare times it is explicitly mentioned in CR.

26   Evidently, a stanza of interpretation is missing: see *Vsaga* 34.

30   Snævar and Sólar are also named in *PrDráp*.

33   Cf. *Gkv I* 23 for a similar kind of self-curse; Vingi does offer to cut a gallows at 39.

36   It is rare in CR to find intrusion of the poet's voice; see also 38.

37   Gunnar and his men signal their acceptance that they will not be returning home.

42   At this point in *Vsaga*, Atli asks for the cursed treasure; this lack in *Atm* is striking, and undercuts the motivation both for Atli's initial invitation and for the nature of Gudrún's warning.

56   Atli gives partial justification for his treatment of Gunnar and Högni: he holds them responsible for Brynhild's death.

57   It is unclear how Atli is implicated in the death of Gudrún's mother Grímhild (see 80, 96); likewise, the 'wise cousin' is otherwise unknown.

58   For Gudrún's tears, see note to *Atk* 29.

59   Apparently a double death is designed for Gunnar; for gallows, cf. 22, 39.

65   Presumably these 'day-workers' are out in the fields, some distance away.

78   'a rest ... brief': even the most vicious vengeance will not make
      Gudrún feel better for long.
81   Cf. Nídud's similar reaction in *Vkv* 31, from where the detail is
      perhaps taken; 'morning' harks back to 68.
97   In other words, Atli is a kin-slayer.
98   Gudrún again takes on the role of a man, by steering her own ship.
103   As in *Sigrd* 34, the rites seem more Christian than pagan.
104   See further *Ghv* 13.
105   Cf. 1; the poem has an envelope-pattern.

Gudrúnarhvöt: Gudrún's inciting

Gudrúnarhvöt (folios 44r–44v in CR) opens with pr that begins with
how Gudrún came to be married to King Jónakr, her third husband.
Just as in *Atk* and *Atm* where she uses her two sons by Atli to further
her vengeance (see note to 5), so too here she incites Hamdir and Sörli,
her sons by Jónakr, to avenge their half-sister Svanhild, Sigurd's daughter.
Jörmunrekk (identified with the historical Ermanaric, an Ostrogothic
king (d. 376)) had sent his son Randvér to woo Svanhild, but when he
is informed by his wicked counsellor Bikki that Randvér has taken
her for himself, Jörmunrekk has his son and Svanhild killed. To egg on
her sons, Gudrún engages in a form of 'comparison between men'
(*mannjafnaðr*), contrasting their inactivity in the face of the provoca-
tion with the heroism of her brothers, Gunnar and Högni, whom Atli
slew. The brothers duly depart for a doomed mission that is played out
in *Ham*, and, despite the title, this incitement only takes up stanzas
2–8. The rest is Gudrún's lament, beginning with the depth of her sor-
row when Brynhild usurped her position on Sigurd's pyre (cf. *Sigsk*
61). As she recounts her many woes and lost children across three long
marriages, it is striking that Gudrún is depicted weeping freely (9; cf.
Gkv I); at the end she orders her own funeral-pyre to be built (20). The
first and final stanzas are the voice of the poet, addressing the audience.
      The poem is in *fornyrðislag* ('old poetry metre'); there is a close
paraphrase in *Vsaga* 41 and Snorri's *Skáld* 39.

pr   That Gudrún cannot sink when she attempts to drown herself
      would seem to indicate that she has become almost a witch (cf.
      13). Other evidence, especially *Ham* 13, suggests that Erp was
      Jónakr's son by another woman; see also note to 5.
1   The poet begins *Ghv* in his own voice to tell what he has heard;
      such a first-person opening is rare in eddic verse: cf. *Atm* 1 and note.
2   Paralleled in *Ham* 3.

4 Parallel passages in the closing pr of *Brot* and *Sigsk* 24–9.

5 The murdered sons are Erp and Eitil, by Atli; Gudrún explicitly acknowledges her guilt (11–12), and the episode is told in grisly detail in *Atk* 34–9; *Atm* 77–85. Hamdir's reference to his lost brothers is somewhat ironic: see *Ham*.

7 Grim laughter is a mark of many eddic poems, notably *Thrym* 31; *Vkv* 29, 38; *Brot* 10, 15, and *Sigsk* 30; *Gkv III* 10; *Atk* 24 and *Atm* 65; *Ham* 6, 20. Gudrún's alternation between laughing (*hlæjandi*) and weeping (*grátandi*) (7, 9) recalls the stark contrast between Völund (*hlæjandi*) and Bödvild (*grátandi*) in *Vkv* 29.

14 The repetition of 'lawful heirs' seems unusual and unmotivated, perhaps simply the result of scribal dittography; for a parallel, however, see *Ríg* 36.

19 The love of Gudrún and Sigurd extending beyond the grave is echoed in the Helgi-lays (*HH I*, *HHj* and *HH II*).

20 In planning her own funeral-pyre, Gudrún follows the example of Brynhild in *Sigsk* 65–8.

Hamdismál: Hamdir's lay

More properly known, according to the concluding pr, as *Hamdismál in forna* ('The ancient lay of Hamdir'), the final poem in CR (folios 44v–45v) puts a haunting and effective capstone on the whole. The tale is summarized in *Vsaga* 44 and in Snorri's *Skáld* 42, and an account of Jörmunrekk's death is given by Bragi Boddason in his *Ragnarsdrápa*. *Ham* begins with the inciting by Gudrún of her two sons by Jónakr to vengeance for their dead half-sister Svanhild, killed by Jörmunrekk, with much of the manner and many of the same words as *Ghv* (see its headnote). Hamdir and Sörli are filled with a sense of their own doom (stanza 10), which they hasten by the senseless killing of their half-brother Erp (15), a terrible mistake they live just long enough to acknowledge (28). Jörmunrekk is a wonderfully grim Victorian music-hall villain, even down to his ironic laughter and moustache-smoothing manner (20); when he has lost all four limbs, he still commands 'as a bear would growl' (25). *Ham* is suffused with a deep sense of fate: all the characters are operating under the malicious influence of norns or *dísir* of ill intent (28–30), from the extraordinary opening stanza (see note to 1) to the defiant last words of the brothers (30). Stanza 29 only is in *ljóðaháttr* ('song metre'), and *Ham* mixes styles, tones and registers with great skill, combining stark accounts of grim heroism with lyrical expressions of Gudrún's grief; it forms a fitting finale to the CR heroic poems.

1   This stanza is usually regarded as an interpolation; its rather baroque style seems out of keeping with the rest.

3   Cf. the similar language of *Ghv* 2.

5   For parallel expressions of solitude using tree-imagery, see *Háv* 50; *Gkv I* 19. For a fine example, see the ninth-century Welsh cycle *Canu Heledd* ('Heledd's songs'), where Heledd mourns the death of her brother Cynddylan, who apparently ruled Pengwern in the mid-seventh century. In one poem she says of herself: 'A single tree in a forest and a blight upon it, / if it survives it is a marvel; / but let God's will come to pass.' For a similar kenning for fire, see *Vsp* 52. There seems to be a stanza missing, where Gudrún would praise her dead brothers Gunnar and Högni: see *Ghv* 3.

6–7 Several lines are greatly abbreviated in CR, where there are correspondences in *Ghv* 4, and I have supplied the missing words from it.

12–14 The stanzas appear as numbered in brackets in CR, where they seem to be out of sequence.

15   It is not clear who this ogress might be, unless one of the *dísir* in 28.

17   Strictly speaking, Randvér, son of Jörmunrekk, is Svanhild's stepson, but he is a 'sister's son' to Hamdir and Sörli, an important relationship in Germanic society (see further note to *Háv* 140). Randvér's double slaying by piercing and hanging can be matched to Odin's in *Háv* 138.

20   On Jörmunrekk's laughter, see note to *Ghv* 7. Jörmunrekk's chestnut hair recalls Erp's (12).

22   Alternatively, Hródrglöd – here translated as 'fame-glad girl' – is a personal name otherwise unattested.

25   In the parallel account in *Vsaga* 42, it is Odin who offers the fateful advice, appearing as he did at the deaths of Helgi and Sigmund. On the invulnerability of Hamdir and Sörli to weapons, see further Snorri's *Skáld* 42 and *Vsaga* 44, both of which say Gudrún supplied the magical mailcoats.

26   CR attributes stanzas 26 and 27 to Hamdir, using the same introduction as at 24; logically, however, 26–7 belong to Sörli, and I have emended accordingly. The 'bag' is presumably Jörmunrekk himself, reduced by the loss of his limbs to a talking trunk.

Rígsthula: Ríg's list

Rígsthula is a breezy and briskly moving narrative that explains the origins of three classes of mankind: the slaves, the yeoman-farmers and the landed gentry. All are descended from the mysterious traveller Ríg, whose wanderings and casual sexual conquests are reminiscent of Odin's, one of whose names is 'All-father'; the initial description of the protagonist as 'a mighty and ancient and much-crafty god' likewise seems more suitable for Odin than for the shadowy figure of Heimdall (in the introductory pr). *Ríg* is in the Codex Wormianus (AM 242 fol.), written about 1350 (and containing the Prose Edda of Snorri Sturluson). The scribe who wrote *Ríg* was responsible for the version of *Vsp* in Hauksbók (AM 544 4to), and it is likely that the introductory pr, composed later, was written specifically to associate *Ríg* with *Vsp* 1, where 'the higher and lower of Heimdall's brood' could be construed to signify the estates of men, although it more likely refers to different kinds of being. Some degree of Irish influence on *Ríg* is certain: *ríg* appears to derive from the medieval Irish word for 'king' (*rí*, *ríg* in the genitive); the standard stay was limited to three nights (more was considered rude); law-codes specified the kind of food to be granted to guests of different social status; and a number of medieval Irish tales attest to a custom of granting important visitors the right to sleep with the woman of the house. Given Ríg's potency, it is surely relevant that the Norse root of his name is cognate with Modern English 'rigid'.

pr   Snorri (*Gylf* 9) describes Odin and his two brothers wandering along a seashore, and creating the race of men from the driftwood; a similar episode of three wandering figures, with Odin as the only common denominator, is found in *Vsp* 17–18.

1   For 'ancient times', see note to *Hym* 1.

2   '[T]he middle of the path' establishes the main setting as Midgard, the 'middle-earth' between the worlds of gods and giants. The name translated 'Great-grandma' here is Edda, on which see the Introduction.

4   The 'boiled calf-meat, the best of dainties', as part of the menu, are delicacies that are out of place here; they are more likely to have been offered to Ríg in his next overnight stay (17–19).

7   Sprinkling with water seems to predate the conversion to Christianity, and may be a kind of naming ceremony; cf. *Háv* 158.

17–19   It is clear that a scribe has omitted a description of Ríg eating, probably through eye-skip from one formulaic phrase to another. See note to 4. Stanza 18 is supplied by the editor.

21   The Old Norse *karl* (here 'carl') signifies a peasant-farmer, though in a derogatory sense, it also means 'old man'; see also 25.

23   Note the more formal marriage-ceremony here, as opposed to the simple shagging in 11.

27   Again, a distinction between the classes: the aristocracy had time
      for romantic love.
43   The phrase translated 'young Kin' (*Konr ungr*) would have the
      connotation of 'king' (*konungr*), the role Kin will assume. For
      the runic knowledge, cf. *Háv* 137–63; *Sigrd* 5–19.
48   Dan and Danp are presumably the eponymous kings of Denmark;
      cf. *Atk* 5.

Baldrs draumar: Baldr's dreams

Baldrs draumar, also known as *Vegtamskvida* ('The song of Way-
tamer'), is in AM 748 Ia 4to, written around 1300. The opening is
identical to *Thrym* 14, and the parallels with *Vsp* 31–5 indicate that
this is a deliberate extension of its Baldr episode; the format is similar
to other wisdom-dialogues such as *Vaf* and *Alv*. As in *Vsp* (31–3), Odin
communes with a dead seeress in order to gain wisdom from her inter-
pretation of Baldr's troubling dreams. The surly seeress answers with ill
grace three questions, two of which are about Baldr's death at the hands
of his brother, Höd, and Váli's revenge (stanzas 8–11). But when Odin
asks an enigmatic question (12), the seeress immediately identifies him
as Odin, and the two part with malice (13–14).

2   CR reads here *alda gautr* ('men's sacrifice'), which seems an unlikely
      description for Odin, even given his self-sacrifice in *Háv* 138 and
      the fact that the name Gaut ('Sacrifice') is given as one of his
      names in *Grím* 54. Here I prefer the reading *aldinn gautr*
      ('ancient sacrifice'), as in 13. For Sleipnir, Niflhel and the whelp
      (if it is Garm), see *Vsp* 44; *Vaf* 43; *Grím* 44.
3   For the noisy journey, cf. *Thrym* 5, 9.
4   Odin claims to know runes for communing with hanged dead
      men in *Háv* 157.
9   If 'glory-tree' is a kenning for 'warrior', it refers to Baldr, or it
      could mask a reference to the fatal mistletoe (see *Vsp* 32–3).
11   Cf. Váli as Baldr's avenger in *Vsp* 33.
12   There is no clear solution to Odin's question – though it resembles
      a series of riddles he (calling himself Gestumblindi ('Blind Guest');
      see also headnote to *Vaf*) gave to King Heidrek in *Heidreks saga*
      (stanzas 62–4, 67), where the solution each time is 'waves' – nor
      is it obvious why this should reveal his identity.
14   For the binding and loosening of Loki, see *Lok* and pr; *Vsp* 34–5.
      Baldr's death is one of the events that will trigger Ragnarök.

Hyndluljód: Hyndla's poem

Hyndluljód is in Flateyjarbók (GkS 1005 fol.), written 1387–94. Stanzas 29–44 are also called *Völuspá in skamma* ('The shorter Völuspá'); Snorri knew this title and quoted part of 33 in *Gylf* 4. The main narrative frame of *Hynd* is a genealogy for Óttar 'the Simple', identified as the son of Innstein and a lover of the goddess Freyja (6). His ancestors consist of a curious mixture of known kings of Hörthaland and others acknowledged elsewhere as descendants of King Halfdan 'the Old' of Norway, with a further sprinkling of legendary heroes. By their very nature, such genealogical texts were prone to addition and interpolation, so identification of the real-life Óttar is uncertain, but he might be Óttar Birting, who, though modestly born, nonetheless rose to marry Ingrid Ragnvaldsdóttir (d. after 1061), the widow of King Harald Gilli of Norway (Harald IV, ruled 1130–36). Ingrid, a member of the Swedish royal family, married into the Danish and Norwegian royal families successively, and then Óttar Birting. It has been suggested that *Hynd* lampoons his plight. Little good it did him: he was assassinated in the 1140s.

In *Hynd*, the goddess Freyja transforms her human favourite, Óttar, into the shape of a boar, Battle-swine, and rides him to visit the giantess Hyndla ('Little Bitch') to discover his genealogy. Beyond the bitchiness at either end of the poem, as well as an interpolated section on the Æsir (29–44), Óttar does indeed hear his whole family history.

1 '[T]wilight of twilights' (*rökkr rökka*) is perhaps a reference to Ragnarök, which in one form, *Ragnarökkr*, means 'Twilight of the powers'.

2 On Hermód and Sigmund, cf. Heremod and Sigemund in *Beo*, and *Hákonarmál* 14 and *Eiríksmál* 16. The sword that Odin gave to Sigmund is Gram, which Sigurd inherits.

4 Freyja speaks of herself in the third person; the same slippage between third- and first-person references is also found in *Vsp* (see its headnote).

5 Freyja's brother Frey is more usually associated with boars; see, e.g., Snorri's *Gylf* 49; *Skáld* 8. Freyja usually rides in a chariot drawn by cats (see *Gylf* 49); troll-wives customarily ride wolves (see, e.g., *HH I* 54; *HH II* 25; *HHj* 30 pr).

6 On the choices among the dead, see *Grím* 8, 14; in the latter, it is Freyja who chooses half the slain, sharing the booty with Odin, so raising the question why she does not take her lover to her

own hall, 'Battle-field'. The inconsistency highlights the difficulty of extrapolating a unified system of belief from the eddic corpus.

7   For these dwarf-names, cf. *Völuspá* 11 in the Hauksbók version. There is an elf called Dead-one in *Háv* 143, and the same name is given to a hart nibbling Yggdrasil in *Grím* 33.

10   Presumably the stones have become glassy through the heat of repeated sacrificial pyres.

11   A tally of some of the noblest folk of the North, echoed in 16; see further Snorri's *Skáld* 64.

13   For Fródi, see *Grott*.

17   It is not clear if Sváva ('the Swabian girl') is the same woman as in *HHj*. The repeated refrain 'do you want still more?' echoes that of the seeress in *Vsp* ('Do you know yet, or what?'; 33, etc.).

27   On Gutthorm, see especially *Sigsk* 20.

29   On the death of Baldr, see further *Vsp* 31–5 and *Bdr* 11.

30   On Gerd, cf. *Skírn* and *Lok*. The word translated as 'cover-keen' is obscure, and may refer either to a fondness for disguise or for sailing. For Skadi and Thjazi, see *Hár* 19 and *Lok* 49–52.

32   On Brightness, with a connection to *seid*, see *Vsp* 21–2 and notes.

33   For Ymir, cf. *Vaf* 21, 28.

35   This mysterious figure may be Heimdall, since Snorri (*Gylf* 27) quotes from the otherwise unknown *Heimdallargaldr* ('Heimdall's spell'), where Heimdall claims that: 'I am sprung from nine mothers; of nine sisters I am the son.' But the nine mothers/sisters might also be the roots of the World-tree, Yggdrasil, of which Heimdall is often a personification.

37   Valkyrie names; elsewhere, notably *Skáld* 17, Járnsaxa is the mother of Magni, son of Thor.

40   For these monstrous creatures, see further *Vsp* 50, 51; *Grím* 44. This explicitly confirms that Loki has been both a mother (to Sleipnir) and a father (to the wolf Fenrir); Snorri (*Gylf* 34, cf. 42) also credits him with fathering the World-serpent and Hel on the giantess Strife-bidder.

43–4 These stanzas connect material that is elsewhere implicit in *Ríg* and in *Vsp* 53, 64. Odin's name appears in many royal genealogies, both in Scandinavia and in Anglo-Saxon England; he may be the 'One' referred to in 43. The language in 44 seems to prefigure Christ; cf. *Vsp* 65, as supplied by Hauksbók.

45   Cf. the memory-ale of *Sigrd* pr 2, and the drink in 50.

47   This may be Freyja's husband, Ód ('Frenzy') (see *Vsp* 25; *Gylf* 35); the name is suspiciously close to that of Odin (cf. *Lok* 30).

Grottasöngr: Grotti's chanting

While many of the poems of CR have a rather lofty view, *Grottasöngr*, preserved in three manuscripts of Snorri's *Skáld*, is refreshingly low-brow, and has a close affinity with the work-songs found widely in later Old Norse–Icelandic literature and in eddic poetry in the ominous and fascinating *Darraðarljóð* ('The song of the spear': see note to *HH II* 19–24), chanted by the ghoulish dream-women weaving with the guts and entrails of doomed men before the Battle of Clontarf (1014), as reported in *Njáls saga* 157. The legendary Danish King Fródi is widely associated with peace, and that he acquired the two giantesses Fenja and Menja and the magic mill Grotti in Sweden attests to its later reputation as an area of peculiarly potent pagan and magical power (as well as Finland and Lappland). The 'wish-mill' is a common folk-lore motif, and the question of how the sea became salty is likewise a staple. The poet of *Grott* combines all these ingredients ingeniously, and adds the piquant detail of the otherwise unknown viking Mýsing, first wished for by the giant slave-girls, and then wished away in a destructive frenzy of over-production. While the structure of *Grott* is relatively simple, with the chanting of the giant captive-women (stanzas 5–22) mainly framed by narrative (1–4 and 23–4), the issues of hidden power, female subjugation, and the relentless and arbitrary workings of fate are masked in a dark tale of subversive revenge. The closest parallel in CR is *HH II* 2–4.

pr   This enquires about the origins of a specific kenning: how gold can be called 'Fródi's mill'.

9   On Hrungnir and Thjazi, see the notes to *Hár* 14 and *Grím* 11.

19   The word translated as 'war-tidings' (*vígspjöll*) is found only here and in *HH II* 12; *HH II* 19 mentions a 'red glow of battle' (*vígroði*).

22   'Yrsa's son' is the legendary King Hrólf kraki; his doubly incestuous and dubious birth as the son of his half-sister Yrsa and Helgi, who raped Yrsa's mother Thóra, is told in detail by Saxo Grammaticus in his *Gesta Danorum* (*History of the Danes*, chapters 51–4). The stanza is likely an interpolation.

Index of Names

358   INDEX OF NAMES

	Atk 1, 3, 6, 9, 11, 14, 18, 20, 22, 23, 24, 25, 30, 32, 43; *Atm* 6, 7, 21, 32, 59, 66; *Ghv* 3, 17; *Ham* 7; *Hynd* 27
Gunnar (2), ancestor of Óttar	*Hynd* 22
Gunnlöd, giantess, seduced by Odin	*Háv* 13, 105, 108, 110
Gunnr, see **Battle**	
Gunnþorin, see **Battle-bold**	
Gunnþró, see **Conflict-keen**	
Gust, dwarf (?), former owner of Andvari's hoard	*Reg* 5
Gut(t)horm (1), brother of Gunnar (1) and Högni (2)	*Gríp* 50; *Brot* 4; *Sigsk* 20, 22; *Gkv II* 7; *Hynd* 27
Guthorm (2), warrior	*Grott* 14
Guy (*Seggr*), son of Carl and Daughter-in-law	*Ríg* 24
Gyllir, see **Golden**	
Gymir (1), giant, father of Gerd; identical with Ægir?	*Skírn* 6, 11, 12, 14, 22, 24; *Lok* 42; *Hynd* 30
Gymir (2), another name for Ægir	*PrÆg*
Gyrd, ancestor of Óttar	*Hynd* 18
Hábrok, see **High-breeches**	
Haddings, sea-kings (?); kinsmen of Óttar	*HH II* pr end; *Gkv II* 22; *Hynd* 23
Hæming, son of Hunding	*PrVöls*; *HH II* 1
Hagal, foster-father of Helgi Hundingsbani	*PrVöls*; *HH II* 2
Haki, son of Hvædna	*Hynd* 32
Hákon, Dane	*Gkv I* pr; *Gkv II* 14
Hálf, Dane	*Gkv II* 13
Hálfdan (1), father of Kára	*HH II* pr end
Hálfdan (2), ancestor of the Skjöldungs	*Hynd* 14
Halr, see **Fellow**	
Hamal, son of Hagal	*HH II* 1, pr, 6
Hamdir, son of Jónakr and Gudrún	*PrGud*; *Ghv* 4, 8; *Ham* 6, 21, 24, 27, 31
Hámund, son of Sigmund	*PrSin*

Vár ('Oath'), goddess of   *Thrym* 30
  marriage-vows
Varin's Bay (*vik Varins*), place   *HHj* 22
Varinsey, see Varin's Isle
Varin's Fjord (*Varinsfjörðr*),   *HH I* 26
  place
Varinsfjörðr, see Varin's Fjord
Varin's Isle (*Varinsey*), place   *HH I* 37
Vé, brother of Odin   *Lok* 26
Vegsvinn, see Way-swift
Vegtamr, see Way-tamer
Veigr, see Swig
Verðandi, see Becoming
Verland ('Man-land?'), place   *Hár* 56
Vestri, see West
Vetr, see Winter
Véur, a name for Thor   *Hym* 11; *see also* Thor
Victory-father (*Sigföðr*), an Odin   *Vsp* 54; *Grím* 48
  name
Victory-god (*Sigtýr*), an Odin   *Atk* 30
  name
Víð, see Wide
Vídar, son of Odin   *Vsp* 54, 55; *Vaf* 51, 53; *Grím*
                                           17; *PrÆg*; *Lok* 10
Viðófr, see Forest-wolf
Vidrir (*Viðrir*), an Odin name   *Lok* 26; *HH I* 13
Viður, see Killer
Víf, see Wife
Vígblær, Helgi (1)'s horse   *HH II* 36
Vígdalir, see Slaughter-dales
Vigilant (*Vakr*), an Odin name   *Grím* 54
Vígríd (Battle-field), site of the   *Vaf* 18
  last battle at Ragnarök
Vili, brother of Odin   *Lok* 26
Víli, see Slogger
Vilmeiðr, see Wish-giver
Vilmund, lover of Borgný;   *PrBorg*; *Odd* 6
  slayer of Högni (2)
Vin, see Dwindle
Vína, see Dvina
Vinbjörg, fortress   *Gkv II* 33
Vindálfr, see Wind-elf

PENGUIN CLASSICS

THE PROSE EDDA
SNORRI STURLSON

'What was the beginning, or how did things start? What was there before?'

The Prose Edda is the most renowned of all works of Scandinavian literature and our most extensive source for Norse mythology. Written in Iceland a century after the close of the Viking Age, it tells ancient stories of the Norse creation epic and recounts the battles that follow as gods, giants, dwarves and elves struggle for survival. It also preserves the oral memory of heroes, warrior kings and queens. In clear prose interspersed with powerful verse, the *Edda* provides unparalleled insight into the gods' tragic realization that the future holds one final cataclysmic battle, Ragnarok, when the world will be destroyed. These tales from the pagan era have proved to be among the most influential of all myths and legends, inspiring modern works as diverse as Wagner's *Ring* cycle and Tolkien's *The Lord of the Rings*.

This new translation by Jesse Byock captures the strength and subtlety of the original, while his introduction sets the tales fully in the context of Norse mythology. This edition includes also detailed notes and appendices.

Translated with an introduction, glossary and notes by Jesse Byock

Penguin Classics

THE SAGA OF GRETTIR THE STRONG

'The most valiant man who has ever lived in Iceland'

Composed at the end of the fourteenth century by an unknown author, *The Saga of Grettir the Strong* is one of the last great Icelandic sagas. It relates the tale of Grettir, an eleventh-century warrior struggling to hold on to the values of a heroic age as they are eclipsed by Christianity and a more pastoral lifestyle. Unable to settle into a community of farmers, Grettir becomes the aggressive scourge of both honest men and evil monsters – until, following a battle with the sinister ghost Glam, he is cursed to endure a life of tortured loneliness away from civilization, fighting giants, trolls and berserks. A mesmerizing combination of pagan ideals and Christian faith, this is a profoundly moving conclusion to the Golden Age of saga writing.

This is an updated edition of Bernard Scudder's acclaimed translation. The new introduction by Örnólfur Thorsson considers the influence of Christianity on Icelandic saga writing, and this edition also includes genealogical tables and a note on the translation.

Translated by Bernard Scudder

Edited with an introduction by Örnólfur Thorsson